# THIRD TIME LUCKY

### AIMEE BROWN

**B**

Boldwood

First published in Great Britain in 2025 by Boldwood Books Ltd.

Copyright © Aimee Brown, 2025

Cover Design by Alice Moore Design

Cover Images: Shutterstock

A CIP catalogue record for this book is available from the British Library.

Paperback ISBN 978-1-80426-851-3

Large Print ISBN 978-1-80426-852-0

Hardback ISBN 978-1-80426-853-7

Ebook ISBN 978-1-80426-849-0

Kindle ISBN 978-1-80426-850-6

Audio CD ISBN 978-1-80426-858-2

MP3 CD ISBN 978-1-80426-857-5

Digital audio download ISBN 978-1-80426-855-1

This book is printed on certified sustainable paper. Boldwood Books is dedicated to putting sustainability at the heart of our business. For more information please visit https://www.boldwoodbooks.com/about-us/sustainability/

Boldwood Books Ltd, 23 Bowerdean Street, London, SW6 3TN

www.boldwoodbooks.com

*To those who believe in happily ever afters – here's two for the price of one.*
*This world sucks right now.*
*I hope this story helps you escape the chaos, if only for a moment.*

# 1

## ASHER

Under the kaleidoscope glow of neon lights, Aaron and I weave our way through the labyrinthine casino, dodging tipsy tourists and high rollers alike. The casino floor hums with the electric energy of high-stakes gambling, clinking glasses and lively chatter. A cacophony of slot machines sing their siren song, while a group of women in the distance erupt in laughter.

Aaron – my little brother – with his devil-may-care grin, points them out. 'Bachelorette party,' he announces, his finger slicing through the air toward the group of giggling women. 'Let's invite ourselves, shall we?'

His eyes sparkle beneath the fluorescent glow of Las Vegas – a technicolor dreamscape where fortunes are won and lost in a heartbeat. His mischievous grin cuts through like a beacon, acting as both an adrenaline shot and a warning.

I follow him hesitantly. 'Word of warning, if you make this a weekend I'll regret, I'm never coming to Vegas with you again.'

As we enter the bar from the casino floor, opulent decor featuring rich velvet furnishings, shimmering chandeliers and eye-catching art installations greets us. Everything in Vegas is over the top, and this place is no exception. The bar's lighting is dim and sultry, with a mix of luminous accents that reflect the vibrant energy that is Glitter Gulch. The sound of music and lively chatter fill the air.

'Says the guy who ended up with a busted lip and in jail the first time we came.' Aaron says as he side-eyes me, cocking his head like he's mister innocent.

It was my twenty-sixth birthday, and I only hit that guy first because he burst into the bathroom, already rearing back to beat the hell out of me. That's about my only defense – hit first so as not to be unexpectedly destroyed in a family bathroom that I was lured into by a beautiful woman. Also, don't go to Vegas with your twenty-one-year-old little brother – I'd say lesson learned but here we are again.

'Asshole,' I grumble, unsure if I'm talking about Aaron or the offender that ended up with no charges at all. 'That could have been prevented had that woman said she was married before she invited me to the bathroom with her.'

He laughs heartily, slapping me on the back. 'We're in Vegas, man. No one tells the truth here. The entire goal of Sin City is to see what you can get away with – and you got caught.'

We may be brothers, but Aaron and I are as unalike as our parents. He's our dad. And I am the early version of our mom (the one who wasn't terrorized by our father's shenanigans). We are opposites. But even with our differences, Aaron's my best friend, co-worker, business partner, and the guy I spend pretty much every moment with. I only regret it sometimes – mostly when we're in Vegas or while he's speaking.

As we reach the group of women, he stops talking. Probably because most are wearing very short dresses in varying shades of pink – each leaving little to the imagination of what may lie beneath – and it's melting his mind.

Except for the girl in the middle: her outfit is stark white, with a long trailing see-through lace skirt open in the front and covering a shorter skirt underneath. She's dainty, her head just about shoulder level on my six-foot-two frame. Her hair falls in silky waves, framing her face and cascading down her shoulders. The rich, chocolate tones highlight her warm complexion. Her eyes are large and expressive and an icy blue that sparkle like diamonds under the lights. She's beautiful – the prettiest one of the bunch – easy, and oddly familiar.

Most eyes are on Aaron, because out of the two of us, I'm not afraid to admit he's the 'looker.' I'm no dog, but women naturally gravitate toward him based solely on his eye-candy looks. To use words he's previously spoken, 'Zac Efron has nothing on me.' He's not entirely wrong, either – he's got the 'Zac in his bleach blond era' likeness. The dude has taken photos with fans and never corrected them; he looks so much like him. His downfall is when he opens his mouth and lets his inner douchebag show. At that point, most women back away.

'Oh my gosh,' the woman in white says with urgency as she spots us.

'Yes,' Aaron says to her in his bedroom voice, nodding his head like a horny creep. 'We *are* single, ladies...'

The woman furrows her dark eyebrows at his words, then looks back at me – a slightly tipsy smile on her face. She hands two shots of tequila – one in each French-tip manicured hand – to Aaron, who gladly accepts them.

'Ash?'

I stop mid step – intending to leave Aaron to the women and head to the bar for my own drink – when my name leaves her lips. I turn back, looking her up and down again. Those blue eyes. Her small frame. The smile with one dimple showing in her cheek. Holy shit – I do know this woman. This is Lucy Gray, all grown up. How in the hell did that happen?

'Asher Wright? Of Portland Oregon?' she continues since I'm lost for words, like she's almost sure but not completely.

I've wondered about this woman for years, hoping her life got easier. And here she is getting married. Wow. That must mean she's happy – and that's all I ever hoped for.

'Yeah!' Aaron exclaims. 'Damn, you're good. Do me next,' he requests, already having downed both tequila shots, and is now sipping a pretty drink he definitely did not order.

Lucy shakes her head, looking at him like he's lost his ever-loving mind. Her gaze moves back to me, and the beauty gives me a familiar smile.

'Lucy Gray,' she says, planting a hand on her chest, only directing attention to her low-cut dress, which Aaron has certainly noticed. 'Don't tell me you forgot I existed?' she teases.

Even cleavage can't distract from what's going through my head right now. Forgetting this woman exists would be impossible. We've got history. Some good, some absolutely terrible, most of it unforgettable. We may have lost touch after high school as people do, but because of what we went through, I've never quit thinking about her. Worrying about her. I just never thought I'd see her again.

Lucy dated my best friend, Kris, when we were in high school. We did some double dating. Caused some chaos. Drank underage. Snuck out of our houses to wander the city. But hell, this – never in a million years did I expect her to turn into this.

'Luce?'

She nods. 'What're the chances?' she asks, wrapping her arms around my neck.

Without hesitation, I hug her, lifting her off her feet and

holding her tight. Every memory I've ever had with this girl comes racing back.

'How are you?' she asks as I set her back on her feet.

'Eh,' I mumble, stepping away from her and shoving my hands in my pockets. She's caught me on one of those self-deprecating days where I've convinced myself my best days are over. 'Turning thirty tomorrow. So—'

'He's depressed,' Aaron speaks for me, frowning dramatically and then tapping the side of his left eye like he's pointing out a tear.

'And he's douchey,' I say, shoving him an arm's length away from me.

'Thirty, flirty and thriving! That's how you say it,' Lucy remarks, lifting me up instead of beating me down. 'You're in your best years!'

I chuckle at her positivity. 'Says the twenty-nine-year-old bride-to-be standing before me,' I comment, looking her up and down. 'Looks like you're in your best years for sure. I had no idea you were getting married. Congratulations. When's the big day?'

'Tomorrow our Lucy becomes Mrs Kruzie, trophy wife,' one of the women in pink says proudly, lifting her drink to cheer the most ridiculous name ever.

'Lucy Kruzie?' I ask, thankful Aaron is preoccupied with someone else. He would have a hay day with this.

She smirks, biting her bottom lip. 'I'm not taking his name, obviously. I'm smarter than that.'

'Good.'

'Who cares about last names when your Prince Charming rides in?' the woman who spoke for her previously says.

Wow. That's big. 'He's your prince?'

'My prince?' she asks it as if she's confused. 'I du— well, he's—'

Another of the women overhears her stumbling over her answer and grabs Lucy's left hand, flashing me a rock so big he either loves her an enormous amount or knows her family wouldn't settle for a carat less.

'What she means to say is she is *his* queen.'

Lucy blushes as I take her hand, inspecting the rock. 'Looks as flawless as the woman wearing it.'

'Stop,' she says with a slight giggle, waving a hand my way and then admiring her ring. 'You were always such a sweetheart.'

'Not really, just telling the truth. So, you ran off to Vegas to get married and brought a dozen of your closest friends?' I ask, glancing around at the women surrounding her.

'Oh, no, everyone is here. You know my family, they spared no expense.'

'I can imagine they wouldn't.'

Honestly, I don't know a lot about her family, but I do know her grandmother is beyond loaded. Yet Lucy never acted like a spoiled brat like some of the other rich kids I've met in my lifetime.

'Anyway, back to why we're here – old man turns thirty tomorrow and wants to lose his virginity,' Aaron butts in, his arm now around a gorgeous blonde in pink. 'Any of your ladies-in-waiting interested?' He glances at the girl hanging off him. 'Not you, sugar, you're mine.'

She beams back at him.

'Congratulations,' I say to his top-choice woman. 'You've just won the fuckboy lottery.'

'Dude!' Aaron moans as if he can argue it. 'I'm trying to get you laid,' he grumbles towards me under his breath.

I punch him playfully in the shoulder, causing him to grimace and rub at it.

'Luce and I are old friends. We go way back.'

'Waaay back,' she says. She then furrows her brows. 'Gosh, how long ago was it I last saw you?'

'Twelve years,' I remind her.

Aaron was too young to have ever met Lucy. My siblings and I are all five years apart, so we didn't really keep up with one another's friends. He and I weren't more than average brothers until after he graduated high school and neither of our parents showed up to watch. That's when I stepped in. I doubt he remembers anything about Lucy.

'Twelve years,' she repeats my words under her breath, staring at the floor. 'It's gone by so fast.' When she looks up at me, it's with sadness and I know exactly what's going through her head.

I'm glad our last memory together wasn't Kris' funeral, but instead her prom. Though with her eyes glazing over the way they are and the excessive blinking to prevent tears from spilling over, maybe she's not as over him as I expected. It's a hard thing to forget, that much I know. Perhaps I'm not the only one he haunts over a decade later. Does she talk to him like I do, as if he's guiding her through life? I doubt it.

'Very fast. But, no,' she says suddenly. 'I promised myself I wouldn't think about him this weekend, so I'm changing the subject; how've you been? Why are you here?'

She promised herself she wouldn't think of him? Jeesh. Now my heart hurts. I rub my chest uncomfortably. Thus far, the tragedy that brought Lucy and I closer together has been the worst day of my life. I honestly hope it always is – and that's selfish as fuck on my part. Grief and me, we aren't besties.

'I'm not here to—'

'Lose your virginity?' She finishes my sentence with a chuckle. 'I wasn't buying it for a second.'

I laugh. 'Good. No, he signed me up for a blackjack game.'

'You're a professional gambler?' she asks with surprise, now sipping a drink one of her friends has handed her.

I shake my head. 'Professional chef. First-time blackjack competitor. Aaron thought, win or lose, playing in a tournament would be a thirtieth birthday I'd never forget.'

She sips her drink through a tiny straw, nodding her head. 'Huh. When's the tournament?'

'Tomorrow night.'

'Ooh. So, are you free right now? Because I have a sure-fire way you'll have a birthday eve you'll never forget.'

'Indeed, we are free right now,' Aaron says, popping in out of nowhere like a fucking genie in a bottle.

Does the man have super hearing? Jesus. I wish he listened like this when we were at work.

He slings an arm over my shoulders to remind me that anywhere we go this weekend will be as a duo. Whether I like it or not – because he paid for our plane tickets this time around.

Lucy opens a white glittery wallet-type purse. 'How do you feel about partying Vegas style tonight at Brandon's bachelor party? It's the talk of the town. Mitzi paid for everything, as usual, and she spent lavishly.' She holds out a gold key card. 'Penthouse suite: this will get you there; just scan it in the elevator. *And* you should come to the wedding tomorrow! It's been so long; I'd love to have you there!'

'Um—'

How do I feel about watching this woman get married – on my birthday – after sitting graveside next to her after losing our best friend and being so severely heartbroken? What if Kris was meant to be standing at the end of that aisle and our stupidity fucked up her whole life? I can't watch that.

'We'll be there,' Aaron says, happily taking the key card from her.

My God, why didn't I see that coming?

'Well then, there you have it. I guess we'll be there,' I say, slightly unsure.

She hugs me again. 'It's seriously so good to see you. I'll find you tomorrow after the wedding, and we'll catch up!'

'Alright,' I say, a little stunned for words. 'I look forward to it.'

What are the odds I'd see someone from Portland in Vegas and have a history with her? About as high as me winning this blackjack tournament tomorrow.

'Come on,' Aaron says, grabbing me by the bicep and practically dragging me from the bar. 'I can't believe you knew someone who could get us into a penthouse party. Damn, bro! You got connections.' He slaps me on the back as we enter the elevator, then kisses the key card like it's real gold before swiping it across the reader. The doors close, and our destination flashes in lights on the screen above the door frame: Nobu Penthouse.

But my emotions are sword fighting within. 'Listen, I don't know if this is a great idea,' I say as we ride upward. 'I knew Lucy in high school and haven't seen her in over a decade.'

'So?'

'So, it feels weird to hang out with her new fiancé, whom I've never met. I can't picture her with anyone but the boyfriend I once knew.'

'Time marches on, my friend.'

'Real empathetic, Aaron.'

He rolls his eyes. 'Why would that offend you?'

'She dated Kris.'

His eyes go wide. He knows the story. But he doesn't know the details. 'Ah. Kris.'

'Yeah. We were teenagers,' I say. 'And that's just it – how well do you know a teenager? What if I was a serial killer now? I mean, chances are slim but not zero. Maybe her judgment isn't what it used to be, and this Brandon is a total psycho? I don't wanna know if he is.'

Aaron is bouncing in his spot but suddenly stops, frowning at me. His disappointment practically oozes off the walls around us.

'Who fucking cares if he's the next Ted Bundy? Don't spend alone time with the guy, and I'm sure we'll be back in our room by sun up. Jeez. The older you get, the less fun you are. Who says no to this?'

'You don't feel the slightest bit awkward walking into a party we weren't *actually* invited to?'

'It's what you go to Vegas to do,' he insists. 'Party with people you don't know and never speak of it again.'

I laugh. If I even say the word Vegas back in Portland, he shushes me like we've got secrets. Trust me, all we have is a collection of bad memories and paid fines.

The elevator dings as it stops, and the doors slide open to a private suite filled with so many people I momentarily check the elevator status to ensure we haven't ended up at a bar. Nobu Penthouse flashes again on the screen above the doors.

Christ on a pogo stick.

'*This* is her fiancé's bachelor party?'

'Ha!' Aaron motions to the crowd. 'Dude's not even going to notice us because half of Vegas is here. This is insanity,' he says, leading me out of the elevator and into the loud, packed room.

'Absolute insanity,' I say, leaning into him so he can hear me over the music playing. 'Jesus.'

'Can I get an Amen?!' is Aaron's response as he lifts his hands into the air.

'What? No. I mean, Jesus, this place easily violates the hotel's fire code with the number of people here.'

He rolls his eyes dramatically. 'My God, Grandpa, stop thinking lawfully and start channeling Sin City. Look at the number of strippers!'

They are everywhere. Literally, there isn't a crowd of people that isn't accented with a scantily clad woman dancing. A curved staircase with a second-story terrace is front and center – including a stair-top stripper. Sleek leather sofas are filled to the brim with people dressed to the nines – some getting lap dances – all holding a fancy drink. Everywhere you look there's more and more people. Out one window, I spot dozens mingling on an outdoor terrace overlooking the strip. A few people are in the hot tub, and the private pool is far from vacant. The music is loud, and every room is jammed full. The place is mad.

'Can I offer you a drink?' A man in a tuxedo approaches us with champagne on a silver tray.

'Seriously? A fucking butler?' Aaron practically dances as he freaks, then elegantly takes two champagne flutes, one in each hand, never offers one to me, downs them one at a time, and then places the glasses back on the tray. 'Thank you, my good sir —' He reaches into his pocket and pulls out a handful of one-dollar bills. I wonder what those are for. 'This is to keep them coming.'

'Sorry,' I apologize to the man as he stares at a handful of ones. 'Vegas him is kind of a monster.'

His pinched smile says he knows very well what Vegas does to people.

'Word of advice,' Aaron says as we approach a loaded bar. 'Put that Lucy Loo girl on speed dial right now.'

'I don't have her number,' I say, ordering a Jack and Coke.

'Get it,' he demands, taking the Corona he asked for. 'Maybe she's into you?'

'She's getting married tomorrow.'

'Which means she's still single tonight.'

'Not how that works.' I heave a sigh. 'Go. Party. We're in room 4007 – do I need to write you a note and put it in your pocket, just in case?'

I know he's going to disappear because we've been to Vegas before. I've learned to stay ahead of him.

'Text it to me,' he says with a wide grin as he backs into the room, disappearing into the crowd.

Get her number. Yeah, I'm sure her husband-to-be would love that. Of course, looking around it's clear he didn't just invite guys to this party, so I doubt one in her phone would worry him. And he knows a *lot* of people. Damn.

I wonder who he is. She said his name is Brandon. Who here looks like a Brandon? I'm picturing a teenage football quarterback superstar, maybe the coach's kid, who models for GAP commercials on the weekends and hangs out at REI downtown, even though he's never stepped foot off the city sidewalk. Or, based on this party, I'm looking for a Scott Disick type. Which is sort of what I'm afraid of, and pretty much accounts for the whole damn room. Hell, the man himself might be here.

*Why* do I know who Scott Disick is? Freaking Alyssa, my older sister, a fan of all things reality TV – that's why. And since she pretty much raised Aaron and me when our mom was too self-occupied, I can't complain about the girly shit I've watched because of her too much.

'Hey cutie,' a woman's voice earns my attention. 'You bored? 'cause I could help with that,' she says, running her fingertips down my arm, her eyes glued to my many tattoos.

The last thing I want to ask is how.

'Nope,' I say, downing my drink. 'Not interested.'

The brunette huffs at my response before disappearing into the crowd.

I promised myself after the arrest, that Vegas would be for drinking, gambling, and babysitting my brother. I learned my sleeping around lesson last time I took advice from Aaron. That's his game, not mine. But, drinking alone is no fun, so I stay for a while, but after way too many strippers offer me a private show as I meander around looking as lonely as a guy can get, I hop onto the elevator and swipe my card to get to my room.

I wonder where Aaron is. Actually, I probably don't want to know. I search my pockets for my phone, but I left it in my jacket, which is on a table in the penthouse. Shit.

I jab the doors open button and emerge at the party once again.

'I guess I don't understand why you're getting married if this is your hobby?' A woman's voice catches my attention as I stroll into the suite.

Oh? This sounds interesting. What sort of hobby is she referring to?

'She's paid her dues, honey. She's earned it. But that doesn't mean the fun is over,' a man says, his hands all over the very scantily clad young woman – the same woman who offered me a way out of boredom earlier.

It doesn't?

There it is! My jacket. I grab it from the table, slide it on, and pull my phone out to text Aaron before he ends up in the lost and found.

ASHER

Sleep? Room 4007

If I know Aaron, he'll mistake that as 'sleep with,' and he'll be back before midnight if he's not successful at bagging a secret.

'I can't get *emotionally* involved. But I can spend my money any way I like.'

'Which is why I charge you double,' the woman says with a snicker.

Charge what to who now? I glance back to look at this dude. Designer suit. Gel. Possibly an hour of skin care before bed every night.

'Come on, honey, time to pay the piper...'

Ew. Man to man, this one's a douche.

I act as if I'm just checking out the suite, but when I turn to where this couple is chatting, I notice her hand on his package, and much to my dismay, what I'm seeing is not an optical illusion – he's beyond into her.

'Oh, Brandon,' she says with a giggle, allowing him to lead her into one of the bedrooms, closing the door behind them.

Brandon?! Holy shit. Is this Lucy's Brandon?! Please, God, no.

Luckily, the door didn't catch, and when I lay my hand on it, it pops open just enough for me to be a total perv and peek in.

*Please don't get caught. Please don't get caught.*

Whoa. I step back. I didn't realize that position could happen so quickly. And aggressively – my God. This cannot be the Brandon Lucy – sweet little Lucy Gray – is marrying.

*Breathe, Ash.*

I pace the hallway like I'm waiting on the bathroom. Man, I hope there's a bathroom over here; otherwise, this looks so sus. What do I do? I guess I should find out if it's him for sure. But if it is how could I prove it? Only one thing pops into my head, and I don't like it one bit. Videos don't lie – but do I want this video on my phone?

*For Lucy, Ash. You have to do this for Lucy.*

Carefully, while glancing around with worry, I hit record on my phone and slip it through the crack. I look only long enough to make sure he's on-screen then look away, pretending everything is normal, but honestly, I might be in over my head here. This could land me in jail. If I'm not careful, I'll soon be on a first-name basis with the Vegas PD.

'Sexy Lexy, you are hot as fuck,' Brandon growls the words, making me look at my phone with sheer disgust. He slides a hand into her hair at the back of her head. 'Can I hire you to give my Lucy girl some tips?'

I gasp. No. Fucking. Way. The words alone are offensive and disgusting, but the worst part is the creepy chuckle afterward that says he's not kidding. I pull my phone from the door and hit stop, swiping out of the camera and heading straight for the elevator. Lucy *cannot* marry this asshole.

## 2

### ASHER

What a fucking tool. How did Lucy even meet this Brandon? What does she really know about him? Clearly not this – I hope.

I lie in bed, alone in the dark hotel room, staring at the ceiling. My head is churning with a jumble of bullshit – all the times I've been cheated on (by almost every single girlfriend, for the record), broken hearts and what Kris would want me to do.

'You just had to go and die, didn't you?' I snap the words out angrily into the empty room. 'You realize if you hadn't wrecked or if we didn't drink, or if *I* had missed the corner instead, it could be you waiting for Lucy at the end of that aisle tomorrow. What if that was supposed to happen and I fucked up the timeline with a terrible idea?'

I groan. *Stop thinking about it, Ash.* This never leads anywhere good.

I squeeze my eyes closed – *please fall asleep now. Like, right now.*

The room is quiet, besides the random drunk giggle as someone walks past. Yet my mind is loud – and filled with flashing lights, horror and Lucy's face as I told her what happened after EMTs declared Kris deceased on arrival. Her house was the first place I went after the police were done questioning me. Needless to say, she was devastated. And I was crushed almost beyond words. It took me ten minutes of her panicking before I could actually explain what had happened. I still feel bad about that.

'She still thinks about you—' I say, unable to rid the situation from my head. 'Considering it feels like you're always sitting on my shoulder, I'm sure you heard that. She misses you the day before she marries someone else. That's fucking heartbreaking, man. Now she's ended up with some cheating asswagon and *I* get to be the one to break her heart. Again.'

Only silence fills the room. Obviously, considering I'm the only one here. And for that I am thankful. I've never told Aaron details about this part of my life. He only knows what our parents told him, and we've never spoke of it. In fact, I've never told anyone willingly. The pain is too deep, rooted right through my heart and soul, and at times, even now, it tears me up.

\* \* \*

We were eighteen. After a few more sips from my dad's bourbon bottle than was smart, we decided to go race around the city in our souped-up cars – BMWs. We worked our asses off through high school to buy them. His was cherry red. Mine was white. At every red light, we'd pretend we were race car drivers and burn out, attempting to beat the other to the next light. On a slightly damp evening, we took our shenanigans just outside the city to the curvy roads of the west hills. As we raced the roads taking curves like we were in that movie *The Fast and the Furious,* we were having a blast and everything was going great. Until it wasn't.

Unexpectedly, I witnessed Kris miss a corner and go head-first into the most enormous tree I've ever seen at probably eighty miles an hour. He didn't stand a chance. I nearly skidded off the road as I screeched to a stop about a hundred yards past him. I still don't know how I had the brainpower to get the car into park, I was so frantic, but somehow, I did. While parked in the middle of the road late at night, my car engine still running without me in it, I ran to where he was, but there was nothing I could do. Kris was gone and all I got was a core memory that changed me forever.

'Why did I live just to be the one who has to break her heart repeatedly?'

The words 'save her' echo in my mind with haunting clarity, sending chills down my spine. I sigh, running my hands through my hair as the weight of the situation settles in.

'She's gonna hate me if I do that, you know...'

What am I doing? Having a conversation with a fucking ghost? How much did I drink tonight? Not enough for this shit.

How do you tell someone this? I'm sorry your husband-to-be is upstairs boning what I suspect to be a prostitute. I mean, no judgment; everything's legal in Vegas, and people gotta make a living; the fault is not hers. She's just doing her job (or, from what I saw, *a* job) and charging the guy double – that part makes me laugh.

But that fucking Brandon deserves to have his ass kicked a million times over, and considering I don't want to go to jail again, words seem more efficient. Maybe I should just go to her room and tell her. Get all the terrible news out there so she can start processing. What room, though? The front desk isn't going to happily announce to a stranger where a wealthy heiress is sleeping.

Goddamn it. I need Aaron's warped mind to figure this out.

He might be a bit over the top and misdirected, but I know he's always got my back, and despite the shock of his actions and words at times, I trust he'll have a perspective on this that may trigger a solution... I hope.

* * *

I barely slept, knowing what I know. Not to mention seeing what I saw. I actually Googled how to get an image out of your head, and apparently – I'm fucked. Short of a lobotomy or brainwashing, I'll be seeing that image in my mind's eye for the rest of my life. Lucky me.

Finally, I gave up sleeping, decided to shower and go for a walk. I ended up at a restaurant that wasn't packed to the hilt with people but still within our hotel. I texted Aaron so he'd know where to find me, but I got no response. I'm on my second plate when he finally rolls in wearing sunglasses inside – the best way to hide a hangover.

'Morning, sunshine. Where were you all night?'

'Bridesmaids, birthday boy,' he says, flashing me two fingers as he slides into the booth, laying his head against the back of the chair. 'It. Was. Awesome.'

Blech. I nearly gag at the thought of it. The mental image is bringing back 'Brandon does Sexy Lexy,' and I wanna vomit.

'You're sleazy.'

'Yes, I am,' he says proudly. 'You order any coffee? My head is pounding.'

I push the full pot his way. 'Speaking of head—'

He smiles wide, suddenly interested in somebody beside himself. 'You?'

'No.'

I slide my phone across the table to him, the video already

pulled up and on mute because I don't need that kind of attention. I hit play and Aaron immediately picks it up for a better
look.

'What the—? You filmed a guy getting a hummer and didn't
order your own?'

'No, king of fuckboys, I didn't order my own – as classy as
that sounds.'

He looks at me like I'm the one who's nuts. 'You're into
watching? That's wei—'

'Brandon,' I point out. '*That* is Brandon, the groom-to-be of
the wedding you said we'd attend.'

Aaron looks at my phone again, now zooming in on the
video. He laughs. 'Shit... and this is your friend? Lucy?' He taps
the screen, restarts the video and watches it again. 'Lucy's got
some skills.' He looks up at me with sudden sympathy on his
face. 'This coulda been you – I told you. Why didn't you invite
her up to the room to catch up?'

I snatch my phone from his hand. 'That's not her.'

His eyes go wide, and for a moment, he looks less hungover
than he did two seconds ago. 'Shit. I suppose – good guy that
you are – you're going to show her this?'

I shrug. 'Don't I have to if I consider myself her friend?'

'Old teenage friend – your words. Is that something old
friends do?'

I've asked myself that question at least thirty times since
sitting at this table.

'I think I have to.'

He sighs heavily, running both hands through his hair. 'Can
you do it without ruining what may well be the love of my life
with her maid of honor, Madi?'

'You slept with her maid of honor?'

'Guilty,' he says with a not-so-sheepish shrug.

'Wait, I thought there were two women?'

He laughs, pouring coffee from the pot into one of the mugs on the table. 'One maid of honor, one bridesmaid. Bridesmaid's got a boyfriend back home, so she wasn't as into me as she was Madi – which I was totally cool with because those girls together were – Jay-sus.' He lifts a hand like he's praising God. 'That, Madi – wow. She did this thing with her tongue—'

I hold up a hand. 'Do not utter another word of that story.'

He smirks. 'Jealous much?'

'Of the fact that we'll need to stop by the Planned Parenthood before we leave here to get you tested for bugs? No.' I roll my eyes. 'Madi's not the love of your life.'

'You don't know,' he says defensively, stealing a slice of bacon from my plate.

'I know ya said the same thing last month about a Sara, and that didn't exactly pan out, did it?'

He smirks, then shrugs as if he doesn't understand how women don't love him the morning after, even though they are drawn to him at first sight. But I know he knows, and I can't wait for the day some girl ropes that asshole's heart in a way he can't escape, and I get to watch him writhe for his life before falling hopelessly in love with someone and promising to only sleep with her for eternity. Though, I'll never tell him that.

'How in the hell do I tell her this?'

Aaron groans, running a hand over his head. 'Why you gotta tell her at all? She's not your girlfriend. *You* didn't cheat.'

'This might surprise you, but because I'm not an asshole?'

'Oh yeah.' He rolls his eyes. 'Almost forgot you're the goody-two-shoes in this relationship.'

'Someone's got to keep you alive.'

'And even though I hardly ever say it, I do appreciate that. One question. What if she thinks you're full of shit?'

'In that case, I show her the video.'

His eyes go wide. 'Ah, amateur porn produced by the groom himself, what every bride dreams of seeing the morning of her wedding.'

'Why don't you use that twisted mind of yours to figure out how we get in to see her so I can ruin her day before she says "I do." I'll think of what to say while we look for her,' I suggest, standing from the booth.

Aaron grabs the rest of the bacon from my plate, following behind me as we head toward the hotel's lobby.

'I'd just say it – "your husband-to-be, blowjob Brandon, has a tab with a girl from the Red Light district."'

'Less hurtful.'

'OK... how about – "your fiancé has a wandering penis, and I've got proof."'

'The words "wandering penis" aren't leaving my lips.'

'Lame, but I think I just got an idea,' he says, grabbing a huge bouquet of flowers from a vase and shaking the water from the stems onto the carpet. 'We're now flower delivery guys. Vagabond Brandon is about to be outed. Play along.'

'Good morning, sir,' the dark-haired middle-aged woman at the front desk greets Aaron as we approach. 'How can I help?'

'I've got flowers for the Lucy—' He glances at me, eyes wide.

'Gray,' I say under my breath.

'The Lucy Gray wedding,' he finishes his sentence.

She motions toward a sign off to the left of the desk.

Gray – Kruzie Wedding

I beeline that way, walking past the next sign pointing into a large ballroom where a woman in a black tuxedo stands outside the door with a tray of champagne flutes. Instead of going in there, I follow a man with a camera who appears to be on a mission.

'I'd bet money this photographer is headed toward the bridal suite.'

'Smart!' Aaron says, now at my side downing a glass of champagne. He tosses the glass into a garbage can on the way.

'Are you even a hint sober?'

'A hint, yes. But that's about it,' he confirms.

'God, those flowers look like they belong in a Vegas-themed funeral.'

'Isn't that what this is about to become?' he asks sarcastically.

Photographer dude lingers near a potted palm tree across the hall from a door labeled – *Bridal Party*. This must be the place.

I inhale deeply, then knock. I've only been this nervous a couple of other times around this woman. God, I hope she's not completely ready already.

Aaron steps up next to me, the flowers covering his face. 'This could go tits up quickly.'

'I'm very aware.'

The door swings open suddenly and a tall slender woman stares us down.

'Can I help you?'

'Um— I'm looking for Lucy Gray? Flower delivery,' I say, motioning Aaron's way.

Her gaze moves to the flowers, and she lifts a curious eyebrow. 'Lucy?' The woman pulls the door open all the way and at the far side of the room, standing in front of a mirror, is Lucy. Our eyes lock through the reflection. Her sparkling white gown glitters when she turns my way. Shit.

'Ash?'

I stand, silent, my mind wiped clean at the sight of her.

'Earth to Ash,' Aaron groans under his breath. 'Say, Brandon is a jezebel and you're too good for him.' From behind the flowers, he mutters a sentence he thinks will fix all, jabbing me in the ribs with his elbow as I realize I'm staring with my jaw hanging open like a goddamn cartoon character, my gaze on Lucy.

'W-WOW,' I stutter. 'You look… beautiful.'

Pink fills her cheeks as she smiles softly, running her hands down her sides and admiring her dress. 'Thanks. Though I do believe it's bad luck to see a bride before the wedding?'

Finally, Aaron lowers the bouquet and shakes his head. 'Only if you're marrying him.' He throws a thumb in my direction.

Since when is he an expert in wedding traditions? 'How do you know that?'

He smirks. 'You may not realize this, but I'm a very romantic man,' he insists, winking toward a woman standing near Lucy. 'Deep down. Very deep.'

The man just used two of her friends – there is obviously a bone in his body, but it's not the romantic type.

I glance back at Lucy, who also doesn't look convinced. I'm sure by now she's heard the story.

'Didn't you— uh—' Aaron clears his throat, looking to me. 'Have something you needed to say?'

All eyes snap my way. 'Yeah,' I say with a nod. 'I, uh—'

I swear she's somehow staring into my soul. She looks so beautiful. And I haven't seen her for twelve years – why am I about to ruin this woman's life?

'Congratulations, again,' I say, the words tumbling out of my mouth unexpectedly. 'You look even prettier than you did at prom.'

Her smile is bright. 'Thank you. And today's the dreaded day, right? Thirty?'

I nod. She remembered even though she must be preoccupied with wedding things.

'Happy Birthday,' she says. 'I'm sure both of our days will be amazing.'

But her face doesn't match her words. Sure, I haven't seen this girl in twelve years, but I once knew her well enough to see when there was doubt all over her, so, I'm not convinced she thinks today will be amazing.

Silence hangs between us like a heavy, invisible cloak, weighing down our conversation with unspoken tension and repressed memories. This is the exact confused, worried look she gave me the night Kris died as she waited for me to find the courage to speak.

'I—'

'OK, that's all the time we have for this,' the tall woman who answered the door says, cutting me off while taking the bouquet from Aaron, furrowing her brow when she realizes the stems are wet. 'Thanks for stopping by, but we're on a tight timeline. We appreciate the sentiment.'

With that, she closes the door in our face.

Aaron and I both stare at the door silently for a second before he starts to laugh.

'Dude, smooth as butter.'

'Shut. Up.' I run a hand through my hair. 'The dress, the sparkles, seeing her again, the words I have to say – it all distracted me.'

'Don't worry. I'm sure she'll catch him with some woman on their honeymoon and then your part in all this is over. You won't have to be the bad guy 'cause men like that always get caught.'

'You realize you're talking about men like you, right?'

'No way. I'm no cheater. I just sleep around. There's a difference.'

I shake my head. 'I'll give ya that. But no. I've walked in on exactly what I saw last night, in my own bedroom. I know how that feels, and I do not want her feeling that. I have to tell her. *Before* she says "I do."'

'We can't get in! She's got security,' he reminds me, motioning behind us where the room is.

'I've got to find a way,' I say as we walk away, running my hands over my head and clasping my fingers behind my neck. 'Jesus on a fucking pogo stick. I'd rather deturd a ship full of shrimp.'

'And you hate shrimp.'

'Exactly.'

'Well, if you've got to do it, there's only one thing that'll make it easier. Booze.' He points toward one of the bars opened twenty-four hours a day.

'It's barely noon.'

'Somewhere it's drinking hour, so let's pretend we're in that time zone so you won't pussy out and hate yourself later.'

I stop at the bar, stupidly letting him order for us. 'I don't do that.'

'Yes, you do. When have you ever spoke for yourself and told off one of these women who fuck you over?'

'I'm no longer dating any of them, so clearly I ended it somehow,' I defend myself.

'Yeah, but which have you told to get fucked? 'Cause they all earned it, but if it happened, I've never heard the story.'

Talking about my feelings isn't my favorite thing. But surely there's one I've told where to go. Let's see.

Megyn, my first 'adult' girlfriend at nineteen – while in college – didn't like my love language – touch. I was too touchy for her. Yet a guy she met in class felt her up in the corner of the kitchen one day, and word got back to me pretty quickly, so – insert confusion here. I broke up with her the same day I found out, and she walked away like I was nothing. Those two are now married – happily, so I'm told. I did not tell her to fuck off like I should have.

Next up was Heidi. She was a bit older than me, turning thirty while we dated. Maybe her ticking biological clock is why she wanted to move so quickly – like 0 to 100 in sixty days. I hadn't even met her family – whom she claimed were a tad 'unhinged,' to put it nicely. So, when I found a box of ovulation kits in my bathroom, I decided to take a hard pass on Heidi. Last I heard, she was married with three kids under three. Sounds exhausting. I was afraid to piss this one off, so no exit words for her either.

Jeneva – aka Jen, is up next. Aaron set me up with her – which I should have known would lead to a terrible ending. But she seemed into me, and I was beyond into her. She was gorgeous and interesting, but she liked to disappear on me a few days a week. It took me a couple of weeks to find out she was busy because she was keeping up with six boyfriends dispersed across the city. That was fun to find out when I ran into her and one of them downtown, hand in hand (hard to deny there's nothing going on when you're clinging to one another like you're in a windstorm). Yet again, I was nobody special in her life but rather one in a long line of men attempting to woo the girl as she built herself a secret harem. I got an invitation to her wedding last year. I didn't accept. No exit words for her either. It's hard to yell at a woman when she's got a huge man on her arm.

Then there was Melissa – the most serious and recent of the women I'd consider 'girlfriends.' Absolutely beautiful, sophisticated, and exactly my type, or so I thought. But after two years of dating (that's right, she's also my longest relationship), she suddenly decided she was no longer feeling it. However, I had a 'friend' visiting, and she *was* feeling it with him.

When I walked in on them in my bed, she was cold as ice. You'd have thought I was the landlord there to ask for late rent. Her exact words were, 'I told you I wasn't feeling it any more. Staying with you feels like tossing a golden ticket into a fire just to admire the sparks. With Justin, he starts the fire.' Jesus, Justin. So, another one bit the dust – and they left my apartment together, him still buttoning his pants. I was once again wordless. I'm not sure of her relationship status now, nor do I care.

So, to sum it up: Cheated. Tried to knock me up. Cheated. Cheated. That's my serious dating history in a nutshell – and Aaron's right, I didn't say what any of them deserved to hear. And that's why I have to tell Lucy about Brandon. I know the feeling of being betrayed too well, and I don't want her to feel like a fool after making their relationship legal.

'Fine, you're right. I didn't tell even one of those women off because I hate confrontation. So, sue me, I'm a nice guy.'

'It's OK that you're soft inside,' Aaron says gently, leaning in closer. 'Now, this isn't exactly a manly thing to do, but we're brothers, *and* we're in Vegas where anything goes, so if you need me to hold your hand while you man up and grow a set so you can save this girl from a nasty future divorce, I'll do it,' he says, grasping my hand and holding it tightly.

I pull my hand from his. 'How about you just have my back in case it all goes wrong?'

'What could possibly go wrong?' he says with a laugh.

I know he's being sarcastic, but he's also buzzed so, I feel like I need to prep him for what could be.

'I imagine the groom's going to be pissed at what she's watching if I've got to break out the video.'

Aaron nods. 'Agreed. We may risk a fight. But two against one, we could take him.'

'I've hit one person in my life and that's plenty. We're not fighting anyone. Should things implode, we run.'

'Run?' Aaron's jaw drops. 'Like a couple of pussies?'

'Exactly like that. You saw that party last night. It appears everyone in Vegas knows this couple, and it would not be two against one.'

'What about your phone? If you hand it to her to watch the video and we run, you lose it.'

I shrug. 'I'm due for an upgrade. No big deal.'

He shakes his head as if he's disappointed that he even knows me. 'You don't have to do this, you know? We could just disappear into the crowd and go on with our lives.'

'Sorry, I can't. She deserves to know.'

He groans. 'Man, I don't even know how you still believe in love.'

'Everyone believes in love, and if they pretend they don't, they're just afraid to admit it.' I side-eye him, but he's shaking his head.

'Maybe she already knows about his shenanigans and gives no fucks?'

I shake my head. 'Not the girl I knew.'

'Alright then, maybe she's only looking for a first marriage in the guy? I mean, considering what I saw when I met her and then walked into that bachelor party – it's going to be a hell of a first marriage.'

'No. She's not like that. This girl has already had her heart ripped from her chest in the worst way possible. I can't let her marry some cheating douche.'

He sighs heavily, dropping his shoulders with defeat. 'Right. The dead guy,' he says with a roll of his eyes, as he sips his drink. 'Alright then, drink up, cause there's only one place left to do this.'

I drop my head as I sit at the bar next to him.

'Let's blow up this girl's wedding,' he says, lifting a fist and splaying out his fingers as if a bomb exploding.

Not the option I was hoping for, but here we are. Fuck. This may well be a birthday I never forget. This could also be my second official arrest in this godforsaken city.

# 3

## LUCY

'Where are *my* flowers?' Madi snaps, inspecting the bouquet. 'I slept with one of them. Wait a sec. Is it just me or do these look oddly similar to the flowers in the lobby?'

We're in an ornate room in Ceasar's Palace, packed to the brim with bags, clothing, shoes, makeup, hair supplies, food and dozens of people helping get me and my bridal party ready for this blessed event. I haven't had a moment of silence since I woke up, and it's all to celebrate me. Well, my wedding. *Our* wedding.

I glance at the bouquet. I suppose they do seem last-minute at best, but the gesture was still sweet. Odd, and unexpected, but sweet. For some reason, my breathing was difficult as we stood in silence, waiting for Asher to speak, but he's probably just stunned to see me, just like I am him. It's been so long and I'm suddenly getting married. Last he saw me, I was in love with his best friend, the boy who taught me what love was – Kris.

Jeesh. There he is again. In my head, with my heart lassoed to him. Why is he suddenly haunting me like this? I was over him.

*Relax, Lucy.*

Today is a good day. Some might even say the best day of their life. I wonder if they make that call before or after they say 'I do,' I guess I'm about to find out.

'They are familiar, dear,' my grandmother, Mitzi, says, now standing beside Madi as they inspect the bouquet. 'And wet.'

'You guys, it's the thought that counts, right? It's not like he knew I'd be here getting married this weekend so he pre-bought flowers. He's just trying to be a nice guy. That's all.'

I'm a 1,000 per cent certain I'm right about this. Yet I can't help but wonder *how* this happened? How strange is it that we'd run into one another the day before my wedding? In a city neither of us lives in? After twelve years. And why do I feel like he had more to say earlier than the words that left his lips? It's not just randomly running into him that's weird either.

Just last week during a pre-wedding meltdown that Madi titled 'cold feet week,' I thought of Ash. Not directly or intentionally, but while I packed up my apartment in preparation for moving in with Brandon, I came across my childhood bedroom boxes. When I got to the one labeled: Kris & Lucy 4Ever.

I cried all the tears, told Madi parts of the story as I drank a lot of wine, and wondered why people think it's better to have loved and lost than to never have loved at all, because looking back that is certainly not how I felt in that moment. It still hurts twelve years later and if I was to let it, like I did last week, it would consume me and my anxiety would swirl through my soul like thick smoke and convince me that I am meant to be alone.

The past is meeting my present in a strange way and that's making it really hard to let go of the version of that girl Asher once knew. She no longer exists, and it's too hard to remember her any more. I have a new life, a new man, and I love nearly every second of it. But after seeing Ash, I'm panicking that perhaps I didn't pack away that girl and her demons as securely as I thought I had.

A sudden knock at the bridal suite door stops my heart. Did he come back?

'Awe, look at you,' he says as he walks in with his gaze on me. 'I always knew you'd be a beautiful bride, but this beautiful? I didn't expect that,' my father gushes as he inspects me. 'You're getting married today, sweetie.'

'I'm getting married today,' I repeat nervously.

Here I am, promising *one* man that I'll love him for as long as I stay alive. Til death do us part. Never expected to have already experienced that at twenty-nine.

'Seems like just yesterday you were eight years old marrying off your Barbies. I can hardly believe today is the day,' he says, kissing me gently on the forehead.

'Me either,' my voice shakes.

With a simple glance of concern, Dad takes my hands in his and squeezes them tightly.

'Take a breath, honey,' he says, sensing the tidal wave of fears. 'You love Brandon and he loves you. It's fate.'

'You know I don't believe in fate, but you're sweet,' I say, fanning my face to save my makeup from tears. 'And you should rein it in because I can't cry.'

'Someone grab her a tissue!' the makeup artist yells from across the room, where he's working on one of my bridesmaids.

Like an order, a box of tissues is passed between people until my dad hands me one. I fold it, gently pressing it to the corners of my eyes, hoping not to dislodge the lashes I am not used to wearing.

'How am I going to ward off tears all day?'

'I don't think a few tears can ruin how gorgeous you are, sweetie.'

'Thanks, Dad.'

He's always been my biggest fan, talking me up and reminding me how beautiful I am inside and out. Just like my mother was – according to him. I don't know much about my mom. What I do know is that she didn't die – but she also wasn't present in my life after I was about six years old. I remember her. I adored the woman, like all little girls probably do. But even at that young age, she always felt disconnected. It's sad because I'd love to have her here for my wedding. But she didn't even respond to the invite, and Mitzi paid a guy to track her down. Oh well.

*Focus on who is here, Luce – everyone you love.*

'Isn't she the most gorgeous bride?' Madi, my BFF, maid of honor, and Brandon's cousin (how Brandon and I met), says. 'It's like the dress was made for her.'

'It cost ten grand,' my dad says, still looking me over. 'It was made for her.'

That's right, ten grand. However, I feel like I need to say *I* didn't choose the ten-thousand-dollar dress. No. That was my grandmother, Mitzi, Dad's mom. She wasn't sparing a single expense for her only granddaughter's wedding. Anything I wanted, I could have, so frugal me picked a dress on the clearance rack for eighteen hundred dollars, and Mitzi (that's what she's always insisted I call her – she's no one's 'grandma') wasn't having it. She thought I deserved designer chic.

'She's never been prettier,' Mitzi says, admiring my gown, covered in Swarovski crystals that sparkle with each movement I make.

The straight-neckline mermaid gown with sheer corset bodice, dramatic tulle skirt and matching arm cuffs does look beautiful, both on and off. I've been dreaming of it since we finalized its creation, and today, when I saw it waiting for me, it took my breath away. I hope it does the same for Brandon.

'For once, I agree with you, Mitzi. That Pnina Tornai knows how to make a head-turning wedding dress.' I glance at myself in the trifold vintage mirrors in the corner. They've even got a pedestal, just like a dress shop, for proper wedding gown viewing before walking down the aisle. I feel like a Portland royal – the reality TV kind.

'I told you diamonds were a girl's best friend,' Mitzi says with a grin, wearing her own impressive set of diamonds. She's got a closet full of glitter. I wouldn't know her if she didn't sparkle somehow.

'Speaking of best friends, guess who I ran into?' I ask Dad, who will surely remember the man who showed up in a full vintage tuxedo, ruffles down his chest and all, at the last minute when I had no date for my senior prom I'd been anticipating for months. Yes, I'd had another gorgeous custom dress, but tragically, no date.

'Elvis?' he asks.

I laugh, shaking my head. 'Technically, yes. But no, not him. Asher.'

Dad furrows his brows. 'I should know this name?'

I nod. 'Asher Wright? Kris' best friend?'

He looks confused.

'He took me to my senior prom after the accident?'

'Oh! Kris' best friend, Asher. Right,' he says, suddenly realizing. 'Nice kid, if I remember correctly. He's here?'

'He showed up at the bar where we were having the bachelorette party, out of the blue. I could not believe it.'

'He also stopped by a few minutes ago and brought her flowers,' Madi says, pointing to the bouquet sitting on the table near the snacks. 'Isn't that sweet?'

'A blast from the past. That is sweet,' Dad says, glancing over at the bouquet. 'What did Brandon send?'

I glance to Madi, whose eyes widen.

'Um, nothing?' I ask, suddenly filled with worry.

Dad frowns. 'Tradition says you send your bride a meaningful gift,' he informs us.

I know he's right, because I did that for Brandon. Madi knows it too because she was with me when I bought him the watch he'd been eyeing. Along with it, I sent the most romantic note a bride-to-be could write her fiancé. With all the thoughts swirling through me, I'd forgotten all about it until just now.

'Oh no. Is this a sign?'

'A sign of what?' Madi asks.

'That maybe he doesn't want to do this?' I ask with panic in my voice.

'What? No. He's besotted with you! Maybe it just hasn't arrived yet?' she says, marching through the suite, yanking open the door, and glancing into the hall looking for a gift we've missed. 'Nothing,' she says, shutting the door, now walking toward me.

'Although, I will say I'm a little jealous you got flowers from a guy you didn't put out for because, after last night, Aaron probably should have stolen me flowers too,' she says with disappointment. 'And maybe Jess as well,' she mumbles, glancing guiltily across the room at Jessica, who is currently in the makeup chair. She grits a smile as she looks my way, insinuating that maybe they didn't give me every detail earlier.

'I don't want to know what any of that was about,' I tell them as Madi adjusts my dress to perfection. 'I want no worries today. At least no more than I already have.'

'What worries do you have?' Dad asks with concern.

'Just...' I glance around the room at the people I love the most and shrug. 'I'm getting *married*. It's scary, considering I don't know anyone who's successfully pulled that off. Especially with *Here Comes the Bride* magazine featuring it and expecting every detail, including the happily ever after, to be perfect. That's a lot of pressure.'

'Luce,' he says with understanding. 'Your whole life you've been talking about this day. About finding Mr Right, walking down the aisle and living happily ever after. I thought you were sure you'd found him.'

'I know. But I also thought I'd found him in high school, and we know how that worked out. Now my worry is, is *this* the dream I had? Is Brandon *that* man? Does he really want to marry me? I don't know any more. How do you know?'

Dad shrugs. 'If I knew that, I'd probably be standing here with a wife.'

That's an excellent point, made at the exact wrong time. I don't know if there's a single person in this room who can honestly say they're happily married. Why on earth would 'fate' allow me to have it?

'Do you think I shouldn't do this?' I ask, wondering – aka worrying.

That's all I've done since I got engaged. Wondered. About everything. Is this the right dress? Do I really want to get married in Sin City? *Are* diamonds *my* best friend? Can I love someone forever? Do I even know what love is? What if he dies? Or leaves? My breathing speeds as my heart gallops through my chest, probably trying to escape.

'Darling, take a breath,' Mitzi says, approaching. 'Everything will go down exactly as it's supposed to, and no matter which way that falls, you will be just fine, trust me,' she reassures me.

'You're right, I'll be fine. Everything is fine.'

Dad nods approvingly. 'Mom is a smart woman,' he says. 'Also, not to build the pressure, but I spoke to a Todd from the magazine just before walking in here, and his photographers are waiting on the OK to get photos. I said I'd let you know.'

Butterflies or maybe bumble bees flutter through my body, making me almost sick. My God, it's nearly time.

'Are we near ready?' I ask Madi, who looks around the room and nods.

'Jessica is the only one left in hair and makeup. Should be good for photos on time. How's Brandon and his gang doing?' she asks my father.

'They're fired up and slightly drunk, I suspect. But ready to go.'

'Whew,' I let out a relieved breath, my emotions going wild. 'At least he's showing up.'

Madi rolls her eyes. 'Stop expecting the worst, Luce. Like he wouldn't show, he's obsessed with you.'

'As he should be, this is forever,' Dad says.

He's very protective of me. When Brandon asked him for my hand in marriage (Dad expected it), he had a list of questions to be answered before he gave his approval, along with a stern *'if you hurt her, I'll kill you'* warning. Hopefully, that last part won't be necessary.

'They're so adorable together. I'm going to be a sobbing mess up there,' Madi says.

'That makes two of us,' Dad says, pulling his handkerchief from his pocket and dabbing at his eyes. He shoves it back in his pocket, then takes me aside to speak without other ears listening in. A daddy-daughter moment, you could say.

'Sweetie, it's normal to be nervous at your wedding,' he reassures me. 'So normal, they've got a name for it – cold feet. My advice is to wear thick socks and not overthink things. Follow your heart, Lucy – it always knows what to do.'

If it was only that easy.

I nod; thankful he's always on my side.

With a hand on my chest, my eyes closed for focus, I practice my breathing for a few.

*Brandon loves me unconditionally. He tells me all the time. I've got nothing to worry about.* I repeat the words my therapist concocted to help with my wedding anxieties until I hear a knock on the suite door.

'Floral!' someone calls.

'Good! The actual flowers are here! I've been dying to see them,' Mitzi says, flittering her eighty-year-old self to the door and allowing the florists in to deliver bouquets.

I don't even know what they look like because she picked them. She planned almost every detail of this wedding while I worried about everything else. Luckily, I trust her judgment.

According to her stories, Mitzi was a ritzy socialite way back in the sixties, before they were cool. She's mingled with the stars for most of her young life, throwing lavish parties that national news has reported on. She's slowed down over the years, but I trust that this wedding will be the talk of the year because of her. She's also the one who got the magazine interested. Without Mitzi, my life would be boring because I didn't inherit her outgoing personality. In truth, I'd have been OK with the discounted dress and just the two of us on a beach in Hawaii. But I've agreed to this and it's too late to turn back now.

# 4

## LUCY

Not even an hour later, we're standing in the nearly empty hall, waiting for the wedding planners to open the doors and reveal us to the room.

'What if I'm making a mistake? What if he leaves in a month? Or worse, *dies*?' I whisper the words I didn't want to say out loud to my father.

He's holding my hand to the crook of his arm, patting it softly.

'Everybody dies, sweetie, but I promise no one is dying today. I know you've been traumatized, but I think it must be fate that Kris' best friend unexpectedly showed up on your wedding day. A sign he's always with you. It's OK to move on – he'd want you to.'

I nod, thankful he's able to read my mind because if I attempt to speak, I'll lose it. He's right, though; it *is* OK to move on. It's time. Kris would want me to be happy, that much I know. I pull the tissue hidden in my gown, dabbing at the corners of my eyes.

Dreaming of marrying your boyfriend as a teenager is

ridiculous, but something I did well. After his death, he haunted me for a long time. So, when Brandon first proposed, I said no – out of fear of losing him unexpectedly like I did Kris. But after therapy and working through some things, the second time was the charm, and here we are, about to tie the knot in front of family, friends, Vegas, and everyone who reads *Here Comes the Bride* magazine. Despite my past, I live a life every girl wants; I can't overlook that.

'You ready?' Dad asks.

My head's ready. My heart... *might* be. I can't figure it out, but the hesitation between the two is maddening. Like something's wrong, but I don't know what it could be? It's got about ten minutes to figure itself out.

I blow out a shaky breath. 'As ready as I'll ever be.'

The doors open, and the room stands as the music changes to a classical piece played by actual stringed musicians. Oohs and aahs fill the room as we walk, and inside, my heart thumps almost audibly. I plaster on a smile at beaming faces, some of which I know, but most of which I do not. God, there are a lot of people here.

Suddenly, one stands out: Asher. He came! I give him a slight wave.

Until now, when he's crossed my mind, he's been eighteen years old and taking me on a pity date. Now he's a grown man, taller than I remember, and handsome with his chiseled jawline, complemented by a neatly groomed five o'clock shadow. He's got the same sandy brown hair cut short, with more green than brown hazel eyes that sparkle like gemstones under the Vegas lights, and cute half-moon crinkles parenthesize his smile. I knew him immediately. It was sort of comforting to see someone from my past. Besides my family, he's the person who knows the pain we both went through when losing Kris.

Today, his smile is soft and a little unsure, and I'd bet money he's experiencing the same thing I am in the pit of his stomach – nostalgia mixed with grief. Did anyone ever think I'd get here? Certainly not me.

'You look beautiful,' Brandon says in a whisper when we make it to the front of the room.

'Thank you, handsome,' I whisper back.

He beams – the exact smile you want to see from your groom-to-be on your wedding day. My heart warms a little. Maybe it's not so undecided.

'Welcome,' the hotel's hired magistrate speaks to the packed room as Brandon and I take our places next to one another, my now sweaty hand securely wrapped in his.

'Relax, Lucy girl,' he whispers, shaking my hand.

I nod, taking a deep breath.

*Everything is fine, Lucy. People get married every day, and rarely do they die from it. You're letting your anxiety get the best of you.*

I glance behind me at the full house of people now seated, and all eyes are on us. I didn't expect this many people to show up to an out-of-state wedding. Did Mitzi invite the entirety of Las Vegas, too? Jeesh. And here I was, worried about inviting two extras at the last minute. I can almost feel the piercing gaze of expectations that I'm afraid I'll fail at. I see Asher and his friend sitting on the right, near the middle of the outside pews. What must they think?

The magistrate's voice has me turning back to Brandon. 'We're here today to witness Lucy and Brandon's happily ever after. Marriage isn't created by a law or a ceremony but rather by the hearts of two people in love. Marriage grows by loving, caring, and sharing ourselves with another – which these two have done for two years now. Of course, this ceremony isn't magic; it won't create a relationship that doesn't already exist.

Our couple have made commitments to each other in the days since they met, and today, we tie the knot. But first, let's get the big scary question out of the way: if anyone can show just cause why these two should not be wed, speak now or forever hold your peace.'

I glance around the room, hearing silence. A peace falls over me – un*til* someone clears their throat and stands: Asher.

'I, uh…' He swallows hard, raising his hand awkwardly. 'I've got just cause.'

'Who the hell are you?' Brandon asks, staring at him with his eyes narrowed.

'Name's Asher Wright; I'm an old friend of Lucy's, a new enemy of yours, I suspect.'

Brandon's glance snaps to me. 'Friend of yours?'

I nod, unsure what to say. 'What are you doing?' I ask Ash. If I wasn't mistaken, I'd say he is sweating right now. Why? Something is very wrong.

'You can't marry him, Luce.' He shoves his hands in his pockets, clearly uncomfortable.

'Luce?' Brandon mimics like he hates this guy using my nickname.

I ignore him for now. 'Why not?'

Asher looks at the ground, then back to me. 'He's not who you think he is…'

The fact that he seems unsure is making me doubt him. Maybe he's not the same Asher he was. I mean, I haven't seen the guy in over a decade; perhaps he's changed.

'I… don't understand.'

His friend, still sitting, nudges him. 'Show her, you're gonna have to show her,' he says, pretending to be coughing between words. Slick.

'Show me what?'

Brandon sighs heavily, shaking his head. 'Jealousy, it comes in all forms, folks. Can we get on with this?'

I touch his shoulder, stopping him from performing a one-man show by putting down a former friend. 'Let's hear him out,' I suggest.

With a roll of his eyes, Brandon crosses his arms over his chest. 'Fine. Speak, stranger. Let's hear it.'

'Trust me,' Ash says, his eyes on me while ignoring Brandon as he approaches, pulling his phone from his pocket as he walks. 'The last thing you want to do is hear it. I think seeing it will be enough.' He hands me the phone, tapping the screen before letting go. 'I couldn't not tell you – I'm sorry.'

He's sorry? Crap. I can see it in his eyes. They're prying and pained, and practically the exact look he had when he showed up at my door the night Kris died. Jeez – how bad is this?

I'm almost afraid to look at the screen. But I do. Loaded is a video. I press play and almost immediately regret it. Instinct tells me I'm not supposed to see this, so I cover my eyes but then force my hand away to ensure I'm seeing what I can never unsee.

As Brandon glances at the phone, he gasps. 'What the—? No-no-no. Give me that.'

He tries to swipe the phone from me, but I grip it with an iron fist, staring him down between glances at the screen. My breathing speeds the longer I watch, and my chest tightens with each second the video plays. Panic sets in like fast-set concrete. This can't be happening.

'What *is* this?' I ask myself in a whisper.

Brandon shrugs like he knows nothing at all. 'It's news to me.'

I shoot him a look. News to him? I glance at the video again to confirm that this is most definitely him. But the flush of his cheeks, the lightning of a storm brewing in his eyes as he watches it with me, tells me this is not news to him.

'Where did you get this?' I ask Asher, who is now backing down the aisle, his friend Aaron doing the same on the other side of the room.

'Bachelor party,' he says nervously. 'I stumbled into it and wasn't even sure he was the right guy at first. Once I figured it out, I knew I had to tell you, and I spent all night figuring out how. I hadn't planned on doing it here, but I got distracted this morning, so here we are.'

Oh my God. That's why he brought flowers this morning. He was trying to tell me then.

The life seems to drain out of me, and I'm freezing to the point of shivering (there you are, panic attack), yet only on the surface. Inside, I'm raging like a volcano has just smothered my heart in hot lava.

'Sweetie,' Dad stands, approaching the altar. 'What's the problem?'

Right as I feel like my heart will explode through my eyeballs, I hand the phone to my father, who accidentally turns up the volume to excruciatingly loud, and I hear the words that send the flood over the edge. *'Can I hire you to give my Lucy girl some tips?'*

A sudden gasp escapes my lips, but it is drowned out by the deafening thud of my own heart pounding in my ears. A bolt of electricity surges through my body, leaving me physically shaken and mentally scrambled. It's as if I'm living out the 'naked in public' nightmare, suddenly stripped bare and exposed for all to see, only this time it's happening at my own wedding, in front of everyone I know and love. And many who will tell this story until the end of time and probably not even remember my name.

I stare at Brandon, with the glare of a woman scorned. How dare he do this to me!

He attempts to take my hand, but I jerk mine away. Tears roll down my cheeks, burning through the makeup that was perfect only seconds ago.

'Tips? Seriously?'

'That's not me,' he says half under his breath.

'Dear God!' Dad bolsters, his gaze still on Asher's phone as his cheeks turn pink, obviously sickened by what he's seeing and hearing. He jabs at the screen to stop the video, dropping the phone onto the floor while it plays on repeat somewhere under one of the chairs – loudly. When he looks our way, the rage in his eyes most likely matches my own. Maybe someone is dying today.

Brandon holds a hand out toward my father. 'I did not say that.'

The tears burning the back of my eyes turn to rage. 'Did you *do* it?' I snap.

'No!' he insists.

'It looks like ya did.'

He shakes his head repeatedly.

'Brandon. You're a grown-ass man. Tell the truth. Is that you?' I ask, demanding an answer, even though I *know* it's him. But, considering what I feel right now, the asshole deserves to have to admit it to everyone in the room.

He presses his lips into a flat line, glancing back at his best man.

'Answer her question,' my dad says firmly stepping up behind me.

Brandon's face is pained, and honestly, he looks like he'd like to run; instead, he exhales heavily and answers calmly as if he can talk himself out of this. 'I was *really* drunk last night—'

My chest ignites in a blaze of pain, each breath scorching my lungs like fire. My mind screams in agony as I struggle to hold on to any semblance of sanity, but it slips through my fingers like sand. My grip on reality falters as I struggle to breathe, suffocating under the weight of his deceit.

'Are you saying this is Tequila's fault?!'

'Yes!' he insists like it's a valid excuse.

'Ha!' I laugh manically. Jeesh. My emotions are all over the place. 'Were ya so drunk you don't remember saying yes to a blowjob by another woman the night before your wedding?'

He nearly chokes on the lie he's holding back.

'Blowjob?' He laughs uncomfortably, shaking his head. 'That's not what that was.'

'That's what it looks like,' I say. 'But please do explain if that's not what I just witnessed.' I cross my arms over my chest, awaiting his story.

'I— I—'

He's speechless – perfect.

Along with me, the entire room seems to pulse with shock, the air thick as if charged with electricity, every silent breath a struggle against the storm within.

The night before our wedding, ugh. No way was this the first time either, that much is obvious. He thought he'd get away with this probably because he's done it a dozen times before. Jesus. My heart plummets to the ground, shattering into a million pieces, as I realize the depth of his betrayal.

'You cheating piece of fucking garbage.'

Each syllable that escapes my lips is a razor-sharp blade, dripping with venom straight from my wounded heart to his. But it's not just my words that are enraged – my entire being is consumed by fury. And in a moment of uncontrollable rage, my clenched fist connects with his nose, the satisfying crunch echoing through the room.

'Oh!' the whole room groans audibly.

'Ouch,' I say, rubbing my fist as he hits the floor with a thud.

'Good Lord,' Madi says, rushing to my side. 'You just laid him out. Are you OK?'

His best man kneels to Brandon, taking his pulse in the wrong spot. 'I think he's dying!'

'God-fucking-speed then, ya cheating asshole,' I snap, grabbing the skirt of my dress and marching down the few steps back to the aisle, Madi hot on my heels like the amazing maid of honor she's been. Despite the fact that half this room is her family, too, she's loyal to me because that's what best friends do when their family are cheating assholes.

'I'm not dying,' Brandon groans, stopping me in my tracks.

I turn to see if he has an explanation. Our eyes meet for a second – and my heart does nothing. No spin. No skipped beats. Just 'Ave Maria' playing as it crawls into a shallow grave.

'That *was* me,' Brandon says finally, admitting it. 'But at least I never hit you,' he says, reaching up and touching his nose, realizing he's bleeding and nearly passing out at the sight of it. His best friend reaches down to help.

'At least you never hit me?! Keep talking and I'll hit you again. And *don't* help him!' I command. 'Do the world a favor and let the sleaze-bag bleed out.'

The minister shakes his head and does a quick hail Mary, probably attempting to absolve himself from this entire day. God, I wish I could do the same.

'I *am* going to kill him,' my father says, now marching toward Brandon. Each shirt sleeve is uncuffed at the wrist and shoved to his elbows, revealing his clenched fists.

I take a few steps back as Dad reaches down, grabbing Brandon by his jacket lapels and jerking him from the floor.

'What did I tell you the day you proposed, you stupid son-of-a—'

Before he can publicly murder the man or finish his sentence, the family he's referring to jumps to Brandon's rescue, and I watch as the whole room combusts to defend their loved ones, all as *Here Comes the Bride's* photographers snap pictures.

That's my cue.

With a determined glint in my eye, I stride toward the back doors like nothing is wrong, refusing to let my soul die over this nonsense – at least right now. I delicately wipe tears from my face, while Madi and I retreat. As we get to the back doors, I meet Asher's gaze one last time.

'I'm so sorry,' he mouths, lifting his palms into the air before allowing his friend to pull him from the hall entirely out of my gaze.

Me too, Ash. Me-freaking-too.

'Come on, darling,' Mitzi says from behind, taking my hand and leading us toward the elevators.

'How could he do this?' I ask the two of them, shards of my shattered pride settling heavily in my gut.

'I don't know.' Mitzi squeezes my hand tightly.

'Because he's the biggest dick alive,' Madi blurts. 'My God, Luce, I am *so* sorry. I had no idea he was capable of this. If you want me to kill him, just say the word. I'll even bury his dumb ass in his parents' front yard.'

'And I'm sure if it needs to go that far I could get involved and we could convince your father to help,' Mitzi says with half a smile.

I laugh, sort of hysterically, unsure of what's funnier: killing him or having my grandmother and lawyer of a father help with the body?

Our steps echo in the long hallway as we make our way toward the elevators that will take us back to the bridal suite. The light casts long shadows around us, each one a mirror of the doubts and insecurities swirling within like a growing hurricane. How did this turn into the second worst day of my life so unexpectedly?

# SEVEN MONTHS LATER

# 5

## LUCY

Mitzi sits in her favorite chair at the dining-room table, a purple laptop open in front of her. 'Darling, what shall I search to hire a professional chef?'

'Professional chef Portland, Oregon,' I say, peeking through the fridge.

Cheese – many kinds. Bottled water. Strawberries. Lunch meats. Milk. Eh, I can see the need for her sudden interest in a chef.

'You're hiring a chef? Do I get to eat with you?'

It's not that I can't feed myself, but I moved in with her just after Vegas, and considering I'm not a chef, we don't eat a lot of 'meals' together. We sort of just survive on whatever is easy, as the nearly empty fridge is proof of.

I didn't plan to move in with my grandmother. But shortly after the nightmare that was Vegas, Mitzi had a very minor TIA that I blame myself for. Why? Oh, you know, loads of money was lost, and the police were called to a wedding with a guest list of 350 folks. And there wasn't just one fight. There were five. We made the local nightly news – and were banned from the hotel for life. Dad was right, the groom and his gang of idiots were slightly beyond drunk at the ceremony, and that didn't help.

Mitzi was so stressed but played it off beautifully and kept me from completely losing it until we'd locked ourselves in the bridal suite with a table full of food. After that I cried, laughed and mourned what I thought I had until we got the all-clear that every last guest (and everyone with the magazine) had gone, and we could escape without further issues.

When my father suggested that maybe she needed round-the-clock care, I volunteered. No way was I allowing her to go into a retirement home. She deserves so much more than that. And I couldn't exactly go back home, to a place I was supposed to share with the douchiest man I've ever known, so why not take care of someone I actually love in a house I grew up loving and it's hardly a hardship living here? Mitzi and I need each other.

If she hires a cook, I can finally see this over-the-top professional kitchen in action. Trust me when I say this is a chef's kitchen that's never seen a chef – or anything resembling one. If you've dreamed of it, it's in this kitchen, and I don't know how to use it. Except the espresso machine. I finally resorted to watching a YouTube video on the brand, and now we have shop-style coffee every morning. I can't imagine what the rest of these appliances could cook up.

'Of course, you get to eat with me, darling. I'm hoping they'll rub off.'

I shut the fridge, shooting her a confused look. 'You want them to what?'

She looks at me with a gray eyebrow cocked. 'Influence you to learn how to cook, dear. Since you moved in, you've not once used the oven.'

I cross my arms over my chest, a little offended. 'Mitzi, might

I remind you that you are against a woman being confined to the kitchen.'

These are words she's said to me a million times over my life. Also, never let a man steal your soul— er, identity. I may have misheard the word soul because I'm currently on a man-hating bender. Rightfully so.

'That's why I'll hire a man.'

I should have known she'd have an answer for anything I threw her way. She always does.

'Can I request an age and type, or is that taboo?'

'Off-the-charts taboo,' I say. 'However...' I tap my index finger to my bottom lip. 'You are eighty. And you deserve to have some fun in life – we could play the elderly, nutty grandmother card?'

She laughs. 'You're absolutely right. I'm an old woman who could die tomorrow. I deserve some fun, you genius girl.' She waves my way approvingly and then turns back to her laptop. 'Twenty-five to thirty-five, male professional chef Portland, Oregon,' she says as her fingers tap the keys. 'Here we go.' She scrolls the screen, nodding every so often. 'Now we're getting somewhere,' she says, jotting names on a paper pad beside her. 'On with your night, darling, I am setting a date with some men.'

'And I am going on a date with one.'

Her gaze shoots over the top of the laptop and meets mine. 'I thought you still wanted to kick love in the teeth?'

Not gonna lie; I said that. And a whole bunch of other things that I'm sure will come back to haunt me.

'I do. And if one day, love proves to be true, which I doubt, he'll probably screw me over, and I will. For tonight, I've set my expectations low. I'm not looking for love, just a piece of cake from the dessert menu with a cocktail for dinner. Is that wrong?'

She shakes her head, her eyes back on her laptop and her pen in motion. 'It's exactly why I'm hiring a chef, darling. Maybe you could bring Mitzi a piece?'

'Of cake?'

'Yes, dear. Life is short. Eat the cake. I like all kinds. Surprise me.'

'OK.' I nod, opening the lid on the bottle of water I'd grabbed. 'I'll leave it in the fridge for breakfast.'

'Perfect,' she says with a smile, still occupied by young hot local chefs.

Yikes, that sounds like an X-rated site that might actually exist. I hope she doesn't stumble across any. If I have to rid her laptop of porn (again – it's a long story – computers are hard when you're elderly – the first time was horrifying enough), I will die.

The last time I had to see a dirty movie, I was wearing a ten-thousand-dollar gown while watching it in front of an audience of hundreds, next to the male lead. That asshole. Thanks to him, every second of that film is burned into my brain in a way that makes me want to stab out my own eyes with a dull pencil each time it crosses my mind. But that is a terrible idea, so instead, I curse him internally and continue smiling outside. That's what you're supposed to do, right? Fake it 'til you make it? I wonder how long that takes to work.

The honk echoing through the living room jolts me from my thoughts.

'That's my Uber,' I say, grabbing my purse and heading out the front door.

'Make him work for it!' Mitzi calls after me.

'Will do!' I say before closing the door behind me.

I'm such a liar. If she knew it was just me and Madi indulging in an exorbitant amount of alcohol, calories, and gossip, she'd be so upset. Mostly because ever since Vegas (that's what we call it now, so we don't say the devil's name out loud), she's been insistent that the love of my life is still out there – he has to be because I'm such a sweet girl and I deserve it – her words.

I don't think I'm as lovely as my family acts like I am. A man defiled my trust and let me believe he was good until the truth was forced out of him in front of everyone we know – that doesn't happen to sweet girls. Or maybe it only happens to sweet girls? Crap. There's one more thing for me to worry about. Truthfully, at this point, I'll probably die a childless cat-lady, and I'm OK with it.

Anyway, Madi and I have plans (and possibly reservations) at Papa Haydn for raspberry lemon drops and the most to-die-for desserts. Their regular food is good too, don't get me wrong, but the bourbon ball – a tiny chocolate cake soaked in bourbon, glazed with dark chocolate ganache – for real, I'd sell my soul for a dozen.

* * *

'How are you?' Madi asks as I approach the table she's sat at in Papa Haydn.

The building sits on a corner lot, with seating inside and out. People are buzzing around the city streets, soaking up the summer evening at the different restaurants and bars along 23rd Avenue – one of my favorite Portland streets.

Fun fact, it's also known as the Knob Hill neighborhood, and considering I'm meeting a woman who reminds me of my ex, that's perfect.

Knob Hill has almost everything you could ever need. Bed sheets worn? There's a Pottery Barn. Wanna sing karaoke?

They've got a bar for that. Looking for whatever McMenamins is trending? Check out Ram's Head. Spill a little sauce on your shirt? Hop into the Urban Outfitters for a new one. Need to replace a lock to keep out an ex? There's a hardware store. Looking for the best Chinese food in the city (in my opinion)? It's on 23rd.

'Just trying to survive my own mind. How about you?' I ask, sitting across the small bistro table from her.

'Already ordered our drinks, so I'm about to be great. Any topic off the table tonight?'

'Just the usual.'

'Will not mention the dickweed.' Madi nods, her curly blonde hair bouncing with her movement.

She's adorable, a total reincarnation of Marilyn Monroe on the outside. It's uncanny. She has been hired as a Marilyn impersonator at a couple of local piano bars, and I went to see her perform once. If I didn't know, and Marilyn wasn't dead, I'd think she was her. She was that convincing, with her wispy voice and gestures.

Madi and I met in college. We had exactly one class together the entire time we were there, and somehow, the friendship stuck. She's breezy, beautiful, loyal, and when necessary, a complete badass. If I'd have ordered that hit on Brandon like she suggested in Vegas, I don't doubt she'd have followed through. She's a great person to be friends with because her attitude is very *c'est la vie*. What happens, happens. Everything is fixable. Things will work out. Live life like today is your last day. The opposites attract thing is true for us. After the wedding, she was so terrified that I was going to dump her, too, just for sharing blood with the dickweed. I couldn't have done that; she didn't choose her family.

Thankfully, since she and Brandon are only cousins, she

doesn't remind me of him looks-wise. If she did, seeing her would hurt more than it already does. He had us all fooled, including his family, who were upset after Vegas. Rightfully so. They'd already paid for our honeymoon – three weeks in Thailand – which he went on with his brother without a budget. I don't even want to imagine what went down on that trip. All I know is that he wasn't murdered or thrown into a dungeon somewhere to rot. Unfortunately, he made it home safe and sound and has been seen around the dating apps my friends use.

'Ladies,' a waiter stops at our table, sets our drinks in front of us, and takes our order – which is borderline embarrassing as we each order two desserts, no actual food. 'I like how you two think,' the man says before walking to another table.

'How's Mitzi today?' Madi asks.

'She's hiring a private chef because, apparently, I need to learn how to cook.'

She laughs. 'She said that?'

'No. She said she's hoping he rubs off on me.'

'Ooh! That's dirty and fancy all at once, isn't it?'

I nod. I'd say the dirty part was unintended, but Mitzi can occasionally throw shocking things out that surprise me. Like, can she search for a hot young male chef? Jeesh. If she actually hires someone fitting that description, I don't know what I'll do.

'What kind of food?' Madi asks.

I shrug. 'No idea. But I'm hoping he comes with a suggestion box.'

'Jackpot,' she laughs. 'Maybe he'll be cute too?'

'That'd be a bonus, considering I work from home and have to look at him all day.'

That's gonna be weird.

I'm a graphic designer who freelances. Dad was thrilled

when I told him I was changing my major from pre-law to the arts. That's a lie. He was so mad. '*You could offer the world so much more!*' he insisted. But did I want to? What's wrong with what I already offer the world? Nothing – in my mind. Finally, after months of explanation, I got him to understand that my worry-wart nature wouldn't let a lawyer become one of my personalities. He recoiled and got on board. Anyhow, now I work right from Mitzi's place and mainly focus on creating visual identities and marketing materials for companies. Boring. But every so often, I get to work on fun projects like designing book covers and album art. That makes up for the rest.

'Good thinking,' Madi says in a proud tone. 'Note to self: start visiting Mitzi more.' She acts as if she's writing it down on a pad of paper. 'Also, take her advice and let the man rub whatever he wants. You deserve it.'

'Sure,' I laugh. 'Nothing weird about three grown women ogling a guy as he cooks for them dreaming of him rubbing things.'

'Men have been doing it to us for centuries,' she says. Her gaze suddenly darts from me to something behind me. 'Speaking of men, that one there seems to have an eye for you.'

I freeze – hoping I disappear. 'Are you serious? No.'

She cocks her head. 'Stop acting like you're some sort of troll right now, Missy. It's not at all shocking that a man would admire you. You are a catch.'

'No, I'm not. Though, if catching turds and labeling them my fiancé is a talent, I'd win first place.'

Madi laughs loudly. 'All I'm saying is you need an outlet. He seems interested, give the guy a joy ride.'

'Uh...' I laugh nervously. 'That's you joy riding men, not me.'

She nods, not disagreeing at all. 'And I haven't been sad in ages. Maybe we should switch personalities *Freaky Friday* style? You use men for your pleasure, and I'll look for love. Deal?'

'Ha! No deal. Should I look?'

She shrugs. 'That's up to you. If you do, he's going to think you're eyeing him back.'

'He's staring? At me? Are you sure?'

Madi nods, unable to wipe the goofy smile off her face. 'He hasn't looked away since you sat down.' She sips her drink, acting casually like we're not speaking of him.

I grit my teeth. 'Does he *look* like a turd?'

'You think the entire male species looks like turds right now.' She reminds me. 'But no time to overthink it because he's on his way over.' The words leave her lips quickly, telling me he's en route as she speaks.

'Crap!'

'Hi,' a male voice to my left says.

Madi and I both sit up straighter as we look up at the man. Tall, dark, and handsome.

'Hi,' we say in unison.

He glances between us, his eyes stopping on Madi. 'I apologize, but I couldn't help but come over and tell your friend how gorgeous she is.'

His gaze meets mine, and for a second, a flutter of something floats through my chest. It's been a hot minute since anyone called me gorgeous.

Madi rolls her eyes with a chuckle. 'Don't fret, hon. I know how beautiful she is. I've got eyes. But definitely you should tell her. She needs to hear it.'

'You're beautiful.' He does as he's told and smiles wide as he says the words, not even attempting to tear his eyes from me. 'I'm Tanner.'

Tanner is beautiful, with dark hair, dimples, tan skin, and

big brown eyes staring at me in a way that I haven't experienced in many months. Is he undressing me? Or admiring me? The line is fine.

'She says "thank you,"' Madi says, kicking me from under the table. 'Tanner, this is Lucy Gray. She's in her thirty, flirty and thriving era as of sixty days ago and beyond single. You two should definitely chat while I run to the little girls' room.'

With that, she stands from her seat, offering it to Tanner, who happily sits.

On her way to the bathroom, she glances back and mouths the words, 'Talk to him – he's cute.'

Oh my God. She set this up.

'Lucy Gray,' Tanner repeats. 'That's a good name.'

I laugh nervously. 'I've got no complaints about it.'

But I do have a complaint for my BFF for once again setting me up and surprising me. She did this with Gabe a few months ago, only he met us at a nightclub when she insisted I drag myself out of bed, dress up and go out. '*Out is good for depression*,' she claimed. It wasn't. Gabe called me every day for weeks after I'd had one too many cocktails and let the guy kiss me. Big mistake. Total turd. Terrible kisser. She means well, but her matchmaking ways have been revoked after Brandon and Gabe, so pass.

'Ladies.' Our waiter stops at our table, second glancing Tanner sitting where Madi was, carefully setting four desserts and two fresh drinks down, filling our small table.

'Wow. You two have a sweet tooth, eh?' Tanner asks, reaching into his back pocket and pulling out a wallet. 'How about I just leave you with this and say – call me sometime?' He hands a business card my way.

I take the card and read the words to myself. 'Tanner Scott – Attorney at Law.' Ugh. Of course, he is. He's dressed to the nines, professional and gorgeous, I should have guessed. Please, Lord, don't let my father find this business card.

'Maybe?'

'Call me maybe?' he says with a smirk, lifting his phone to his ear.

Now it's awkward.

'Yeah... I'm not gonna lie, you're very pretty. However, I'm sort of on a dating hiatus right now, bu—'

'Buuuut,' Madi comes buzzing back over as if she wasn't in the bathroom at all but hovering somewhere just out of sight listening. 'She'll reconsider that and shoot you a text in the coming days. Sound good?'

'My phone's always on,' he says, winking.

Tanner looks like he doesn't get shot down a lot, but he doesn't press and just waves before leaving the restaurant altogether.

'Did you set this up?' I ask Madi as she sits back down, her eyes on the chocolate in front of us.

'What?' she asks, her tone saying everything. 'I don't even know the guy.'

'Might I remind you that lying well doesn't run in your family?' I say, noticing the flash of stormy waters in her eyes. 'I told you, Mads, you're banned from all future set-ups. You're two to zero, my heart is long gone, and I'm over dating. Romance or love or even a strong liking – whatever you want to call it – I'm no longer looking for it.'

'You're officially on a man ban?'

Ooh. I like that. I nod. 'That's right. From here on out, man ban. Got it?'

'Fine,' she says with a sigh. 'But for the record, that one found you.'

'No,' I say, pretty sure I'm right about this. 'At some point in the not-so-distant past, I'd bet money Tanner Scott found you, and you thought of me, and here we are.'

She laughs, stabbing her fork into one of her desserts. 'You're having some wild thoughts. Now, catch up to me; I've already started my second drink. And don't lose that card. One night at two in the morning, you'll think of Tanner, and from my lips to your ears, he's not opposed to booty calls.'

'For the record, if I booty call him, you start looking for love.'

Her smirk says everything – that is never ever happening.

I drop my head toward the ground with a groan. 'The fact that he pulled off chivalry so well when all he wants is to get laid is a tad disturbing. How is a woman ever supposed to trust again?'

'They can't all be gentlemen,' she says through a bite of chocolate ganache that she closes her eyes for. 'Sometimes we need someone to ravish us to remember how we should be worshipped.'

A thought that hadn't crossed my mind. Have I ever been worshipped by a man? Once. But I'm not sure teenage puppy love counts.

'You are something else,' I say, knocking back the rest of my drink so I can make it through the evening.

# 6

## LUCY

The delicious scent of mango and cherry wafts through the steamy shower as I lather my hair with my favorite shampoo and conditioner. I've got a big evening planned (not really). Dinner (surely there's something in the fridge that's appetizing) and Netflix's *Love is Blind* – which I'm not sure that it is, if I base my opinion solely off this show. My favorite part is seeing the newly engaged couples meet in person for the first time; after that, it becomes a wild race to the altar – if they even make it that far. It's oddly comforting to watch the train wreck it usually becomes, especially since my own love life has been less than successful.

I let out a contented sigh as the warm water washes over me. Rinsing the conditioner from my hair, my mind wanders. I've warded off Tanner's texts three times over the last seven days. That's right; Madi gave him my number because she suspected I'd never call him, and she wasn't wrong. I'd planned on staying single for at least the next decade, but she just has to throw a wrench in my plans – because I 'deserve' more. But until a man rides in on a white horse, wearing a crown or his kingdom's family crest – and saves me from the dragon that is life, I'm out. The man ban is now in full swing. Plus, I could use the time to figure out who I am again without the stress of worrying about finding Mr Right. I don't need a man. I can woo myself better.

Lost in my thoughts, I absentmindedly reach for the body wash and start to lather it on my skin, relishing in the sweet scent of coconut and vanilla. A knock on the bathroom door startles me out of my reverie, and I hear a familiar voice calling out to me.

'Darling, I'm sorry to barge into your room, but remember the take-out sample meals you tried last week?'

I quickly rinse and shut off the shower. Do I remember? I tried them in order (she had them numbered, not named, so I didn't know who the chefs were) and I swear when I got to three, it was orgasmic. Seriously, that man knows how to cook. I've never had flavors dance on my tongue before. I didn't even know what I was eating besides pork, pears and cashews, and those are just the ingredients I could see, but it's going on the list of soul-selling foods.

'Please tell me you hired number three and trashed the other guys? My taste buds fell in love with him.' I shout so she can hear me from my en suite bathroom while the door is closed.

I twist a towel over my hair, and with a second towel pulled tightly around my chest, I buzz by Mitzi, who's standing in my room, the door wide open to the house behind her, and into the closet, where I pull the door partially closed, so I don't flash her, dressing in whatever is most comfortable for binge-watching after eating a meal that will make me believe in love momentarily.

'I did hire chef three,' she says. 'I came to tell you he's here.'

'Oh!' I coo excitedly. Now I don't have to eat cheese and

crackers for dinner like I'd previously planned. 'Is he cooking?' I ask, sniffing the air as I walk back into my room from the closet.

'He is cooking—' She stops mid-sentence, looking me over from head to toe with her eyebrows furrowed. 'Oh dear. Is this what you're wearing?'

I glance down at the oversized emerald-green hoodie that hangs on me like a dress over two-tone gray heart print leggings and fluffy pink socks because this house is big and drafty sometimes.

'To have dinner and spend an evening in my room binging Netflix? Yep. Why are you surprised? This is always how I dress for a night in.'

'No surprise. I just expected us to be in daytime clothes when we met him.'

'Based on the one meal I've had, the man is a genius in the kitchen,' I say. 'Because of that, I wanted to wear my stretchy pants in preparation of overeating. You didn't have a single opinion on them at Thanksgiving. What's the problem now?'

Her eyes go wide as I speak. 'I think perhaps—'

Right then, I get a whiff of something. Garlic? Maybe. I can't wait to find out. 'Do you smell that? Come on, Mitzi, we have a private chef to entertain us. Why are we standing in my room worried about my outfit when we could be ogling a young, hot chef,' I say with excitement.

She grimaces. 'That is sort of the problem.'

'He's not hot? Or young? Is he elderly? That'd be good for you!' I approach, taking her hand and leading her through the house toward the kitchen.

'No dear, it's not that – it's—'

'Mitzi, you're never this hard up for words. Just say whatever it i—'

Suddenly, I have a stroke. Not a real stroke or anything, but

I've lost all my words as I reach the kitchen – stopping as if my feet have been glued to the floor, partly because my brain has malfunctioned at the sight of him.

Our eyes meet, and there's a flicker of something in his expression that mirrors the shock swirling within me. Memories flood back – him standing on my doorstep at one in the morning attempting to stay stoic as he gave me the worst news I've ever gotten, his terrible dancing at my senior prom, the ten-thousand-dollar gown, the scent of flowers from the wedding bouquets, and the sound of my heart pounding furiously as I stood at the altar watching a video I still can't unsee. A shiver runs down my spine as I recall the commotion, the surprise of the guests, and the look of determination in his eyes as he uttered those unforgettable words – '*I couldn't not tell you – I'm sorry.*'

'He happens to be the man who interrupted your wedding,' Mitzi says, squeezing my hand tightly as my gaze lingers.

My God. Has the man saved my life twice now? It's possible.

Over the months, I've tried to bury the memories deep, along with all the haunting nightmares that go with them. That's going to be harder to do now that he's standing in front of me.

'W-wh-*why* is he here?' I manage to whisper, my voice barely above a breath.

'He was sample number three, darling,' she explains, her voice low.

No freaking way.

'He was number three?' I repeat, trying to wrap my head around the surreal situation unfolding before me.

Mitzi nods solemnly. 'Yes. It would seem fate may be trying to tell you something,' she suggests, leaving me in the spot where my feet feel locked to the floor as she takes a seat at the kitchen island.

'Fate?' I mumble, not believing in its supposed 'goodness' for even a second. It's screwed me over one too many times.

Tension fills the room, suffocating us both as we stand there, lost in a moment suspended between the past and present.

'Hey, Luce,' he says softly. His voice breaks through the tension like shattering glass.

I take a deep breath, attempting to steady my racing heart. 'Hi, Ash.'

# 7

## ASHER

'Before you think I set this up, let me explain. I honestly didn't realize this job was for Mitzi until I got here today. If it's uncomfortable for you, I can leave...' I say, fidgeting nervously with the pan in my hand after nearly dropping it on the gas stove that I'm not sure has ever been used, as she enters the room.

'No,' she forces out. 'Don't go.'

'Don't go?' I ask, as if I heard her wrong.

Mitzi and I exchanged words as we both realized my connection to Lucy when I got here. I couldn't predict how my presence would affect her, but Mitzi assured me it would be positive – after her initial shock, that is. And now, as she stands there, speaking in short sentences with confusion written all over her face, I can't help but wonder how this may unfold.

Despite mentally preparing myself, her presence catches me off guard. She looks nothing like the glamorous woman I saw in Vegas – somehow, she's even more stunning, casually dressed in leggings and a hoodie, her damp hair is tucked behind her ears, which are adorned with multiple silver earrings. Not a stitch of makeup is on her face, and the slight freckling over her nose that I remember from our youth, catches my attention. I always thought her freckles were adorable, but as a teen she was pretty insistent on finding makeup that had *'full freckle coverage'* – her words. Today, her skin glows like it's made of glitter, and half a shocked smile sits crookedly on her pretty face. She's absolutely having an out-of-body experience at this moment.

'I want you to stay,' she says, clearly unsure of herself.

I set the pan down on the stove, the sizzling sound fading into the background as I turn to face her. Her eyes search mine like they're hunting for a hint or clue in my expression – but there are only a couple of things going through my head right now.

One – she's more beautiful than I remember. And two – she's OK after Vegas. Thank God.

The smile on my face is probably ridiculous. 'OK. I'll stay then,' I say, taking a step closer, closing the distance between us. 'But you, sit,' I say, guiding her to the barstools.

She allows me to help her into her seat but remains silent, fixing her gaze on me for what feels like an eternity before speaking.

'I, uh— I didn't realize you were a chef?' she asks the statement as a question – like maybe she'd forgotten.

'I mentioned it briefly in Vegas,' I reply.

Her eyes go wide.

Shit. Why did I say that?! Maybe she'll punch me for reminding her. I can only imagine the memories it'll trigger.

'But, uh— I'm sure you don't want to talk about that shitshow. Sorry, I shouldn't have even mentioned it. Worst trip, ever, by the way.'

I didn't play in the blackjack tournament that weekend. Aaron and I just drank, for about twenty-four hours straight.

Until she and what had happened wasn't at the forefront of my mind. On the plus side, I didn't get arrested that time.

'Understatement of the year...' she mumbles as her cheeks pink slightly.

Thick silence falls over the room as I continue to cook. Occasionally, as I caramelize the onions, I glance in her direction, and each time, she's got her eyes on me, but I'm not sure she's seeing me with whatever is going through her head. She's reeling, it shows all over her face and I might be the one to blame.

'Should this be weird?' I ask.

Her eyes unglaze with a slight shake of her head. 'Um... do *you* feel weird?'

'Sort of,' I admit. 'As if I've done something wrong.' I hesitate, unsure if I should keep speaking, but I have to know, because I've spent countless nights worried about this woman. 'Did I?'

'I—er... you—' She tries to speak but clamps her mouth shut, then opens it again, but no words leave her lips.

The last thing I want is her hating me for what I did. What I *had* to do. The smell of something 'off' earns my attention, and I race back to my pan.

'Please tell me I didn't ruin your life. I've thought about it – about you, a lot.'

'Really?'

'Yeah, I've been worried. Like, did I do the right thing? Should I really have gone so public? Was the video actually necessary?'

She shakes her head, her face softening. 'Don't worry, *you* didn't ruin anything. That was all Brandon,' she says his name with a sad sigh. 'But it's in the past. Now, I'm doing great. Totally over that tool. And despite the fact that I'm dressed for bed at six in the evening on a Friday night, I am also over all that Vegas crap. In fact, I have a date tomorrow night. So, that's proof I'm not just sitting around here mourning what I thought I had.'

Mitzi suddenly coughs, covering it up with a sip of water from the bottle on the counter in front of her.

'You have a date?' Mitzi asks once she's recovered.

'Um... *yes*,' Lucy insists. 'I told you all about him recently, remember?'

'No,' she responds.

The way her eyes go wide and panicky says Mitzi is blowing this story for her.

'Her memory isn't what it used to be,' she says to me behind a hand covering her mouth so her grandmother doesn't see. She then turns to Mitzi. 'Remember the lawyer I met with Madi that night we indulged in cake and cocktails?'

With a look as suspicious as suspicious gets, Mitzi nods. 'Papa Haydn, right?' Mitzi says. 'I didn't realize you'd called him yet.'

'Didn't I tell you? We've been texting all week.'

'What's his name?' Mitzi challenges her.

'Tucker— *er*, Tanner?'

I chuckle to myself, my eyes on the stove. This is awkward.

'You're not sure? You've been chatting him up all week, and you haven't memorized his name?' Mitzi asks.

Lucy bites her lip, avoiding the question. She could be lying. But why? Let's take a shot in the dark, shall we?

'This is your first "date" since the wedding, isn't it?' I ask, pouring the contents of one of the many bottles of cooking magic I brought with me. Flames shoot toward me and the gasp from Lucy is adorable. I shake the pan, killing the flames.

She cracks a guilty grin, glancing at Mitzi, then back at me. 'Sort of – how did you know?'

Interesting.

'Legit, just a good guess.'

'Well, this is exciting,' Mitzi says. 'You're ready to move on. That deserves the finest of champagnes to celebrate.' She attempts to leave her seat, but I stop her.

'I'll get it,' I say, throwing the towel I just wiped the counter with over my shoulder. 'Direct me.'

'Thank you, sweetheart. Wine Fridge. Bottom shelf.'

I kneel down and pull open the wine fridge tucked under the island countertop full of wine and champagne bottles – and not the cheap stuff.

'Glasses?' I ask.

'Cupboard on the far right,' Mitzi says.

I meander the kitchen, pulling open cabinets and drawers, looking for what I need to pop the top on this champagne. Lord knows I could use a glass right now, and that's coming from a guy who usually refuses to drink on the job.

Once we all have a glass, Lucy smiles softly, visibly relaxing in her seat.

'I can't believe you were chef three. I don't understand how it's even possible.'

'You should tell him what you told me a few minutes ago about his sample dish,' Mitzi suggests as she lifts her glass.

'Mitzi,' Lucy says under her breath.

'What was it that you said? *"Trash all the others. My taste buds have fallen in love with chef number three."* I believe you used the word orgasmic,' she says through a chuckle, sipping her champagne as cover.

I laugh but rein it in when I notice Lucy's look of mortification at Mitzi's repeating the words I couldn't quite hear from out here earlier.

'Orgasmic,' I repeat, a smile creeping through. 'Well, that's a high compliment. Thank you.'

Lucy rolls her eyes playfully, flashing me an uncertain smile. 'You're welcome – I suppose. So, what smells so good?'

'That is the savory scent of garlic sizzling, onions caramelizing, and the buttery goodness of chicken breasts roasting in the oven.'

Lucy lets out a small sigh, resting her chin on her left fist as she leans forward, watching me intently. 'I don't remember you being into cooking back in school?'

'I wasn't,' I admit. 'After I moved out, I realized I needed to eat, and I wasn't a fan of the fast and frozen food my mother loved to serve for every meal, so I learned. Then, I got into it, learned more and more – went to college, and now, I'm in the transitional period between working for someone else and opening my own restaurant.'

She gasps with surprise. 'You're opening your own restaurant?'

I nod. 'I am. Downtown, Knob Hill area – my favorite.'

'Mine too,' she says softly.

'Best neighborhood in the city if you ask me. The building is currently being remodeled, and I'm on the hunt for a suitable name. Maybe you two could keep that at the forefront of your mind as I work for you, and if you think of anything fitting, let me know.'

'Copper and Clover? Saffron and Sage? Cocktails and Cake? Fork and Flame?' Mitzi throws out options – the champagne not taking long to do its job – none of them bad.

'I like the idea of "something" and "something,"' I say. 'Not sure those are the right words, but great brainstorming, Mitzi.'

She smiles, nodding proudly at Lucy.

'I'm gonna think about it,' Lucy says. 'I feel like I need to know you— er, your cooking better first.'

She wants to know me better? Huh. Why do I like the sound

of that? I glance her way, catching her gaze and flashing her a grin. Lucy Gray has suddenly become a mystery I can't wait to unravel, yet her caution reminds me to be careful of how I handle this.

* * *

I pick up my buzzing phone without bothering to check the caller ID because I already know who it is. Every night at 11 p.m. sharp, he calls me – unless we're together, which is often.

Aaron's not only my brother, but also my business partner. He's almost as brilliant in the kitchen as I am. Unless you ask him, then he's the best there ever was, and he's just waiting for a moment to knock my ass out of place – and yeah, never happening.

'Aaron,' I say, feigning annoyance.

'Bro. How was the side gig?'

I let out a laugh as I stretch out and prop up my feet on the soft ottoman, crossing one over the other. It's good to be back home, relaxing in an outfit almost identical to the one Lucy wore this evening – comfortable gray sweatpants and a cozy black hoodie. But I admit, my head's on her. I think I officially have my first-ever crush, and it's got some baggage – not her, but us, our history. How in the hell do I navigate that?

Despite not wanting to leave tonight, I did, and I'm back at what I now see as a dingy dude's apartment compared to Mitzi's mansion. I don't live as luxuriously as Lucy does. My place is a single bedroom. Literally, you walk into a big living room/kitchen/dining combo and look left at the small hall with three doors all facing one another. One goes to the bathroom big enough for one. Another is my only closet. The third is my bedroom, which I am pleased to say was big enough for my king-sized bed, so I'm not complaining. But the place is quaint. And filled with thrifted crap that a grown man needs to live. A couch – black leather, purchased nearly new. The matching ottoman turns it all into one big La-Z-Boy. A giant TV because I'm a dude, and that matters. There may be a gaming console or three (millennial who didn't get this shit as a kid here – don't judge). I am somewhat sentimental, though. I didn't buy everything via Facebook marketplace. I've got a vintage Bentwood rattan rocking chair (and know what that is) straight from my grandmother's estate. It was the one item she left for me. I don't have a lot of great childhood memories. My parents were a mess and worked a lot to pay the bills and just barely kept food on the table, so my favorite memories are of my nana rocking me as a child in this chair. Looking at it brings me a sense of comfort and realization that I don't need to relive the mess I was raised in. I can be anything I want to be.

In the makeshift dining room, there is absolutely nothing on the walls. But there is a robin's egg blue sixties dining table set. On top of that, I've decorated with a stack of cookbooks, an out-of-control pile of unopened mail (again, dude) and a spot for me to eat like I'm not a caveman if I prefer. But, usually, I don't, because the ottoman makes a great table while binge-watching whatever I'm in the mood for.

Overall, think small, clean (c'mon, I'm a chef), sparse yet cluttered rental apartment on the second floor, overlooking the sidewalk and a parking garage that's always got some kind of shenanigans going on across the street. I hear a lot of sirens, if you get my drift.

'Remember the wedding we imploded in Vegas?' I ask.

'Like I could ever forget. That might be the proudest I've ever been of you – standing up for some woman you barely know – doing the right thing even when it felt really, *really* wrong. I still can't believe you went through with it.'

It was easily the second scariest thing I've ever had to do. I was forced to listen to Kris – the ghost that connects us – and I had to save her. In honor of him, but also because she deserves so much better. It was sort of like an itch you have to scratch – you'll excuse yourself from a crowded room to take care of it – and that's what I did. I scratched the itch. And yeah, I felt better, at first – then I let my mind take over on the flight home and have pretty much worried about her ever since.

Never have I felt like that, besides the night I took her to her prom. She couldn't sit at home, and no way was I letting her cry over Kris when she could be out making a memory that started her life over when grief made her feel like she had nothing left.

'My gig is with the jolted bride, Lucy, and her wealthy grandmother.'

I can hear the phone shuffling as he probably drops it or stands up, giving his full attention to our conversation. Aaron is ADHD-positive. And he hates when I say it like that, which is why I do it. We're brother's, we razz one another, it's fun. I can picture his hands in his hair right now.

'Say what?' he asks, his voice low and wary.

'You heard me right.'

'How do you feel about that?' he asks as if I'm paying for his opinion.

'I'm not disappointed.'

'Interesting – why?'

'No clue,' I say honestly. 'But I'm looking forward to it – and not entirely for the paycheck. It could be fun to catch up after all these years.'

'In that case, holy shit! What'd she say when she saw you?'

'At first, absolutely zero. It was terrifying. She just stood there, staring at me. I thought she'd died standing up.'

It was like she'd seen a ghost as she stared through me – glued to the floor at the sight of me – and for all I know, maybe she did. I know I do at times.

'But then she started talking. At first awkwardly, then her grandmother got out the champagne and that helped. Though, I have a feeling she's not handling this breakup as well as she pretends.'

I'll never tell Aaron this, but I want to know why. Partly because I feel somewhat responsible for having thrown a live grenade into her wedding ceremony. But also because Lucy has had two serious relationships that I know of, and I've been there to witness the heartbreaking losses of both of them. Again, why?

'Even I wish I had less details.' He audibly shivers. 'I hope you deleted that video.'

'Was on my old phone.'

'But is probably saved in the cloud,' he says.

'Then it's safe, because I have no idea how to get to the cloud, so one day, my loved ones will find it and wonder.'

Aaron laughs. 'That's beautiful. You fuckin' perv. Where you at?'

'Home, and I'm not leaving. Where are you?'

'Bar a block from my apartment.'

He goes there at least three times a week. If he eats one more of their loaded cheeseburgers, he's going to need to get his cholesterol checked, and he's barely twenty-six.

'Bartenders know you by name in there yet?'

'They have my drink ready by the time I reach the counter.'

'Classy.'

'Very.'

# 8

## LUCY

What a freaking loser I am! Ugh. Why can't I stop thinking about this? I flip on my bedside lamp, hoping the light will chase away the thoughts from my past that are now storming my head after the awkward night I just endured, refusing to let me sleep. It doesn't work. But you know what might? More booze. I'm sure I've had enough, because my mind evaded me most of the evening, while champagne filled my word hole. It was a disaster. I can't imagine what Asher thinks of me.

I navigate through the dark house to the kitchen, unsure if I truly want to drown my thoughts or face them head-on, flipping on the lights over the kitchen island. It doesn't really matter which bottle I choose – Mitzi has exquisite taste, and I know every one is exceptional.

As I close the wine fridge after making my selection, I notice a business card held up by the yellow smiley face magnet on the refrigerator – something I hadn't seen before. Which makes sense because everything from earlier now feels surreal, like I was outside my own body watching two trains collide.

Grabbing the card, I read the words aloud. 'Asher Wright –

Private Chef & Catering.' My gaze then lands on the numbers beneath his name.

Oh my God, this is his phone number. Should I call and try to explain myself, or would that just make things worse? I floundered through this evening, and I can't even recall exactly what I said. There's no way he didn't notice me almost have a stroke at the sight of him in my kitchen. Humiliating.

I place the business card on the island counter and open the bottle of wine, feeling the corkscrew twist into the stopper until the satisfying pop of the cork brings a fleeting smile to my lips. I skip the glass and take a swig straight from the bottle, my eyes fixed on the card.

Did he intentionally leave this, or was this Mitzi's doing? I could wait until morning and check with Mitzi – *or* I could just ask him? I take another swig, conflicted. Honestly, what do I really have to lose? He's already witnessed me at my worst. How much more awkward could things get?

Another sip, dang this is good. The crisp, refreshing taste of the white wine lingers on my tongue, a perfect choice since it doesn't need to breathe – thankfully, because I don't have a minute to spare. I need to make this phone call before my courage dwindles away like a fading sunset.

I flick off the kitchen light, casting the room into shadows, clutching the bottle and Ash's card tightly as I head back to my room. The door clicks shut behind me, sealing me in my own little world. Settling cross-legged on my bed, I take another long, satisfying drink, feeling the cool liquid slide down my throat as I gather my resolve and courage.

He probably won't even pick up, especially since it's so late, but the least I can do is leave him a voicemail. I'll explain that I'm actually quite normal – if such a thing exists – and it would mean a lot to me if he didn't judge me based solely on the situations he's witnessed me in.

That's it. Just one more sip, and I'm going through with it. At the very least, I owe him thanks for getting into a tricky situation in Vegas on my behalf.

I hesitantly tap the phone number into my cell phone, placing it on speaker, my heart racing with uncertainty as I take another swig of wine, trying to calm my nerves. But once I hear it ring, I slightly panic realizing I can't take it back. One way or another, he'll know I called.

'Hey, you've reached Asher. If it's not an emergency, text.' BEEP.

'Oh, thank God, voicemail. OK – this works. Hi, this is Lucy. I, uh, wanted to explain why I was so weird earlier, but I'm slightly torn about what to say. Partly because I'm sure I said I was fine. But obviously, I'm not fine. Now I've got both of my worst memories weighing me down and I'm not sure how to— Ugh! Should I even be doing this? It's not like you gave me your number personally, I just stole your card off the fridge and invited myself to call you because I feel like an idiot. But you don't have to answer. I mean, call me back if you want to...? God, this is so embarrassing. How do I delete this?'

As I speak, my fingers fumble to exit the call, my mind racing with urgency to Google how to delete a voicemail. Suddenly, a tremor runs through my hand as my phone vibrates insistently, displaying a number not stored in my contacts. My eyes dart to the business card on the bed, its crisp edges and bold print confirming exactly who I suspect it might be.

'Hello?' I ask, feigning ignorance.

'Lucy?'

'Um— no...?'

He laughs softly. 'Are you sure? Because I just heard your message, and I swear you sound just like a Lucy I know.'

I take a swig from the wine bottle and exhale heavily, feeling caught.

'Fine, yes, it's me,' I admit. 'I found your business card on our fridge, and even though you didn't ask me to call, I did. And to be completely honest, since you appeared in my kitchen earlier, my mind's been in a whirl. I can't sleep, and here I am, halfway through a bottle of wine I opened just five minutes ago.'

'You've got my attention,' he says, clearly entertained.

'Tonight sort of unraveled not at all how I'd envisioned. Not that I'd pictured it. In fact, I didn't because I wasn't expecting chef three to be you, so it's completely thrown me off balance. So, fair warning, in case you didn't notice earlier, I've got issues.'

'Issues, eh?' There's a warmth in his voice that puts me at ease. 'We all have our quirks. It's what makes us interesting.'

I let out a nervous laugh, feeling the tension in my shoulders ease slightly.

'Well, I can guarantee I'm more than just interesting. I'm a whole mess of worry, overthinking and awkwardness.'

'Worry, overthinking *and* awkwardness, you say? That sounds – relatable.' There's a pause on the other end, but it's not uncomfortable. It feels like he's taking a moment to process everything I've said. 'You don't need to worry because I'm sort of a mix of the same things.'

'You are?'

'Yeah,' he says. 'I'm surprised you didn't find me weird, to be honest.'

'Pretty sure I stole the show.'

He laughs. 'You know you caught me off guard when you mentioned you'd like to get to know me better. I think I like the idea of that. We used to have fun together, why not now? How about dinner at your place tomorrow night?'

I burst into laughter, almost disbelieving. 'You still want to come over here and watch me scramble through another evening like a newborn calf struggling to stand?'

'Interesting way to put it, but yeah. If your date with Tucker slash Tanner will allow it?'

Crap. My date. I forgot about that lie. I swallow a large gulp of wine, trying to calm my racing thoughts. He can't think I made this phone call to clear things up but still lied or he really will think I'm nuts.

'Right, my date. Maybe we plan our already planned dinner for the next night?'

'I probably won't say no to any night.'

I laugh again, more out of nervousness. 'Are you sure? Because I feel like a fool. The past has been breathing down my neck for months and piqued at the sight of you tonight, if you catch my drift. I'm so embarrassed.'

'You're not a fool. In fact, I might be the only person who truly understands what you're feeling.'

I lay back, staring at my ceiling, my breathing finally slowing. Maybe he will understand my wildest worries.

'Do you think—?'

I pause; unsure I should even mention him but unable to keep the words in because it feels like he's standing in the same room with me.

'Do you think Kris would be disappointed in me?'

'Um...' He hesitates. 'Why would he be disappointed?'

'Because I chose an obvious loser to marry and, if it weren't for you, nearly went through with it without a clue.'

'He'd probably be more ready to kick the guy's ass for you.'

I sit up. 'You think?'

Ash laughs softly. 'I remember an unfortunate teenager named Grant who followed you around until Kris chased him through town to a cemetery and threatened that he may never leave.'

'Oh my God, Grant! I'd forgotten about him! Poor kid. For the record – Kris did apologize after I made him.'

'I remember. Look, Lucy, one thing I absolutely know, is that Kris was smitten with you. You could do no wrong in his eyes. And I think deep down you still know that. He was so in love with you that I had to set a rule limiting him to gushing over just one cute thing you did each day.'

A slightly tipsy chuckle escapes me. He was annoyed that Kris would gush about me? That's sort of adorable.

'Really?'

'Yeah – otherwise, he'd endlessly go on about how he was the luckiest guy for finding "the one" at sixteen.'

'He thought I was "the one?"'

Of course, I knew this, Kris told me, but hearing he shared it with his friend is unexpected. I didn't realize teenage boys had such conversations. I take a deep breath, caught between the warmth of remembering and the ache that it brings.

'Never doubt that Kris loved you. If he were still here, he still would. As for Brandon – well, even the smartest of us make mistakes. Lord knows I've made some.'

It's quiet for a moment before I finally reply, my voice soft. 'Thank you for telling me all this. I needed to hear it.'

'Anytime, Luce, anytime.'

There's a heaviness in the air, a weight of shared grief and understanding that somehow feels comforting and raw at the same time.

Ash clears his throat, breaking the silence that had settled between us.

'And I promise things won't be as awkward the next time I cook for you, because now I know to serve the wine first,' he says with a laugh.

'Ha-ha. And I promise I won't call you in the middle of the night again while drinking.'

'Actually, feel free. I enjoyed this. Is that weird?'

'You enjoy talking women off cliffs after midnight?'

'Not all women... But you're welcome to call me at any hour, anytime.'

'OK... thanks. I guess I'll see you when I see you,' I murmur, my words trailing off as the rich, velvety wine begins to weave its gentle spell, clouding my thoughts and pulling me irresistibly toward the comfort of my pillow.

'Day after tomorrow,' he says. 'Sleep tight, Lucy.'

'Night, Ash.'

# 9

## LUCY

I did it. Against my better judgment and because I was afraid of turning myself into a total liar after claiming to Ash that I had a date, and him reminding me when I drunkenly called him last night, I texted back Tanner (not Tucker – oops) and asked him to meet me at a bar, which is where I am now.

'What do you do for work?' Tanner asks.

'Graphic design. You're an attorney?'

He nods. Getting words out of this man is like pulling teeth, and I'm tempted to remind him that my eyes are a bit north of where his gaze keeps falling.

'What kind of law?'

'Divorce.'

'Wow. That must be stressful.'

'Not really,' he says, knocking back the rest of his drink. 'I help people get what they deserve.'

'Interesting way to put it... so you're a retaliation lawyer?'

He chuckles. 'I like that.'

Huh. I bet that's a detail Madi doesn't know about this guy.

He's a divorce lawyer. Or maybe she did and thought: he hates marriage, he's the perfect guy for Lucy to joy ride.

'Did a bad marriage send you that direction?' I ask.

'Nope. Just a hopping business. The average length of an American marriage is eight years. So, safe to say people jump into loveless marriages all the time and leap back out practically as fast. I've had one client five times, and he's engaged *again*.'

The roll of his eyes tells me he's not on board with the engagement.

'But his wedding failures just keep adding to my bank balance, and a guy's got to make a living.'

How classy.

'Maybe sixth time's a charm?' I suggest.

'I'll cross everything for him,' he says, not sounding serious at all.

He raises a hand, getting the bartender's attention, then lifts his empty bottle, turning it upside down to prove he needs another.

We sit awkwardly, waiting for his second beer. This place is a dive. The food is greasy. And the drink menu is lacking because they only serve canned and bottled brews and have zero fruity drinks to cloud my mind and help me see past this man's boring personality.

'Can I get you anything?' the woman delivering his beer asks, glancing my way.

'I'm good,' I say, a Coke sitting in front of me.

He didn't offer to feed me; he just asked what I wanted to drink. Something in the form of a double was my first thought. But that wasn't an option because I refuse to go back home tonight and risk Ash still being there to see me drunk – again – so soda it is.

He takes a big sip and then leans my way. 'Have I told you that you're gorgeous?'

I nod. 'Twice. Thank you.'

It's about the only thing he's open with – that I am beautiful. It must be his 'line.' Tell a woman she's beautiful enough times, and she'll start paying attention to you – eventually. But I'm more than just a pretty face.

I glance at my phone, willing it to ring, but it only sits there silently, its screen black – taunting me. Even checking my email, likely filled with unwanted sales ads, would be more interesting than this conversation.

'I heard *you* almost needed a divorce,' he says out of the blue.

No, she didn't tell him about Vegas. Dang it, Madi.

'It was a close call,' I admit. 'Had we made it another fifteen minutes, an annulment would have been necessary, but luckily, a friend saved me.'

'Interesting,' he says.

'It was more humiliating than interesting, but yeah.'

'I'm sure there were red flags,' he says as if I'm an idiot.

Sadly, I don't entirely disagree. I've thought about this a lot. Red flags. Green flags. And invisible flags. I see none of them. Love makes you blind – that much I know.

'Riddle me this,' I say, earning his attention. 'Considering your profession, you probably know a lot about bad relationships. Got any advice on how not to let that happen in the future?'

Maybe he's got wisdom. It can't hurt to find out.

'My advice is always to keep things casual,' he says before setting his beer on the table, his gaze finally meeting mine, but it's strange, like he's trying to read me or hear something from across the room. '*Or* if you insist on wedded bliss, marry the friend – seems like he's got your best interests at heart.'

I cock my head, confused. The first part I get, that's his vibe. But marry the friend? Huh?

Finally, my phone buzzes in front of me. That took forever. I snatch it from the table before he can glimpse Madi's face.

'Hey,' he says, holding up a hand before I can answer. 'Real quick, is this going anywhere?'

'What do you mean?'

'I live right around the corner.' He nods toward the front door, waggling his eyebrows.

For a second, I'm stunned. He wants to take me back to his place? I'd bet money he doesn't even remember my name. But he can't be that brazen. He probably just wants to show me his law book collection... not. What a piece of work. He's spent twenty minutes with me, and he's ready for me to drop my dress on his bedroom floor and give it up. Absolutely not.

I answer the call, ignoring his question indefinitely. 'Hello?'

'Seriously?' she says. 'Didn't you guys just get there, and you already hate him?'

'Loathe.'

She sighs heavily. 'Not even for a stress relief?'

'No, thank you.'

I smile sweetly at Tanner, who, for once, is looking me in the eye. Wouldn't want him to know I'm looking for a way out of this mistake.

'Fine, I'm five minutes away. Can you wait that long, or do you need me to call in a bomb threat?'

'I think you've done enough.'

'Oh my God, Luce. I was kidding!' she laughs. 'Please, don't be mad. I'll pay for dinner *and* drive you home. He was only a suggestion.'

A suggestion. Next time, text those to me; don't invite them into my life unexpectedly. I'll tell her that later.

As I hang up, Tanner is downing his drink in one swallow. That's a bit of an ex-frat boy giveaway.

'Emergency?' he asks.

Wow. He's done this before.

I nod. 'My hamster. He's not got long, and I'd hate for him to be with strangers after all he's done for me.'

The smile he first greeted me with slowly grows on his face, reminding me that while he isn't engaging in the slightest, he is handsome – a waste of a good face.

'Your hamster,' he says with a laugh. 'That was good. Honest opinion?' he asks as he stands, tossing a fifty-dollar bill onto the table.

'Uh— sure?'

'I read people – family gift – and I don't think you've got to worry about the next one breaking your heart. It seems pretty guarded,' he says. 'However, take off your blinders because I predict the third time will be a charm for you.'

He reads people? What in the heck does that mean?

'You *predict*?' I ask with the most disbelieving tone ever.

Had he been interesting like this ten minutes ago, maybe I wouldn't have had to drag my imaginary hamster into this.

He nods. 'I'm never wrong.'

I'm not buying that for a second.

'Shall I set a reminder to text future you so you can keep track of your bet?'

He shakes his head. 'Completely unnecessary, I've got no question about it. You hate love, but you also crave it – always keeping an eye out for Mr Right – and I am not him. Your third try is the one that will end the way you want.'

How offensive that I'm this easy to read.

'What if there is no number three? Maybe I've permanently given up at two?'

He chuckles. 'Good luck with that,' he says, giving me a military salute and heading out the door.

My jaw drops in confusion. What does any of this mean? He has a family gift of reading people? Is he some kind of psychic? If he were, he wouldn't have had to ask if this was going anywhere.

But I don't have time to think about that because a vaguely familiar man has danced through the bar as he made his way to my booth and is now sliding in across from me still rocking to the beat, staring at me like he's got something to say.

'May I help you?'

'You like Flock of Seagulls?'

'No. But I've felt like running away since I walked in here, so perfect mood music.'

'You're Lucy Gray, aren't ya?' the stranger asks, grinning at me oddly.

'Perhaps...'

'I'm here!' Madi says, rushing through the front door and stopping when my table guest turns her way.

'Well, well, well,' he says, his attention averted.

Madi stops in her tracks, her gaze on him.

'I was hoping this would happen when I saw her sitting here. Hello there, gorgeous,' he says, arm resting on the back of the booth as he stares all heart-eyed at Madi.

Her jaw drops open as she glances between us. 'Shut. Up! *Aaron*!?'

Aaron? Oh my gosh. Wasn't that the name of Ash's friend in Vegas?

'What up, girl?' he asks, scooting in and pulling her into the booth with him.

'Do you know who this is?' Madi asks me, setting her purse on the table and staring at the man beside her. 'Vegas! Your friend's friend, what was his name?'

'Asher,' Aaron and I say in unison, causing his head to snap my way with interest.

'It *is* you!'

I shrug, glancing around the bar. Surely, Ash isn't here because he should be at my house right now cooking without me.

'He's not here,' Aaron interrupts my thoughts. 'And for the record, he's my brother.'

His brother? I guess I knew he had siblings, but I never met or knew them.

'But, despite his absence, I hear you saw him recently?'

My God. If one more person reads my mind tonight...

'Who are we talking about?' Madi blurts.

'Turns out sample meal number three was Asher's. He started last night.'

Number three? No. Dang it, Tanner. Now I'm going to see threes everywhere. This'll be fun to overthink.

'The hot private chef is Asher?!' she asks, her jaw dropping as she looks between Aaron and me. 'Your brother?'

Aaron nods proudly.

My jaw drops with her words. Hot? *What* are you doing? You can't say that in front of his brother, he'll tell him.

Aaron's eyes are on me, and he is interested in every word. 'It's him. Also, he will be thrilled as fuck to hear someone call him hot.'

'No!' I blurt out, causing him to jump. 'You can't tell him that because when I said it, I was talking in general, hoping our "new chef" was easy on my eyes so I could enjoy watching him cook for me.'

'So, you *don't* think he's hot?' Aaron asks, head cocked, eyebrows lifted, clearly confused.

I glance at Madi, but she's no help, quietly admiring the man who defiled two of my friends in one night (she told me on the plane ride home).

'No,' I say without thought.

Aaron frowns.

'I mean, yes, he is... very. I just didn't expect it. See in my head I'm struggling because I've always remembered him as eighteen and my boyfriend's best friend. Making that transition in Vegas was mind-boggling. But now, seeing him again, I... My eyes don't hate it.'

My biggest question is, why didn't I notice him like this at the wedding? Brandon certainly had no problem noticing beautiful women. Where was my head? Wholly consumed in that cheating bastard.

Aaron laughs. 'Women gotta be so damn complicated.'

'What I'm trying to say is, you *can't* tell him I'm attracted to him because I never intended to *be* attracted to him. It hit me out of nowhere, and if I have to explain it, it'll just make things more awkward and, trust me, I've already made that bed.'

'What did you do?' Madi asks, a beaming, goofy, wide smile plastered on her face.

'I—' Should probably shut up already. My nervous chatter is making this so much worse. 'You know what? For this conversation, I need a drink,' I say, my gaze landing on Aaron, who has his chin on his fist as he listens intently.

I can guarantee that no matter how much I ask him not to tell Ash my words, he's saying them – as soon as possible.

'Would you be a dear and grab us one?'

'Yeah!' he says with a nod, not waiting for Madi to move, just crawling right up over the back of the booth and hopping onto the floor enthusiastically as he makes his way to the bar.

'Did you invite him too?' I ask sarcastically but sincerely wondering.

'No,' she says, her gaze following him. 'He's a happy surprise. I haven't seen him since Vegas. We've texted a time or two, but I just couldn't fit him into my schedule.'

'Oh,' I say, pretty much to myself because her eyes are on him. 'I'm guessing your schedule just opened up?'

She nods but never looks my way, so I reach across the table and poke her shoulder hard.

'Ow!' she says, turning to me. 'What was that for?'

'Tanner, firstly – I'm gonna have to change my number. But also, *yes*, I am attracted to Asher. When I saw him yesterday, my head shut down, so imagine that scene. I had to call him in the middle of the night and explain that it wasn't him, but all me.'

'You called him in the middle of the night?' she asks, her attention now on me.

'I've got to face this guy every day now that Mitzi's hired him. I had to.'

'How late?'

I shrug. 'I dunno. After midnight.'

'Were you drunk?'

I hit my fist on the table. 'Damn it,' I moan. 'How do you know me this well?!'

She laughs. 'Because you only make late-night phone calls when wine suggests it. Did you booty call him, Luce?'

'No!' I insist. 'I just apologized for being a psycho. I don't know what's gotten into me. I'm perfectly happy on my new man ban and now my eyes are deceiving me. What do I even see in him? Sure, the outside is pretty, but so was Tanner's and Brandon's and look at the twatsicles those two are.'

'Oh, Luce. My naïve, sweet little Lucy. What do you see in him? Well, he is adorably handsome, can cook, stole flowers for you to soften bad news, and he pretty much saved you from a life of sharing your husband with multiple mistresses.'

'Madi, that *is* the problem; he's beautiful in every way – his outside and his heart. Not to mention the fact that he's tall, talented, sweet and tattooed.'

'He's tattooed?'

I laugh at the speed of her response. Tattooed is usually her type, not mine.

'Yep. He was wearing a T-shirt, and has sleeves of colorful tattoos on both arms, shoulder to wrist. My mind nearly melted. Then I ate his chicken and swear my soul left my body. My palate adores him. I want him to cook for me every day. And I want to watch him do it.'

'Then do that,' she says.

I groan, dropping my head before sending her a stare she can't look away from.

'I can't *do that* because we have history. A weird, tragic, history.'

She presses her lips into a flat line as she nods her head. 'Right... hmmmm.'

'We were only ever friends. It's weird to have my body react to him this way.'

'In that case, maybe remind yourself that you can't date him because not only does he work for you, but you're on the man ban. Which I am assuming is why you sent Tanner away so quickly?'

'No, Tanner left because he's a horny psychic weirdo. But that's a story for another day. For now, when Aaron gets back, change the subject to anything else. Make him forget I said the word hot. I can't have that thrown into the ring right now. I'm not ready.'

Madi smiles softly, resting her hand on mine. 'Are we ever ready to meet someone who might turn our world upside down and make us vulnerable?'

'*What*?!'

She only shrugs.

Whose side is she on here? I thought we agreed that a dating pause was the right thing to do at this point in my life. I need to clear my head, heal my heart and evaluate what I want out of love. She's supposed to give me good advice, and instead, she's setting up booty call interviews and suggesting I be vulnerable.

'Ladies... if I remember right, you two were cocktail drinkers? They don't sell those here, but I pulled some strings,' Aaron says, setting two tangerine-colored drinks before us. 'Screwdrivers in fancy glasses. Because you're pretty.'

Madi giggles. Seriously, like a schoolgirl.

'That is adorable!' she coos, snuggling into his side once he slides in beside her again. 'You're cute.'

Aaron lifts a shoulder, smirking my way. 'That's what my mom says, too.'

The way Madi looks at him explains her statement earlier. She likes him. And not just one-night-stand likes him either. She's been thinking about him since Vegas, has him on the back burner by keeping him interested via text, and seems to be sincerely happy to see him. My God, have I lost her? Am I going to have to figure this out on my own?

# 10

## LUCY

The evening air hangs around me as I approach the house, its facade softened by a gentle glow from the streetlights. The scent of fresh rain clings to everything, making the sidewalks shimmer under the silver touch of moonlight. Light spills from the kitchen windows, painting ethereal beams across ivy vines that cling persistently to the brick walls.

When I enter, I expect to find her in her usual chair, but Mitzi's laughter isn't there to greet me as it usually is, a subtle symphony that has become as much a part of this place as the weathered doorknob. Instead, I encounter only shadows and stillness, broken occasionally by the soft clinks of utensils in use from the next room.

'Hello?' I call out, hesitant considering I don't know who I'm hearing.

'It's just me,' a voice says gently.

As I walk in, Asher stands surrounded by a spread of ingredients and jars on the pristine white marble island. He's here late.

'Hey,' he greets me, looking up briefly from his chopping board, his smile wide.

'Hi. Where's Mitzi?' I ask, only slightly worried.

'Said she was turning in early to watch her show.'

Laughing softly, I throw my purse onto the dining table and take a seat opposite him at the bar.

'She's obsessed with streaming services and has subscriptions to all of them. Did she tell you what show she's currently binging?'

'Nope.'

'Multiple things, but mostly, *Game of Thrones*.'

He pauses mid-cut before shaking his head. 'Damn. Mitzi's braver than I am. Aaron tried getting me into it, and I barely stumbled through Season One.'

'Same here! The cringe factor is high with that one,' I commiserate. 'Last year, she devoured *Sons of Anarchy* – twice – because she's head over heels for Charlie Hunnam.'

'Well, who isn't?' Asher lofts with a hearty chuckle.

'Did you know he's British?'

He nods knowingly. 'Yet he nails being an American biker far better than I'd ever manage.'

'And you've actually got the tattoos!'

My eyes wander over the vibrant ink snaking out from beneath his shirt sleeves right down to his wrists – mysteries inked across skin, each one possibly holding a story untold. And secretly I wonder how far they might extend beneath that shirt. Yep, he's beyond hot and now it's all I see.

He glances down at himself, suddenly shy.

'Yeah... I got swept up in the Portland ink-nado fest of the twenty-teens – did I overdo it?'

I dismiss his concern with a shake of my head.

'Would you even be a PDX chef without them?' I laugh.

'Truthfully, I didn't expect them, but somehow, they fit perfectly.'

His gaze sends jitters pattering throughout when meeting mine again, suddenly serious.

'Good to know,' he says with an appreciative smile.

As I grab a bottle of water from the fridge, he works quietly, his eyes flicking to me every now and then. Climbing back onto my stool, he breaks the silence.

'Should I ask how your date went, considering it's not even nine?'

I exhale a long sigh, slightly more humiliated than before. 'It was... interesting.'

His eyebrow arches curiously at my choice of words. 'I feel like that's not a compliment to Tucker-Tanner.'

'You remember his name?'

His smile is warm as he nods. 'Did you ever nail it down?'

'Tanner. And no, "interesting" is not a compliment.'

We're just going to skip over the puzzling mind-reading aspect of him. Even I can't wrap my mind around that. And no way am I telling him I ran into Aaron. I'm hoping with everything in me that he and Madi keep my words to themselves.

The artistic arrangement of vegetables on the counter beside him catches my eye: vibrant colors organized meticulously in clear packaging like a painter's palette before the inception of a masterpiece.

'I didn't think you'd still be here.'

'I prefer prepping everything the night before,' he explains with an easygoing grin. 'Mornings and me, we don't jibe. I'm definitely not here because I wanted to stick around and see how your date went, if that's what you were wondering?'

'Ha!' I blurt a nervous laugh. Did he stay to find out exactly that? Now I want to know. 'Well, uh – do you need a hand with anything?'

'Um—' he says after scanning the kitchen around us for options. 'If you insist, I'd love your help slicing vegetables?'

'I insist,' I say, washing my hands before joining him at the kitchen island. 'Who should I cut first?' My playful tone makes him smirk and shake his head slightly.

'Let's start with celery – it's ready to go, just needs a chop.'

Equipped with a sturdy butcher knife, I slice through the celery stalk with such verve that it reverberates against the cutting board – a sharp echo ringing through our cozy culinary corner. Ash jumps slightly at the sound.

'Brutal,' he remarks, with amusement edging his voice.

'It's a great frustration reliever. The Tanner in my head totally just shut up,' I say, going a little easier on the rest of the celery.

He smirks.

'Should I know this is celery when I'm done?'

His laughter is genuine and brightens up our small cocoon within this late-night hour. 'Knowing what it is makes it easier to know what I've got when cooking. So, yes, please.'

Continuing at a softer pace than my initial hack-job cadence; all that's heard are steady rhythms being carved into wooden surfaces – creating music solely owned by shared focus amidst kaleidoscopic veggies.

'Can I ask you something? About men?'

Without uttering a single word, he pushes aside his task and leans against the counter facing me, ready to listen. His hip casually rests against the edge, and his arms are folded over his chest. Every intricate tattoo adorning his skin and the well-defined biceps I hadn't previously noticed are displayed. They certainly weren't as pronounced when he was eighteen, and they definitely didn't possess the same definition they do now, with his shirt sleeves embracing them snugly.

My God, I bet he's firm in *all* the right places.

*Snap out of it, Lucy. You've had enough of leering eyes on you like you're a piece of meat tonight. No way are you imagining Asher that way; he's your friend.*

'I'm an open book,' he says with a warm smile. 'Ask me anything.'

'Is getting laid your people's only objective?'

He lets out a chuckle. 'Jumping right into the fire. OK, well, for some guys, yeah, they're only looking to get laid. Others? Not so much.'

'How can I tell the difference?'

He side-eyes me. 'I'd bet money the second you saw Aaron and me in Vegas; you knew who the fuckboy was.'

'Well, yeah,' I say. 'But I've known you before, so I assumed you were the good guy.'

'I'm still a guy – I just don't consistently have X-rated scenes playing through my mind like I suspect Aaron does,' he replies.

'I apparently knew a guy a like that once,' I tease. 'Almost married him...'

He half smiles, but part of it's sad. 'My advice, watch out for the narcissistic or overly flirtatious.'

I bite my lips together, focusing on the celery not the words that now remind me of Brandon. He was both of those things.

'Tanner spent thirty minutes admiring my chest – then randomly let me know his apartment was just around the corner.'

One of Asher's eyebrows arches sharply upward with amusement mingled with disbelief. 'Eye contact with your nipples is always a red flag. Unless that's the game you're playing.'

'What's a red flag?' I ask. 'And I'm going to need you to explain it to me like I'm five, because I've failed this class before.' A laugh escapes me despite myself because it's better to joke about it than get frustrated over it all again.

Brandon flashes through my memory – a painful reminder wrapped up perfectly with a bright red bow that I never saw until Vegas.

'I think I'm color blind in the flag department...' I say with a shrug.

'I'm sure you're not, Brandon was just a douche.'

I nod slowly, absorbing his words. 'I'm not disagreeing, I just don't understand how I didn't know.'

'He was a great liar.'

I nod. 'And if it wasn't for you, he'd have gotten away with it and I'd be none the wiser.'

'Nah,' he says gently. 'You're a smart woman; you'd have figured it out.'

His words seep into me like gentle rain on parched soil. I meet his warm, understanding eyes – the same ones that seemed so apologetic in the past – and feel a comforting wave settle over me. He's still a good guy, as I thought.

'Doing what you did couldn't have been easy. So, in case I haven't said it yet, thank you. You saved me from a lifetime of deceit. And probably a handful of STDs.'

He grimaces, shaking his head. 'I'd say the pleasure was mine but repeatedly giving you bad news isn't my favorite part of life.'

'It makes you a saint, though.'

'Nah,' he says. 'I'm definitely no saint. Remember the issues you mentioned the other night?'

I nod.

'I've got 'em too. And they've taught me all kinds of shit I never wanted to know.'

'Really?'

He nods. 'Wisdom stems from trauma.'

'That it does,' I agree. 'I don't even know why I expect more from men or why I even bother with this dating game any more. Everyone I love eventually leaves.'

Ash frowns, visibly conflicted on how to respond to that.

*Take it all back, Lucy. You sound like a loser.*

'Anyway, Tanner wasn't a "real" date, he was just Madi setting up another pity date while urging me to use him for my pleasure. But using guys isn't really who I am and Madi doesn't have the best taste. Brandon is proof of that.'

'Another pity date? Who was the first one?'

How could he possibly forget? It's one of those memories that cling to you, refusing to fade.

'Come on, Ash. You were the first.'

He grimaces slightly like its unwelcome news. '*Me?* I was your first pity date?' he asks, placing a hand on his chest. 'When?'

'Prom?' I reply, torn between surprise and hesitation.

He shakes his head repeatedly. 'That wasn't a pity date,' he presses back.

I tilt my head, pointing the knife in his direction. 'You wouldn't be lying to me, would you?'

'No,' he insists earnestly, 'I did that—'

'For Kris,' I interject, completing his thought.

His name tumbles out more easily this time, the result of one tipsy phone call. Naming him out loud doesn't feel as awkward any more, yet it stirs a mix of emotions within me. We share this connection, after all; we should be able to talk about it.

He looks at me puzzled but affirms softly, 'Mostly, I did that for you.'

He did that for me? No way.

I return my focus to the celery, chopping it meticulously. My mind, however, drifts through a tangled web of memories and emotions, unsure of where I stand.

Sure, Asher and I had seen one another a lot in those two weeks, with the funeral and events that come along with a sudden death. But the last thing I ever expected was for him to call and tell me to get ready; he was taking me to the prom I'd been looking forward to for months.

I was as delighted as a teen in mourning could be not to miss my senior prom. But at the same time, I was torn, feeling like I was doing something I shouldn't be – cheating on a boyfriend who no longer existed, and afraid the night would be like walking on a tightrope of fragile glass, where every word threatened to shatter and leave us tumbling into a pool of grief-stricken tears. It didn't, though. If I remember right, Asher kept me laughing most of the night. My God, do I miss green flags too?

'Why would you do that for me?' I ask, my curiosity battling with the hesitation in my voice.

His smile is bittersweet. 'After weeks of relentless tears and heart-wrenching mourning, I knew you needed to find your smile again. And I felt responsible, so I wanted to help you do that.'

Our eyes meet, creating a bubble of shared reflection.

'You felt responsible? For what?'

His face crumbles, his brows knit tightly, and he nods solemnly. 'Everything. The accident. Your shattered heart. My shattered heart. All of it.'

My heart sinks through my chest. 'Ash, that is so much to take on as a teen. You weren't responsible for any of it.'

'My mind knows that. But here...' He presses his hand against his chest with a sense of desperation. 'My heart refuses to accept it. But enough about that. On prom night, you managed to smile more than you cried and that helped me more than you'll ever understand. That night transformed me, etching itself as one of those pivotal memories I sometimes despise, because I remember everything.'

He remembers everything? I am at a loss for words. His heart stubbornly clings to the belief that he is to blame, and mine is racked with sorrow at the thought of him bearing this burden for so many years. Yet on prom night, despite his torment, he summoned every ounce of strength to keep me smiling. He wielded humor like a sword, danced with reckless abandon, and mastered the art of distraction with unmatched skill. But I never would have guessed he was feeling this way inside.

I'm tempted to delve into this right now, but my heart screams to leave that Pandora's box tightly shut until he's ready – and for now, I'll heed its warning. It's time to wield my magic power and steer the conversation elsewhere.

'Do you like cooking?' I ask as I dice.

He gives me a sideways glance, aware that I've abruptly switched subjects mid-conversation. Yet, he's gracious enough not to question it. 'Love it.'

Right then, punctuating his words, my stomach lets out a howl loud enough to make Mitzi stir.

Without missing a beat, Asher heads to the fridge, retrieves a plate wrapped in foil – stripping away the cover as he crosses the kitchen – and puts it into the microwave.

'I saved you a plate. Sit,' he instructs, pointing at the island bar.

He saved me a plate?

'Thank you,' I say sincerely. 'I probably shouldn't tell you I hoped you'd do exactly this. My taste buds were in mourning.'

He seems pleased by my confession.

'Well, I wouldn't even think of leaving until both the ladies of the Gray household have been fed. It's my job right now.'

Settling down where I'm directed, he catches sight of my haphazard attempt at dicing celery.

'Uh – do *you* enjoy cooking?' His tone carries more than a hint of doubt.

'Not even a little bit, does it show?' I admit, glancing at the celery before the smells coming from the plate now sitting in front of me distract my mind.

'A little bit,' he laughs.

'Yeah, well, Mitzi had high hopes when hiring a chef that he would inspire me to learn.'

'Is that so?'

I nod, my mind on the dish in front of me. 'What magic have you woven here? It smells amazing.'

'That is chicken tikka masala over white rice.'

I take the first bite, dropping my head back as I chew.

'Holy everything. I didn't lie before. My taste buds are in love with your cooking. You're a culinary wizard, Mr Wright. How do you do it? I've had this before, and yours is leagues above.'

My compliments cause him to light up. 'Actually, this one was Aaron's recipe. I swiped it.'

'Well, Aaron is a freaking genius then.'

'Never tell him,' Asher quips with a smile that could turn saints into sinners.

As I savor each mouthful of food, I notice his curious stare directed at my celery handiwork again.

'Taking Mitzi's hopes into consideration, along with this celery massacre, maybe you should come along with us tomorrow night.'

'Who's us? And what's happening tomorrow night?'

'Me and Aaron. Aaron and I?' He questions his words. 'Ya know, us.'

'You two are a real team, aren't you?'

'He's my little brother and best friend. He drags me to places like Vegas, and I force him to things like baking classes.'

Realizing how much losing Kris affected both our lives hits home; I'd never thought about how he had to form new friendships after everything turned upside down. And he's chose his brother.

'You're going to a baking class? But I thought professional meant you taught the class?'

He smirks. 'Sometimes it does. Other times – like when it comes to baking – legends know more than me, so I listen and learn. What do you say? Want to come with and learn something new?'

Do I say yes to this? Because I want to.

'Um...'

'Mitzi would be thrilled to hear you're honing your culinary skills,' he adds persuasively with mock innocence. 'I'll even pick you up and drop you off.' His sly wink confirms what he's up to – and maybe it's working, because now I'm tempted beyond resistance.

I can't stop staring at him unless I'm busy stuffing my mouth with his delicious dishes. It's clear that I should say no before I embarrass myself further. But if I agree, he's right – Mitzi will be happy. Plus, I'll have the chance to steer conversations and ensure Aaron doesn't blurt out anything inappropriate.

'And it'll be a great way to get to know me— er, my cooking better, too,' he says, cutting through my thoughts by skillfully using my own words against me.

I bite my lip, trying to contain a smile as he grins back at me, bashfully charming.

'Guess there's no escaping now, is there?'

'Nope. You're roped in. We leave after dinner tomorrow night.'

Unexpected excitement bubbles in my chest like champagne fizzing up in flutes. And the deal is sealed. I'm joining him and Aaron for a baking class with a legend. But first, I finish the masterpiece he's made in front of me before I starve to death.

# 11

## ASHER

The restaurant is a maze of exposed wooden beams and metal scaffolding, its walls still unfinished and rough. Debris and construction tools clutter the floor, while the skeleton of a kitchen can be seen through a wide-open doorway that will eventually be closed with swinging double doors. Sounds of construction fill the air, from the buzz of power tools to the clanging of metal and the thumping of hammers. The windows are covered in opaque plastic sheets. Once I figure out a name, I'll post a 'coming soon' sign facing the sidewalk to entice future diners.

We walk around the torn-apart building, plastic taped to different areas as the contractor we've hired repairs walls. One corner holds the appliances I ordered – all top-of-the-line and designed to make Aaron's and my life easier once this place opens.

'This is gonna be nice!' Aaron boasts. 'I like the flow.'

'Me too. Maybe we won't constantly be running into one another.'

We most recently worked together at a restaurant named

DINE. Yep, original. The kitchen was small, hot and a B-health code at best. Aaron still works there – he took my spot when I left after taking on so many private jobs during my off time that I couldn't work both. Catering, line work, private chef work, you name it, I've done it. It was nice to cook anything that wasn't greasy diner food served as 'four-star cuisine.' I wanted to be a five-star chef. A culinary genius. Now, my clients know I am – Lucy's orgasmic compliments prove it.

My grandmother – who helped Alyssa raise us kids when she couldn't handle us boys – sent my siblings and me to college. To my surprise, there was enough money to send me to the dreamiest culinary school on my list, right in the heart of Napa Valley. After the tumultuous years of my late teens, I needed to escape and find a new environment to save myself from self-destruction. So, I headed south to an unfamiliar city where I could start fresh. Finally, it's paid off, and I'm on my way to where I want to be – owner and head chef of my own restaurant. And I'm doing it with Aaron – yapping like he's Gordon Ramsay – by my side.

He turns my way with a growing smirk and it's not because he thinks I'm funny. No. This is a look I know well – he's got a secret.

'Speaking of running into things,' he says nonchalantly. 'I bumped into Lucy last night.'

I turn his way, confused. 'How? I saw Lucy last night.'

'Before that, she was in my bar on a bizarre date, I think. Or maybe it was a job interview? Pretty sure if it was, she didn't get it. Who knows. Anyway, I suspected it was her, so when the guy left shortly after he'd arrived, I decided to see if I was right. I was.'

He says 'my bar' like he owns it when he just spends too much time there.

I wonder why she didn't mention this last night.

'What did uh—' I clear my throat, suddenly nervous. 'What'd she have to say?' I ask, unsure if I want to know what they spoke of.

'She likes you—' he says, walking away from me, his fingers trailing along the countertop near him.

'— as friends,' I finish his sentence.

He shakes his head.

'Stop,' I command, watching him come to a halt. 'Why are you saying no to that? *You* didn't talk about me, did you?'

He turns, making an about-face toward me. 'Maybe?' he says with a shrug.

'Aaron, spill it.'

He laughs. 'She thinks you're "hot."'

She thinks I'm *hot*?

'And "tall, talented, sweet, and tattooed,"' he continues.

'Please tell me she didn't use the air quotes you just did.'

He rolls his eyes, shaking his head. 'That was me because those were *her* words, and obviously, I don't see it, or I'd be dating you. Congratulations, buddy. Somehow, you've hooked her.'

My jaw drops. I've hooked her? How did I not notice it?

And then I realize he's messing with me.

'She didn't actually say any of that, did she?'

He scrunches his face, silently insinuating that I'm a moron.

'Yeah, she did,' he insists. 'Even told her friend she's unexpectedly attracted to more than just your cooking.'

She said *that*? My insides are fizzing with this news. Is that why I kept catching her staring at me last night? I'd convinced myself it was nothing but low-key hope on my end. Our conversation flowed much easier than the night before, but how did I misread this part?

'Oh, also, I'm not supposed to tell you. She doesn't want you to know until she understands it, which could be never, so keep your fat trap shut.'

I'm so confused – yet psyched? My heart is dancing in my chest, and my head is all over the place. I walk across the restaurant to the boxes full of booze waiting for opening day, pull out an unopened bottle of Jack and crack the seal, tipping it to my lips without using a glass.

'I guess that bottle is yours now,' Aaron says as if I'm costing him money.

'You asshole. How am I supposed to keep this to myself?'

'Asshole? You should be thanking me that you've got a heads-up, ya tool! And whaddya mean "*how do you keep this to yourself?*" Pffft – easy, just don't say anything.'

'Says the gossip queen himself,' I remind him.

He motions locking his lips and tossing an invisible key over his shoulder. 'I can be quiet if I want to. Any other questions?'

'A thousand. You do realize I invited Lucy to our class tonight, right?'

'What? *Why*?' he moans.

'She seemed interested.'

Shit. Maybe I misread that, too? She seemed interested in helping me prep, so I thought maybe she'd like a baking class, but maybe now I'm the pity date? Don't get me wrong, I was serious before. Taking Lucy to prom wasn't out of pity; it was because I respected the girl enough to know she needed a break from trying to process feelings she shouldn't have had to experience at such a young age.

My God, I'm going to hyperventilate. I lift the bottle again, grimacing at the black licorice-tasting tranquilizer. This is so much better in something else.

'You shouldn't have told me,' I say, feeling the weight of the new information settle heavily on my shoulders. 'Now I've got to hold that information while figuring out how to approach it.'

'Why you gotta approach anything? Just let things evolve,' he suggests, as if it were that simple.

I shake my head, torn between the desire to take action and the fear of what that might do to her.

'Did I ever tell you details about Lucy and my past?' I ask, hesitating, because this is a line I never cross. I don't talk about Kris. To anyone but my therapist. Ever. Until now.

'She dated Kris, your only friend. Now deceased from teenage tragedy.'

'Want to know the details?'

He looks at me confused with his head cocked. 'You wanna talk about it?'

In the past, I've enforced the 'don't ask' rule. It's the one topic that's always off the table. But that is eating me alive right now.

'I dunno,' I admit, a chaos of emotions swirling inside. 'It's all coming at me pretty hard lately, and it'd be nice to have someone on the outside's opinion.'

He hops up onto the countertop, signaling his readiness to listen.

'You know how firm I am about not drinking and driving?'

'I know you'll spend the next three hours here so the very small sips of Jack don't affect you later, so yeah...'

'Well, that's because Kris and I had been sneaking Dad's bourbon earlier that night, and made a really bad decision. I was in the car behind him when it happened.'

His jaw drops in disbelief. 'You *witnessed* it?!'

'I'm the guy who called 911,' I say, feeling the memory crash over me like a wave – suffocating me as it always does. 'Then I volunteered to tell his girlfriend, which was way harder than I'd anticipated. A couple weeks after the funeral was her senior prom, and I'd heard through the grapevine that she was going to stay home. I...' I drop my head, the past unexpectedly clawing at me. 'I couldn't let that happen so, I borrowed one of Dad's old suits and took her.'

Aaron's eyebrows are raised in shock. 'Are there photos?'

'Somewhere, I'm sure.'

'Wow.' He rubs the back of his neck. 'Dad's suits were bad.'

'The suit isn't the point of the story,' I say, tipping up the bottle. 'I'm now caught in an endless maze of regret, one moment feeling suffocated by his ghostly presence, the next finding a strange comfort in a woman he loved.'

'Yikes,' he says as he shakes his head, trying to process this information. 'Wait a second.' He grabs me by the arm, turning me around – his finger jabbing at the back of my left bicep. 'Kris,' he reads the name tattooed on my arm out loud. 'He still haunts you? That's why you've got the dude's name tattooed on you in big bold letters?'

'He was my friend, assface, that's why I got it. I try not to remember the rest.'

He walks around to face me, giving me a severe look. 'Where's my name? I'm your brother, don't I deserve a spot for eternity on your skin?'

'Die, and I'll tattoo Aaron across my chest.'

'Deal. Write that down,' he says, grabbing a piece of scrap paper and a pen. 'I want a guarantee.'

'Shut up,' I say, rolling my eyes while shoving his paper out of my face. 'This is serious. I've always felt responsible, especially as I told her what happened that night.'

'I probably would of too,' he says, staring at me awkwardly. 'Vegas is suddenly making much more sense.'

'See. My history and Lucy's is complicated to the point that I don't know if "feelings" are allowed.'

'I mean, I kinda see it, but it's been twelve years. It's only still complicated if you let it be.'

I shake my head, taking another swig. 'What am I supposed to do now that I know she likes me?'

I groan, now pacing the restaurant, one hand clasped on the back of my neck and the other gripping this bottle of Jack like it's bringing some peace. Memories I've attempted to forget flood through me, and I'd do anything to have a stop button on my brain right now.

Aaron scrunches his face in confusion. 'You were a teenager.'

'Yeah.'

'Rough as it was back then, it sorta seems like it's something you should both be over by now.'

I sit in one of the many chairs around the room, leaning forward, my elbows on my knees and the Jack in my hands. 'People don't get over death, douchebag. It sticks with you, painfully forever.'

'Well, I guess you better pull up that therapy app from your phone and tell your psychiatrist because I think you're being ridiculous.'

'That's great. You're helpful. So glad we talked,' I say sarcastically.

He reads the room, shooting me a glare, then letting out a heavy sigh as he walks closer towards me.

'What if I invite Madi tonight, too? That way, it's not weird because we'll both have dates.'

'I didn't ask Lucy as a date. I just thought she might like to get out of the house. But that's not a terrible idea.'

'See, I'm a genius. You're welcome.'

'Don't speak too fast,' I say sarcastically. 'Actually, don't speak at all tonight.'

'What?'

'That's right. Button it up, buster,' I say, taking one more sip while my heart slows from nearing cardiac arrest. 'If you say one word about any of this, in her presence, I'll have witnessed two deaths.'

He furrows his brow. 'You're scary sometimes.'

'Also, no romance. No touching. No lusting. We're just a group of friends passing the time.'

'Jeesh, OK, Bossy Betty.' The way he nods his head suggests that he probably won't follow any of my rules, so I need to be prepared in case he throws out a bomb.

'Please, Aaron. I just talked to you about my feelings, which is code for this is a lot for me to work through, so don't make things worse.'

He heaves another sigh, his heart taking over for his spitfire head. 'Fine,' he groans. 'I'll try to tame my tongue. And you should take that bottle home,' he says. 'You could use some liquid courage to shut up the ghost that lives in your head.'

'No thanks. I've reached my limit already.'

'Lightweight,' Aaron teases.

I hang my head, exhaling deeply. This quickly spiraled out of control. How on earth am I supposed to process this information? She's actually into *me*? Romantically? My heart races, my mind reeling as I try to make sense of the situation. Could it be possible that the tension between us wasn't one-sided? That the sparks I felt weren't just figments of my imagination? I think I'm about to find out.

# 12

## ASHER

As the sun gently dips below the horizon, a breathtaking canvas of vivid orange and deep purple hues is painted across the sky, casting a serene glow over the rushing scenery outside. The air is filled with the aroma of fast food drifting in from roadside diners, carried by the breeze wafting through the slightly open windows.

I can feel the tension in Lucy, who's sat beside me as I drive, her gaze fixed on the passing scenery. What's going through her mind? Are her thoughts consumed by what she may have said to Aaron? How do I navigate this? I've no fucking clue.

'I don't know if I can fit even a morsel more into my already full stomach,' Lucy remarks.

But her body betrays her words. It doesn't faze her, but it's great for me because I'll always know when she's hungry and I like to feed people.

'Your stomach seems to disagree,' I tease.

'It's one of those organs I have no control over,' she says wistfully.

A smile tugs at my lips; curiosity piqued. 'And what are the others?'

'My head and heart,' she answers with a rueful chuckle. 'Those two never agree.'

The mention of hearts makes me acutely aware of mine, which is currently beating out of control. I've been thinking about this woman every second of my day, even when I'm with her, trying to decode her body language and read between the lines. But I'm no closer to figuring out if Aaron is telling the truth than I was right after he told me. I push those thoughts aside as we approach Audrina's house.

'Luckily, this is a baking class. I'm attempting to build our dessert menu.'

The smile that crosses this girl's face... wow. I swear she gets prettier every time I see her.

'We're making dessert?' she asks.

Before I can answer, we pull up to the front of Audrina's house and are greeted by Aaron and Madi standing outside his car. They wave their arms wildly like two crazed fans at a concert.

'Madi's here?' Lucy exclaims, her confusion evident on her face. 'Why?'

'Aaron heard I invited you and insisted on bringing Madi along,' I reply with a shrug.

'I can't believe she didn't tell me,' she mutters as we exit the car.

The chatter and laughter grow louder as we approach.

'Ready to get this party started?' Aaron beckons, taking Madi's hand then catching my gaze and suddenly dropping it, sparking a confused look on her face. He steps ahead of her, heeding my earlier directions and leading the way toward

Audrina's vibrant pink front door, leaving Madi behind. He knocks a melodic tune.

'Wow!' Lucy marvels as we walk up the front steps. 'This place is stunning. And here I thought Mitzi's mansion was impressive.'

'Mitzi's place is gorgeous,' I say.

The door swings open to reveal Audrina standing there, welcoming us in her characteristic style.

'Boys...' her gaze shoots from us to the ladies, 'and unexpected girls?'

The middle-aged woman stands in her doorway, her back straight and head held high. Her hair is perfectly styled, a rich chestnut color with subtle highlights. Bright blue framed eyeglasses stand out on her face and she wears a dress that matches them, covered with a full-length apron tightly tied around her waist.

'Come on in – kitchen's ready to go.'

Aaron takes the lead, Madi trailing closely behind, followed by Lucy, who intercepts them before I can cross the threshold. The trio leisurely stroll into the living room, casting occasional glances toward the kitchen, engaging in whispers. I can only imagine Aaron receiving a stern talking-to based on his prior remarks. Little does Lucy know, it's far too late.

I've only been here twice, but the house is still a stunning fusion of old and new, a masterpiece of architectural design and artistic expression. The clean lines and bold colors transport you to a time of great creativity and exploration. Every inch of the interior is flooded with natural light, pouring in through floor-to-ceiling windows that offer breathtaking views of the surrounding landscape.

Smooth wooden floors gleam underfoot, contrasting with the softness of the large blue plush shag carpet in the living room. The furnishings are a perfect blend of modern leather and textured fabrics, inviting you to sink into their comfort while taking in the view through the expansive windows overlooking a pristine garden. And then there is the kitchen – a true highlight of the home. A mix of faux-retro and modern design, it boasts sleek navy-blue SMEG appliances (that I've never been able to afford) and playful, colorful decor.

'Who are your guests?' Audri stops me, touching my arm as I walk in, her gaze on the three of them ahead of us.

'That is Lucy and Madi.'

'Are these women your girlfriends?'

I laugh, but it's a bit uneasy. 'No. Well, Aaron and Madi have been spending some time together – both vertically and horizontally – but you know how that usually goes?'

Audri laughs. 'He'll probably wind up with another scar to add to his collection, I'm sure.'

The incident she's referring to was not one of Aaron's finest moments. We were working the closing shift for her that night. He had arranged to meet a girl at the end of the night to break things off with her because he suspected she was a bit nuts and didn't want her knowing where he lived. After I'd left, I realized I'd forgotten my keys, so I went back to retrieve them. As I made my way through the dimly lit establishment, I heard a commotion – loud banging and yelling echoing through the corridors. Following the sounds, I discovered the source behind the heavy metal door into the walk-in freezer.

I pushed the lever and swung the door open to reveal a bizarre scene: there Aaron was, standing stark naked, alone, and handcuffed to a metal shelf. The frigid air was clearly biting, and the harsh fluorescent light cast sharp shadows on his shivering form. His right hand was bleeding, and despite the urgency of the situation, I couldn't suppress a laugh at the absurdity of it all, even as I hurried to free him and get him the medical attention he desperately needed (six stitches and an hour under a heated blanket).

Needless to say, the girl hadn't taken Aaron's news well. And she took his clothes, phone, and wallet. He'd dodged a bullet for sure. Had I not forgotten my keys he could have been dead by the time either Audrina or I could make it back. Yet he's still an idiot for reasons I've yet to unravel.

'And the other one?' Audri asks.

'Uh— that is Lucy. She and I are old friends, going way back to our high school years. We recently crossed paths again when fate intervened – in its usual "holy shit" sort of way, and then, unexpectedly, her grandmother brought me into their lives as a personal chef.'

I refuse to delve into every intricate detail for the sake of my own sanity, or else I'll be trapped here, unraveling the complex web of our past all night long because Audrina is a fixer.

'Lucky her to have you cooking for her.'

I grin, remembering her word 'orgasmic.' 'She's beyond thankful for that too,' I say with a wink.

'Smart girl,' Audri says. 'The last time I saw anyone from high school was at a class reunion I went to just to shove my status in their faces.' She smiles proudly. 'It worked, they used to bully me, and now they all think I'm a total culinary bitch.'

'A total "known around the world for your amazing culinary skills" bitch.'

She nods, her smile never leaving. 'This is why I adore you, Ash. Shall we get started?'

\* \* \*

Approaching the three of them, Lucy appears visibly more anxious. I wonder what was said. Aaron better have kept his mouth shut. But obviously, I can't ask. That would prove I know what she doesn't want me to know, and I'd hate to make her uncomfortable. Sure, she can't trust Aaron. But she can trust me.

The four of us stand in the warm, inviting kitchen, enveloped by the comforting aroma of freshly brewed coffee. Our eyes follow Audrina's graceful steps as she makes her way to the front of the room. The last of the day's sunlight streams through the windows, illuminating her features and casting a golden glow across her.

Her hands rest lightly on the countertop as she looks us over, tilting her head and evaluating the four of us with a calculating gaze.

'Since there are unexpectedly four of you,' she begins, her voice laced with amusement, 'we're going to make two teams.'

Aaron and Madi immediately lock elbows, their competitive spirits already flaring.

'Team!' Aaron calls out as if we are in a playground, choosing sides for a game that is sure to end in victory.

I can't help but laugh at their antics, my nerves melting away as I look over at Lucy. I flash her a nervous smile.

'Wanna be my partner?'

She feigns hesitation. 'I dunno,' she drawls. 'If you're all that's left... I guess.'

Thankfully, I can tell she's kidding; otherwise, my racing heart may have flatlined there.

'Team!' I call out with almost as much competitive nature as my brother did, glancing at Aaron with renewed confidence.

'We're going to kick their asses,' I say quietly in Lucy's direction only.

She grins mischievously. 'Then count me in,' she says. 'But, seriously, how do you know Audrina Leighton? I watch her show.'

'We're in the same business,' I say, proud to call someone like her a colleague. 'She's mentored me for years.'

'Wow,' Lucy says, looking impressed.

The sudden clap of hands interrupts our conversation.

'Alright, teams are set! Aaron and Madi, you're a team. And Lucy and – what's your name again?' she asks me with a playful glint.

'Funny.'

I met Audrina at my first kitchen job. She was the head chef, and I was her sous. The number of things this woman taught me is insane. Basically, she created a protégé in me, and we've been friends ever since – even now when she has her own national cooking show. She sends me a text, checking in a couple of times a month. And she can't wait until the restaurant is opened – she's requested to be on the permanent VIP list.

'Lucy and Asher, you two are a team,' Audri declares. 'Whose dessert will wow me? Let's find out.'

As Audrina gives instructions and advice, I catch Lucy's eye and nod confidently.

'We got this –I measure, you mix. Mid-speed, easy.'

She follows directions and works the mixer, pouring in each ingredient as I hand them to her; our movements synchronize as we dance around each other in the small space.

'Too much!' Aaron yells excitedly at Madi. 'Too freaking much – unless you like cakes that taste like the main ingredient is salt-water, you beautiful maddening minx,' he says through a laugh, trading places with her and demoting her to running the hand mixer as opposed to measuring out ingredients.

'Problems?' I inquire, not really caring if they have them or not because, so far, Lucy and I are killing it. Of course, we're only five minutes in, but I'm calling it now – we will be the ones to wow Audrina.

'Just mind your business, asshole,' Aaron responds.

Lucy laughs. 'Do you two work together too?'

I guess we haven't really talked much about Aaron. Usually, my little brother isn't the topic with women I'm steadily earning a crush on.

'We're business partners, and he's been my sous chef off and on. But occasionally, he pretends he's the boss.'

'Occasionally, I have to be the boss,' Aaron claims.

'No, he doesn't,' I correct him.

'You don't get sick of one another?' she asks. 'Friends, brothers, and co-workers seems like a lot of time together.'

'I hate him,' Aaron says, laughing.

'And I'm sick to death of him,' I tease.

'But he's a hell of chef,' Aaron follows.

'And he's OK too, I guess...' I say, reluctantly.

Lucy chuckles and her smile brightens the room. At least my side.

'How are you two old *friends* handling working together?' Aaron interjects. 'Everything running smoothly over there? No feelings out of order or anything?'

I shoot him a glare.

'Smooth as butter,' Lucy snaps back. 'Ash knows what he's doing, and I can follow instructions. Can you?' she asks sweetly, directing her question at Aaron.

He stops what he's doing, meeting her gaze. 'When I want to,' he responds, pulling Madi from measuring out flour and planting a kiss on her lips just to piss me off.

'Pay attention to each ingredient you add,' Audri says from the island bar she's now seated at, watching us as she sips a large glass of red wine. 'Notice how it changes your mix. Knowing how ingredients react to one another will make it easier in the future to create your own recipes.'

'Mads, you're overmixing!' he exclaims, pointing at the bowl with a grimace. 'We aren't whipping the eggs.'

Madi rolls her eyes, but takes a step back, allowing Aaron to take over once more.

'Fine, Mr Perfectionist. Show me how it's done,' she retorts, a hint of competitiveness in her tone.

'He's no perfectionist,' Audri says with a smile as she approaches Aaron and Madi.

She and Aaron have always play clashed. Aaron tends to grind on people until he's become the annoying little brother you never had. The guy's never been uncomfortable a day in his life.

'I intentionally chose hand mixers because they're harder to use. You've got to pay more attention and that's Aaron's goal tonight. To pay attention. I won't eat one more half-done dessert at our Friendsgiving this year.'

'Hey,' Aaron snaps back. 'My desserts are the bomb.'

'Yes, last year's caramel pecan pudding—'

'Bars,' he corrects her.

They've been having this argument since last Thanksgiving.

'In my world, melting in your hand is a good thing,' he says, his eyes on Madi.

Gross.

I glance over at Lucy, who chuckles softly at the exchange. 'Their dynamic seems fun,' she remarks sarcastically, a twinkle in her eye.

'If awkward was fun...' I tease. 'I know I'm having more fun than I expected,' I say, leaning into her slightly. 'Could be the fact that he's not my sous right now.'

Her gaze meets mine, a hint of curiosity in her eyes, and I wonder if, in that handful of words, I've said too much.

The corners of her lips upturn in a way that makes my heart skip a beat.

'I'm glad to be your partner,' she says softly, her eyes warm and inviting. 'I think we make a pretty good team.'

I nod, unable to tear my gaze away from her. 'Yeah, we do.'

As we put the finishing touches on our dessert, I can't help but steal glances at her, admiring the way her brow furrows in concentration and the gentle curve of her smile as she tastes our creation.

'Oh my god. We made this?' she asks.

She raises a glass of wine – poured by Audrina – her slim fingers curled around the stem. I watch as a lock of her hair falls over her eyes, interfering with the curious gaze she's fixed on me. I want to know what's going through her head – it frustrates me in ways it shouldn't. Why doesn't she want me to know what she said to Aaron? Why can't we explore those feelings?

'Incredible,' Lucy moans, the taste test she just did mesmerizing her.

Audrina saunters over to our station, a curious expression on her face.

'How are we looking here?' she inquires, peering at our cake mix with interest.

'Wait until you taste this,' Lucy declares confidently. 'It's to die for.'

'Yes, I know,' Audri says. 'I created this recipe.'

'Oh!' Lucy says, suddenly wiping a hand on her apron. 'I've seen your show. You're amazing. I've always wondered how good your food would be and now I know – heavenly.'

'Remind me to give you a cookbook before you leave.'

'I'd really be on Mitzi's good list if you come home with one of those,' I tease.

'Then I'll buy two! One for me and Madi. Perhaps I'll even ask to learn how to use the oven in the coming weeks.'

Yes, please.

Audrina shoots me an approving nod before turning to Aaron and Madi's station. 'And how about you two? Any break-throughs yet?'

Aaron wipes his brow dramatically and exchanges a sheepish glance with Madi before shooting a glare my way. 'We may have hit a small hiccup or two, baking doesn't appear to be either of our specialties – but it's nothing we can't handle,' he replies with a grin, trying to exude optimism despite the setbacks. 'Because of that, I officially designate Ash as our baker at the restaurant. If you win, I'll get you a trophy.'

I pour our mixture into a baking pan that Lucy prepped and slide it into the top space of Audrina's double oven, feeling confident in our creation. Lucy stands beside me, wiping her hands on a dish towel as we wait for our dessert to bake. The scent of chocolate and vanilla fills the air, making my stomach growl in anticipation.

'I think we nailed it,' she says, her eyes sparkling with pride.

'Audrina won't know what's hit her.'

\* \* \*

As the timer chimes, signaling that our dessert is ready, I carefully pull it out of the oven. The cake looks perfect – moist and fluffy with a golden crust.

'You know what frosting is good for, right?' Aaron asks Madi, not at all under his breath, dabbing a bit on her lips and then sucking it off in a way that feels dirtier than ever.

'Mmmm,' Madi moans, licking her lips once they've parted. 'We could use that when you make up for being a bossy asshole later.'

'Ooh-hoo-hoo,' Aaron moans gleefully. 'You hear that big brother, she wants frosting in our make-up se—'

'Stop,' I say firmly. Shutting him up. Is he trying to get bitch slapped?

Lucy glances at me, an awkward grimace on her face. 'Ew.'

She laughs nervously.

'Don't even pretend like you're not jealous,' Aaron calls out. 'We're adorable.'

'You're cringy,' I say.

He flips me the bird.

After what feels like hours of intense concentration and teamwork, both teams are done and we present our desserts to Audrina for judging. She surveys our cakes with a critical eye, her expression unreadable.

She takes a bite of our offering first, savoring the flavors before looking at us with a knowing smile. 'Impressive. But it's you, so I knew it would be. Now let's see what your brother has to offer.'

'We *have* to win,' Madi says to Aaron. 'We made this cake twice.'

I laugh. 'Is that what took so long?'

Another finger flung my way.

Audrina teases us as her gaze shifts between our creations, her expression inscrutable.

Lucy grips my arm suddenly. An electric current surges through my body, but I know I need to keep my cool.

I pat her hand lightly.

'We've totally got this,' I say softly, leaning into her.

'Aaron better buy you that trophy,' she teases.

Finally, Audrina sets down her fork and clears her throat, the suspense thick in the air. 'After careful consideration,' she begins, drawing out the moment, 'the winning team is...'

I exchange a glance with Lucy, silently willing Audrina to announce our names.

'Asher and Lucy!' Audri proclaims, her smile lighting up the room.

'Boo!' Aaron says, tossing a towel from the counter aggressively my way. 'She's always liked you more. Where's the unbiased judge?'

'Yours wasn't *bad*,' she counters Aaron. 'Just not as good,' she says with a smirk.

She turns to us. 'Congratulations on a truly exceptional dessert, you two.'

I wrap Lucy in a tight hug, overcome with happiness and pride. We did it. We impressed Audrina Leighton.

She hugs me back, pulling away after a second and giving me a high-five.

'Good job, partner!' she says, beaming. 'You are an excellent instructor.'

'It was a team effort. You did better than a guy who graduated culinary school.'

Aaron's lips curl into a mischievous smirk.

'FYI for the future, he likes that in the bedroom, too.'

Lucy's eyes widen in shock at his comment, and she glances between him and Madi, disbelief written on her features.

'He's, uh— kidding,' I say, pitching the towel back at him while shooting him a sharp glare, silently warning him to stop before he goes too far. 'Aren't you?' I press, all heads now his direction. I convey the message with a subtle hand gesture across my throat.

'Oh, yeah. I'm kidding,' he says, half a guilty grin on his face.

'Ash doesn't know what he's doing in the bedroom, so guide him.'

That douche.

I clear my throat, but Lucy speaks for me.

'Better make that trophy big,' she says.

'It'll be as big as his—'

'No,' I bark. Silencing him once again.

'I think we should all clean up our stations,' she suggests.

I nod, thankful for the change of subject. 'Great idea. Let's get this kitchen back in order.'

After the kitchen is once again sparkling clean, we gather our things and prepare to leave; I catch Aaron's eye and give him a knowing look. We'll be talking about this at some point.

As the tension dissipates, Audrina claps her hands together to get our attention.

'Congratulations again to Asher and Lucy on a well-deserved win,' she says, her voice filled with pride. 'But remember, it's not just about winning – it's about being the best bitch you can be.'

'Words of wisdom,' Lucy says with a laugh as she dismisses us. 'This was fun, thank you. I'll never watch your show the same way again!'

'Any friend of Asher's is a friend of mine. Let me go grab you some books,' Audri coos, a sign she likes this one. She did always love to give suggestions on who I should date. I never listened, but she gave them.

As we make our way out of Audrina's kitchen, me carrying our cake in a pink bakery box and Lucy with her armload of books, the warm night air greets us like an old friend. Aaron and Madi are discussing their plans for the frosting they're stopping by the store for (and other spreadable things to be used in ways I don't want to think about) and completely ignoring us. Thank God.

Lucy links her arm through mine, a contented smile on her face. 'I can't believe we won,' she says, her voice filled with wonder. 'Audrina Leighton said I made the best cake.' She suddenly glances at me. 'We,' she corrects herself. '*We* made the best cake.'

'Mitzi will be proud.'

'Proud and shocked that I didn't burn the place down for sure. I'm going to leave this on the island for her to discover. Maybe she'll give you a raise.'

I laugh, shaking my head because there is no way I'm accepting more money from her. She's paying me quite well, and the pleasure is becoming all mine.

'Spending time with you is payment enough,' I say.

The streetlights cast a soft glow around the car, creating a peaceful atmosphere as we make our way back to Mitzi's place. I glance over at her, staring out the window, with a slight smile on her face. She is gorgeous. Inside and out. I wish I could tell her that without scaring her off.

With each passing second, the closer we get to Mitzi's, the more I'm gutted that the night is over. I just want to spend every second with her. Wait. Every second? My God. I'm never going to be the same.

# 13

## LUCY

'That was an absolute blast,' I exclaim, practically bouncing in my seat. I have definitely had too much sugar. Or maybe it's him? My heart's been racing all evening in the best, most unexpected way.

'Yeah. I've never baked competition style, but it was fun,' Asher says.

The adrenaline from winning still pulses through my veins. I'm about as non-competitive as people come. I don't even watch a single sport. But tonight was a nice break from my usual, hanging out and binge-watching Netflix while scrolling my phone by myself. Plus, Audrina Leighton! I love her.

'We should hang out more often.'

*What* am I doing?

*You can't be questioning why you're attracted to this man and then suggest spending more time together.*

'Yeah?' he asks, rubbing his chin – a bit uncertain, but his slight smile suggests he may be up for it.

*As friends, Luce. Put that boundary out there. It's safe. You need safe relationships right now.*

'The universe keeps pushing us together so, why not? It's what friends do, right? I've always considered you a friend. We're bonded by trauma. Plus, it's sort of fun hanging out with someone from way back when, you know? We know teen Lucy and Asher – could it be fun to get to know the adult versions of us, too?'

'That's hard to argue, especially considering you've become one of the best parts of my day. I guess hanging out is what friends do.'

Oh. That felt dangerously flirty, and I didn't hate it.

Dang it. Why am I looking for this?

*Come on, Lucy. Snap out of it – you two have established you're just friends. He is not flirting. It's been seven months, and your vagina is just lonely, and Asher's presence is somehow waking it up. Man ban. MAN BAN!*

'So, what do you think of Aaron dating Madi?' I ask, once again flawlessly changing the subject before even attempting to leave his car after pulling into Mitzi's driveway.

Freaking Aaron. The guy promised to keep my secret, but his words were loaded with innuendo. Asking about feelings and dishing out 'future bedroom' advice. Not cool, Aaron. I need to know if he said anything. So, talking about him and Madi may provide me with that information.

Ash nervously presses his lips together. 'Honestly? Aaron's sort of a chronic dater, to put it nicely. And, usually, he picks unforgettable ladies, if you catch my drift.'

'Madi's memorable. I mean, she's never made the nightly news, but she brought a friend to their first night together. Most guys would never forget that.'

He laughs heartily. 'I have heard the story – more than once, unfortunately.'

'Yikes,' I grimace.

'Yeah,' he concurs with a serious nod. 'Let's just hope Madi isn't planning on forever.'

'She's not,' I say hesitantly. 'Off the record... she stopped husband-hunting a few years ago. She's more about living life to the fullest and forgetting yesterday ever happened now. Rarely does she worry about tomorrow either.'

'That's pretty much Aaron's mantra too. Uh-oh,' he says, his eyes narrowing with concern. 'I think we've got double red flags on the dating field.'

'You think?'

I rarely worry about Madison. She's a force of nature, perfectly capable of handling herself and anyone daring enough to cross her. Sure, she might look like the ultimate girly girl with her sweet voice and stunning looks, but underestimate her at your peril – one of those stilettos she loves might just find its way into your skull if you wrong her.

'I don't need to hear more to see they're basically clones. Who hurt her?'

'What do you mean?'

'I mean, everyone who shuns love has been shattered by someone – could be family, could be romance. It happens to the best of us, but some people crack harder,' he comments, his gaze meeting mine.

I wonder if he thinks I'm one of those 'crack harder' types? I wanna say no, but—

'Someone did hurt her,' I say, hesitant to tell Madi's secret.

He listens so intently when I talk. Brandon never did. He'd cut me off with some great idea or somehow respond in all the right places, then not remember a single thing I said. I like feeling heard.

'She's only had one long-term boyfriend, and by "long-term," I mean six months. When she uttered those three magic words, he arrogantly declared he couldn't date a "little girl" who didn't know the difference between love and lust. Then he dumped her, claiming his feelings for her were the latter. In that moment, she doubted her own heart and vowed never to fall again.'

He winces sharply. 'Ouch.'

'Yeah,' I say, clutching my chest as if I could soothe the ache I still have for her.

'I daydreamed out loud over wine about erasing him from existence. I tried to convince her—' Asher laughs. 'But Madi wouldn't let me. She and Mitzi both know I'm all bark and no bite and in some corner of my mind, I'm relieved I'll never stoop to kick a man in the teeth.'

'I dunno,' Ash says, his voice dripping with admiration. 'I watched you once break a guy's nose. That was seriously badass in my book. And in front of a crowd while wearing a ballgown too...'

I let out a laugh, memories of that day flooding back.

He raises his hand, eyes gleaming. 'High five for nailing that jerk?'

I slap his hand decisively. We did this earlier but this time he squeezes my hand with a gentle grip before releasing.

'Thank you. It was my first time. I heard it was actually broken too. Not just blood.'

'Bravo,' he says with genuine pride in his voice. 'So, Madi's got some baggage... who doesn't? Aaron's carry-on probably has the plane tilting.' He rubs his neck, staring out the windshield of his SUV. 'You know, they're practically the same person once we drag 'em out of the bedroom. Maybe they're meant to be?'

'Maybe.'

'You know,' he says with this tone I've never heard from him. It's soft and sweet and... suggestive? 'I've got a wild idea just to keep everything on track, we could date *with* them. To – you know – ensure they don't stumble and hurt one another? To give love a fighting chance...'

A surge of nerves dances in my stomach as he awkwardly suggests the idea of double dating with our friends.

'They do seem incredibly into each other, and sometimes people catch feelings fast and live happily ever after.'

'Who would we be to stand in the way of love?' he asks.

'Exactly.'

'Double dating,' he comments, as if recalling a distant memory. 'We haven't done that since high school.'

He's right. We double-dated as teens – Ash with a girl named Isabella and me with Kris. We did all the typical teenage things. Bowling, movies, stalking the dying mall, ate greasy food, and even snuck out a few times for some underage clubbing.

It was so much fun – except for that time I fractured my ankle ice skating. I was not a natural, and Kris could barely stand himself. So, after one particularly hard landing when I thought turning around would be easy, Ash skated over like a pro (apparently, he'd learned to skate to play hockey as a kid) and carried me back to the side of the rink, getting me help in no time. He's always been a total saint.

'As friends on our side – just like before,' I say, mostly to remind myself.

'Yeah.' He nods. 'We may just be the perfect candidates for this kind of operation. And getting to spend more time with you doesn't sound terrible either.'

A slight gasp leaves my lips as he throws that *obvious* flirt into the ring. Do I flirt back? No. Do I want to? Yes?

I catch his eye and hold his gaze, feeling the tension crackling between us like electricity. A flicker of something more is in his eyes, something that mirrors the flutter of excitement in own chest. It's dangerous territory, this dance we're doing, flirting on the edge of friendship and something deeper. But as I look at him in the dim glow of the city lights filtering through the car window, I can't deny the pull I feel toward him.

'Spending more time with you sounds pretty great to me, too,' I admit softly, my voice barely above a whisper.

He smiles a slow grin that reaches his eyes, lighting up his face like the stars above us.

'Let's make it happen then,' he suggests eagerly.

'Let's,' I say with a grin.

Before I can exit his car, he beats me to it and walks around the front to my side, pulling open my door like a gentleman. Brandon never opened any doors for me. This is sweet.

The summer evening air wraps around us, tinged with the scent of the nearby blooming flowers planted around Mitzi's front porch.

'Thanks for bringing me tonight,' I say softly, meeting his gaze.

He smiles back, his eyes sparkling under the moonlight. 'No, thank you for coming with me,' he replies sincerely. 'I had a great time, and I can honestly say that it's been a while since I've had that with a woman.'

My heart skips a beat at his words, but I try to play it cool.

'Are you implying that you're not the man-whore your friend is?'

*Please, say no. Please, say no.*

A laugh bursts out of him, shaking his head repeatedly. 'Not even a little bit.'

'Thank God,' I say through a sigh of relief.

He raises a single eyebrow.

'I mean, that's refreshing to hear.'

*Smooth, Luce.* I'm sure that saved it.

He laughs, shaking his head, looking as stunned by what's going on between us as I am.

'Yeah, my last girlfriend was a couple of years ago, and since then, I think I could count my dates on one hand.'

'Well, that's *not* refreshing,' I say, as we walk toward the porch together. 'How come?'

'Work is my girlfriend,' he says with a shrug like he just can't help it. 'I've got a goal and can almost see the light at the end of the tunnel. Trying to stay focused.'

'I get it,' I say. 'Work has become my boyfriend too. It's safer than laying my heart out for someone who could crush it in an instant without warning.'

'That it is,' he says with understanding.

It's strange how easily we fall into conversation after being practically strangers just days ago. Now, we're spilling secrets, eager to spend more time together, and date with our friends, while we linger unnecessarily on Mitzi's front walk under the stars like teenagers dabbling with the rules on curfew.

'Well, here's to better times ahead, minus the drama and heartbreak of our past,' I add, raising an imaginary glass between us.

Ash mirrors my gesture, clinking his invisible glass against mine. 'To drama-free adventures with a new old friend.'

'New old friend,' I repeat as I walk the half-dozen steps up Mitzi's porch toward the front door. 'I like that.'

'I'll see you tomorrow?'

'Absolutely,' I reply. 'Nothing can make me miss another dinner you create. And that's a promise. I'm officially your biggest fan.'

He's got his hands in his pants' pockets, and he's standing at the bottom of the stairs, smiling up at me like— well, like Ash.

I turn and slide my key into the front doorknob.

'Lucy—'

I leave my key in the door and turn back. My heart races as his smoldering gaze bores into me. Every nerve in my body is on edge.

'Yeah?'

'Use my number *any*time,' he says, his voice is low and tempting.

Jesus, I want to call him right now just to hear that voice again, and he's standing right in front of me. My mind is reeling, trying to process his words, tones and face. I've never seen him look at me like this before. I bite my lip, attempting to stop the rush of desire. But, I can't resist playing along.

'Right back at ya,' I say, my tone laced with equal parts flirtation and challenge.

Ash nods, the smile on his face undeniable; he's leaving here as happy as I am.

Once he's safely in his car and pulling out of Mitzi's driveway with a honk, I unlock the door and enter the house, leaning against the front door while my heart slows from nearing cardiac arrest.

Well, that felt like a date. Not at first. But, just now. And I didn't hate it. This double dating thing might be something special going by what I feel right now.

## 14

## LUCY

I close my bedroom door, emotions fluttering inside me like a swarm of fireflies. Do I truly feel something for Asher Wright? Is that allowed given our situation? Is there a book I can buy to help?

After I've undressed and crawled into bed, my phone dings on the nightstand. I grab it seeing Madi's familiar face light up the screen as she calls me on FaceTime, her delicate features framed by a soft glow. I half-expected her to be wrapped up in bliss and covered in frosting right now.

'Hello...'

'What's the news?' she asks eagerly, clearly fishing for some juicy gossip.

'No news, he drove me home. It was fun,' I reply, my words feeling like a betrayal to the tangled feelings inside. 'And we got to meet Audrina Leighton!'

'I know, she's amazing. We had fun too. I just wanted to call and check in... you know, make sure everything went alright after you left?'

'Why wouldn't things go right?'

'Luce,' Madi's tone shifts to serious as she says my name, 'he knows.'

'Who knows what?'

'Asher. He knows what you said. About you thinking he's hot.'

I gasp. He *knows*? No, no, no. A sinking feeling grips my chest as I sit up.

'You told him?!'

'*I* didn't,' she says defensively. 'But Aaron did.'

'Ugh!' I groan, lying back on my bed and staring at the ceiling. 'That freaking ding-dong! Why would he do that?'

'Because they're brothers and friends, and it's exactly what we'd have done.'

I groan, tormented by the fact that she's right, yet torn apart by the conflicting feelings of betrayal and understanding swirling inside me.

'You don't have to throw technicalities in my face.' I stand, my feet automatically pacing the room as I wrestle with how to handle this emotional storm. 'Well, this is just great. What am I supposed to do now? Wait—' I stop pacing. 'What— uh— what'd he say?'

Should I even be considering what she says if it didn't come straight from his lips? Is second-hand – or even third-hand – information only questionable in courtrooms, or does it apply to matters of the heart as well?

'He's interested,' she says.

'He's interested – romantically?' I ask, bewildered.

I mean not completely bewildered. I suspected with the low-key flirting tonight. But he knows and he never said anything when he had every chance?

Suddenly a new voice enters the chat.

'Yeah. Despite you acting completely unhinged, Ash likes

you, with more than just his penis,' Aaron confirms, lacing his words with a touch of sarcasm.

'Don't say it so crudely, she's my best friend,' Madi counters, nudging him with her shoulder. 'Anyway, yeah, he likes you, with his heart,' she insists. 'He even called you gorgeous – but then again, who doesn't? It's really too bad your kitchen is closed.'

I gasp, then laugh, unsure if she's complimenting or mocking me.

'You two just made this weird.'

'Honestly, Luce, we didn't mean too.'

I'm so annoyed by this. And also intrigued? I don't know.

'Well, you should know we talked about you two as well. Ash thinks I should warn you that Aaron never follows through with relationships. He said he's a chronic dater.'

Aaron snorts laughter in the background. 'I guess that's better than fuckboy, which is usually how he describes me.'

I try not to laugh.

'He said for some reason Aaron always bolts when things start to get serious. And it reminded me of someone, but I can't quite figure out who?'

Madi's smirk tells me she's fully aware of my silent accusation. She falls quiet, but the sound of her manicured nails drumming on something lingers in the air.

Are we passive aggressively fighting right now?

'It's sweet that Ash cooks for you while you admire him, saved you from a bad marriage, treats you like royalty, and on top of all that, he's incredibly handsome – and you act like none of it impresses you.'

'I've no idea where you got that, I'm beyond impressed. I just — I—' My phone buzzes with a new message, and I see Asher's name flashing on the screen. My heart leaps into my throat as I hesitate before opening the message.

'Gotta go,' I say, tapping the end call button before she can speak.

I open the chat and read.

ASHER

You still up?

I grip my phone, tapping the response bubble and typing with my thumbs.

LUCY

Yep. You?

It's after I hit send that I realize how stupid a question that is. Obviously, he's awake, his phone isn't texting me on its own.

ASHER

Like a damn owl.

LUCY

How come?

ASHER

Tornado of thoughts.

I gasp, slightly relieved that he's an overthinker like myself. He seems so solid emotionally and grown-up. Is that a mask? I don't know, but if so, maybe he'll understand the nonsense my head comes up with.

LUCY

We have that in common then.

ASHER

Yeah? Tell me about it. No judgment.

LUCY

Will you tell me about yours?

ASHER

If u really wanna know, sure.

LUCY

I know you know what I said about you being... hot.

Hot. God, it's so high school. After this I'll never use the word hot for anything besides something coming out of the oven. The '...' typing bubble torments me as I wonder what exactly he's saying that's taking so long.

ASHER

I think Aaron and Madi also have gossiping in common. I do know. And I should have told you but had no clue how to say it and Aaron made me promise I wouldn't. I'm sorry.

LUCY

Are you kidding? If you had told me, I'd have been an outline in Mitzi's front door. Truth be told, I'm a little scared.

ASHER

What are you scared of? Me? Being friends with me?

LUCY

Being friends with you. Being attracted to that friend. Dating that friend with our friends. Possibly falling into more than friends. All of it. I feel like he's watching us...

ASHER

How often do you think about him?

My chest fills with storm clouds, affecting my ability to breathe at the memory of him.

> LUCY
>
> Often. You?

ASHER

Every day lately.

> LUCY
>
> Because of me?

ASHER

Maybe? Truthfully, the survivor's guilt is very much back – I feel like I ruined all our lives.

I pause, rereading his last message multiple times. Survivor's guilt? He mentioned this the other night too, but I thought it was in the past. I knew he was there when the accident happened. Never once did I consider he felt guilty for living.

> LUCY
>
> I'm not ruined. I don't think you are either. That accident was NOT your fault.

ASHER

That's what my therapist says too.

He's going to therapy? That's mature. I did, too, for a while.

> LUCY
>
> I've never blamed you. He wouldn't either. That much I know.

ASHER

Thx – I needed to hear that.

> LUCY
>
> Do you think he's happy wherever he is?

ASHER

Yeah. He's probably laughing that we still have
to deal with this world.

LUCY

LOL! And now it's thrown us together in a way I
never expected.

ASHER

I suspected u were feeling this way. So, I just
wanted to remind u that I'm always here to
listen even when things seem complicated.
Night, Lucy. See u tomorrow.

Tomorrow... the word dances in my mind, igniting a spark of
excitement at seeing him again.

LUCY

Thank you. Until tomorrow, then. Goodnight,
Ash.

My phone lies forgotten on the nightstand as I try to process
the unexpected depth of our conversation. Talking about Kris is
like opening old wounds, ones that I've kept hidden for so long.
But with Ash, it's different. He gets it. And he listens in a way
that no one else ever has and somehow that's got my heart
digging itself out of its shallow grave, bit by bit. He's amazing
and sort of unexpected.

## 15

### ASHER

As I stroll through Mitzi's museum of a house, my arms laden with reusable grocery bags, the faint sound of a door opening and closing reaches me.

Lucy appears in front of me, gracefully gliding out of her bedroom. The room brightens as she enters, like a ray of sunshine bursting through the clouds. Or maybe that's just how I feel when I'm around her. I swear it's gonna take a while before I get used to seeing her again.

'Oh! My gosh.' Her hand flies to her chest with a gasp. 'I didn't realize you were already here,' she says with a shaky laugh. 'I thought I could hear Mitzi.'

'I'm sorry I scared you.'

She waves a hand as if it's no big deal. 'Can I help you?'

Her hair cascades over one shoulder in a perfect braid, accentuating her delicate features. A diamond stud necklace sparkles in the mid-morning light beaming through the kitchen windows. Silver bands haphazardly adorn her fingers, and her nails are painted a vibrant blue, adding to the energy radiating from her. She's wearing a charming floral print sundress that hugs her curves – curves I shouldn't be noticing, but am. And her sandals are laced up her calves in an intricate pattern. With each step she takes, her smile grows brighter, and her eyes dance excitedly. She is breathtaking.

'Bringing all the groceries into the house in one trip has been a challenge I've enjoyed since I was a child,' I joke, offloading the six full bags hanging off my arms. One bag wobbles – causing me momentary grief that I'll have to pick up a dozen oranges if it falls – but instead, it stabilizes, and I exhale a relieved breath. 'Looks like I still got it,' I say, winking Lucy's way.

She laughs, shaking her head. 'You're just full of hidden talents I never knew you had, aren't you?'

'You've got no idea,' I tease. 'How's your day been?'

The warmth of the sunlight streaming through the windows casts a cozy glow over us as we catch up. I don't cook on the weekends, so it's been a couple of days since I've seen her.

Her shoulders rise and fall with a nonchalant shrug. She seems more relaxed around me today, which I didn't expect after learning she knew I knew what she'd said. Thank God she doesn't know what it's doing to me internally. Yet.

'Just the usual,' she replies, her tone hinting at boredom. 'Zoom calls that could have been emails, a handful of deadlines – some met, others pushed back. And a new client was thrown into the mix.'

Curiosity kicks in, and I realize I haven't yet asked about her job. 'What do you do, exactly?'

Her pink lips quirk into a small smile. 'I'm a freelance graphic designer.'

I nod, impressed. 'That's cool. Do you work from home?'

'Yeah, I have the flexibility to set my own schedule, so I often work on weekends because Mitzi is usually out with her friends at one of their many social gatherings. Sometimes, the peace can be quite refreshing.'

'Mitzi's active still, is she?'

'Oh, yes,' she confirms, perching on a barstool at the kitchen island as I unpack bags. 'What day is it today? Monday?' She taps her phone screen to double-check the date. 'Right now, she's at an upscale Catholic church for Monday morning Mass with her friend Kitty, probably lighting a candle to bless our family with whatever she deems necessary. Tonight, she'll call me into her room to tell me she prayed for me and got an immediate answer – then she'll try to imprint that answer in my mind because she believes she's doing me a favor.'

I chuckle. 'Are the prayers at least good ones?'

Lucy tilts her head. 'After Vegas, she prayed that a man would enter my life and sweep me off my feet by Christmas.'

'By Christmas?' I repeat her words.

We were in Vegas the week after Christmas, so her deadline for answering that prayer is this upcoming Christmas. I'm curious if Mitzi remembers this. I also wonder how often she's right.

As I continue unpacking groceries, Lucy leans back on the barstool with a wistful expression. 'You know...' she starts, absentmindedly swirling the water bottle in her hand. 'I sometimes envy Mitzi's optimism – her unshakeable faith that everything will work out. She swears that people get what they deserve because karma's never wrong.'

I pause, meeting Lucy's gaze. 'Do you believe in all that? Prayers being answered and fate intervening?'

She shrugs, a small smile playing on her lips. 'I don't know if

I believe in prayers per se, but I do believe in the power of hope. Sometimes, when everything seems bleak, a glimmer of hope is all you need to keep going. As for fate, I don't think it likes me.'

'Why wouldn't fate like you?'

'You've seen my life.'

I glance around the mansion of a home she's living in.

'Not *that* – I know I'm blessed. Trust me. I could be lounging around here all day, doing nothing and never worrying about anything. But that just isn't me. I was born a worrywart. It felt weird to live my life on someone else's dime. I know the money is there, but it's nice to say I made a difference in the world. Even if it is in a tiny way, like business branding.'

'That's not tiny. Every great brand has a graphic that people know them by. The Golden Arches. The black swoosh. The green mermaid. And one of my favorites, the black apple.' I hold up my iPhone. 'I'd be lost without this thing.'

Yes, I'd upgraded my phone after we left Vegas because no way was I going back in for the one I'd brought with me. But she doesn't need to know that.

Her smile exudes sweetness and a touch of humility as she responds, 'Excellent point. However, my jobs are slightly less important than the classics. I was recently commissioned to design a logo for a bunny ranch near Reno, Nevada.'

'A bunny ranch?' I inquire, my curiosity piqued. 'For meat?'

'Sort of...' she replies with a mischievous smile. 'It's like a modern-day brothel.'

My eyebrows shoot up my head. 'A brothel? So, *for* meat, but not as I intended – interesting. What was your design?'

She blushes as she shakes her head. 'I passed on the job. It's difficult to compete with their current logo – a pair of bunnies humping.'

I burst out laughing, causing her to laugh with me.

'Wait,' she says, now scrolling through her phone. 'I've got photos.' She turns the phone to me, displaying a bright yellow roadside sign with two bunnies fornicating.

'Wow! There it is. Two bunnies, doing it doggie style – unmistakable. Jesus.'

'Doggie or bunny style?' she laughs.

Her mischievous smirk dances on her lips. At that moment, it's impossible to hold back laughter. Hers is infectious, bubbling up deep within her and pouring into the world.

'What's so funny?' Mitzi asks, causing both of us to straighten up like we're in trouble.

'Oh, Mitzi, you're home. I was telling Asher about that bunny ranch job I passed on.'

'Gracious, darling, don't remind me,' Mitzi groans dramatically as she drops her designer handbag onto the kitchen counter. 'Kitty was scandalized when I told her. I think she thought you were moving into the Playboy Mansion. It took me a week to explain it to her. Though, I must confess, I can't imagine what logo you would have created for them.'

'I'm thinking something with a rod...' I tease.

At this point, Lucy is practically glowing with amusement.

'I'm sure your next project will be much more... family-friendly,' Mitzi suggests. 'Maybe Asher needs to design some cutting-edge menus!'

I glance Lucy's way. That's a thought.

'Actually, I do need menus,' I tell her. 'I'd never thought to go with a graphic designer, though. Aaron suggested a boring old print company. Is that even something you could do?'

Her eyes light up with excitement at the prospect. 'Of course, I can do menus! It's all about capturing the restaurant's essence and enticing people with more than just words.'

Mitzi claps her hands together in delight. 'Oh, I love it when creative minds come together! Asher, you must let Lucy work her magic on your menus. She's a genius with designs.'

This is a great idea.

'We'll have to discuss it,' I say, my words low and almost conspiratorial. 'Do you take private appointments?'

Lucy nods affirmatively, a small flirtatious smile playing on her lips. 'Yes. My usual meeting spot for local clients is Queue Coffee, off of twenty first. Do you know it?'

Isn't that ironic? She's been meeting clients just a block away from my new restaurant, and I had no idea. I wonder if, eventually, we'd have run into one another. Perhaps fate is at work here? I'd say that had to be it, but Queue Coffee is in the lobby of the Q21 apartment building, and one of my exes lives there. Or at least lived there when I knew her. I haven't taken the chance to go by it since we broke up and without her suggestion not sure I ever would have.

'I know the area well,' I say, a twinge of excitement filling me. Exploring my favorite part of town with Lucy would undoubtedly be an adventure.

Suddenly, our phones simultaneously ding with a message, interrupting our thoughts. We both check our devices.

'Is this some sort of -A situation from *Pretty Little Liars*?' Lucy asks, her tone laced with both amusement and intrigue.

> AARON
>
> We're double dating bro!!! STD – next friday, we got a hot 1 – lucy loo's got the deets.

My eyes scan the message before looking up at Lucy. 'It's from Aaron.'

She nods. 'Madi. I told her our idea this weekend... word's out.'

'Not sure we got the same text 'cause I think Aaron's telling me he's got an STD?' I say regretfully. 'Please tell me yours says something different?'

'An STD? Mine says, save the date—' Lucy glances at me with a smirk. 'You're officially busy next Friday. Meet us in the Woodstock neighborhood at 8 p.m.; there will be a pop-up SBDP.'

'STD clearly doesn't mean what I suspected, thank God. But what the hell is SBDP?' I repeat.

'No idea.'

Mitzi chimes in from across the room, now sitting at the dining table with her laptop opened. 'Silent bubble dance party and it seems there's one happening next Friday night in Woodstock. Dancing!' she coos. 'I remember going dancing. It was so wonderfully freeing, letting the rhythm take over.'

Asher and I both turn toward her, intrigued by this new information. She danced, huh?

'How did you figure it out so fast?' I ask.

'Mitzi's obsessed with Google,' Lucy says.

'Google knows everything,' Mitzi confirms. 'I wish it was a thing fifty years ago. My nonstop Google searching got you here,' she tells me directly.

'Dancing,' Lucy says, glancing my way. 'That's fun.'

'You'll need a new dress,' Mitzi suggests to her.

'Maybe.'

I notice Mitzi's interest in our conversation and can't help but wonder about her younger years. Maybe she wants to come with? I'm sure Lucy wouldn't mind considering how close they seem.

'What do you think, Mitzi? Going dancing with us?'

'Pardon?' she asks, her head cocked like she didn't hear me.

She closes the laptop, getting up slowly and making her way to the bar.

Lucy beams. 'Are you inviting my grandmother?'

'Psshhh,' Mitzi shushes her. 'If the answer to her question is yes, I would love to go dancing with you, Asher.'

'Then it's a date.'

'Can I come?' Lucy asks with a laugh.

'I hope you do,' I say.

'Of course you can, darling,' Mitzi says. 'He'll need a dance partner when I'm tired. And when I'm not, we'll have a three-way dance party.'

I laugh at her choice of words.

Lucy's eyebrows shoot up her forehead. 'She's a little filthy-mouthed for eighty,' she teases, leaning into her grandmother, her arm around her shoulders now as she hugs her to her side.

'It's settled then,' I declare. 'Next Friday, we dance.'

'Oh, how exciting!' Mitzi coos. 'We'll go shopping, darling. I can hear Nordstrom calling us already.'

'Thank you,' Lucy mouths.

I nod. The pleasure is all mine because I am just a man who has a slightly huge crush on the woman sitting in front of me, and bringing her grandmother will keep me honest.

* * *

'You asked her grandma to come? *Why?*' Aaron balks during our nightly phone call.

'Because she seemed interested,' I reply with a casual shrug he can't see over the phone.

'Did you also invite the girl you like?'

I laugh, but there's an edge to it. 'Obviously.'

'Do you plan to date the both of them forever?'

'Why? Does the idea of me dating two wealthy beautiful women make you jealous?'

He laughs heartily. 'Not when one of them is a hundred and two.'

'I dunno. Truth be told, I'm a little nervous, It's been a while since I've been on a date and now, I've got two women to manage.'

A sigh sounds through the phone. 'You're reminding me of me and Mads' first date.'

'Do *not* tell the story again,' I command. 'This is all your fault, by the way.'

'What is?'

'Me being worried. You own that.'

'How?'

'You're a gossip queen. Had you kept your trap shut this could have evolved naturally.' I shoot back, unsure if I'm more annoyed or thankful.

'Maybe in twelve more years... you two don't seem to move quickly,' Aaron interjects, rudely.

'You don't get it,' I say, dropping my head against the back of my couch. 'She's scared.'

'Of *what*? My pussycat brother who won't even tell a woman he's just walked in on having an affair with his friend to go to hell?' he moans. 'Clearly, she's been too influenced by the mass amount of ink under your skin. You look like a badass, but a pussy, you are.'

'I'm going to hang up on you.'

'OK – wait,' he laughs. 'Lemme ask, are you scared of her?'

'Um—' Am I? Is this feeling fear? 'I dunno. Not her directly but possibly the overall situation,' I admit, feeling the tug of uncertainty. Kris is still in my head, influencing my thoughts with words he'll never really say.

The phone fills with him groaning. 'Dude. What is wrong with you?'

'Nothing's wrong with me,' I counter, unsure if I believe it myself. 'Listen, Tin Man, you don't get it 'cause I've actually gotta heart. I'm struggling. Shit's complicated. I've watched this woman be destroyed, twice now. I can't add to that.'

There's silence across the line.

'You know what the Ash I know would do?' he says suddenly, clearly suggesting I've changed somehow.

'What?'

'He'd own that shit and charm the pants off this girl to prove there's nothing to be afraid of. I've seen you be smooth, man. You got it in you. I've heard the stories. You take dead friend's girlfriends to prom. You cook for women on first dates. You stand up to cheaters while they stand at the altar. The only person you don't stand up for is yourself. Around her – you're suddenly a knight in shining armor saving a damsel in distress.' He's half-goading but sincere beneath it all. 'Girls love that shit. If you're that into her, be *that* guy.'

Rarely does Aaron think something through to a conclusion that makes complete sense. I close my eyes, letting his words sink in, torn between the person I've been, the teen I was, and the man Lucy suddenly makes me want to be. He's right – I've always been one to go the extra mile for those I care about. And Lucy... damn, she does something to my insides no one else ever has. She makes me want to go above and beyond while becoming a better version of myself – for her. I finally want to take the risk and put myself back at love's door – for her. Yet, the fear of failure looms, and I'm caught between wanting to be that guy and doubting we can overcome the ghost standing between us.

'Also...' I say, almost ashamed the words are coming out of

my mouth to the guy who learned some of the eighties hottest dance trends when he was a tween – for fun. 'Why in the hell would you choose dancing?'

'Because I'm a disco dancing fuckboy. I do believe you've said those words before.'

'Yes, when you danced your ass in front of the mirror while I was in the shower,' I remind him.

He laughs. 'You weren't getting ready fast enough, and we had a timeline that day.' His laughter fades. 'Do you need me to come over there and give you a dance lesson?'

'You want to teach me how to dance?'

I lean my head against the back of my couch, almost certain I should say no to this.

'I guess it couldn't hurt. But only if we can *not* focus on one decade's vibe. No routines. No lifts. And I'm not grinding on this girl.'

'That outs one of the best movie scenes ever. You're so boring, Grandpa. But fret not, I hadn't planned on giving you all my best moves. I could probably keep it PG-17.'

'Alright then. Come over and teach me, Mr Miyagi.'

'Ha-ha... you sound so much cooler than you are when you mimic me.'

'Sure. Just come over and don't tell anyone, Madi included, or I'll start telling her stories from the vault about you.'

He gasps suddenly. 'You wouldn't.'

'I so would.'

Sometimes being the older brother is fun.

'I'll be there in ten.'

\* \* \*

I drop the phone onto the couch cushion next to me and unmute the TV. What did I just do? I asked my brother to teach me to dance. Shit. I'm dancing for this woman? I guess my two left feet would sink me, and she's already seen me flounder around a dance floor once. But still, this feels big. Considering I've not dated in a long time; I didn't expect such big moves from the heart so quickly.

'Oooh, isn't he fancy – driving a white Range Rover? What a stud.'

I laugh. 'Please don't use the word stud around him.'

'Why not, darling?'

'I just— can't...' I shake my head, worried about three people and their mouths now: Aaron, Madi and Mitzi. This could be super-fun or overly humiliating – let's pray for the former.

'All I'm saying is that the man drives a nice car, it means he's not some sponge.'

'Sponge?'

'Sixties slang, darling. Brandon was a sponge.'

Blech. Why'd she bring him up? Not that I disagree, but...

'No sponge either,' I say in a sing-song voice, making her laugh.

'Picky, picky,' she says, stopping suddenly to turn my way. 'Lucy,' her tone changes to one I know well, motherly. 'It seems as though you don't want me to embarrass you because you might be feeling something for Asher?'

'What!?' I say, glancing at her and knowing right away she's not buying it.

She nods her head, staring me down. 'I understand. He's only handsome, talented, and respectful. What's there to love?'

'*Love*?' I practically choke on the word. 'I mean, sure, I don't disagree with anything you just said; he is all those things. I'm just trying not to get in over my head here. Of all people, you should understand. You've nursed me back from heartbreak twice now.'

'Very true. But I *know* you, darling.'

That she does, which is why it's hard to lie to her.

'Mitzi, you look lovely this evening. You were right, that is the perfect dress.'

She's wearing a lilac dress adorned with delicate lace and embroidery of the same color. The fabric drapes loosely over her slight frame, a constant reminder that she is slowly diminishing with age. But in my eyes, she remains timeless.

Her lips are painted a warm pink, adding a touch of vibrancy to her otherwise mature appearance. Her long, graying hair is carefully styled into a sleek low bun at the nape of her neck, accentuating the graceful slope of her shoulders. As I admire her, my heart aches at the thought of losing her one day. She's been my rock through all of life's ups and downs. The mother I never had, and she's never hesitated to take on that role.

After Vegas, she worried about me. I swear she paced a path from her room to mine, checking on me so often. She brought me coffee, scones, tea and cakes and would climb into my bed and turn on a movie that reminded me you can love after heartbreak. But I wasn't convinced it was worth it any more.

As days turned into weeks and weeks into months, I slowly began to see a glimmer of hope on the horizon. I was worth so much more than Brandon's asswipe ways made me feel. And it was Mitzi's gentle nudges and quiet strength that guided me back to a place where I could envision happiness again. As the seasons changed, so did I, thanks to her constant presence by my side.

'Ladies,' Asher says, stepping out of his car in all black – jeans, T-shirt, shoes and even a suit jacket.

'Wow, you dressed up?'

'Mitzi was a low-key starlet in her youth,' he says as if I don't know.

He extends a hand to her. 'I Googled you, young lady. You've got quite an impressive résumé.'

'Thank you, sweetheart,' Mitzi says, carefully maneuvering the front steps, her hand in his. 'I've had a wonderful life.'

'Gotta dress the part, I figured. Good?' Ash asks, glancing back at me.

Too freaking good.

'Young, hot, Portland chef,' Mitzi says. *Out loud.* 'Lucy and Google were right about you.'

I laugh nervously as Asher's brows raise in curiosity.

'That's the phrase I simply suggested she enter into Google that got you hired. I didn't realize she was going to *tell* you, so that's only slightly embarrassing.'

He looks elated to hear this, and his smile is so sincere like he's genuinely here because he really wants to be. Just like he was on prom night. I thought I'd spend the night bawling over our loss like we had the week of the funeral, but he never once stopped being fun, so I had no chance to dwell on what I'd lost. We just danced and had a great time. My gosh, I think he's right – that wasn't a pity date for him.

Once Mitzi is buckled into the front seat, he turns, and I'm practically next to him when he does, so we end up closer than intended. He stops, not backing away but leaning in.

'I'm sorry you have to sit in the back.'

'It's OK,' I say, through nervous laughter, climbing past him into his SUV.

He flashes me an adorably flirty smile before closing the door and hopping into the driver's seat.

As we drive through the city, the lights of downtown Portland flicker like stars against the night sky. Ash's choice of music fills the car with a mix of old classics and modern beats, creating a comfortable atmosphere that makes it easy to forget the world outside. Mitzi sits in the front seat, chatting away with Ash about her past adventures as a young starlet, while I can't help but steal glances at him when he's focused on the road. A couple of times, our gaze meets in the rearview mirror, and the static once again fills my insides. I wonder if he's feeling it, too? He seems to read my mind, so I wouldn't doubt it.

Asher manages to park on the street only a block from the dance. Not sure how that happened, but lucky for Mitzi because she's wearing kitten heels, and I'd hate to make her walk blocks.

The warm summer breeze carries a gentle mist from dozens of bubble machines as we approach, Mitzi on Ash's arm and me off to his side.

'This looks fun!' Mitzi coos, as she admires the bubbles floating lazily through the air.

'This *is* cool,' I say, stopping next to them.

Silhouettes sway to music only they can hear because everyone is wearing big bulky headphones in front of a small open-to-the-sidewalk bar with a counter labeled: Music to Go.

A garage door has been rolled up into the ceiling, revealing standing tables scattered across the sidewalk outside.

Bartenders expertly mix drinks, filling to-go cups with vibrant liquids. The air is sweet with hints of vanilla and citrus, thanks to the bubbles. String lights zigzag above us, connecting the building to a closed second-hand furniture store across the street. It's like stepping into a sparkling wonderland where fireflies have come to life and dreams are made real.

'Very Portland,' Ash replies with a smile. 'Full disclosure, until recently, I haven't danced since prom.'

'Until recently?'

He looks stunned at my words.

'Uh, that part was supposed to be silent. I didn't mean— oh, what the hell. Aaron offered me a dance lesson and I may have taken him up on it.'

'That Aaron,' I ask, spotting him and Madi across the dance floor, off to one corner, grinding like they're in a dark club.

Ash grimaces. 'Yeah... that one. But we didn't practice the art of scaring a woman.'

'Sure...' I laugh, but I'm reeling. He had his brother give him a dance refresher course? Is that what he's saying? For me? No.

'Maybe you should run now,' he kids.

'You guys made it!' Madi exclaims as she wakes from her daze and spots us. 'And you brought Mitzi!' she says, gently giving her a hug. 'Great idea.'

She's looking adorable in a flowing skirt slit up the front, crop top, flip-flops and her hair pulled up just on top. The oversized black headphones stand out, and she has one ear uncovered so she can hear.

'Don't you seem happy!' I say, noticing immediately. 'Could it be this guy?' I ask under my breath as the guys greet one another behind us.

'Perhaps...' she drawls. 'I think I feel things for him—' she leans back, her jaw dropped.

'North or south?' I ask.

She drops her chin staring me down with shock on her face, not wanting to give me the details right now but if I had to guess, I'm thinking north. Wow. That, I didn't expect.

'Fine, tell me later,' I whisper.

'OK, how does this work?' I ask. 'We're SBDP virgins.'

Ash chuckles. He's standing close enough that I can feel his warmth, giving off the impression to others that we're a couple – on a date with my grandmother. It's totally not weird.

'Easy-peasy,' Madi says. 'Go to the MTG counter, check out three sets of headphones, and pick one playlist; they'll sync you. They have dozens to choose from – from hits of the year to genres – even mood playlists – everything you can think of. Then grab your drink and come back here to dance with us!'

Asher leans in close to me, his cologne filling my senses. I swear it's the scent you imagine Portland to have: blackberries, cedar, sweet tobacco and rain. I can't get enough of it. 'But do we have to speak in acronyms all night?' he whispers.

'IDK,' I tease.

He pokes me in the side with his finger, activating the fire-flies again.

'What's the problem?' Madi asks, picking up on our conversation.

'MTG?' I inquire.

She laughs and points toward the counter. 'Music to Go,' she clarifies.

'Where'd Aaron go?' he asks. 'He was just here.'

We all look around, our gaze stopping near one of the rooftop-mounted bubble machines and we see him dancing under a waterfall of bubbles without a care in the world. Eyes closed, headphones on, he's lost, pumping his hands in the air and swaying his hips like the tune is something sexy.

'Never mind,' Asher chuckles. I grab three drinks and let Asher and Mitzi rent our headphones and pick our playlist. As soon as we put on the headphones, the music starts playing in our ears, transporting us into a world where only we exist.

'May I have this dance?' he asks Mitzi. 'I'm coming back for you soon,' he tells me as she accepts.

He leads her to the dancers, swaying to the beat, letting Mitzi lead him for a bit. He's doing remarkably well, until he isn't.

Before I know it, he's doing the sprinkler before pretending to rope me in. He's a tornado of awkward limbs and exaggerated movements, but he wears his lack of grace with a pride and confidence that makes it endearing.

I match his moves, laughing the entire time.

'Your brother may have done you wrong,' I laugh as he reaches me.

'That last part was all me,' he says, proudly. 'Mitzi convinced me that the only way to dance is with your soul, so, I let it lead and here we are.'

My breath catches in my throat.

'Wooo! You guys are so bad you're good!' Madi yells over the music, relieving me of coming up with a response to his incredibly sweet line there.

She clinks her cup to both mine and Asher's before dancing her way over to Aaron, who gleefully accepts her into his arms.

The two of them take to the dance floor, their bodies immediately drawn together in a heated embrace. I don't know what they're listening to, but we definitely didn't choose the same playlist. Their movements are fluid and sensual as Aaron holds her close, his hands gripping her waist as she sways her hips to the rhythm of the music on his thigh.

'Oh, how I wish they were a little more prudish,' I say to

Asher, who laughs. Right now, I'm glad Mitzi left to use the ladies' room.

'Don't look directly at them,' he says, covering my eyes jokingly. 'You know what they're doing, right?'

I shake my head.

'Aaron's obsessed with eighties movies. When he was a kid, our mom spent most of her time in her room. So, Aaron hung out with her, and they watched VHS tapes all day. If it was hot in the eighties, he's probably got it memorized. I'm pretty sure he learned this from *Dirty Dancing*.'

My eyebrows shoot up my forehead, and laughter emerges loudly. 'I think you might be right!? Ew.'

Suddenly, our song changes to something slower. We turn to one another, wide-eyed as if we've got caught in the air before a summer storm. Do we stay on our own side of the gym, or do we come together and take advantage of a romantic situation like adults?

Asher sways closer amid bubbles, offering me a hand that I accept. He twirls me before pulling me close, his hand resting on the small of my back. His touch sends a shiver down my spine as we sway to the romantic melody playing in our ears. It's a waltz of sugar and spun glass, our delicate movements weaving a tapestry of sweetness and grace. The world around us fades into the background, and all I can focus on is the warmth of his touch and the steady rhythm of our hearts beating in time.

'I feel like teenage Ash again,' he whispers, his voice warm on my neck.

'Can you imagine being teenagers without the weight of tragedy crushing us?'

'I can.'

'Sort of a dangerous feeling, isn't it?'

'Like walking onto a minefield,' he says, his eyes searching mine, a silent question lingering in their depths.

'We could get seriously hurt,' I say, picturing the aftermath of one wrong step.

'Or we won't,' he suggests, hope in his eyes.

How are we saying so much without actually saying anything at all? The world around us blurs into nothingness, leaving only us in our private bubble of shared emotions. The moon casts a gentle glow over us, adding to the enchanting atmosphere of the night. The heat of his touch seeps into my skin, igniting a fire that spreads through every fiber of my being.

'We need refills, join me?' Madi interrupts.

My heart stalls in my chest. Now?

'It's cool,' Ash says, releasing me. 'I'll check on Mitzi and Aaron while you're gone.'

I nod, sad to walk away from him.

'You two looked cozy,' Madi says as we reach the bar. 'How's it going?'

'We were having a very vague conversation, beating around the bush about how we were feeling?'

'Oh? What'd ya land on?'

'Don't make a wrong step while on a minefield?'

She scrunches her face.

'I'm pretty sure we were wondering "what if" without actually saying it?'

She smiles sweetly as if I deserve every second of this.

'Luce, here's what I know. People come into your life for one of a few reasons. To teach you something. To offer you something. Or to take something.'

'And what do you think Asher's here for?' I ask, my gaze drifting back to him. Mitzi's talking animatedly with him and

Aaron. Ash's eyes light up with every word she says. She looks so happy. I'm so glad she came.

'I think he's here to teach you,' Madi replies.

'What, though?'

'Maybe about trusting your instincts? Or maybe he's here to push you to follow your heart even when your head says "no." I think he could be good for you.'

I nod slowly, absorbing her words as I watch him, laughing at something Aaron has said. He glances my way, his eyes crinkling at the corners when he smiles at me.

'Look at the way he looks at you,' Madi says, gazing his way. 'It's what every girl dreams of.'

'Yeah,' I say. 'I definitely don't hate it.' I love the way his smile makes my heart skip a beat.

'By the way, you *never* looked at Brandon like this.'

'I didn't?'

Hmmm, I had no idea.

'Nope. Plus, he invited your grandmother. That's possibly the sweetest thing I've ever witnessed.'

Maybe she's right. Asher may be here to teach me something important about myself. I'd be an idiot not to accept the lesson. But what if he's just being polite, and I'm mistaking kindness for something more? He never really said how he felt about me when I told him I knew. What if I want to be loved correctly so badly that I'm turning this into something it's not? Seeds of anxiety sprout in my mind, and the last thing I need is more of those taking root.

# 17

## ASHER

Mitzi looks absolutely lovely this evening. But Lucy is breathtaking – literally. From her short V-neck lace spaghetti-strap dress that ties in the back to the white Converse shoes on her feet, ready for dancing, her makeup is soft, and her hair is down, wavy and tucked behind one ear; she is gorgeous. Truthfully, it's making me a little nervous, considering she's undoubtedly the prettiest woman I've ever laid eyes on.

But I'm choosing to focus on the intoxicating feeling that consumes me when she's close – like a raging wildfire, burning through my chest and leaving me gasping for air. I can't get enough. I don't want to resist her alluring pull, even with the uncertainty it brings.

She's at the bar with Madi but turns to glance my way. Once our eyes meet, a small, knowing smile plays on her lips as if she can sense the internal turmoil I'm grappling with.

'I'm going to go check on the girls,' Mitzi says, excusing herself from Aaron and my presence.

Aaron's voice breaks through my thoughts, jolting me out of

my trance. 'You gonna bring grandma on all your dates with her?'

'Probably not.'

He laughs, raising an eyebrow.

'Seriously, Aaron,' I urge him, grabbing his arm to ensure he's listening. 'In the last hour, something has clicked for me.'

He looks at me curiously.

'I don't care what happened in our past, all I know is that I am *really* into Lucy. So, she'll probably meet someone better in mere months. That's how my life seems to go. But, until then, I think I want to know where this goes.'

'Or, maybe you're the someone better. I've met one of her exes; you're definitely more of a man than that guy.'

I suck in a breath, wanting to be hopeful, but my heart is holding back. 'That scares the hell out of me too.'

'So you are afraid of her?' he remarks. 'I thought you were afraid of nothing – remember the time you yelled that at me?'

'We were in the Shanghai tunnels with a tour guide who'd wandered off and left us in a room that felt like it was breathing down my neck. Either I said I wasn't scared out loud, or I ran out of there like a fucking girl.'

He laughs – exactly like he did that night. Never again will I go on a haunted tour. I walked in a skeptic and walked out feeling like I'd been touched by the other side and desperately needed a shower.

'So, basically, you're scared of each other?' He shakes his head. 'You two make shit complicated. Look at her,' he says, motioning her way. 'She's like five-two or five-three and weighs maybe a buck twenty. The girl's fine as fuck, pretty as hell, rich to boot, and laughs at all your lame jokes. Seems pretty harmless to me.'

'*She's* harmless,' I reply with a sigh, wondering how

someone can suddenly be afraid of their feelings. 'But she has this affect on me that I just don't understand – and there is no translation book.'

'Your heart needs subtitles?'

'Around her, yes.'

'That's weird, man.'

I shoot him a glare. 'Better than my heart needing an STD test...'

He rolls his eyes.

'By the way, before you drink yourself into oblivion this evening, we've got a delivery at the restaurant tomorrow and I expect you there before ten.'

'Shit, I didn't know my boss was coming tonight.'

I glare.

'That sucks. But you know I'll be there.'

'Good.'

'We off the clock yet?' he asks.

'Sure.'

'Man, my boss,' he says leaning into me. 'Guys a fucking slave driver.'

I wanna smack him, but out of the corner of my eye, I see Lucy move, and she's all that exists. She glides effortlessly through the crowd, drawing people in with her infectious energy and radiant smile. I gravitate toward her, unable to resist her magnetic pull on me.

'Hey there,' she greets me warmly, bouncing with the beat in our heads, her eyes sparkling with mischief. 'Got you a refill.' She hands me a new drink.

'Thanks, I was parched,' I lie, sipping the fruity beverage through the straw. I remember why I drink whisky – these cocktails are dangerous.

'Do you think they'll crown a queen and king, like prom?'

she asks as we hang out against the cool brick wall, watching dozens of strangers and our friends dance the night away.

'That would be a fun incentive for this place. Who will earn the title of Lord of the Dance? Definitely not me.'

We both laugh.

'I am glad you were crowned queen back then. You deserved it.'

'It was a pity win,' she says, a twinge of disappointment in her tone.

Her and this pity bullshit.

'Nah.'

She chuckles. 'I'd believe you, but they crowned you the honorary king in Kris' memory. Pity wins for both of us.'

It was weird, but at the same time, I felt him there. I could see the guy wearing the crown.

'You were a beautiful prom queen and a gorgeous bride, Luce. You deserve to wear a crown everywhere you go.'

Her cheeks are pink as she bites her bottom lip. 'You sure know how to flatter a girl.' The announcement of the bar closing fills our headphones when the song ends, filling me with dread.

'Ohhhhh...' Lucy moans with a frown, her brows furrowing in disappointment. 'It's over!?'

Exactly what I was thinking.

'Afraid so,' I say, gently releasing her even though I'd rather not. I pull off my headphones, taking hers as she hands them to me.

'Here you go, sweetheart,' Mitzi says, now standing nearby, handing her headphones to me.

But my gaze is on Lucy as she runs her fingers through her hair, tousling it into perfection as the twinkle lights dim, and the moon casts a soft glow over her.

'I'll be right back. Don't you ladies disappear on me,' I tease, turning to approach the bar to pay tabs and turn in headphones. Something changed tonight in the best way possible, and not just for me, that much I know. I'm ready to charge onto that minefield without armor. For her.

# 18

## LUCY

**ASHER**

What u up to this morning?

How can a text from him make me feel giddy? He has been the only thing on my mind since the dance – and I like it. My plans for the morning were derailed as the client I was supposed to meet with canceled at the last minute. Of course, there are things I could be doing instead, but as usual, my head is elsewhere.

**LUCY**

My schedule is clear today.

My fingers drum nervously against my desktop as I wait for his response, eagerly anticipating those three little dots indicating that he's typing. Finally, they appear. The suspense is almost palpable as I anxiously await his reply. Why is he curious about my plans? What is happening between us?

ASHER

Wanna help shop for this week's menu? I'll buy
u coffee.

LUCY

I was ready to say yes before you even
mentioned coffee... now it's a hell yes.

ASHER

Precisely what I wanted to hear. Be there in 30.

Thirty minutes? I glance down at myself, still clad in my
wrinkled pajamas and my hair is a tangled mess. Panic sets in as
I realize I have to shower, get ready and be dressed in – I quickly
recheck the time – twenty-nine minutes!

Frantically, I rush to the bathroom, shedding my pajamas
and stepping under the hot spray of the shower. Ah. The warm
water soothes my nerves as I hurriedly wash away any hint of
sleep from my skin.

Determined not to make Ash wait, I move through my
morning routine with practiced speed, pulling on a simple yet
stylish outfit (cut-off jean shorts – not the booty kind, my check-
ered Vans and a sky-blue V-neck top). I've no time to dry my
hair, so I run a brush through it, add a dab of product, and
scrunch, hoping it'll air-dry fast. A swipe of lip gloss, mascara,
and a dash of perfume, and I'm ready just in time.

Stepping outside, the morning air fills my lungs. Just seeing
his SUV running in the driveway sends a flutter through me.

Before I can approach his car, he steps out, his quick smile
putting me at ease.

'Hey,' he greets me, his eyes warm and inviting.

'Hello,' I say, attempting to keep my cool.

'Be honest, what are you most excited about, grocery shopping, coffee or me?' he asks while opening the passenger-side door.

'Obviously, coffee,' I reply with a teasing glint in my eyes, as I brush past him to slide into the passenger seat. 'But having you as company is a close second.'

'I suppose that's the right answer,' he says, winking before closing my door.

As he pulls out of the driveway, I steal a glance at him. Today, he's clean-shaven, smells fantastic, and I'm not the only one who did the shower-and-go thing if I had to guess by his slightly tousled hair.

\* \* \*

'So, what's on the menu this week?' I ask once we both have to-go coffee cups in our hands, breaking the comfortable silence between us.

'How do you feel about taste-testing some new dishes for me?'

'If I ever say no to that, get me to a doctor asap because I'm delusional.'

He chuckles at my response, his gaze lingering on me longer than necessary before returning to the road – and I like it.

'I'm attempting to build my menu for the restaurant.'

'Count me in then. Always. Anytime you cook anything, count me in.'

I love the way he laughs at my words like they make him feel good. But I'm only being honest.

As we arrive at the grocery store, Asher grabs a cart, and we start our leisurely stroll down the aisles. His expertise in choosing fresh ingredients and unique spices is evident as he explains his vision for each dish he plans to prepare. I find myself hanging on to every word of his, fascinated by his passion.

'Any favorite foods or requests?' he asks, glancing at me with genuine interest.

He wants my opinion? The woman who practically mashed celery?

'Um... I like to try new things, but I also have a soft spot for Italian food.'

'Italian food,' he repeats my words, somehow making them sound alluring. He's standing next to the cart, one hand in his pocket, the other resting on the cart handle.

'Yeah. There's just something about a hearty bowl of pasta that warms my soul.'

'Tomato or cream-based?'

'Cream,' I say without question.

He nods thoughtfully, reaching into the refrigerated cheese display we're standing near and tossing mascarpone and mozzarella into the cart.

'Italian for dinner tonight, then – just for you.'

*Just for me.* Why do I like the sound of that so much? My taste buds are bouncing with joy right now at the thought of it.

We continue our grocery shopping, and by we, I mean him, because I'm mostly admiring him while sipping my coffee and attempting not to get caught.

He turns to me with a sly grin as we approach the register. 'Prepare yourself,' he whispers, leaning into me. 'I have a feeling that this check-out girl is into me.'

'Really...?' My curiosity piques.

'Yeah, she's always checking me out.'

I glance at him, watching his grin widen, becoming almost

ridiculous, and realize he's messing with me. With a burst of laughter, I play along with his game.

I nudge him with my elbow. 'Wow, Mr Popular! Can't blame a girl, though; who could possibly resist your charming personality and incredibly addictive cooking skills?'

He lifts a single eyebrow.

'Or perhaps she's fallen for your handsome face?'

His gaze is tied to mine, and his face holds a captivating heat, like embers waiting to burst into flames, which adds a dangerous allure to his already striking features. There is no doubt we've crossed into 'I like you and you like me, let's flirt,' phase of this new old friendship.

'Flattery will get you everywhere,' he teases, winking at me.

'Is that so?' My words dance like a butterfly, teasing and light.

Flirting with Ash feels right, amazing even. But deep inside there's a voice screaming, *what are ya doing?!* Here I am, partially still brokenhearted, on a man ban, fighting off memories of my past yet succumbing to his charm so effortlessly.

We're silent as we load the groceries into his car. As we drive back to Mitzi's, a Sirius Radio station plays softly in the background, but my mind is on our flirtatious grocery trip. Perhaps, I should change the subject to lift the tricky fog surrounding us.

'Um— I've been considering your menu design and had a few questions,' I mention.

He side-eyes me, flashing a slight smile. 'Ask me anything,' he says, before returning his focus to the road ahead.

'What type of restaurant will it be?'

His eyes glint with excitement. He really loves his job, and it shows. 'Fusion meets comfort,' he says. 'I like melding different flavors together to create something entirely unique.'

I nod in agreement. 'And you do it well. Will there be a bar?'

'Yes, but with custom drinks. We won't be serving something you can grab anywhere.'

'If someone falls in love with a specialty cocktail, they'll keep coming back. I've done that myself. Genius.'

And it's true – those irresistible bourbon balls always manage to find their way into my life.

'Will it be an all-day-service restaurant or dinner only?'

'Five to midnight. Dinner, desserts, drinks.'

'Dress code?'

'No shoes, no shirt, no service,' he jokes, cracking a smile my way.

'Funny.'

'Seriously, upscale casual.'

'OK... dinner party attire. Nice. Music vibe?'

He tilts his head to the side, pondering my question. 'Nothing too loud but enough to set the mood. Maybe something upbeat and happy? I'd want to make everyone feel welcome, so a mix of genres and songs from different years might be wise. I dunno; I'm picturing a lively atmosphere with diners chatting and enjoying themselves without a care in the world. Does that make sense?'

'It sounds absolutely lovely. I would love for the menu to reflect that vision.'

'Do you want to see the place?' he offers.

'Your restaurant?'

He nods. 'We're one exit away. I usually stop by once a week to check out the progress. It could be fun to get an outside perspective.'

'Yes,' I reply with a smile I can't contain. 'I would love to see it.'

The car glides off the highway and into a quieter part of town, where the streets are lined with quaint shops and cozy cafés – Knob Hill – my favorite.

'Here we are, the restaurant with no name,' he announces with a grin, turning off the ignition after parking along the curb out front.

As I step out of the car, my heart quickens. It's obvious he's proud of this. He can't quit smiling. And he chose to show me. Wow, I'm seriously honored because this place seems like his baby.

The building stands like a charming beacon of the past, blending into the cityscape with a familiar coziness that promises warmth and comfort inside. Its walls are a welcoming brick, worn with character and history, and its large front windows hold secrets behind their opaque coverings.

'It's adorable,' I say as he pulls open one of the double doors.

'This will be the dining area,' he explains, walking me through the space.

Tables and chairs are stacked along one wall, waiting for their final places. The soft glow of hanging pendant lights casts a warm ambiance over the room, making it easy to envision the lively atmosphere he described. I can already see the potential in the space. I imagine guests laughing and clinking glasses as they devour his carefully crafted dishes.

'A handcrafted bar with a vintage blue subway tile base and a countertop made from local barn wood will line this wall with open glass shelves so the early-evening light can do its thing through the front window, and after dark, there will be deep blue LED lighting.' He motions along the brick wall as if he can see it. 'Black back barstools,' he says, nodding at the wall of furniture and pointing them out. 'And my mother suggested greenery to take advantage of the large front windows.'

'So, no dark, dingy restaurant for you.'

'No way,' he says. 'Mood is key.'

I bite my lip, forcing away the ridiculous smile at how enthused he is. 'I love that. How is your mom, by the way?'

I didn't know her well – or really at all. But I did meet her at Kris' funeral; she was a mess, like everyone else. I was surprised when she hugged me with the force of my father.

'She's – her usual self – not into parenting at all,' he says, his smile soft but sad. 'Her and my dad divorced when I was nineteen. I don't see much of either of them any more.'

I frown. 'I'm sorry.'

He shakes his head. 'Don't be. They taught me the valuable lessons of never overdoing things and never giving up. My dad was the king of pushing the limits. And my mom was queen of disassociation. There were some battles in my house on a regular basis. But that is so depressing to relive and I'm sure you don't want to hear my problems so, on with our tour.' He changes the subject flawlessly.

I'm depressed for him. He seems like he should have had an amazing life to become the man he is, but from the sounds of it, things were anything but.

He leads me through the rest of the space, pointing out where the kitchen will be located, the cozy private dining area in the back for special occasions, and even a small stage for live music performances on weekends.

'You've thought of everything,' I say, gazing at the partially set up kitchen that could give Mitzi's place a run for its money. 'I can already tell this place is going to be something extraordinary.'

'I hope so,' he says earnestly, his eyes alight with an unmistakable passion. His gaze doesn't waver as it shifts to meet mine. 'I can't wait to see what you come up with for the menu design.'

His excitement is contagious, a fever that courses through me and sets my heart racing. This might be my most exciting project ever, and mostly because I want to know every single thing about Asher Wright – the good, the bad, the sooner, the better – and taking this on may help me do that.

# 19

## ASHER

'There you are, darling. I was starting to worry that you wouldn't make it,' Mitzi calls out from the kitchen island.

'I'd have to have lost my mind to be a no-show to one of Asher's dinners.' Lucy's voice is soft, luring me in with every word.

My eyes dart over, and the sight of her causes my grip on the wooden spoon to loosen. It falls from my hand with a clatter, landing in the sizzling pan below.

Sweet Jesus. She's dressed in a form-fitting, high-waisted blue pencil skirt that stops just below her knees, a cropped white top revealing her toned midriff and white Converse shoes. I can't help but notice every curve of her body, and my thoughts come to a standstill. Her hair is styled in loose waves like a mermaid, her eyeliner perfectly winged, and she's wearing a bold shade of pink lipstick that is absolutely mind-melting.

A smile creeps up on her face as I admire her, and then she glances at the pan nearby, which – is now on fire. Shit.

I twist off the gas burner, grab the burning pan that just

sprayed me with hot oil and race it to the sink – throwing a towel over it.

'There's a fire extinguisher under the sink!' Mitzi exclaims, pointing wildly.

Without second thoughts, I fling open the cabinet door and snatch the extinguisher. I quickly aim and release a single burst of thick smoke onto the furious flames. The kitchen now is filled with smoke and the smell of charred onions. The fire alarm blares, its urgent call piercing the air and surprising everyone. I am so glad this place isn't set with a sprinkler system.

I grab another dish towel and fan the offended alarm until it quiets. If only I could spontaneously combust right now and finish the performance.

I turn back to the two women a tad sheepishly to see their reactions – Lucy with a mischievous grin and Mitzi with a stunned expression. Well, this is embarrassing. A beautiful woman enters the room, and I nearly burn her fucking house down.

'I'll have to uh— start that one over,' I say with a nervous laugh.

'It happens to the best of us, dear boy,' Mitzi says, now turning her attention back to the newspaper folded in half in front of her. 'You should ask Lucy about the time she attempted a tuna melt in the toaster oven...'

Lucy cocks her head, looking at Mitzi with half a smile on her face.

'I didn't know you had to choose a "how toasted do you want this" setting. I also didn't know it was already set to ten.'

I smirk, her sending one right back.

'It stunk up the house for the entire day,' Mitzi laughs. 'We had to open all the downstairs windows.'

The two laugh, taking the attention off of me and giving me a chance to admire Lucy.

'You, uh— you look nice,' I say, my mind finally settling.

Her lashes flutter down, grazing her cheeks before returning to meet my gaze. 'Just nice?'

'More than nice.'

'Thanks,' she says with a proud smile.

'Overlooking the fact that we almost just had to make an emergency call – you do look nice, dear,' Mitzi coos. 'What's the occasion?'

She shrugs and sits down. 'Just thought I'd dress up instead of down, that's all – no need to scare Ash away every night. I didn't realize he'd become a fire hazard at the sight of me,' she teases, glancing at me with a crooked grin.

'Sorry about that. I guess I got a bit distracted,' I say with an apologetic smile, trying to regain some semblance of composure.

Mitzi lets out a light chuckle from behind her newspaper, clearly amused by the situation. 'Oh, don't worry, sweetheart. We've had worse disasters. Paul insisted he fry a turkey for Thanksgiving dinner a few years back. Remember that, darling?'

Lucy nods. 'And that's my dad's "nearly burned down the house" story that influenced Mitzi's decision to remodel the kitchen,' Lucy says with pride. 'Don't worry, you're only the third person to attempt burning down Mitzi's house.'

She hops off her stool and joins me, opening the cupboard that stores the best pots and pans money can buy.

'What can I help with?' she asks, handing me another frying pan.

'Nothing,' I insist. 'It'll take me five minutes to get back to where I was. You sit.'

After pouring three glasses of wine and handing one to each of us, she follows the instruction.

'You know,' she says, sipping her wine. 'I was thinking about your menu, and I have some ideas.'

'Oh yeah?' I ask, slightly terrified to look away from this pan. 'Do I need to make an official appointment?'

She shakes her head. 'I could just show you really quick,' she shrugs.

'No way. I'm hiring a professional to work for me and I'd rather witness your graphic design skills in action. Let me schedule an appointment formally.'

She presses her lips into a tight smile. 'Alright, I'll text you with the details.'

'Perfect,' I say.

At that moment, as she holds her phone in her hand, both of our devices chime with incoming texts. We share a laugh, knowing exactly what it is. Our goofball friends are taking this double-dating challenge to the extreme.

'Do you want to read it or shall I?' Lucy asks.

'I've already had one near-distracted disaster, so you go ahead.'

She clears her throat, reading right from her phone. 'Saturday night. 9 p.m. 99W. Newberg. BYOC.'

I stare her way. Again, with the acronyms. 'BYOC?'

'Bring your own... cell phone? No. Obviously, we're bringing those,' Lucy says.

'C,' I say, flipping through words that begin with the letter. 'Candy? Candles? Cake?' I say, shaking my head.

'Condoms?' Mitzi throws in causing us both to freeze.

Lucy and I glance at one another, then at her.

'You two act like I've never lived. Back in my day, birth control wasn't as easy to get, so I bought condoms by the case sometimes. We had to march the streets to have it as easy as you kids do today.'

'Well, we're still marching those streets for the same reasons decades later. But, fun,' Lucy says, scrunching her face. 'A detail neither of us needed to know about your love life.'

Mitzi smirks, now intently staring at Google on her phone. 'It's a drive-in theater!' she exclaims.

'A drive-in theater...' I repeat. 'Bring your own – car?' I question with a laugh. 'They don't want to share a vehicle with us?'

'That seems like the right answer, knowing those two. You saw them at the dance, remember?' Lucy says. 'I don't think we want to share a car with them.'

I laugh. She's not wrong about that. So, not condoms, although knowing Aaron, he may have been silently insinuating that, too. My God, these two aren't even a little bit subtle.

'Sounds romantic,' Mitzi says, her eyes glued to the paper before her, not even glancing in Lucy's or my direction.

It does sound romantic, being in a car, alone, with Lucy, at night, for hours.

'Are you OK with that?' I cautiously ask, desperately hoping for a positive response.

She nods, a hint of excitement twinkling in her eyes. 'It sounds like it could be fun.'

Whew. Seriously, my heart just took a relieving beat. We've been alone, but never for long. Maybe this will be the thing that breaks what feels like a curse? Surely, something's got to give with all the passive flirting and silent conversations. Lucy's right: this could be fun.

## 20

### ASHER

Aaron and I make our way through the bustling restaurant, filled with contractors attempting to meet their deadlines. After what feels like ages of waiting, the kitchen is finally installed. It's not yet functional, but it's getting easier to picture. The sleek metal countertops gleam under the warm lighting, and every inch of space is optimized for efficiency.

We pass by the double butcher-block islands on opposite ends of the kitchen, and Aaron stops.

'These individual islands are a stroke of genius,' he remarks.

I nod, letting out a sigh of relief as I take in the sight. 'Now I can pretend you're not constantly turning everything into a race.'

Aaron chuckles, his eyes alight with amusement. 'Oh, I'll still be racing you – and winning,' he responds playfully, 'you just won't see me doing it.'

I roll my eyes, knowing his competitive nature all too well. But as I look around the nearly finished kitchen, a sense of pride washes over me. My vision for this space is coming to life, and it's even better than I imagined.

'It's going to be a dream cooking in here,' I say.

As we reach the industrial-sized walk-in refrigerator, Aaron swings open the door and takes a quick peek inside.

'We could fit a dead body in here, easy,' he observes with a smile.

'Or just one live naked one, handcuffed to the shelving,' I remark.

He purses his lips glancing around. 'On second thought, maybe we should keep a stool and a blanket in here – just in case.'

I roll my eyes, closing the door once he's exited. 'We definitely need a section for our collection of knives,' I add, picturing the gleaming blades neatly arranged in a custom-made slot above the workstations.

Aaron's eyes light up at the mention of the knives. 'Ah, our babies,' he says, his voice tinged with reverence. 'We can't forget about them.'

This is about as dorky as we get, daydreaming about kitchen knives. We stand there momentarily, imagining the finished walk-in with all its compartments and details.

He leans into me. 'Which of us do you think will have sex in here first?'

I scrunch my face. 'You, for sure – no doubt behind my back. That said, no girls in the kitchen – let's make it our first official rule. You keep your shenanigans to the bathrooms or alley out back. Because I don't need the health department up my ass after you run your mouth about your conquest.'

Aaron chuckles at my response, a mischievous glint in his eyes. 'You know me too well,' he teases, giving me a playful nudge. 'But I promise to behave... mostly.'

I shake my head with a smile, knowing that his idea of behaving usually involves chaos. But as I look around the kitchen once more, I am completely grateful to have him by my side in this venture.

'Let's make a pact,' I say, facing him. 'No matter what happens, we don't do anything that risks us having a falling out and losing the place. While we're here, it's about the food, the creativity and the joy cooking brings us and others.'

Aaron's face relaxes, his usual joking attitude replaced with a more solemn one. 'I'm in,' he states, reaching out to shake my hand. 'We are brothers first, friends second and business partners third. Also, bros before hoes.'

'Like you've ever followed that rule.' I roll my eyes with a chuckle, shaking his hand firmly.

My phone buzzes in my pocket. 'That's me,' I say, pulling it out and silencing the alarm. 'I've got to meet Lucy about the menus.'

* * *

The walk is short, five minutes at best, and the sun is shining, so what better way to diminish these nerves? Every time I know I will see her, my insides fizz like pop rock candy, and I'm starting to enjoy it.

Queue is a coffee shop on the ground floor of the Q21 Apartment building, across from the New Seasons grocery store off of 21st (not far from my beloved 23rd Ave). Its tall ceilings and industrial vibe are complemented by a pop of color at the front counter – a bright purple that immediately catches your eye. The spiral chandelier adds a touch of movement, and the wooden menu boards set the down-to-earth vibe. Scattered around the space are funky couches, chairs, and bar tables. Along one side, near the entrance, you'll find a double-sided wood-topped bar with seating on both sides that offers a glimpse into the Q21 lobby, an upscale, ritzy apartment building where my ex-girlfriend, Melissa, used to live.

'Hi,' Lucy greets me with a smile as I enter the coffee shop. She's already sitting at a wood-topped table, her iPad lying on the table in front of her.

'How's the restaurant?' she asks.

'It's coming along.'

'You're so humble. Even unfinished it's amazing. Aren't you excited?'

'Yeah,' I say with more enthusiasm. 'It's literally my dream come true.'

'Everyone will be talking about you.'

I cautiously flash her crossed fingers, not wanting to get ahead of myself, but trust me, girl, I've got the same feeling.

She chuckles. 'I ordered you a house blend with cream and sugar.'

'That's exactly what I needed.' I grab a sugar packet and shake it to loosen the contents before tearing it open and pouring it into the coffee mug.

As I mix my drink, she picks up a stylus that resembles a pencil to navigate through the screens.

'I have a few more questions,' she says, tapping away on the device.

'Hit me.'

'List out prices or simply state a number?'

'Just a number.'

'Feminine or masculine?'

'Somewhere in the middle.'

'Separate drink/cocktail menus or all in one?'

I rock my head back and forth. 'Let's separate because we'll be offering full bottles as well as by the glass.'

'OK... Here's what I'm thinking...'

When she swivels her iPad my way, I am stunned.

'I'm leaning toward shades of blue. The sections – such as Dinner, Cocktails, House Specials and Desserts – will have a more masculine font to represent you and Aaron. There won't be any harsh lines; everything will flow seamlessly, with simple sketches to draw attention to specific dishes, particularly on the cocktail menu, which will be in a lighter shade of blue to stand out.'

I stare at the iPad, comparing her two menus side by side. Everything she has put together perfectly matches my vision – like she got into my head.

'What do you think?' she asks with a hopeful smile.

'I think you nai—'

'Oh no, Brandon!' Lucy hisses, panic lacing her voice as she clutches the iPad like a shield in front of her face.

Brandon? It can't be.

I whirl around, and a cold dread grips my heart. There he is, a malevolent aura radiating from him like the toxic cloud he is as he strides purposefully toward us from the entrance. He halts at our table, his gaze piercing through me.

'Just a friend, huh?' he snaps at Lucy.

Well, hello there, double standards.

She lowers the iPad slowly, her jaw set with defiance against his accusation, yet she remains composed.

'Oh,' she retorts, feigning surprise. 'I thought I heard the growl of a demon, but it's just you.'

'Funny,' he sneers, his eyes flicking toward me with a predatory gleam. 'Friend of yours?' he asks, nodding his head in my direction.

'Since you feel entitled to know to the point of asking repeatedly, yes. Asher is both my friend and a hero that saved me from the worst-behaved boy I've ever met,' she replies coolly, glancing at me meaningfully.

I meet her eyes with a firm, reassuring smile, silently willing her to remain unshaken by Brandon's venomous presence.

'Boy?' he snaps back.

'Cheating bitch is more fitting, but yes, boy works,' I respond for her, without hesitation. Their eyes snap toward me. 'Men don't do what you did. Boys do.'

Brandon glares. 'Yeah? Well, she didn't have to humiliate me in front of everyone I know. My whole family's seen that video!'

'Holy—!' Lucy stands suddenly, pressing her finger against his chest, causing him to take a step back. 'You think *I* humiliated *you*? Are fucking you kidding me?'

The woman rarely swears, but when she does, it's top tier.

'That wasn't even me in the video.'

'Might I remind you that you've already admitted it was?' she snaps.

'I lied because I suddenly realized I'd end up in an abusive relationship if I didn't get out when I had the chance,' he insists, his eyes meeting hers with a blatant lie, defiance etched into every feature. He's trying to see if he can manipulate her. That piece of shit.

Lucy gasps. 'I'd *like* to hit you right now—'

I gently touch her hand.

'Trust me, doucheknocker, I was unfortunate enough to catch the live show; it was you. No lie necessary.'

Lucy's lips curl into a slight, confident smile, her resolve and disdain for this cockroach intensifying by the second.

'You've chosen a pervert, Luce. He stood there and watched. That's sick. I thought you had better taste.'

Her eyes flash with fury at Brandon's words, but she remains calm and collected, determined not to show how deeply he's hurt her. 'You do realize I despise you, right? I purposely chose to be here with Asher – someone who actually behaves like a real man,' she declares, then suddenly spins to face me with a saccharine smile. 'By the way, that's a refreshing change. Thank you.'

I nod and return a tight, measured smile, ignoring the prying eyes of Brandon.

Her head snaps back to him. 'Why are you even here? The unspoken rule for couples left at the altar is silence and distance. If you run into one another, you walk away without words. Yet, here you stand. So, are you lost? Or just profoundly stupid?'

Ouch. Damn. This woman is absolutely incredible.

Brandon's expression shifts dramatically, from swaggering confidence to stunned, with a hint of hurt. Bullseye.

I doubt she spent much time in their relationship speaking to him this bluntly. Which only makes him a bigger asshole in my book. She was good to him – I'd stake everything on it – yet he likely betrayed her repeatedly.

'Relax, I was just having some fun with ya,' he insists, forcing out a laugh that rings false, a pitiful mask of deceit. 'I saw you from across the street and thought I'd drop by and say hello,' he purrs, his voice dripping with insincere sweetness as if they're old friends.

'Next time, don't,' Lucy shoots back.

'You don't even want to know that I'm engaged?'

With that unwanted proclamation, he thrusts his phone toward me, then her, flaunting a picture of a woman with a ring that glistens with malicious intent. Lucy's gasp of horror is a dagger to the heart. She's stunned silent, like a statue.

Uh-oh.

'Now you can move on and know you didn't destroy me.

Closure, I thought we could use some. So, there ya go. I'm off the market.'

The woman at the table next to me gasps in disbelief at his brazen words. I agree. Shit. This dude is a bigger fucking moron than I thought.

I glance at Lucy, her hands clenched into fists as she averts her gaze my way, unable to even look at him. I've got a feeling she's at a crossroads, deciding this man's fate. Will she choose life or death?

I impulsively stand, just in case she hits him like she did at the alter. Which, I'm totally on board with if that's her move, but I don't think the coffee shop will approve. I'd hate to have this girl banned from her favorite coffee house and hauled off to jail for assaulting a prick who deserves to be buried alive.

But she raises a calm hand, calling me off silently. As I sit back down, she turns to Brandon, her hands now clasped in front of her.

'Well, congratulations,' she says with a tight smile that doesn't quite reach her eyes. 'How classy of you to recycle the same ring, she must feel like a true second-hand princess. I do hope your new victim has taken the necessary precautions to keep you in line – microchip, tracking device, or at the very least, a leash. Considering you tend to stray.'

Brandon releases an exaggerated sigh, rolling his eyes with dismissive arrogance. He glances at me, scoffing, 'She thinks she's funny.'

'She's brilliant,' I reply.

'Can I see you—' Suddenly, Lucy's hand clamps onto his bicep with a grip that likely bites into his skin. 'Over here,' she commands, dragging him a few feet away, just inside the edge of my hearing.

I take a sip of my coffee, scanning the shop, when I suddenly feel the weight of eyes staring back at me.

'It's all good,' I say, nonchalantly to their audience. 'He needs closure or something. I don't think she'll murder him right here.' I shrug, lifting my palms as if hopeful.

Lucy inhales sharply, her breaths deliberate, as the electric tension gradually unwinds. 'I want you to listen without words. Got it?'

He nods once.

'I don't forgive you,' she declares, her voice edged with a steely resolve, as if she's rehearsed this moment a thousand times. 'Unfortunately, I did truly love you, and now I'm convinced more than ever that you never felt the same. Honestly, it's a little freeing because I've been ready to let my heart out of mourning, and I think your idiotic words have finally sparked that liberation. So, thank you.'

That was so grown-up. I'm proud of her. Not sure what my reaction would have been if this was me, but according to Aaron it'd likely be silence.

She takes a breath, dropping her shoulders and relaxing her clasped hands. A slight sweet smile crosses her face, and she continues.

'I wish you nothing but the absolute worst. May your mattress become a torture device for your spine. May your water heater become your daily nemesis, scalding your pathetic manhood with every shower you take. May you accidentally wash your hair with Nair. And if this girl is truly the one for you, I hope you treat her the way she deserves, have the perfect life, and then she cheats.'

Ah… there she is. Closure. I'd bet this is what Aaron means that I've never told off a woman who hurt me. And she did it in one breath, expertly.

He just stares at her. Wordlessly. Painfully.

'Consider this goodbye, Brandon. I can't wait to never see you again.' With that, she turns on one toe and heads back toward me.

As she settles back at our table, the café around us buzzes with the usual chatter. She takes a sip of her coffee, calmly as if nothing just happened.

And Brandon just walks away.

We sit in silence, the buzzing of the café around us providing a comforting backdrop. I raise my coffee cup in a silent toast to her. She – an absolute badass in my eyes – returns the gesture, a newfound sense of freedom shining in her eyes. I am falling for this girl so freaking hard.

## 21

## LUCY

My God. I think I had a breakthrough. Yesterday, I told Brandon to be gone, and he left. And it felt... pretty good. Then, this morning, I successfully used the oven. Of course, Ash wrote down very detailed instructions, but still, I think my luck's turning around.

Morning sun rays dance across the room, illuminating every surface as they stream through the windows, painting us in warm hues. The enticing smell of freshly made espresso wafts through the air, accompanied by the delicate hint of cinnamon emanating from Asher's homemade rolls.

He's not here right now, as eight in the morning is too early for his liking. But the cinnamon rolls he could sell on the sidewalk to strangers, now sit, fully baked, on a serving place in the middle of the dining table, tempting us all.

'Where did you say you got these?' Dad asks, helping himself to his second.

He stops by before work a couple of times a month to catch up, make sure everything is in order, and ensure Mitzi is still kicking. We'll worry if she ever loses her biting wit.

'Asher, our chef, made them,' Mitzi says, sipping her coffee.

'You have a chef?' he asks, then lifts his head, looking right at me. 'Asher? How do I know that name?'

'Kris' best friend.'

'Right!' he says as if it were on his tongue's tip. 'Do you see much of him?'

'He's here Monday through Friday,' Mitzi says. 'A wonderful young man.'

Dad looks my way. 'Do you think so too?'

He's always trying to marry me off. Or at least hoping I find a man who will take care of me, so he doesn't have to worry.

After Brandon and I broke up, Dad stopped by every morning on his way to work just to make sure I was eating and leaving my room. He'd bring me coffee and breakfast, and Mitzi would check on me in the evenings, ensuring I had dinner. I was depressed, to say the least. Humiliation masked some of it. I never wanted to show my face again anywhere. But the world doesn't work like that. Sure, I can order pretty much anything I need and have it delivered right to my door but a girl's got to get out of the house at some point.

'If we compare him to the last guy I spent time with, he's a saint.'

'Wouldn't take much to outrank the Antichrist, would it?' Dad says with a chuckle.

Should I tell these two I ran into Brandon? How dare he act as if I was the problem in our relationship. Like I'm the reason he got caught. That bastard. And he gave my ring – a custom-made diamond that I personally picked out – to someone else? That seems wrong on so many levels.

'No, it wouldn't,' I say, hesitating. 'Question for you—' I summon the courage to bring it up – vaguely – at least. I need to know.

'Let's say you're a man whose engagement ended badly, and you find a spark with someone else, so you propose. Do you use the ring you already have from the failed engagement or buy a new one specifically for this relationship?'

Both Dad and Mitzi turn their gaze to me, Dad with a cinnamon roll mid-air to his mouth.

'The ring is a promise. Giving that promise to someone else might curse the whole darn thing. So, I say, you return the ring you had and buy a new one, no question,' Dad answers.

Mitzi eyes bore through me. 'Did this happen, darling?'

I nod. 'Yes. Ash and I ran into Brandon yesterday, and he's engaged. Again.'

Dad nearly drops his coffee cup but saves it. 'Someone else agreed to marry that tool?'

Another nod.

'That's not right. Are you OK?' he asks, quickly looking me over.

'She broke his nose, Paul. I'm quite certain she can take care of herself,' Mitzi pipes in, saving me from his worry. 'You were with Asher yesterday?'

'We went to Queue to discuss the menus.'

She smiles sweetly, her face wrinkling. 'Fate may once again be trying to tell you something,' she says with a slight smile. 'Again.'

'Well, as you know, I don't speak the same language as fate, so please translate it for me.'

She sets down her coffee cup and folds her hands on the table before her. 'Brandon's moving on, and you seeing him in a new and even more hateful light might signify that you should let go of any lingering doubts or regrets about him. He is who he is – a wet rag.'

Dad laughs to himself.

'And if the wedding didn't prove that, handing over your engagement ring to a rebound girl should.' Mitzi reaches across the table and covers my hand with hers, her touch grounding me.

'I know. It was just – hurtful. Like one more knife to my back, ya know?'

Mitzi nods her head slowly, sipping her coffee. 'Letting go doesn't mean erasing the past, dear; it means making space for new beginnings.'

'Mom's right, Lucy. Life is too short to let ghosts hold you back, sweetie. Embrace the present and look forward to the future,' Dad says, nodding in agreement, his eyes reflecting understanding.

Neither of them realizes how fitting their words are. I don't have to forget where I've been or what I've learned. I just need to pave a new path, so making trips down memory lane isn't as easy.

I take the final sip of my coffee, a sense of clarity washing over me like the morning sunlight filling the room. Perhaps it's time to heed their advice and truly start looking forward. What might a future without the shadows of yesterday clouding my vision look like? I think I want to find out.

Dad gets up from his seat, stretching his arms above his head. 'Well, on that note, I should really get going. Work beckons.'

Mitzi stands up as well, tightening her robe around her. 'Thank you for stopping by, Paul. It's always a pleasure to have my baby boy here.'

The two briefly hug as she sees him out, closing the door behind him. Then she turns to me.

'Have you told him?'

'Told who what?'

She shakes her head. 'Sweet girl, you do not play an idiot well. *Asher*,' she says. 'Have you told him how you feel?'

I'm caught off guard a little. 'How do you think I feel?'

She fixes me with a knowing look. 'More than you're letting on, dear.'

'I dunno... he sort of accidentally knows I'm attracted to him, and we have fun together. I don't know what I'd say, really. "Hey, I'm a mess, wanna fall for that?" Seems like that might scare him off.'

'Sometimes the heart knows before the mind catches up,' she says sweetly. 'You'll figure it out.'

I exhale slowly, the weight of emotions pressing down on me.

'I'm not sure if now's the right time anyway... He's busy opening a restaurant, and I don't want to distract him.'

Mitzi places a gentle hand on my shoulder, her touch comforting. 'Darling, there's never a perfect time for matters of the heart. But there comes a point when holding back becomes heavier than taking the leap.'

'What if my feelings change everything between us?' I ask.

'It happens to the best of us.' She offers me a reassuring smile. 'Love has a way of reshaping our world in ways we never expect. And sometimes, it's worth the risk.'

I wonder if it happened to her.

The doorbell echoes through the house as if on cue, pulling me from my thoughts. Saved by the bell.

I open the door to Asher standing on the porch, a bright smile on his face, a take-out tray holding three Queue coffees, and that familiar twinkle in his eyes that makes my insides fizz like shaken champagne.

'Hey,' he says with a grin as if he's happy to see me.

Perhaps the universe *is* aligning the stars in my favor.

'Hi,' I say, my voice surprisingly steady despite my heart racing.

Hanging from the crook of his elbow are his brightly colored reusable grocery bags, packed to the brim. I glance at my Apple Watch: 8.27 a.m.

'You're not supposed to be up so close to daylight.'

'You're not wrong. And trust me,' he says. 'There were four coffees on this tray, but I drank one on the way over.'

'Well, my dad left already,' I tell him.

'Perfect, because I'm going to need a second cup to make it through the afternoon.'

I take the tray of drinks he's handing me.

'So, you just came over early to bring coffee?'

He walks past me into the house.

'That, you, and I knew you were having company and thought I'd come help clean up.'

He came to help clean up? What planet is this man from?

'See,' Mitzi says leaning into me once we reach the kitchen, taking a coffee from the tray in my hands. 'Brandon is a wet rag. Asher is a dream boat, darling.'

'All aboard?' I say under my breath, causing her to grin with pride.

As Ash follows me, his eyes catch the nearly empty plate on the table, and a proud grin spreads across his face.

'I see you nailed the cinnamon rolls,' he says, winking playfully.

'The oven was surprisingly as easy to use as you said.'

He's unpacking groceries as I set the tray of coffee onto the counter and perch myself on one of the stools at the island.

Mitzi has disappeared, probably because she suspects there are underlying feelings between Asher and me, and I know she's giving me the space to work that out and possibly find my words at last.

'I'm sorry about yesterday. I can't believe I embarrassed myself in front of you once again.'

Asher pauses, setting a container of fresh strawberries on the counter before turning to face me, his expression serious.

'You didn't. All's good,' he says. 'Cheaters don't worry me because usually they're also liars, schemers and losers.'

Brandon fits the bill.

He reaches into the bags and takes out a few more items, placing them on the kitchen island. Then, he looks at me carefully as if trying to gauge my reaction.

'Are you alright? That couldn't have been easy facing evil again unexpectedly.'

I give a small shrug. 'I had nightmares about it last night, and pretty consistently for many months, but thanks to you, I'm not overthinking it as badly as I expected I would be,' I state. 'Had you not been there, I'm unsure I would have been able to find the right words. But now that it's over, I feel like I said what I needed to say.'

His smile widens. 'You were incredible. I wanted to give you a high-five.'

I laugh. 'He definitely knows how to push my buttons.'

A chuckle escapes him, filling the room with his warmth.

'If he's the reason for that fierce and fabulous version of you, perhaps we should send him a thank-you card,' he suggests, a playful glint in his eyes.

'Or a bag of dicks,' I suggest. 'There's a website that does that.'

'A dick for a dick, genius. Can you request small, misshapen penises?'

'Maybe?'

We share a laugh as Asher arranges the groceries he brought into the fridge.

'I've never done what you did,' he says suddenly.

'What's that?'

'Told off a cheating ex. Aaron reminded me of that recently. I usually just break it off, walk away and bury it deep.'

'Someone's cheated on *you*?' I ask, instantly mad at this mystery woman.

He chokes out a laugh. 'Multiple someones. You inspired me yesterday. If it wasn't rude as hell, I'd call each one of them and tell them my actual feelings right now.'

'They deserve it. Who hurts a guy like you? You're perfect! Give me their numbers and I'll do it for you. I owe you a few favors at this point.'

A shy but curious grin grows on his face.

'You know what I think?' he says as he leans against the counter, his palms supporting his weight. 'You're worth so much more than Brandon,' he says, his gaze intense and unwavering. 'And I know there's a man out there who would love to give you the stars, the moon, and the entire world if given the chance.'

The lump in my throat grows at the weight of his statement. God, I'm beginning to hope that man is him so badly.

## 22

### LUCY

The drive-in theater is a vintage gem. Its marquee is adorned with playful neon lights that flicker to life as the sun sets. Large trees surround the perimeter and provide a natural barrier against the outside world, leaving the theater in an idyllic bubble. In the back is a cute turquoise snack shop that stands out with its bright and cheerful color. The air is heavy with the scent of pine and fresh-cut grass, mingled with the familiar aroma of buttered popcorn.

Aaron and Madi pull into the spot in front of us, giving us prime seats for whatever entertainment is about to unfold from their vehicle. BYOC did, in fact, mean bring your own car – apparently, they didn't want us interrupting whatever they'd planned by being in the same vehicle. Considering I know Madi – and now Aaron – too well, I'm not excited about what awaits us from their car.

As the sun sets below the horizon, the sky turns a warm orange hue, and the giant screen in front of us lights up with rules and reminders before teasing us with sneak peeks of upcoming movies.

Couples settle into their cars as evening falls, children bouncing excitedly in the back seats. The sound of laughter and chatter fills the air as friends share popcorn and soda while waiting for the feature film to start.

'I haven't been here in ages,' I confess. 'But it's still just as charming as I remember.'

'Would you believe it when I say this is my first time at a drive-in theater, ever,' Ash admits, easily tossing a piece of popcorn into his mouth.

'You're a drive-in virgin?' I tease.

He nods. 'Teach me the ways, oh experienced one?'

'Well,' I say, suddenly shy. 'Usually, you come to these with someone you want to be alone with.'

He looks at me with a hint of surprise, a tempting smile on his lips.

'Looks like we've got that part down,' he says in a low voice.

I try to come up with a witty response, but before I can, the screen flickers to life with the movie's opening credits. The chatter around us dies down as everyone settles in, their attention captured by the film unfolding before them.

As the main feature starts playing, I steal a glance at Ash. The soft glow of the screen illuminates his profile, casting shadows across his features and making him look as handsome as I've ever seen him.

'I'm assuming fogged windows within seconds of the movie starting is considered pro-level theater going?'

I look ahead and instinctively cover my eyes. 'Oh my. Yes, that's a professional – very ballsy level of romance – with amateur moves, if I had to guess,' I say with disdain.

Freaking, Madi. I get that she's overly horny, but man, it's hard to ignore what they're doing right in front of us.

We stare at the screen for fifteen minutes, but I am in my

head. He wants to spend alone time with me? Is he the man he mentioned who wants to give me the stars, moon and world?

Unable to bear the uncertainty any longer, I turn to face him fully.

'Ash,' I begin, my voice barely a whisper over the movie's soundtrack.

'Yeah?' he replies, equally quiet.

'Do you think he'd be mad?'

'About what?'

I like how when one of us refers to 'him' or 'he,' the other just knows who we're talking about. *He* (Kris) is the common denominator that connects us and the person who changed both our worlds. He taught me what love was, and I've been searching for it ever since he left.

'Mitzi said something recently that made me realize I haven't said this out loud yet...' I inhale sharply. 'I – *like* you. As in, I can't quit thinking about you. I'm excited to see you every day. When your name pops up on my phone, I get giddy. And, secretly, I'm so glad we're not sharing a car with those two right now.'

I look at the car ahead of us, its windows still fogged, a single handprint now visible. Ew.

'Really?' he says as if this surprises him.

I nod. 'I feel safe with you. And you *are* incredibly hot, that wasn't a lie. But to be completely honest, I also feel Kris, right here,' I motion over my shoulder between us. 'And because of that, I wonder if he'd be mad over what's possibly happening between us.'

Ash's slight worry turns to a crooked grin. He looks back to where I'm motioning as if he sees him, too.

'I know exactly what you mean.'

'Yeah?'

He nods. 'I got his name tattooed on the back of my arm.' He leans awkwardly, pointing out one of the many tattoos on the back of his arm. 'Because I too feel like he's always looking over my shoulder.'

I touch his name with the tips of my fingers. My God, that is sweet. Sometimes, I forget that he truly loved Kris as much as I did, possibly even more, because they had been partners in crime from a young age. It must feel like he lost a brother.

'I'm forgetting him. I know how he made me feel. But I don't even remember his voice any more.'

'That part hurts, doesn't it?' he says with a frown.

I sigh heavily. 'More than I expected.'

He shifts in his seat, turning my way. 'Do you feel like you two would still be together all these years later?'

I've considered this before and came to the conclusion that, no, we probably wouldn't still be together. Teenage love rarely lasts because we change so much throughout the years. I'm not the same girl I was at eighteen or even twenty-eight. Thirty-year-old me wants to find what teenage me thought she had, but I'm not sure I believe I ever will. Or at least I didn't, until Ash.

'No,' I say, honestly. 'Like all my other high-school friends, I'm sure he'd have faded into the background eventually. Why would he be any different than my relationships since him?'

'Do you ever wonder if your life would be different had he lived?'

'Yes,' I admit. 'I'm terrified that anyone that means anything to me will leave without saying goodbye; that started the moment he died.'

'He'd have said goodbye, given the chance. I promise he would have.'

Would that have made the whole thing worse? Knowing he

didn't want to go, he had to and got one chance to say goodbye to the people he loved. Probably.

'And to answer your earlier question,' he continues. 'No, I don't think he'd be mad at whatever this is turning into. We were his best friends. He loved us; he'd want us to be happy. I think that's why he's always around. Maybe he's to us what we're hoping to be for Aaron and Madi? Just from beyond.'

Never have I hoped someone was right so hard. When we reach *that happy*, will Kris finally move on? I guess there's only one way to find out.

'Another question... where do we go from here? Judging on the car ahead of us, we're doing a terrible job directing those two toward love.' The words tumble out in a rush, my heart pounding.

He takes a moment to answer, his expression unreadable. Then, with a gentle smile that reaches his eyes, he reaches up to tuck a loose strand of hair behind my ear. 'Luce, I've never been more interested in a woman than I am – you. I'm waking up early. And at this point, I'd probably show up at Mitzi's place daily even if she fired me, just to see you.'

He would?! Hope blossoms in my chest like a fragile flower. 'Truthfully, I'm falling in like with you, Lucy Gray. A little more every day. But I don't want to do anything you're not ready for.'

He's falling in *like* with me? Sweet mother of Moses that is adorable.

His words hang in the air, swirling around us like fireflies on a summer night. The weight of our confessions settle between us.

'I may be falling right along with you,' I admit, my voice barely above a whisper. 'And it's scary – like a trust fall exercise. The last guy who said he'd catch me let me slip through his fingers, intentionally, so he could catch someone else.'

Ash's eyes widen ever so slightly, and a soft smile tugs at the corners of his lips. He leans in closer, his breath warm against my cheek as he cups my face gently in his hands. 'I promise, I've got you,' he murmurs. 'With me, there will never be someone else.'

And then, with a tenderness that takes my breath away, he closes the distance between us and kisses me.

It's sweet and soft and unexpected. As his tongue mingles with mine, a rush of emotions swirls between us like a tempestuous sea. I place my hand on his – now on the side of my neck – his thumb grazing my jawline. When we break, he rests his forehead against mine, a sweet, disbelieving chuckle leaving his lips.

'I hope that was OK. The moment felt right, and I just went with it.'

'OK?' I ask in disbelief. 'It was totally wow. Wow-wow-wow-wow-WOW! There aren't enough wows.'

He laughs, lifting my hand and kissing my knuckles.

'Again, wow.'

The man knows how to kiss a girl and leave her longing for more. My lips are tingling. My knuckles are tingling. Hell, my toes are tingling. The air around us is buzzing as we settle back into our seats, our fingers laced together resting on his thigh. Has anyone else done this to me with a single kiss?

The movie continues to play on the screen in front of us, but I spend the rest of the evening with my head in the clouds, stealing glances at him. Each time finding his gaze already fixed on me with an affectionate intensity that sends my heart aflutter.

When the movie ends and the credits roll, signaling the conclusion of our night at the drive-in theater, we breathe.

'So, was that what you expected for your first drive-in experience?' I ask, my tone light.

'Definitely not what I expected, but in all the best ways,' he replies. 'How about you?'

I smile wide. 'Best movie I've ever seen, and I don't even remember what it was about.'

He laughs out loud.

A sense of contentment settles over me like a warm blanket as we drive away, leaving behind Madi and Aaron who likely have to wait until their windows are unfogged enough to see the road. The radio plays a soothing melody, blending with the tires rolling over the pavement. Sultry summer night air swirls through the cracked windows, and the stars twinkle overhead like scattered diamonds against the velvet sky. The night seems perfect.

*Starlight, Starbright, please don't let the end of us be in sight.*

Wishing on a star might be ridiculous and maybe a little bit childish, but it worked when I was seven and asked for a puppy, so why not try again?

## 23

## ASHER

'What in the hell are you doing here?' I ask, opening the door more, letting him in because he'll barge through otherwise.

'A better question is, why is Lucy not half naked on that couch with you?'

'I'm romantic, you asshole. You think I'd have opened the door if she was?' I ask, rolling my eyes, dropping back onto my couch and grabbing the remote. 'Can a man not even daydream about a woman alone in his apartment any more?'

Aaron's eyes move to the TV, but he looks back with a single eyebrow raised.

'I'm not watching porn, you perv.'

I throw the remote at him, which he catches single-handedly. I know what he's thinking because his mind's usually only got one channel.

'We saw you kiss her,' he confesses.

'Not sure how you saw anything through the steam on your windows,' I say, rolling my eyes. 'Do you even know what movie we watched?'

'No clue,' he grins mischievously. 'Was it good?'

'Don't know,' I laugh. 'My mind was elsewhere.'

'Ooohhh. Where was your mind? Fess up, you liar.'

'There's nothing to fess up because it's not a secret. Yes, we talked and we kissed, while we were sitting in a car full of windows. I sort of figured someone would see considering what we saw you doing—'

His jaw drops. 'I thought the windows were fogged?'

'Not enough.'

'Well, consider it a free lesson in the art of lovemaking.'

'Gross.'

'Come on, details, boy. How was it?' he pries, sitting next to me, well and truly interested.

'Soul-spinning,' I reply with a nonchalant shrug, trying to play it cool. But inside, my heart is still racing, and my mind is reeling from the moment's intensity. Kissing Lucy was unlike anything I've experienced before – electrifying, passionate and filled with an undeniable connection.

'Soul-spinning?' he repeats, his voice tight. 'That's girly. Did your heart do cartwheels, too?'

'It did, actually. Does Madi do that to you?'

'Not when she kisses my lips,' he says.

'Ugh, you have a way of ruining the moment,' I groan. 'Why'd you come over anyway?'

'Because you're my lonely brother who can't find a good woman, and I need to hear all the juicy details,' he says with a cheeky grin. 'Plus, I wanted to make sure you were still alive. For some guys, sudden hard-ons after not having one in a while will kill them. So, tell me, was it like riding a bike? Did you still know what to do?'

'No hard-ons were involved. It was sweet. Heartfelt. Intense. Yet completely unexpected, you know? It just felt right.' I admit, resting a hand on the back of my neck. 'One minute we were talking, and the next—'

'Boom, fireworks?' he interrupts, waggling his eyebrows.

'Supernova,' I correct him, a smile tugging at the corners of my lips. 'I never knew a kiss could feel so... perfect.'

'You experience a supernova, and you end it with just a kiss?' he asks, his eyes widening in disbelief. 'You should have invited her back here to show her all your moves. What's the matter with you?'

'I'm not you. We've still got things to work through. And that's OK because I'm perfectly happy where we are. Holding off will just make it better.'

'Boo,' he groans, crossing his arms over his chest.

'Boo all ya want, because she didn't, and her opinion is the one I care about. I guess I'm just more of a romantic than you.'

'Pffft, I'm hella romantic.'

'Please,' I chuckle, shaking my head. 'You're about as romantic as a rock. What you are is hella horny with commitment issues,' I tease. 'But you sleeping with the same woman for multiple weeks is giving me hope.'

'Hey, I'll have you know deep down I'm a sensitive soul,' Aaron protests, putting a hand over his heart with mock hurt. 'Just because I appreciate the physical connection doesn't mean I don't have a romantic bone in my body.'

'Alright, Mr Sensitive Soul, I'm not denying your romantic bone. Relax.'

'Funny,' he says. 'So, what's your next move? You gonna ask to see her bra next?'

I burst out laughing. In middle school, my friends had seen bras, even boobs, but I hadn't. One day, I just asked a girl to see her bra, and without question, she lifted her shirt to reveal a purple one. I'd forgotten I'd told him that story. I can't go the middle school route.

'No, I'm not. Honestly, I'm not really sure where it goes from here. All we've really established is that we like one another and that we're both catching feelings. But that's it.'

'Catching feelings makes it sound like a disease,' he says. 'Maybe ask her out on a proper date and stop tagging along with Madi and me. Your awkwardness is a mood killer.'

'Yet you continue to perform in the most public of places,' I retort sarcastically. 'But you're right, a real date would be a good start.' I nod slowly, considering his advice. 'What if—'

He shakes his head. 'No. Life is too damn short for "what ifs,"' he says. 'I'm right – now stop being a pussy and take the chance. We both know you want to.'

How eloquently said. I guess there's nothing more to consider. Mainly because my heart is ready to dive off this cliff. But my head is worried it might be to my death. It's a battle between my desires and doubts, and I'm unsure which side will win, but I'm rooting for the part that ends up with Lucy.

## 24

### LUCY

Have you ever thought about cloud nine and what it might feel like? Well, I think I'm there and it's fantastical. Glitter blows in the wind as the sun warms you and everything is light, breezy and hopeful. Pretty sure this is my first time here ever.

Tonight, Ash made tandoori chicken sliders, and I ate three. Yep. There's no shame; I should have worn the leggings.

Now, Mitzi has retired to her room to continue her show, leaving just Asher and me in the kitchen while he preps for tomorrow. The smell of food fills the space, but it's the lingering taste of our first kiss that I crave the most.

We haven't talked about it, but I see it in his eyes every time he looks my way. I wouldn't doubt that he's noticed I've touched up my lips three times since he got here with my La Mer lip volumizer. Am I begging for another? Maybe.

He's got me slicing vegetables again, but the tension between us, is like a live wire crackling in the air. As he reaches across me to grab a knife, the brief brush of his arm sends a shiver through me. I can feel his eyes on me, burning into my skin, making me feel exposed and vulnerable in the most delicious way possible.

Each moment stretches taut like a rubber band on the verge of snapping.

'Go on a date with me,' he says suddenly, setting his knife on the island with a clatter. 'Just me, no Aaron or Madi, no Mitzi or Brandon, just us.'

I glance up at him, my heart pounding in my chest. His intense gaze searches mine for any hint of hesitation. With a shaky breath, I nod slowly, a rush of excitement and nerves flooding through me.

*Please, Luce, don't cut off your finger right now.* I slow my chopping just to be safe.

'OK,' I reply. 'Just us. I'd like that.'

'I'll plan everything,' he says, the corners of his lips curling into a satisfied smile.

'Text me the details,' I say, mirroring his expression.

Even the idea of being alone with him again is like being suspended in a cloud of bubbles, maybe it's cloud ten? I dunno. But each one pops with a burst of sparkling excitement as my heart flutters like a hummingbird's wings. My vision blurs with happiness, making the whole kitchen seem brighter – because of him. Why can't I stop smiling? God, my face is probably lit up like a carnival ride. An actual date with Asher Wright. I've never been more excited for anything in my entire life.

'He asked you on a date? Just the two of you?' Madi's voice is enthusiastic, making it clear how excited she is about this news.

As soon as Ash left, I had to call someone and tell them before I burst. I'll never be able to sleep tonight. A smile is plastered on my face, and it's so ridiculous I'm avoiding looking at the small video of myself in the corner of the screen.

*Suppress the giggle bubbling inside you, Lucy. You're not fifteen. Just answer the question.*

I inhale deeply, trying to calm my nerves.

'Just us,' I confirm, a wave of anticipation in my stomach.

Madi's eyes sparkle with curiosity as she leans in toward her phone. 'What are your thoughts on that?'

'I'm anxious, and wondery, and nervous, and my insides are filled with a swirling mass of confetti, ready to burst out at any moment.'

'How very detailed. Want to know something?' she asks.

'Sure.'

'The confetti thing, that's pretty much how Aaron makes me feel. Shhhh,' she lifts a single finger to her lips.

'Really?' I ask, my curiosity piqued. 'And not just when you're on top of him in the back seat of his car?'

She gasps. 'You saw?'

'Not because I wanted to. More because you were in my line of sight while watching the movie.'

A giggle escapes her lips. 'You caught me,' she confesses. 'Just like we caught you two! And yes, especially in that moment,' she admits with a guilty grin.

Yes, they saw us kiss. But I don't care. I hope they see it again. As a payback.

She nods. 'I realized at the bubble dance that despite being a bit of a wildcard – it's part of what makes him fun. He's got a soft side that I could be falling for...'

'Falling? Like into a pit of despair or love?'

'I think, love? Maybe? I dunno.'

'He's a little rough around the edges,' I remind her.

'I think maybe I could be the right woman to smooth those internal edges.'

'You're going to attempt taming a wild stallion?' I ask, arching an eyebrow skeptically at Madi's bold suggestion.

The idea of taming men is nothing but a myth perpetuated by women. It doesn't work. In no world can I picture Aaron, the handsome yet reckless playboy, being tamed by the equally wild and carefree Madi. It seems like a plot straight out of a romantic comedy.

I let out a small laugh, unable to hide my doubt.

'Well, I wish you luck with that.'

Madi grins. 'There's just something about him, Luce. I see beyond the bravado and fuckboy charm. There's a fragility hidden underneath that mask that no one else seems to notice. I want to see it more clearly.'

'I truly hope you're right.'

I'm startled out of my thoughts by a light tapping on my open bedroom door. I turn to see Mitzi, wearing her housecoat, standing in the doorway.

'Hi,' I greet her, flashing the phone her way. 'Say hi to Mitzi, Madi.'

'Hi, Mitzi! Did you hear the news? Asher finally asked our Lucy out!'

Mitzi's face lights up with a broad smile, her laugh lines deepening and wrinkles forming around her eyes. 'I overheard that,' she confesses with a grin.

'You did?' God, I can't imagine what it looked like from the outside looking in.

'Yes, I was standing in the hall listening,' she says as if she does it all the time. 'It's why I'm here, dear. I thought maybe you could use some help picking an outfit. He's seen enough of your stretchy options. You need something that says, "Yes, I'm effortlessly gorgeous, and I've never even tried."'

I laugh.

'Ooh, yes, let's pick an outfit!' Madi says with excitement.

Mitzi claps her hands together like a kid on Christmas morning, taking my phone from my hand as she begins rummaging through my closet. She talks to Madi as she pulls out various pieces of clothing, scattering them onto the bed. I try to protest, but it's too late – half of my wardrobe is already on display.

'How about the slinky black dress?' Madi asks as Mitzi holds up a dress I haven't worn in ages.

'Uh— no,' I say, shaking my head. 'I got engaged in that dress.'

This is that little piece that sticks with me – the memories. I can't shake them because they're everywhere. How do I get rid of them?

'Ick! Burn it with fire,' Madi exclaims, causing Mitzi to toss it onto the floor like hot, contaminated, toxic garbage. 'Ooooh! You know what we should do? Have a dress burning of the wedding kind. I know you still have it, and the thing is cursed. It's only bringing you bad luck with the memories that hit you every time you see it hanging in your crowded closet.'

Mitzi tilts her head, giving me an interested look.

'You want to burn a ten-thousand-dollar wedding dress?' I ask Madi in shock.

'Do you remember when you asked about regifting engagement rings?' Mitzi responds.

I nod.

'The same rules apply to wedding dresses. Madison's right: it may well be cursed. How does one release a curse? Back in my day, it was with fire.'

'Mitzi?' I ask curiously. 'You've burned some things in your lifetime, haven't you?'

She chuckles. 'Everything but buildings, dear.'

'I guess we'll be having a boy burning bonfire then,' I say.

'This is going to be fun!' Madi says. 'And Mitzi, you should write a novel about your life.'

'I prefer to keep some things a mystery,' she replies, meandering into my closet and dragging out the wedding dress I've been avoiding since I put it there. She drops it onto the floor, along with the engagement dress. 'When you do it, I'll ensure my lawn guy is on standby with a hose in case things get too wild. And please, girls, do not post any evidence on social media. I wouldn't want to upset Pnina. Is there anything else we need to take care of, darling?' She glances back at my closet as she asks.

I nod slowly and walk inside, dragging out the suitcase I never bothered to unpack from my trip to Vegas. In my arms, I also carry a box filled with trinkets and souvenirs from Brandon, every gift he had ever given me except for the jewelry – which I will pawn just because.

'Might as well toss in these too...' I say, stacking things on the growing pile.

Mitzi furrows her brows. 'Perhaps I should inquire about a burn permit from the city, just in case.'

The only thing left to do is pick a date for the bonfire. Hopefully, fire can kill what's left of this demon.

## 25

### ASHER

I'm sitting at a newly assembled Ikea desk in the restaurant's office. My laptop is open before me, and I've been browsing endless options for a date idea in Portland for what seems like an eternity. Why do I feel like I have no idea how to plan a date?

'I thought we were stocking shit today. What're you doing in here?' Aaron asks, stopping in the doorway and looking in curiously. 'Studying for a test?'

'I asked Lucy on a date – without you,' I admit, shaking my head in exasperation. 'And now I've not got a clue what to do.'

'Do her,' he says like a creep, nodding his head repeatedly.

'I'm looking for romantic, not offensive.'

'Oh, well then, duh, cook for her then do her.'

I shake my head. 'Cooking's no longer a novelty, considering I do it for her daily. I need something bigger.'

'Bigger, huh? I guess that means sex really is out of the question.'

I roll my eyes. 'You do realize that sex is only one aspect of a relationship, right? It's not the main focus.'

He stares blankly as if I'm speaking in a foreign tongue.

'If you say so, boss,' he finally says with a chuckle, leaning against the door frame.

'I want to romance this woman, Aaron, not do her in the back seat of my car.'

He mocks me under his breath, sounding nothing like me at all. 'Fine, Mr Romantic, let's brainstorm. How about a hot air balloon ride at sunset? Or a hike to a private waterfall for a picnic? Multnomah Falls!'

I shake my head. 'It's not a proposal; it's a first date.'

'You said big,' he argues.

'I meant, first date big, and I really like her but don't want to go so big I'll never top it. What else you got?'

Aaron's eyes light up with an idea. 'What about a pottery class? You could recreate that scene from *Ghost*?'

'*Ghost*? You spent too much time with Mom as a child.'

He nods enthusiastically. 'Dude, the eighties were awesome and Swayze was a God.'

'You never lived through the eighties,' I remind him.

'My God, you're lame,' he says with disappointment. 'The best part of having Gen X parents was the eighties nostalgia they brought with them. Back when McDonald's sold copies of *Ghost* in the nineties, Mom bought one on VHS. She's still got it, and it is worn.'

'Yes, I'm aware that our mother still watches VHS in twenty twenty-five. But it's never been my decade. The only eighties movies I've seen are the ones you've forced me to watch,' I admit.

'Ugh,' he groans. 'You missed so much good shit. Wear your tightest pants, sit behind her, and help her with the pottery wheel. And don't forget to channel your inner Swayze.'

'Eh, no Swayze. In fact, if we can steer clear of anything requiring tight pants or the eighties, that'd be great.'

'You're so dull,' he laments with a heavy sigh. 'How about something adventurous like a nighttime kayaking tour on the Willamette River?' he suggests eagerly. 'You can see the city lights from a whole new perspective, and it's pretty romantic if you ask me.'

'*We* did that once,' I remind him. 'At *your* insistence. Did I miss a big sign there?'

'Actually, never mind. Scratch that thought – it's definitely not romantic. More of a brother sport. Especially when one of us ends up drunkenly falling overboard.' He taps his fingers against the door frame while contemplating.

For the record, the drunk man overboard was him. I had to fish him out with an oar when he was too scared to get back in his boat because he felt something swim against his leg and was sure it was a shark (in a river). I tied the two kayaks together while he sat uncomfortably close, shivering the whole way back to shore. Nope, don't want to relive that with a woman.

'What about a wine and paint night?' he suggests. 'Girls love wine and crafty shit. Plus, you can unleash your artistic side – paint one another, naked – and share a laugh over each other's masterpieces.'

'Why's everything gotta be naked with you?'

He shrugs. 'Naked's more fun.'

It wasn't fun the time I walked into his apartment and found him nakedly attempting to unclog the toilet, but his suggestion sparks an idea.

'Actually, remember the idea we had to graffiti one of the walls in the dining room?'

'Yeah...' Aaron says.

'What would you think of me hiring someone who lets Lucy and me help as our date? Two birds, one stone, it's crafty, and I have boxes of the best wine.'

'Yeah, do it. But pay for the wine 'cause half that shit is mine. Then, bring her to the roof for a romantic picnic under the stars. I'm not done up there quite yet but close. You can tell me what else it needs.'

Aaron designed our rooftop as a private dining experience for small parties and couples. I'm completely out of the loop and don't even go up unless he's invited me. This part is entirely his baby. A romantic date night hot spot – maybe he does have that romantic bone.

Suddenly, a thought pops into his head. He raises a finger and points it in my direction.

'I just remembered something. I recall Madi mentioning that they sometimes like to have dessert and cocktails for dinner.'

'You listened when a woman spoke?'

'Sometimes, I'm a gentleman,' he rebukes.

'A dessert rooftop picnic,' I say with a nod. 'Not a terrible idea, and she's only seen me bake that one time with Audrina.'

'Madi hasn't seen me baked yet,' he jokes. 'Paint and bake – sounds like a hippie date. I'm gonna add that to my list.'

'You're almost good at this romance thing.'

'You act like I'm just a pretty face,' he says with a huff, crossing his arms defensively. 'I didn't choose to look like this,' he adds as if it's his cross to bear.

'Don't fret, love, you're the most handsome man I've ever met,' I say, only a hint of sarcasm in my tone.

'And wait until you see the roof. I've got romance, you too!, it's just all up there.'

'I'll find out soon enough. I owe you for coming up with this plan.'

'You can pay me back with details afterward.'

'Never happening,' I declare, opening up a website for a locally well-known graffiti artist and shooting her an email.

A notification from my phone catches my attention as it buzzes on the almost empty desk beside me. I look over, smiling like a fool, when I see her name on the screen.

> **LUCY**
>
> Fire & Spice – a potential name for your restaurant?

'Hey!' I call to Aaron, standing from my chair to find him after he wandered off. 'What do you think of Fire & Spice?'

'Fire's good. Spices are good. Why?'

'For a restaurant name?' I add.

He nods his head as he contemplates it. 'Fire and Spice... it flows well, and there will be fire and spices.' He claps me on the back. 'I think you just named the place.'

Fire & Spice. I like it too. Simple but telling.

I type a text to her – Aaron doesn't need to know I didn't think of it myself.

> **ASHER**
>
> You are a genius. We love it.

> **LUCY**
>
> Really?

> **ASHER**
>
> Aaron's dreaming up a mock window design now.

> **LUCY**
>
> Yay!

> **ASHER**
>
> BTW – Friday Night, 8 p.m., dress casual, I'll pick you up – date night.

LUCY

!!! 😊 Can't wait!

\* \* \*

'Now that we've sorted out all *your* issues,' Aaron begins, 'I wanted to run something by you.' He jumps on the counter, facing the office with his hands tucked under his knees like a child. 'You think I'm getting too serious with Madi? I mean, like you said recently, it's been weeks.'

'And you're usually a "days" kind of guy...'

'Precisely,' he replies as if it's something to be proud of.

'How exactly are you getting too serious? I thought hooking up was how you two spent most of your time together?'

'That's the gist of it, but we also chat before and after, and sometimes on the phone.'

'You two talk on the phone?' I ask curiously.

Aaron is the only person in my generation who loves talking on the phone, like a teenage girl. He hates texts and refuses to check his emails, but if you answer, he'll talk for hours.

He confirms with a nod. 'Lately, she's been my ten o'clock call. See, with me calling you at eleven that gives us one hour. Otherwise, I'd be tempted to talk all night.'

'You'd stay up talking to her all night if you could? Seems like there's a word for that... what is it?'

'Phone calls?'

'Love? You're falling for her. Why not just admit that you want something more than just a casual fling with this girl? Instead of ending it like all the others.'

'You're wrong, man. This is intense and kind of heavy. Love ain't heavy. Something is nagging the shit out of me right here,' he gestures between his stomach and heart. 'It's encouraging me to focus on this one girl. That's not usually how I roll, so I need your take on whether she's worth it.'

'That's a loaded question I won't be answering. She's Lucy's best friend. I don't really know her, and you tend to gossip. Look, if you like her, focus on her. If she likes you, you won't scare her away. What could it hurt?'

Like the child he sometimes is, he reaches down and rests his hand on his groin.

'Before you speak as if it has a voice,' I say, feeling a mix of amusement and frustration, 'remember your brain is up here...' I tap him on the forehead as I stand up, conflicted about how to help without enabling his antics. 'Try using that one, and please don't do anything dumb that makes Lucy reconsider what she feels for me.'

'No promises...' he replies. 'My mouth does what it wants,' he adds as I walk into the dining room, torn between laughing and worrying, trying to distract myself by imagining how the wall would look painted.

## 26

## LUCY

'This date is a little bit unconventional,' Asher comments as he parks in front of the restaurant.

'There's nothing unconventional about you making me dinner. When you're not around, I dream of it.'

'You dream of me?' he asks, smirking.

'Um... mostly your cooking, but you've definitely made an appearance,' I admit sheepishly.

*Super-smooth, Luce.*

But his expression shows that he doesn't mind; in fact, my words please him.

He quickly exits his SUV, gracefully making his way around to my side to open the door for me. I love that he is a gentleman.

'What kind of unconventional are we talking?' I ask, intrigued by his mysterious proposal. 'Aaron didn't plan this, did he?'

He laughs heartily. 'No. We're painting something.'

I lift an eyebrow. 'Painting something inside?'

He nods confidently and swings open the front door, beckoning me inside before following closely behind me.

The atmosphere in this place is constantly in flux, always evolving. It's almost unrecognizable from my last visit. Thick plastic sheets hang from the ceiling, creating a makeshift barrier between the bustling construction work and the rest of the establishment. All is quiet now, except the rattling of a spray can being shaken at the far end of the room.

With a final click, the door shuts behind him, causing a sudden gust of wind to sweep through the room. The sheets, strewn across the ground, sway and dance like ghosts in its wake.

The sharp, metallic scent of spray paint fills the air, and a woman stands in front of the large blank wall, her body moving fluidly as she creates a masterpiece. Her passion for her craft is evident in every movement, as if she is in a trance-like state, entirely consumed by her art.

'Lucy, this is Kyrie Fitzgerald, a local legend of the PDX graffiti scene,' Asher introduces her to me.

Kyrie has shoulder-length dark curls and caramelly light brown skin, and judging by her incredible spray-painting skills, it's easy to see why she holds such a reputation.

'Hi,' Kyrie greets us sweetly as she turns toward us, still wielding the spray paint in her hand.

'Kyrie, this is Lucy, my date.'

A warm flush spreads over my cheeks as a smile slowly blooms. I am his date, and I can barely contain my excitement over it. I love hanging out with him. My heart has been racing with anticipation and giddiness since he asked me – and that's coming from a woman who'd just about given up on love. It's as if I stepped into a romance novel, where the pages are filled with enchantment, and the words dance off the page, swirling around me in a whirlwind of wonder.

*Back to earth, Luce. Don't get lost daydreaming this early on.*

'It's so nice to meet you,' I tell the woman.

'So,' Ash continues, 'I've commissioned Kyrie to paint this wall. We wanted something fun and different. If you've ever strolled down Alberta Street or pretty much anywhere in northeast Portland, you probably noticed the buildings covered in brightly painted murals; she created a few of them.'

'Wow!' I exclaim. 'I have noticed. How freaking cool. What are you painting here?'

'Well, I've prepped the wall with this deep turquoise color and outlined the words "Fire and Spice" in tag style. Now you two are going to help me bring it to life.'

The name I came up with! This is so cool. No way is he knowing it came to me in one of the dreams he appeared in. One that would make him blush if I gave him details. We used the bar for... well, you could imagine. Anyway, I'm a woman who's not felt a man's touch in many months – so I'm pretty sure dreaming about it is normal.

'Fire and Spice,' I repeat. 'I still love it.'

'Lucy is the one who thought of the name,' he says to Kyrie.

'Cool,' she says. 'It's a great name. You ready to get started?'

With a kind smile, she gestures toward a couple of white painting coveralls. After we are suited up, she guides us through a crash course on the art of spray painting. Showing us how to hold the spray cans and the proper technique for avoiding drips down the walls. With graceful movements, she demonstrates how to keep the sprays even and consistent. It's harder than it looks, but we try to keep up.

'How's it looking?' Ash inquires a bit later, his hands moving with ease as he sprays paint like he sneaks out at night to do this on train cars. He's a natural.

'Kyrie's side is undoubtedly better,' I chuckle.

Thankfully, she's trailing behind us to add her finishing touches and make our amateur contributions blend seamlessly into this floor-to-ceiling masterpiece. With each stroke of her spray can, the wall comes alive with energy and depth, transforming before our eyes into a work of art that commands attention.

\* \* \*

As we step back to admire the finished mural, a sense of pride swells within me. The 'Fire & Spice' tag shimmers with a mesmerizing blend of oranges, blues and purples, forging a visual feast for the eyes. I can't believe we had a hand in creating something so beautiful in a place that I've no doubt will become one of *the* Portland restaurants to visit.

'You both did an amazing job,' Kyrie praises us, her eyes sparkling with satisfaction.

'I am honored you'd let me help with this,' I say to Asher.

He grins. 'I couldn't have asked for a better partner in crime.'

'Right back at ya, handsome.' The word slips from my lips, but how his eyes light up tells me he's pleased by my response. 'You know,' I say, trying to maintain a nonchalant facade – like I didn't just call him handsome, but my stomach is doing somersaults because he is, 'this needs to be the design on the back of the menus.'

'That's a brilliant idea, beautiful. It ties everything together perfectly.'

I laugh at the way he throws a compliment back at me mid-sentence.

'I think it would look fantastic on the menus,' Kyrie says.

'It would be amazing,' I say, grabbing my purse from a

nearby table and searching for my phone. I snap half a dozen photos. 'I can make this work and it'll be so cool.'

After we help Kyrie gather her things as she prepares to leave the restaurant, Asher grabs my hand, sending a jolt of warmth through me.

'This was so much fun,' I say to him. 'I've never been on a better date.'

'Good, because it's not over. There's one more part.'

'One more part?' I ask, my voice rising with anticipation. He really did put some thought into this, and I'm delighted he did because I'm not ready for this to be over.

He leads me to a hidden staircase in a corner of the restaurant. A heavy velvet curtain obscures its entrance.

'Shockingly, this next part *was* Aaron's doing – a private romantic VIP lounge for the warmer months. Welcome to The Ember Lounge, a play-off your name suggestion.'

He leads the way up the stairs, pulling open a heavy door at the top, and we emerge into a cozy outdoor seating area – still under construction but still completely epic, just like downstairs. My breath catches in my throat as I take in the sight before me – city lights twinkling in all directions.

The space is transformed into a romantic oasis, with outdoor loungers, large umbrellas emitting a light glow, a metal fire pit lit with a blue flame, and a table with wine and a picnic basket. Stunning.

'Aaron created this?' I ask, shocked because it's incredibly romantic and he's – not. To be honest, considering he meandered my way while grooving to Flock of Seagulls all those weeks ago, I'd have expected that guy's rooftop to have bright colors, a smoke machine, neon lighting, and MTV playing on a big screen. But this... 'It's beautiful,' I gush.

'Yeah, he surprised even me. I think he might be a little deeper than even I knew.'

'Madi will be so impressed to see he has this side. She's a total girls' girl. She'll love this.'

He stops, our eyes meeting. 'Do *you* love this?'

My smile widens as I reach out, touching his hand bashfully. 'As I said, it's already my favorite date ever.'

He smiles, relief washing over him. 'I thought this would be the perfect place for a nightcap and dessert after our artistic endeavors. Just us.'

'Just us,' I repeat, the fluttering in my chest growing stronger. 'You are incredible,' I breathe out, overwhelmed by his effort to create this surprise.

'I wanted tonight to be special,' he says, his eyes reflecting the flickering light of the fire pit. 'Because you're special.'

His words cause my heart to skip a beat, and his intense gaze washes over me like molten honey.

'Were you this sweet in high school because I would remember if Isabelle had been talking non-stop about this – and just like Kris gushed about me, she did about you. For sure, she would have told me.'

Isabelle was his girlfriend when Kris and I were dating. She was tall, blonde and beautiful – the head cheerleader and once voted 'most potential' of his class. I wonder: whatever happened to her?

He rumbles a laugh. 'Isabelle, wow, I haven't thought about her in a long time. She was my, uh—'

'First?' I ask, with a sly smile. 'Yeah, she did tell me about that. How do you think I knew you weren't in Vegas to lose your virginity?'

His eyes widen, with a nervous laugh. 'Fair enough. Though, I don't know how I feel about her giving you details. I wasn't exactly Mr Romance as a teen. And if she told you the story – I hope to God she didn't – you already know that.'

It's not a terrible story. He got excited it was his first time and well – you know how that goes. But for the record, once he recovered physically and emotionally (according to Isabelle), she was pleasantly surprised at multiple aspects of their 'encounter.' Now that he's a full grown man with experience under his belt – pun intended – it's got me wondering...

*But, no, Lucy. It's date number one. Find your manners. I know it's been awhile and he's incredibly handsome and sweet, but you will not joy ride this man on a rooftop. At least not yet.*

'Now, not to sound impatient, considering I'm all in with anything you cook, but what's on the menu tonight?'

He grins proudly. 'A little bird told me you were a dessert girl?' he says, grabbing the picnic basket.

I smile wide. 'They didn't lie to you.'

'Good, because I spent all afternoon in the kitchen creating my first custom dessert.' He unpacks the basket, pulling out two bottles of wine, stemmed glasses, ice packs, and a closed brown takeout box with '#3' (nice embarrassing touch there) written on it, before revealing two personal-sized chocolate cakes.

'Oh my God, what is it?' I ask excitedly.

'Chocolate cheesecake with fire-roasted homemade marsh-mallow topping,' he says, opening the box to reveal a stack of marshmallows he made.

'You made marshmallows from scratch?'

'Yep, and we're roasting them first.'

'Smore's cheesecake!?' I ask, absolutely giddy over this.

'S'mores cheesecake, exactly.'

He skewers a marshmallow onto a metal roasting stick and hands it my way before making one for himself. We hold them over the flames as they sizzle and turn golden brown while we rotate them over the intense heat. The fire licks at the edges, leaving behind a smoky trail.

'I haven't done this since I was a kid.'

'Me either,' he says, pulling his flaming marshmallow from the fire. He blows it out, then carefully slides it from the skewer and onto the top of one of the cheesecakes, handing it to me.

I exchange my roasting stick for the dessert, and he does the same to the second one.

'Are you ready for the big reveal?' he asks nervously, offering me a fork.

As if he needs to be nervous – the man is a culinary master. I take a bite, and my taste buds are met with an explosion of flavors – the sweetness of the chocolate perfectly balanced with the slight crunch of the graham cracker and the gooey marsh-mallow topping. Sweet baby Jesus, it's heavenly.

'Wow,' I manage to say with my mouth full. 'You have truly outdone yourself, sir.'

I can't help but chuckle at his genuine surprise. The man may be a master chef, but he still has moments of self-doubt like the rest of us.

He takes a bite, exhaling contentedly. 'Holy shit, I really did.' His gaze is curious as he shoots a look my way, a slight smirk creeping up on his face. 'Would you say it's... orgasmic?'

'Oh my gosh, I should have known that would come back to bite me!' I say with a laugh.

'Curious minds want to know...' he teases.

I take another bite, closing my eyes and nodding my head. 'Toe. Curling,' I confirm.

He smiles wide – clearly proud of himself.

'Tell me something I don't know about you,' I say, changing the subject.

He laughs, knowing exactly what I'm doing.

'Hmmm. Something you don't know,' he says, tilting his head as he thinks it over. 'After high school, I went into the CIA.'

I shoot him a glance. 'The CIA?'

'The Culinary Institute of America, in the heart of Napa Valley.'

I laugh at his clever wordplay, shaking my head in amusement.

'You had me going there for a second,' I admit, taking another bite of the delicious cake he crafted.

He grins mischievously, clearly pleased with his little joke. 'Well, a little mystery adds flavor to life, don't you think?'

'Mitzi says something like that.'

'I never asked why you live with her?' he questions.

'After Vegas, she had a very small TIA that I blame myself for because of all the chaos.'

He lifts an eyebrow.

'Stroke,' I fill him in.

'Oh no.'

'Yeah. Dad wanted to hire around-the-clock care – just in case – even though she bounced back like she was a teenager. And I found myself without a place to live, so I volunteered.'

He listens intently, his gaze softening as I recount the unexpected events that led me to share a home with Mitzi.

'She's lucky to have you looking out for her,' he remarks, a hint of admiration in his voice.

I shrug modestly. 'Mitzi has always been there for me, like the mom I never had. It's the least I could do.'

'She adores you,' he says, still devouring his cake. 'Only wanting the best for her favorite granddaughter – her words.'

'I certainly lucked out in the grandmother department,' I say with a smile, grateful for Mitzi's presence in my life.

We eat silently for a few, enjoying one another's company.

'I gotta say, I really lucked out going to Vegas last winter and reconnecting with you,' he says.

I meet his gaze. My God. I want this – with him. But I need to purge my demons before I tell him that.

'Likewise,' I say, giving his hand a reassuring squeeze before setting my nearly gone dessert on the table and lacing my fingers through his. 'So far, you've helped turn every worst day of my life, into something better. I'm for sure the lucky one.'

He doesn't say anything to that, just gently caresses my hand with his thumb. I lie back on the lounger next to him and stare up at the stars twinkling above us.

'Have you ever wished on a star?'

'Not since I was a kid. Have you?'

I nod. 'Recently, actually.'

'Did your wish come true?'

I squeeze his hand tighter. 'I think it's happening right now.'

His gaze softens, a smile playing on his lips. The crackling of the fire and the gentle rustling of leaves in the breeze fade into the background as he brushes a strand of hair behind my ear.

'I better make a wish then,' he whispers, his voice barely above a breath.

The moonlight dances across his face as he leans in, the distance between us diminishing until our lips meet with a gentle pressure that sends electricity down my spine as his hand cradles the back of my head. This man knows how to kiss a woman like he means it. Wow.

As we part, I've no doubt I'm wearing a grin that stretches from ear to ear. The taste of chocolate and marshmallow lingers on my lips, but now it's mixed with the sweetness of him. The crackling fire seems to burn brighter, casting flickering shadows across his face as he looks at me with an intensity that makes my heart flutter.

'Looks like my wish just came true too,' he says, the smile lingering on his handsome face.

Be still my heart. It's at this moment that I know whatever demons or ghosts may haunt me from my past, I'm ready to face them. If it needs to be with fire in my grandmother's backyard, so be it.

## 27

### ASHER

Well, I'm fucked – in the best fucking way ever. My feelings may be steering me down the path of the big L word, and I'm not scared for once. I was a bit fearful Lucy would think I was using her for free labor at the restaurant with the mural painting (which was definitely not my intention), but she seemed to love it. It turned out even better than I had hoped, thanks to the brilliant name she came up with. I always knew I wanted a local artist to design a wall, but I never could have imagined it would perfectly capture the elusive idea that's been floating around in my mind for so long.

My phone buzzes in my pocket, and even though it's after eleven, I know exactly who it is because I've ignored three of his calls in the last hour.

'You can't let me have even a second to consider how this went without your input, can you?' I say when I answer, as opposed to hello.

'Nope,' he states firmly. I can almost see the playful smirk on his lips as he continues, 'Spill it – did you wear those tight pants?'

'I don't even own pants that tight.'

'Liar. You've got skinny jeans. I've seen you wear them,' he argues.

'Skinny is different than ball hugging.'

'You got tiny balls, do ya?' he teases. 'It's not a problem; just stuff a sock down there. Every eighties star did it.'

The image of famous stars from decades past with socks stuffed in their pants to impress women, and probably other dudes, is slightly disturbing.

'Well, four decades later, in the present day, men don't do that,' I state matter-of-factly.

'Pffftttt... I bet they do; our socks are just smaller now.'

A snort of disbelief escapes my lips. Why are our conversations always unhinged? I never know where they will lead, but that's part of the fun.

'Talk,' he commands. 'Did she love the S'mores cheesecake thing? Did she love my rooftop love nest?'

My mind flashes back to Lucy, when she walked onto the roof, her eyes closing with a slight hum of ecstasy as she took a bite of the cheesecake, the way her lips felt on mine. I have to force myself to focus, or I'd have been imagining something very X-rated – Aaron style.

'You nailed it with the rooftop love nest – though please stop calling it that.'

'Yes!' He exclaims. 'I *knew* I was romantic.'

Also, despite how it sounds, Aaron was not the genius behind the cheesecake creation. I was rambling on the phone with him while flipping through my gazillion cookbooks and stumbled upon two recipes that seemed meant for each other – cheesecake and homemade marshmallows. *Voila!* The cake that nearly sent her into an orgasmic state was born.

'She definitely loved all of it. She practically melted in her seat when she took a bite.'

'Hot!' he utters. 'But wait, it's midnight, you're home talking to me, and I hear no heavy breathing or moaning. Couldn't seal the deal?'

'You think I'd answer your call if I was in the middle of that?'

'I dunno why you wouldn't. I do,' he reminds me.

'I know...' I groan. 'But no, I didn't try to defile this woman as soon as she allowed it – I respect her. I'm thinking I want to try to make this into something long term.'

'Ew,' he groans. 'You and your lovey-dovey nonsense.'

'Someone's got to balance out your eternal bachelor vibes.'

We fall into our usual rhythm of banter and shared jokes, the easy comfort of our relationship wrapping around me like a familiar blanket.

As much as I enjoy our conversation, my mind keeps drifting back to Lucy, how she smiled when she saw the mural, and how her eyes lit up when she tasted the cheesecake. I can still feel her hand in mine, our fingers interlaced as a spark of electricity passed between us. Her lips on mine were soft and inviting and tasted like the sweetness of the S'mores cheesecake we had shared earlier. The world around us seemed to disappear as we kissed, and I wanted to stay in that moment forever.

'I gotta admit,' I confess to my friend, 'I think I like her more than you.'

'Pardon me?' he says with exaggerated shock.

'Sorry bud, but Lucy might be stealing your spot as my number one.'

Aaron's gasp is so dramatic that I can't help but laugh.

'You're kidding, right? You're choosing some girl over me? We share blood, bro.'

'She's not just some girl,' I defend. 'She's like... like a piece of me I didn't even realize was missing until now.'

'What the hell am I, then? Chop liver?'

'Chop liver? You are so outdated,' I tease. 'We're bros, man. I am never choosing to marry and spend my life with you in a million years, but I can see it with Lucy.'

There's a moment of silence before Aaron lets out a heavy sigh.

'Shit. Does this mean I have to find a new wingman?'

'I'll always be your wingman. But what about Madi? You didn't seriously pull the plug, did you?'

'Not yet, Madi's cool and all, and the sex is amazing – but I'm not looking for anything serious, and suddenly I suspect she is. We spend every weekend together. She took me to the farmer's market. We bought apples. Married couples do that shit!'

'Are you saying you hated every second of it?'

'No. I liked it. I ate those apples and made the woman a pie! That's the thing. I'm feeling shit in my chest. I'm practicing baking for her. That's the tell.'

'What's it telling you?'

'That it's time to move on because if something fucks it up, it's gonna hurt.'

'It's unbelievable that you can be this much of a moron. Those are the *actual* feelings of falling for a woman. Not a red flag telling you to flee.'

Aaron sighs, his exasperation evident even through the phone line.

'Yeah, Mr Romance, whatever. I'm not the one over here contemplating my feelings like a teenage girl.'

I chuckle, knowing he's just putting on a tough act to cover up any vulnerability.

'No, you're the one who won't admit you're doing exactly that.'

'Shut up,' he moans. 'If you fall in love you'll ruin my life.'

'Well, don't worry. Like you said, we share blood so I can't shake ya that easily. I won't let Lucy steal me away completely. You'll always have a special place in my heart – right next to grandma's lasagna.'

He groans dramatically. 'Fantastic. I'm on par with lasagna now.'

After exchanging goodbyes, I reach into the fridge and grab a cold beer. My eyes are drawn to one of the items stuck amongst the magnetic clutter on the front – reminders, recipes, coupons, and a collection of magnets from my sister's travels. It's a photo of Kris and me on the day we graduated high school. We're wearing black caps and gowns, our arms wrapped around each other as we proudly display the diplomas we secretly wondered if we'd actually earn with as much school as we skipped.

'It's possible that I might actually love her,' I say out loud, but his expression remains unchanged. It's hard for me to picture him as an adult, because, in my mind, he will always be eighteen years old. 'Teenage love rarely lasts,' I try to explain. 'I doubt you two would even still be together all these years later and she agrees. Not to gang up on you or anything. You'd want her to be happy, right? 'Cause I really want to do that for her.'

No answer – but I really like to think he would. And I believe he'd want that for me, too.

## 28

### LUCY

The backyard of Mitzi's place is vast and well-manicured, with a sprawling green lawn surrounded by colorful flower beds and perfectly trimmed hedges. Tall mature trees dot the property, and in the distance, a sparkling pool glows under the starry sky.

In the back corner, away from everything, stands a middle-aged man named Jayson with a hose lying at his feet as he watches a fire he built in a gravel pit he usually uses for burning yard debris.

'I can't believe we got this all in one trip,' Madi says, pulling the suitcase behind her – the box of Brandon mementos gripped in one arm.

'Just tell me if I'm going to faceplant,' I say, unable to see over the wedding dress wadding in my arms.

We're doing this. And I brought marshmallows because when Ash heard what we were planning – after he laughed and wished me luck – he gave me some, knowing how much I adored the cake he made.

'A wedding dress?' Jayson asks, his face contorted in a way

that says – you girls are nuts. 'Please tell me you ladies aren't summoning demons tonight?'

'We're incinerating them. The dress is cursed,' Madi tells him matter-of-factly. 'We've got to break the spell so she can move on. Be glad it's not a body.'

Jayson takes a few steps back, shaking his head in disbelief. He picks up the hose and squeezes the handle, spraying water away from the fire as if testing the thing works just in case.

'Maybe toss things in one at a time so you don't burn down the neighborhood or get the fire department out here,' he suggests.

'Excellent idea,' Madi says, dropping the box without care onto the ground and parking the suitcase beside it. 'Maybe we should chant that Lil Jon song like Sandra Bullock in that movie with Betty White.'

'If we're out here hollerin' about balls to the walls, I bet the police would be called, so – no.'

I drop the dresses from my arms. They land at my feet with a swoosh.

'OK... What do you want to start with first?' she asks.

Without hesitation, I reach for the wedding dress, a strange mix of excitement and trepidation surging inside me. It's still beautiful and looks so innocent, yet it carries a weight of sorrow that I can feel in my bones.

As I hold the cursed garment in my hands, memories flood back of shattered dreams – dreams that, in reality, were nightmares – but it took the most humiliating moment of my life for me to see them. But tonight, right here in this backyard, with the warm glow of the fire casting dancing shadows around us, liberation awaits.

I step closer to the fire pit, the flames crackling and reaching out as if eager to consume the dress. With a deep breath, I let go of all the pain and heartache the dress represents as I toss it into the heart of the fire. The tulle of the skirt catches quickly, and sparks flare into the air around us as flames devour it voraciously.

'My God,' Madi says, clapping her hands with glee. 'It's like we doused it in gasoline.'

'Curses must burn hot.'

'Next up, Vegas,' Madi says. 'Do you want to burn the entire suitcase?'

I shrug. 'It's not like I can't afford to replace it, and the last thing I want is to go on a future vacation and be reminded of the last place it went.'

She lifts the suitcase and tosses it on the dress without another question. The fire roars to life as the leather catches, sending black smoke billowing into the air. I watch as the flames consume the remnants of a life I once thought I wanted, a life that turned out to be a mirage.

Madi and I stand side by side, watching the flames dance and flicker in the darkness. The heat warms my skin, but it's nothing compared to the warmth spreading through my chest, a feeling of release and renewal.

The engagement dress is next. I bought this thing specifically because I knew he was proposing that night, and I wanted to look amazing. I did, according to Mitzi and Brandon. What I don't understand is how he had so much emotion while asking me to be his bride (tears were involved), when later that night, he probably screwed some other girl without a care in the world that his actions could destroy me.

'I can't believe that bastard was so charming while blatantly lying for two years,' I moan, tossing the silky garment into the flames. 'I hope he's feeling this like a voodoo doll right now.'

'By way of a burning bush in his pants – like an STD,' Madi says with a laugh.

For a moment, Jayson's look is pure fear as we cackle like witches around the fire.

The fire eagerly devours the engagement dress, the delicate fabric igniting quickly and disintegrating in a whirlwind of flames.

We glance down at the last burnable. A brown Louboutin shoebox – it's a small size (6), much like Brandon's honesty.

'Do you want to do this one memory at a time, or should we just toss the whole box in?'

In a sudden burst of determination, I grab the box from Madi's hands, and without a word, I fling it into the fire pit. I don't want to see a single thing in it again. The sound of crackling cardboard mixes with the roar of the flames as the box is engulfed. Embers fly into the air, carrying with them the last remnants of a relationship that should have never been.

As we watch the box burn, I feel a weight lifting off my shoulders. A strange mix of emotions swirls inside me – relief, sadness, anger and freedom.

'One more thing,' I say, pulling a pack of photos from my hoodie pocket.

'What's that?' Madi asks.

'The photos *Here Comes the Bride* magazine sent,' I tell her, ready to pitch them into the blaze.

'You got them?!' she asks with surprise.

I nod. 'A while ago. Mitzi paid them to kill the story, but with her generous offer to make up for it, they asked if she'd like the photos.'

'Wait!' she says, grabbing my hand. 'Let me see those really quick.'

I hand them to her.

'Why?'

She speeds through the prints, pulling one from the stack before handing them back to me. 'Proceed,' she says.

'Which one did you take?'

'I'll tell you when this is over,' she answers, holding the photo.

When I toss the photos into the fire, they flutter like a deck of cards landing in random places. The glossy paper catches quickly, curling at the edges as the proof of the most humiliating day of my life is consumed.

Madi's eyes glitter with mischief as she holds the one photo close to her chest, a secret smile playing on her lips.

'That's it,' I say, staring into the flames – a sense of finality washing over me as remnants of my past life turn to ash.

Madi turns to me, her eyes reflecting the fire's flickering light.

'How do you feel?'

'Like Mitzi's a genius and now I want to know what she's burned.'

Madi laughs.

My phone dings in my hoodie pocket.

'Ooh, who is it?'

His words create a bubble of desire inside me.

**ASHER**

Hope the burning of Brandon's soul is going safely.

 Call me later, gorgeous. I'll wait up.

My heart swells in a way that makes me suck in a breath.

Madi reads the text over my shoulder.

I told him we were doing that earlier – burning Brandon's soul – if he even has one. I thought maybe it would scare him from getting involved with me, but here he is, checking in, complimenting me and requesting a call anytime. I am smitten.

'My God, he's exactly your type of cute. Clearly, this worked,' Madi motions at the dying fire.

He is my type of cute, and it's doing something to my insides that I can't explain.

'Here,' she says, handing me the photo she kept. 'Anytime you feel like you can't do something – look at this and remember you are a badass who laid a guy out with a single hit in front of everyone he knows and a magazine to boot.'

I take the photo from her – one I've never seen because after I got the package, I hid it away in the top of my closet and forgot they existed. No way was I looking. My heart couldn't bear it. I probably shouldn't take the bait now, but of course, I'm going to. And I laugh at what I see: me punching Brandon, with fury all over my face – perfectly manicured nails and wearing a ten-thousand-dollar dress.

A smile grows on my face. I am a badass. Never again will I make a mistake as big as Brandon. Every single thing Asher makes me feel is something new to me, which tells me I'm on the right track.

'Thank you,' I say to Madi.

Like the good friend she is, she pulls me in for a hug, and I stare at the photo over her shoulder. This thing is getting framed and going somewhere important.

I am so glad she kept this.

'Pics or it didn't happen?' she asks, holding her phone up.

'Yes,' I say gleefully.

We press our cheeks together, me proudly holding the photo

on display, fire blazing behind us, and Jayson hose in his hand, directed at the fire, watching like we've snapped. Madi clicks a photo, then sends it to me.

'I don't see a single demon,' I say, inspecting the photo.

'Fire works,' she says, impressed as she stares at the fire.

Just for fun, I tap into Ash and my text thread and attach the photo.

LUCY

> Lucy-1 Brandon-0 turns out fire trumps demons.

ASHER

> Maybe flames escorted them back to hell. LOL. Congratulations. I just set that as your contact photo. Never have I ever been more attracted to you than I am right now.

Is that so? I can't say I hate the sound of that. But there's one more thing I need to do.

*God, Ariana Grande says you're a woman, and if that's true, you know exactly what I'm thinking right now. Please – let this work. Maybe let him be the one, too. Asher, to be clear – if you need his demographics and social I could probably get it. I really like him. Like giddy like. He's just... everything I ever hoped for, and at this point, if we don't work out, that's gonna hurt real bad. That's a lot to ask for, I know, especially for a girl who's prayed about a dozen times in my life. Sorry for that. Amen. Namaste. The End.*

I do a quick Hail Mary, just in case – of what I'm unsure.

I stare at the starry sky above, glad I didn't just say any of that out loud. I feel like a new chapter is unfolding – one where Asher is present in a way teenage me could never have imagined. I just need to do one more thing. I type out the text on my phone, hesitating before I hit send – maybe he's not ready for this part?

*Nope. Stop questioning your heart, Luce. Take the leap.*

LUCY

> Meet me in an hour at Tom McCall Park, near the fountain. Bring Kris.

# 29

## LUCY

My heart is racing like wild horses, my fingers trembling as I clutch my taser in one hand and the delicate vial of ashes in the other within my front hoodie pocket.

It's warm out, yet I'm freezing, thanks to anxiety. I'm seeing every shadow and hearing all the sounds the bustling city usually masks. Coming down here alone in the middle of the night wasn't a brilliant idea, but I wasn't exactly thinking when I suggested it – it was a follow-my-heart moment, and all I knew was I needed to do this with him.

But my frightening wait is nearly over as I see Ash drive by, toward the parking garage around the corner, so I know I'll be less alone in mere minutes.

After Kris died, his mom gave both Asher and me a small vial-type urn with part of Kris inside. For twelve years, I've kept it in my nightstand drawer, tucked away in the back, out of sight. Even when I've moved house, he's always near me – like a comfort blanket. I knew he'd always love me because he never got a chance not to. At his funeral, she asked both Ash and me that when the timing felt right, we spread his ashes in the river downtown so he could be a part of the city he so loved. Never in a million years did I expect to be doing this part *with* Asher.

I glimpse him rounding the corner as he jogs toward me, glancing both ways in the dimly lit street before crossing. Worry, and a hint of relief fill his face as he slows.

'You are insane,' he says, slowing to a stop once on the side-walk. 'Out here all alone, in the middle of the night? People get murdered down here. You could've waited in your car, and I'd have found you.'

All I can do is smile as he worries about me while seeing that I'm perfectly fine and he's here now. My anxiety doesn't settle, but somehow, my heart slows with his presence. Unexpectedly, he envelops my small frame in a protective embrace, his tall form providing a shield from the dancing shadows. I sink into him, so glad he's here.

'Are you OK? Got the fire out?'

I step away, nodding. 'Yeah, the lawn guy took care of it. I'm sure Mitzi slipped him a tip to keep it quiet, considering her name.'

'Did it cleanse you of boys gone wrong?'

With a laugh, I nod. I sound insane. I don't *not* see it. But he's not running away from it either.

'It was like being in a burning cathedral with the flames licking at stained-glass windows and somehow illuminating the dark corners of my heart, freeing me of that asshole.'

'That was almost beautiful,' he says, smiling wide. 'You smoked him out. Congrats.'

'Thank you. Now he's nothing more than a pile of ashes in Mitzi's backyard.'

He nods approvingly. 'Good riddance.'

'Exactly.'

'How's it feel?'

Our gaze meets a streetlight illuminating the area around us as I inhale sharply, blowing it out slowly.

'It feels like I got back a very large part of my heart.' I rest a hand on my chest. 'But there's one more thing I need to do, and I think you are the absolute perfect person to be a part of this.'

'Am I?'

'In so many ways, yes. Your text tonight was like a sign from the universe that the metaphorical curse had been lifted – though Madi is absolutely certain it was real. And when it was over, I knew I had to do this next.'

He nods, his face grave as he pulls his vial from his jacket pocket.

'I suspected that's what you wanted to do. Are you sure you're ready?'

An anxious bubble of laughter (not the ha-ha kind) leaves my lips unexpectedly.

'Are you? I sort of just threw this at you without asking. Don't do it if you're only doing it because I am. I *need* to. It's time. But if it's not time for you that's OK—'

He reaches up and touches my waving hand.

'I'm ready,' he says, lacing his fingers through mine and holding on tightly, stopping my rambling instantaneously. His gaze is on Kris in his other hand. 'Truth be told, I've been ready for a long time, but the timing of actually letting him go never felt completely right. Until recently.'

I pull my vial from my hoodie, holding it alongside Asher's. Inside, it's not just Kris – it's a piece of our shared history, our grief, and our love for a friend who left us too soon.

'You have a way of reading my mind. It's sort of scary,' he says, easing the tension as he walks me toward the river railing. Each step feels heavier than the last, as if I'm carrying a vial of ashes *and* my first try at love. I always feel like I failed, but I didn't – he was just taken too young.

As we reach the railing, I realize this is where everything ends. This is it. The final farewell to Kris. Where I let go of the pain that's held me captive for so long and be the person he'd want me to be. Happy.

'Ready?' Ash asks, releasing my hand.

I exhale heavily, raising a shaky hand. 'Ready.'

He unscrews the lid of his vial, gazing at the ashes inside for a long moment. I do the same; a lump forms in my throat as memories of Kris flood my mind. I don't know if what we had was truly love – I was a teenager – but for the two years we dated, I *really* loved Kris wholeheartedly. As much as a teenager could love. And I know he and Ash were inseparable from a young age, so I've no doubt he's feeling the same breathless feeling I am right now.

Together, we turn our vials over, watching as the ashes scatter in the gentle breeze, mingling with the water below. It's a bittersweet moment.

'I hope you're at peace,' I say softly – my voice shaking with each word.

'I'll never hurt her,' Ash says simultaneously as if he's continuing a conversation with him.

I study his face, seeing a mix of emotions flicker across his features before he locks eyes with me.

'I won't,' he says to me. 'Ever – no matter what I am to you – that's a promise.'

Tears glisten in my eyes, and he pulls me into him, holding me tightly. At this moment, I know we will always have a bond – forged in grief, strengthened by shared memories and sealed with a promise to move forward. Together.

# 30

## ASHER

And... I just completely fell in love with the woman. Like there is no coming back from this. She owns me. What a strange feeling to have just released a piece of my past that had been holding me back, and I didn't even realize it until right now while standing at the edge of the Willamette River with the girl he once loved more than anything. I get it. Probably in a completely different way, but I get it, and I love it. Her. Everything about her.

I want to protect her from everything and anyone who ever wants to do her harm. I want to rope the fucking moon and pull down the stars to light her path. There's not a question in my mind, heart or soul that I love this girl. Completely. Having a past with her just makes it a little bit sweeter. We share this core memory with equal loss on both sides and no one else will ever understand it but us. We need each other.

'Come on,' I say after we spend a few moments in silence. 'I'll buy you a coffee.'

She nods, and we start walking away from the river, hand in hand, the sound of water fading into the distance.

The coffee shop is warm and cozy and practically empty this late at night. We settle into a corner booth, our hands wrapped around steaming mugs of coffee.

I watch Lucy as she gazes out the window, deep in thought. She's not the same girl I once knew. She's grown, matured, weathered storms and emerged stronger than ever.

'I need to say one more thing,' she says nervously, picking at the label of her cup suddenly. 'You're the only person in my life besides my dad, Mitzi and Madi who's only ever had my best interests at heart. I know it must've hurt for you to have to tell me the heartbreaking things you have, but I couldn't be more thankful that it was you. I owe you so much.'

'We're completely even, Luce. No debts owed.'

She smiles shyly.

'Wanna hear something weird?' I ask.

She nods. 'Of course.'

'You're literally right in front of me, and I can't quit thinking about you.'

She sucks in a small breath. 'Yeah?'

I nod. 'You said you think about me all the time when we were at the drive-in. Is that still true?'

Her cheeks slightly pink at my words. 'Could be more than that now,' she says as if guilty.

I laugh but shake my head. 'If we're competing, I'll easily win because I've been thinking about you since the funeral. Then, even more after Vegas. Now I'm daydreaming about you as I cook in your kitchen.'

She smiles, dropping her head in the most adorable way. 'Watch your words, mister. You'll get us both in over our heads here.'

'What if I want to be in over my head with you?'

'Wow,' she says breathlessly. 'Never in a million years did I think I'd find myself here with you,' she says, her voice barely above a whisper. 'But it feels right, I can't lie about that. Obviously, we both feel it.'

'I know I do.'

'Maybe we were always meant to find our way back to each other – or is that weird, considering...'

'Not weird.' I sip my coffee.

A few times, I'll admit, I wonder if the paranormal had a hand in this. It wouldn't have been unlike him to meddle in my love life. Kris was usually the reason I had a girlfriend at all. He didn't have a car for a while, and he needed a ride. My rule was gas money or a girlfriend. Classy, I was not. Thankfully, that's changed.

I reach across the table to gently grasp her hand.

'Full disclosure, I am absolutely falling for you,' I say, the words hanging in the air between us. 'I hope that doesn't scare you.'

For a second, she stirs, almost uncomfortably, but settles quickly. An easy smile fills her gorgeous face.

'It doesn't. Not any more.'

'Then how would you feel if I propose giving this a real shot?' I ask, my voice unwavering. 'No more running away or holding back. Just you and me, figuring it out together.'

A smile tugs at the corners of Lucy's lips, and I can see the shadows of her past fading away, replaced by a new light that shines from within her. She squeezes my hand, a silent agreement passing between us.

'I'm all in,' she says softly, her eyes meeting mine with a newfound determination.

'Me too.' The words just fall out of my mouth easily without question. This girl is it.

We finish our coffee in comfortable silence, and both lost in our own thoughts yet connected by an unspoken under-standing.

As we step out into the night air, a sense of anticipation lingers between us, crackling with electricity the second our fingertips find one another.

I walk Lucy to her car. The city is quiet around us, as if holding its breath in anticipation of what's to come. When we reach her door, she turns to face me.

'Here we are,' I say, stopping in front of her blue Honda.

Without saying a word, as if guided by an invisible force, her lips meet mine in a soft, tentative kiss. This is the first time she's kissed me and wow, there's that supernova again. I slide my hand around her neck and feel her lean into me, one hand on my chest, gripping my T-shirt. She deepens the kiss, and I don't know why I didn't let her lead before. Jesus. Mary. And Joseph. This girl is about to knock me off balance.

When we finally separate, her eyes shine wildly, probably matching my own, and a lovestruck smile sits on her face – probably exactly like mine. My God, have I ever loved someone like this?

# 31

## ASHER

Last night was easily the best night of my life. I practically danced back to my car after Lucy left to music only I could hear. Without a doubt, I fell asleep with a smile on my face. I know because I woke up with one. The first thing I did after brushing my teeth was text her. Three words: good morning, gorgeous. But no big deal, just me totally ass over tea kettle, as my grandmother would say.

Even though letting go of what we had left of Kris was emotionally exhausting, I feel so much freer. He'll never be forgotten, but I think it's important to let him rest without me constantly calling upon him for invisible advice. He helped shape me into who I am and introduced me to a woman I'm completely smitten with, and for that, I'm in debt to him forever. One day, I'll get to thank him in person (or via souls – whatever it may be).

Today, I'm home, still reeling over every second I've spent with her. My playlist while I cleaned the apartment was more pop songs than I'm used to, so they've convinced me to buy this woman flowers and pretty much everything her heart desires, so

I'm now sitting on my couch, Swiffer propped against the arm, staring at my laptop balanced on my knees contemplating which of these bouquets I should order. Do I go as big as I feel? Or do I dial it back a hundred notches?

My phone blares next to me as I decide. When I answer, I put it on speaker so I can multitask.

'Hey, sis,' I say.

'Ash! Long time no talk, little brother. How are you?'

'I'm the best I've been in a very long time.'

'Good to hear. What about Aaron, he still alive? I called but he didn't answer.'

'I would assume he's hungover or got a girl in his room.' I laugh. 'But to answer your question, yep, he's alive, annoying, and Aaron. Where are you now?'

'Berlin, Germany.'

'Wow. How is it?' I ask, impressed.

My sister has probably traveled to more than sixty countries alone, documenting her travels on her popular Instagram account. When you grow up as poor as we did, sometimes you want to take life to the extreme when you finally can, and that's precisely what Alyssa did. She's thirty-five, single, and doesn't even have an apartment in the States because she's only ever here for a quick visit, then off again. Pretty sure the girl has never paid for a flight because she purchases everything she buys on credit cards that offer her flight miles.

'Stunning,' she breathes. 'I'm standing in front of a massive apartment complex with a vibrant, floor-to-ceiling painting adorning its exterior. It immediately brought to mind your recent email.'

She contacted me right before my first 'official' date with Lucy, and I mentioned the mural we were painting on the restaurant wall. I sent her a photo when it was done, and she agreed it was perfect.

'How's that going?' she asks curiously. 'I'm guessing well by your previous statement?'

'It's going pretty damn well,' I reply with a grin, unable to hide my happiness.

'Ash,' she says sternly, just like our mother would. 'Are you in love?'

I chuckle, feeling a warmth spread through my chest at the thought of Lucy. She came into my life unexpectedly, like a whirlwind of color and light that chased away the shadows of my past. 'I think I am,' I confess, my voice soft with emotion. 'Lucy is... she's just incredible, Lyss. Kind, funny, smart, beautiful. I could go on for days. Not sure how it happens, but everything falls into place when I'm with her.'

Alyssa lets out a delighted squeal that nearly blasts my eardrum through the phone. 'I knew it! I can hear it in your voice. Tell me everything!'

And so, I launch into how Lucy and I crossed paths again, how my connection was instantaneous, the way she makes me laugh, and how she looks at me as if I hung the moon. It's easy to talk to my sister – she's nicer than Aaron, and she's always been my protector, advice giver and second mother, really.

'It's meant to be,' she says.

'Ya think?'

'Kris' ex – a girl you've helped through two self-destroying losses now – yeah. It's as if your paths were intended to cross, destined by the stars since ancient times, and now's your time to shine. I bet you're soulmates.'

That sounds exactly like a woman who spends her days admiring history would say.

'Soulmates, huh?' I respond with a hint of skepticism.

'No question.'

The idea of having a soulmate has never really crossed my mind before. It seems improbable that out of eight billion people on this planet, *one* person is meant specifically for me. And she just happens to live in the same country, state and city and entered my life when we were both teenagers. The odds seem as unlikely as our existence (1 in 400 trillion says Google) – yet I'm sitting here – so maybe she's onto something.

'Your abrupt silence tells me you're overanalyzing this, Ash. But don't.'

'That's a tad easier said than done,' I laugh.

'Finding your soulmate is rare. Our parents certainly never did. Most of my friends are married and divorced. And I've traveled a small portion of the globe – more than most people ever will – and still haven't found mine despite trying.'

'You've been trying?'

I always thought she was against long-term relationships because she loved being free – traveling the world and doing anything she wanted without another person tagging along and slowing her down.

'Love is the only emotion every single person on the planet craves. Did you think I was the exception?'

'Well, you and Aaron,' I admit.

She laughs. 'I suppose he and I have that in common. One day, you're both coming on a trip with me to see that I'm never *alone*. Good people exist in the world, and they have a way of finding me.'

'Mr Right is the exception?'

'Exactly,' she laughs – ending it with a sigh. 'The thing about a soulmate is that being with them is effortless. Whether it's been a week, a year, or forty, it doesn't matter. Of course, you'll have disagreements and fights; you're human. But deep down, you'll know they're the one practically from the first glance. Did you?'

I think back to meeting Lucy when I was fourteen, via Kris. Then running into her in Vegas. And finally her coming into the kitchen at Mitzi's that day. I wondered if she was having a medical emergency. I realized it was just the affect of my presence on her. And in that same instant, my heart responded in kind.

'Third glance.'

'Ha! That's cute. You know what they say: third time lucky. Sometimes, it takes a little longer for the heart to catch up to what the eyes already see.'

I nod, even though she can't see me. Alyssa always has a way of putting things into perspective, of making me see the bigger picture beyond the doubts and uncertainties that cloud my mind.

'Well, I should go,' she says suddenly. 'There's a bakery around here baking *Apfelstrudel*, and I need one.'

'Alright, get your baked goods.'

'Send her flowers, Ash. Women love flowers. And chocolate. And...' she sighs. 'Be better to her than Dad was to Mom.'

'Of course. Lucy's getting the best of me without question.'

'Good boy, little brother. Tell Aaron to answer his phone. Talk soon. Love ya!'

'Safe travels, Lyss. Love you too.'

Alyssa is right; Lucy deserves the world, and I plan to give it to her. I quickly select a bouquet of vibrant wildflowers from a site called 'The Flower Boy' and a box of locally made chocolates to be delivered to her doorstep this afternoon. I'll probably be there when she gets it, so I send them anonymously.

\* \* \*

'Asher,' Mitzi says my name as she wanders into her kitchen. 'I thought that was you I heard come in. How are you, sweetheart?'

'Could not be better,' I say, buttering the pan I need to make fresh bread that's done rising.

'Look at you,' she says with a smirk, stopping at the end of the island next to the fridge. 'You've got a hanger in your mouth, dear.'

'That I do.'

'Is it someone I know?' she asks, knowing somehow.

'Uh— yeah. It is actually.'

'So, the boyfriend bonfire worked,' she says, seemingly pleased. 'I suspected it would. I had some luck warding off some sponges in my younger years.'

'Sponges?'

'Cling-on men who don't like to work, sweetheart. Lucy's father, Paul, is the result of one.'

Poor Paul. Every day, this woman says something to make me wonder about her young life.

'Did you ward Paul's father off with fire, or is he somewhere in the wilderness beneath carefully selected endangered plants?'

'The latter may have been easier in the long run,' she chuckles. 'But no, he's alive and not-so-well – in a nursing home, to my knowledge, losing his mind.' The smirk on her face says this is a detail she keeps up with happily and it reminds me of Lucy wishing Brandon the worst. Best speech ever.

Suddenly, the doorbell rings.

'I'll get it!' Lucy calls from her room loudly.

I haven't seen her yet, so I suspect she doesn't know I'm here. She races out of her room – barefoot (with neon pink toenails), wearing a simple pair of jeans and a cream-colored T-shirt with words and a logo I don't quite catch as she buzzes by.

'You *are* here!' she says, pointing my way and then looking at the front door when the bell rings again, perplexed.

No way. Her excitement to get the door was for me to be standing on the other side? That is freaking adorable.

'Answer it, dear,' Mitzi says, waving her through the kitchen. 'I wonder who it could be?' she asks me once Lucy's disappeared into the living room.

'Haven't got a clue,' I lie.

There's a slight chatter between Lucy and a male voice at the front door. Once it shuts, my heart starts to speed. I see the flowers before I see her face.

'Someone sent flowers!'

'Oh!' Mitzi coos. 'Aren't those beautiful?'

'I'm glad you think so,' Lucy says, 'because one of them is for you.' She hands her the smaller bouquet of yellow roses, which reminded me of Mitzi for some reason.

Her gaze shoots my way as an approving smile grows.

'How thoughtful,' she says.

'So gorgeous,' Lucy says, setting hers on the counter with a box wrapped in black and white paper and topped with a frilly bow that matches her neon nail polish. I didn't even request that, so well done, Flower Boy. 'I wonder who could've sent them?' she asks, pulling the card from the center of the bouquet, her accusing gaze on me.

I shrug like I don't know.

She pulls the small rectangular card from the envelope, turns it over, and inspects the back. Her whole body drops as her brows furrow.

'You didn't sign it,' she says, certain these are from me.

'What's yours say, Mitzi?' I ask, casually.

Mitzi looks all around. 'No card.'

'Ooh, maybe you've both got secret admirers.'

A heavy sigh leaves Lucy's lips. 'These really aren't from you?'

Disappointment doesn't usually turn me on, but right this second, I'm overheating.

'Let me see that card,' I suggest, motioning her my way.

She hands it to me. I take the card and inspect it, just like she did, and then set it on the counter, leaning into her slightly and speaking just a hair above a whisper.

'I wanted you to see how beautiful you are,' I tell her – motioning to the flowers she thought were so gorgeous mere seconds ago. 'And a card can't say that like I can.'

She stares into my eyes, her frown slowly turning as her eyes sparkle in the sunlight streaming through the windows. Without a word, she stands on her tiptoes and kisses my lips. There is no tongue; it's quick, soft, yet somehow melts my mind.

'Thank you,' she says as she pulls away.

'You know Mitzi is—' I glance at where she was, but she's gone, as are her flowers.

Lucy looks around, glancing back at me.

'When did she sneak out?'

'She has a way of reading a room. Maybe she thought we needed to be alone for this?'

'This?'

The sweet scent of her perfume mingles with the warmth of her hands on either side of my neck pulling me closer. Her lips are like sugary honey, the taste lingering on my tongue sweetly. My hand instinctively slips to her lower back, pressing her tightly against my body. I am so freaking glad Mitzi has left the room because this is R-rated at best. Especially with the soft moan that just escaped her lips. I want to devour her right here in this kitchen. Who cares if I burn the bread?

When she pulls away, I'm left stunned. Did I just have my best kiss ever? Nah. I'm thirty years old. Surely, someone else has— *Shit – focus, Ash, she's talking.*

'...was the sweetest thing anyone's ever done. I don't even care if Mitzi sees,' Luce says. She waves a hand in front of my face, my feet still glued to the floor. 'I'm all in, remember? Uh, hello? Earth to Asher?'

I snap to, unable to hide the likely lovesick grin on my face. 'Wow.'

'Yeah?' she says, slightly proud of herself.

I nod like a fool. 'I heard nothing that you said except that you're all in because that kiss sort of floored me. I mean, if that's what flowers on weekdays get me, I can't wait to try something this weekend.'

She laughs, poking my chest and reminding me I'm here to cook, not just stare at her pretty face all day. 'Ha-ha,' she says with a grin, squeezing my hand before grabbing the mysterious gift. 'What's in the box?'

'Open it,' I suggest.

She peels off the wrapping paper and gasps. 'Creo chocolates?!' she exclaims, opening the box and then glancing at me with a smile. 'The heart ones! So cute. Thank you. This was really nice.'

'You're welcome. I was hoping maybe they'd entice you to go on a second date with me?'

'A text message with only a question mark could have done that,' she says, popping one of the chocolates into her mouth and savoring it. 'Oh my gosh, you have to have one.'

She picks one for me, and because my hands are now covered in flour, I open my mouth, and she pops it in, allowing my lips to close on the tip of her finger. She bites her bottom lip through a smile before giggling.

'So, it's a yes to another date?' I ask, impatiently needing to know so I can properly work myself up over what this is growing into.

'It's a hell yes,' she says firmly. 'Want me to plan this one?'

'Uh, sure,' I say, wondering what an outing planned by Lucy Gray might entail.

I guess I'm about to find out – until then, I will let this woman take over every corner of my mind.

# 32

## LUCY

I went entirely masculine for this date because Ash went totally romantic for our first one. We're at a place called Corner 14. They've got an indoor bar, a covered outdoor eating area surrounded by some of the best food trucks in the city, and the thing I thought he'd enjoy the most, axe throwing.

'This is cool,' he says as we walk through the dining area to choose our cuisine.

'Isn't it? We can eat, drink, and throw sharp objects safely. What's not to love?' I laugh. 'What're you in the mood for?'

'Um...' he glances around. 'You like spice?' he asks, his crooked grin is adorable.

'Depends on the kind,' I say flirtatiously.

The man is pretty much my every thought. Flirtatious Lucy – who has been missing for a while now – has no chance of staying hidden around him at this point.

'For now, the chicken kind?'

Has his voice always been this captivating? I mean, my heart is hanging on his every word, dangling from the tallest building by a thread and not even a little bit afraid of falling to its death. That's for sure new.

'I love spicy chicken,' I say, glancing at Ali's hot chicken and smash burger truck, which is my favorite, alongside De La Hi Barbecue. 'It's what I'd usually pick. Wanna do a swap?'

He raises a single eyebrow.

'You order from Ali's; I'll order from the barbecue place, and we share?'

'My God,' he says, looking as proud as he could. 'You are a goddamn genius; have I ever told you that?'

'Once before,' I remind him, thinking of the restaurant name text thread. 'But you used the word brilliant.'

'I wasn't a syllable wrong either.' Pulling his wallet from his pants as he speaks, he tries to hand me cash, but I shake my head.

'Nope,' I refuse the money he's handing me. 'I know you said no debts owed, but considering you're the heroic type, tonight's on me.'

He shakes his head. 'You owe me nothing because the pleasure was all mine.'

God, he's sweet, and I've heard his conversations with Aaron. He's a guy's guy, but when with me, he softens into a cinnamon roll I want to unroll.

'Effortlessly charming is what you are,' I say, studying him admiringly.

He cocks his head. 'See anything you like?'

A nervous giggle leaves my lips.

'Let's not wander down that road. Yet...' I tease. Sort of. 'Let's order!' I say, blowing past it and handing him a twenty-dollar bill.

He accepts the bill, slightly begrudgingly, with a playful wink.

'Alright, my lady. I will meet you in ten.' With his unhurried swagger, he heads to Ali's hot chicken truck, and once our orders have been filled, we meet back at the seating area, sitting across from one another.

'What'd you get?' he asks.

'A two-meat plate – ribs and tri-tip with beans and mac and cheese. Also, barbecue chicken nachos.'

'Whoa, great minds,' he says, lifting one of the two trays. 'One Nashville Hot Chicken sandwich and fries, extra pickles. And Ali's loaded nachos.'

I gasp. 'Nachos! We both ordered two dishes, and each got nachos. That's it. We're meant to be. This seals the deal.'

'It's definitely a hard-to-miss sign,' he says with a grin, passing me a fork. 'Maybe we're one another's elusive soulmate.'

My jaw drops a bit. A man has never said that word to me – not one. In fact, over the last year, I've wondered if soulmates are as real as Bigfoot.

'Maybe...' I say, but only because it's the only word I can find. Does he really feel that way about me?

*Don't overthink it, Luce. Focus on the food.*

The scent of sizzling meats and aromatic spices fills the air under the canopy.

'This smells amazing,' I say. Once again, avoiding something romantically uncomfortable because I don't know how to approach it yet. I'm sure it'll come to me.

'You're not wrong,' he says, rubbing his hands together eagerly. 'Ready for this?'

I laugh, digging into the barbecue chicken nachos. The flavors explode on my tongue, and I close my eyes in delight. When I open them, he's watching me intently.

'Good?'

'Meh,' I lie. 'You could have done it better, I bet.' That part is not a lie.

'Flattery, I love it.' He cuts the burger in half, handing me part while taking his bite. 'Shit,' he moans, burger in one hand as he drops his head back like he's thanking Jesus. 'Now I gotta add a hot chicken sandwich to my menu.'

'I'd eat your hot chicken sandwich any day.'

'Careful with those words, Luce. You might get more than you bargained for,' he winks as he says it, and my heart twirls.

I like flirty Asher. I like serious Asher. Hell, I liked teenage Asher. I'm in trouble. Really, really good trouble.

'Is that a promise?'

His gaze darkens slightly, a flicker of something primal dancing in his eyes. 'It's a guarantee I'd gladly sign,' he murmurs, his voice low and husky.

The air crackles with electric tension as we continue to share the meal, our conversation flowing easily and comfortably. The food is exquisite; each bite's a symphony of flavors, leaving us both satisfied and eager for more.

The sun dips below the horizon as the evening wears on, casting a warm golden glow over our table. The soft flicker of string lights above us adds to the magical ambiance of the moment. It's almost like the venue knew this would probably become a core memory for both of us, as I suspect it will, just like the bubble dance and drive-in have been.

'Ready to throw some axes?' I ask as soon as I start to regret not wearing the leggings.

'Yes, I am,' he replies, standing up and brushing off any crumbs from his clothes.

We make our way over to the axe-throwing area, caged in for safety purposes because 'people be crazy' according to the waiver we signed as we paid for our time. I don't disagree.

'Want to go first?' he asks.

'Nope. I've got no idea how to throw an axe, so I want to watch you first, so I don't embarrass myself. I'm trying to impress you.'

He grins – grabbing his axes before taking a stance in front of the target.

'I've been impressed for a while now,' he says casually. With a flick of his wrist, he sends his axe spinning through the air, embedding it solidly into the wood bullseye with a sharp crack.

'I like how you worked that in like you're a freaking pro. *And* you hit the target!? Good Lord,' I say. 'Promise me you're not keeping score because my axe will never land in the red like yours. That I can almost guarantee.'

'You don't know until you try it,' he says, handing me an axe. 'Just aim for the middle and don't let go until your hand is almost level with it.' He's got a hand on mine as he stands behind me – like every breath-holding romance movie moment I've ever seen where a man teaches the love interest how to do something – and swings my hand downward, stopping when it's in line with the bullseye. 'Right there.'

Do you hear that? I think my loins have just joined the chat. Crapola, that was hot.

'Got it,' I say, as if I've actually got anything at this moment.

When he steps away, his gaze lingers, and I love it. I swing the way he showed me a couple of times, then, with a deep breath, I pull my arm back and let it fly, watching as it spins through the air. To my surprise, it lands with a satisfying thunk in the ring just outside the center.

'See!' he exclaims – immensely proud of me. 'You're a natural.' He rests his hand on my shoulder while kissing the top of my head.

The urge to pull him to me and taste him is real right now.

But I'm a lady, and ladies do not maul men in public – at least this one doesn't.

'Dude—'

We turn suddenly to the voice outside the cage. Ash's jaw drops as he glances my way and then back at him. What on earth is he doing here?

# 33

### ASHER

'I don't mean to interrupt, but I've got a problem, and I need your help.'

What in the fuck? Why is he here?

'Nice to know you have no respect for personal space,' I mutter, irritated that he's shown up during a date that was going perfectly. 'How in the hell did you find me?'

'GPS,' Aaron says, his fingers curled through the fence he's on the outside of like I'm in jail. He's lucky the fence is there because I just discovered he's probably got a fucking apple tag in my truck, and I'm holding an axe.

'*What* GPS?'

'Life 360. Remember? The time I disappeared for two days with that girl? You and Lyssa made us all download it so we could track each other's locations in case we go missing again.'

I shake my head. 'Only one of us has ever gone missing...' I remind him.

Disappeared – or run off like a rambunctious, horny puppy? It's a tale as old as time in Aaron's world. He met a girl in a bar, and she invited him home. Of course, he said yes. But it turned out her home was in Seattle. Once he was there – he had no way back – had lost his wallet and phone somewhere along the way (I suspect she robbed him, but he insists otherwise). I called the police for advice on what to do when a grown-ass man has gone missing. After asking a few questions about Aaron's lifestyle, they advised me to give him a couple of days. He'd probably surface, they'd said.

Forty-eight hours later, he called me from a number I didn't recognize, and once again, I had to make that phone call to update the police on the actual situation (he followed a woman home) and let them know that I had found him. Then, I had to drop everything to bring him home.

'You're about to go missing right now,' I mutter quietly so Lucy doesn't hear me.

I hear the thud of her axe hitting its target, then falling to the ground below.

'Thank God you're in jail then, eh?' he laughs. 'Listen, I see I've pissed you off and that you're busy. In my defense, I thought you were just here blowing off some sexual tension.'

Jesus, please don't let Lucy have heard that.

'I'll make this quick. I pushed the boundaries with Madi and she's mad, and I don't handle mad women well, so I'm cutting her off,' he says, that last part under his breath.

'What?'

'I wanted to see how serious she was so I may have hit on someone else in front of her. It didn't go well, she wants forever or exclusive or some lovey dovey shit I'm not cut out for, so I'm ghosting her.'

'Can I ghost you?' I ask, running a hand through my hair nervously.

'Nope, you're stuck with me for life 'cause we're brothers.'

'People cut off family all the time nowadays.'

'You'd never,' he says, calling me out.

Holy shit, this moron. He is going to fuck this up for me. Deep breath. 'You are an idiot,' I growl through clenched teeth.

His shoulders tense as he spits out the words. 'Things were getting too real, and I couldn't handle it.'

'This is one of those ridiculous conversations that should have been a phone call or a text I could ignore until I've got time.' I shake my head in exasperation at Aaron's typical behavior. It's always the same cycle with him – getting too close, feeling suffocated, and then running away.

'Tried that, you didn't answer.'

'Because I'm busy.'

'Well, I'm sorry, but I didn't know what to do because now she's blowing up my phone,' he says, flashing me a glimpse at the screen, notifications filling it. 'I don't want to hurt her by blocking her, but love was not our deal.'

I glance over at Lucy, who has retrieved her axe and is now eyeing Aaron with curiosity and suspicion. At this point, I should just tell her what's going on and let her hurt him for Madi.

'You're unbelievable,' I moan. 'How do you chase a girl for weeks and then decide, nope, I like her too much, she might be in love with me, she's got to go.'

He shrugs. 'I'm a complex fella,' he says, arguing back.

'No, you're scared of feelings.'

'No, I'm not,' he says, offended. 'I'm scared of commitment. There's a difference. I need space to do my own thing, you know? I can't have some woman depending on me, I'll let her down. Just like Dad let Mom and us down. Trust me, it's best for both of us,' he mumbles, clearly avoiding eye contact.

'What I know is that you've got some deep-seated relationship issues and fuckboy tendencies and need to see a therapist before you die of gonorrhea, or some pissed off girl kills you.'

He laughs. 'Never had the clap, thank you very much.'

'Not brag-worthy,' I remind him. 'Listen,' I get closer to the fence separating us. 'If you fuck up what I've got with Lucy by hurting her friend, I'll hurt *you*.' I raise the axe.

'Come on,' he says, not believing a word I say. 'You'd never. You're all soft inside, remember?'

I roll my eyes. 'I'm not cleaning up your mess this time, so whatever you're here to ask of me, the answer is no. I'm busy.' I glance back at my date, who flashes me a gorgeous smile.

Lucy strides over, her axe glinting in the overhead lights. She stops before us, her eyes flicking between Aaron and me.

'Hi,' she says. 'Is everything OK, or did I just hear you say you need space?'

Aaron nods, thankful it seems someone is more understanding than me.

'From Madi?' she asks.

He shrugs, suddenly realizing who he's talking to. 'Nah.'

'Oh, so you're not here because something happened with Madi? 'cause I thought I heard you say you'd hit on another woman in front of her.'

His gaze shoots to me, then back to Lucy, who is also holding an axe. 'Nope.' He shakes his head repeatedly. 'Would never do that.'

I roll my eyes.

'Huh, that's weird then,' she huffs. ''Cause I just checked my phone, and I've missed fifteen texts. You got caught grinding up on another woman in a club? Is that true?'

He rears his head back, 'Doesn't sound like something I would do,' Aaron lies.

'You did what?!' I ask, knowing damn well it's true.

'It was just a dance.'

'A Swayze style dance?' I snap.

His jaw drops a bit. 'It's the best way.'

I glance at Lucy, hoping she's not judging me based on his mistakes. But her eyes are firmly on Aaron, and it looks like she might be the one to give him his next battle scar. She steps closer to the fence.

'Well, in case I'm right, you should know I'd never let someone intentionally hurt my best friend, and I've got plenty of space in the dungeon back at Mitzi's if needed. What do you think of *actually* disappearing?' She asks teasingly, clearly having overheard our entire conversation, which is why she probably checked her phone, but a fire in her eyes screams: 'I'll protect my friend no matter what.' Aaron might finally have crossed the wrong women.

He looks slightly intrigued yet terrified now. 'You've got a dungeon in that mansion?'

Lucy nods, but considering this is the first time I've heard of this dungeon, I suspect it's just a basement, likely filled with expensive wine and champagne.

Aaron gulps audibly, glancing between us like a deer caught in headlights. 'I, uh— I'd rather not make the news,' he says sheepishly.

'Too bad,' she says with a smirk. 'It's not been used in ages.'

I laugh under my breath, earning a glare from Aaron.

'Don't worry, Luce. Aaron can figure this one out on his own because he's a grown man and he was just leaving,' I interject, shooting Aaron a pointed look. 'Weren't you?'

'You're not even gonna help me?'

I shake my head. 'I'm not even gonna help you. Time for you to grow up, little bro. Deal with it and leave.'

He cocks his head, looking less than thrilled with me.

'Fine. I'll just figure it on my own,' he says, backing away slowly. 'I didn't need help anyway, I was just... checking in?' He glances around, nodding his head approvingly. 'But everything seems good here, so off I trot.' He turns on his heel and practically sprints away, not daring to look back.

Lucy watches him go with a slight smirk before turning her attention back to me. 'He's a lot of work, isn't he?'

I chuckle, feeling relieved that Aaron is finally out of the picture. 'Like a puppy on his first night in his forever home.'

'One of those hyper types,' Lucy agrees. 'Did he really do this to Madi?'

'I don't know. Knowing Aaron, probably.'

She sighs heavily, throwing the axe in her hand and nailing it dead center. 'Shit,' she groans. 'You know how I wanted this date to end?' she turns, asking me.

'How?'

'With sweet nothings whispered into my ear and a kiss that curls my toes?'

My jaw drops. 'I drove you here. Maybe he ruined the mood at this location, but we can still end this date – the best date of my life with the most stunning woman I've ever met – any way we want.'

Her smile widens into one of pure sweetness, lighting up the dimly lit bar and making my heart skip a beat. She chuckles softly, a blush painting her cheeks.

'Always wise. Let's do that then, handsome.'

## 34

### LUCY

As we make our way back to my house, my phone vibrates for the third time. I quickly glance at the screen and see that it's Madi calling. When it stops ringing, a text notification pops up on the screen.

MADISON

SOS! Seriously, call me, please.

I let out a frustrated sigh.

'I was so trying to wait to deal with this until you dropped me off, but I don't think I can,' I tell Asher, who nods understandingly and keeps his eyes on the road.

'It's OK,' he says. 'You should take it.'

'Thank you.' I dial Madi's number and she picks up on the first ring, sounding frantic.

'Finally,' she says instead of a simple greeting. 'What took you so long?'

'Just enjoying my life to the fullest while the world apparently implodes around me. What's going on?'

Asher smiles at my response, not even glancing my way. He's so cute.

'Have you seen Aaron?' she demands impatiently.

'Uh, no?' I lie with ease. 'Why do you ask?'

'That asshole! I think he's ghosting me.'

'Why would he do that?' I ask as if I know nothing, because I'd rather not.

'You didn't read my texts?!'

'Mads,' I say lowering my voice. 'I was sort of on a date and he had my full attention, so no, I didn't read through the entire book you sent me yet.'

She sighs heavily. 'You were on a date?'

'Yep.'

'Shoot. I'm sorry, I'm just in crisis here. I'm feeling things, Luce. Deep things. And I thought he was, too, but then we were at a club, and I caught him getting cozy with another woman on the dance floor. He played it off like I was making a big deal out of nothing, but I haven't heard from him since. I've left six messages, texted, emailed, nothing.'

I listen intently to Madi's words, feeling a mix of concern and frustration on her behalf. Aaron has always been a questionable character, but I feel for her, knowing what I think I overheard.

I glance over at Asher, who catches my eye and raises an eyebrow in silent question. Ignoring his unspoken inquiry, I focus back on the phone call with Madi.

'I'm sorry. I mean, you did sort of expect this from him, right?'

'Don't remind me.'

'I just mean, usually, you don't care if someone exits your life because if they're meant to stay, they'll do the work. Maybe Aaron's not who you thought he was.'

'I know exactly who he is, and damn it, I like 85 per cent of it, and that's the highest percentage I've liked in a man since... you know... so since things are working out for you, I'd thought I'd at least try.'

'You want to try for love again?'

'If you can, I can.'

'Well, in my defense, previously I haven't set the bar very high.'

'I've heard you go on about Ash like he's our Lord and savior. I want that. And apples don't usually fall that far from the tree. If Asher is the catch you claim he is, Aaron is too, he's just stupid.'

Ash laughs, overhearing her words.

'Do you need me to come over? We can make Aaron voodoo dolls or have another boy burning seance,' I offer.

'If that jerk is ghosting me without an explanation, we'll be burning his doll at the stake. Warn Mitzi now, just in case there's a permit required for that.'

'I always knew a scorned woman would murder him one day,' Ash says under his breath so Madi doesn't hear.

'Is that Asher?' she demands. When she's in private eye mode, her senses are super-powers.

'Um, yes, it is. We were on a date, remember?' I confirm.

'Does *he* know where Aaron is?'

'Nope,' he interjects loudly, covering for his brother. I understand why he's doing it; I'd do the same if I had siblings. But in this case, Aaron is definitely in the wrong.

'He says no,' I chime in, ensuring she heard him.

'Liar!' she exclaims, her voice filled with anger. 'Those two share everything, just like us. He knows – he's just choosing not to tell you.'

Feeling uncertain, I glance over at Asher. Sure, he's

protecting his brother. That I expect. But is it a red flag? In the future would he keep something from me, even if it hurts someone I love? God, I hope not.

'When will you get here? I need to talk this out and come up with a plan because I know he's just freaking out. I told him how I feel with strong words. I should've started softer. Or waited until he was properly sauced up. Ugh. That was so stupid of me! Hurry up. If I freak out alone, you know my bottle of tequila will get lonely, and I'll end up at the man's door in a bad way.'

I'll never forget that night. We don't need a repeat of her choosing not to drunk text but drunk arrive at an ex's house. With a baseball bat.

'I like this one, Luce. I need a plan. Help me.'

I exchange a knowing look with Asher, listening quietly to my conversation with Madi. It's clear that there are deeper issues at play here beyond just Aaron's questionable behavior.

'Of course, I'll help. We'll come up with a plan and won't even need tequila. I promise. I'll be there in twenty, and we'll figure it out, alright?'

Even though I'd much rather go back to Asher's place even if I don't actually have an invite, I need to help my friend. She's done it for me countless times over the years. Plus, she's got anxiety turning in my head like a tornado that maybe all men are shady, including the one I'm actively falling in love with.

\* \* \*

As we pull up to Madi's place, she's in her open doorway, arms crossed over her chest. The worry etched on her face is apparent even from a distance. I haven't seen her like this in a long time.

'I'm so sorry,' I say to Ash.

'No need. Obviously, those two are having some issues and I

totally get it – she's your friend – you should help her. My phone is always on for you, alright?'

I nod. 'You are the sweetest man. I hope you know that.'

'And you are amazing,' he says, giving me a quick but mind-melting kiss. 'I'll plan date number three?'

'Yes!' I say, opening the car door. 'Make it on the weekend?' I suggest, glancing back to see his face at that statement.

Slowly, an adorable smile grows, and he nods.

'Alright then. See ya tomorrow?'

'Absolutely,' I say with a smile, closing the door but wishing our night wouldn't end here.

I trudge up the stairs to Madi's second-floor apartment. She's outside waiting on me, nervously pacing.

'How ya doing?' I ask, stopping near her.

'What's the plan?' she asks, but my head is still buzzing from Asher's lips. Or maybe just Asher himself.

I need to focus.

'Let's go inside first,' I suggest, leading the way into her apartment. Once inside, I make us some tea, trying to calm our nerves and hopefully distract her from the freezer full of booze she has on standby.

'So, what exactly happened?' I ask, settling into her comfortably cozy, thrifted apartment.

She takes a deep breath before launching into the whole story; telling me about their fight, how she tried to talk to him about their budding relationship, and how he seemed to shut down completely.

'I just don't get it. One minute, we're having a good time, and the next, he's telling me he's incapable of love.'

'So, the man-taming isn't going well then?'

'Not even a little bit,' she moans. 'He's probably got multiple women all over the city just like Brandon.'

Her statement lingers in the air, heavy with potential. Would Asher condone this behavior in his brother? He doesn't seem like that kind of guy, maybe she's right and the apple doesn't fall that far from the tree and Ash is just great at playing it smooth. What does he think of his brother betraying my best friend like this? I should probably ask.

'I think Aaron's probably self-sabotaging for some reason only a therapist could help him through,' I say. 'But that doesn't excuse his behavior. You deserve someone who values you and is willing to communicate openly and not cut you off the way he has.'

'Absolutely!' she exclaims excitedly. 'I am a precious diamond, and he needs to recognize that.'

I nod in agreement, taking a sip of my tea. 'A flawless diamond, without a doubt.'

'Can you talk to Asher tomorrow? Please?' she asks, practically begging. 'Find out what he knows and ask for his help. He knows him best.'

Even though this feels a little like a high-school conversation about a boy annoying us outside our lockers, I promise to talk to Asher the next day, assuring Madi that I'll do everything I can to investigate Aaron's behavior for her because she'd do that for me.

We spend the rest of the evening devising a game plan, trying to figure out how best to approach the situation without causing more drama than necessary. Please, God, let this work the way she hopes because I have my doubts.

## 35

### LUCY

As I sit down with a late-morning cup of coffee, I can't help but feel a sense of unease settling in the pit of my stomach. Asher is busy prepping for lunch, and bringing up Aaron and his antics is not how I wanted to start the day, especially after last night. But for Madi's sake, I have to push through.

'Good morning, beautiful,' he says as I make myself comfortable at the bar.

'Hello, handsome.'

He's at the stove, stirring something.

'You know, I realized as I daydreamed about you last night that I never thanked you. Before Aaron ruined things, I was having a blast.'

There's no way my face is going to betray this man; it smiles uncontrollably at practically his presence alone. 'Me too. I never expected axe throwing to be so... sexy?' I say, unsure that's the word, but based on his sudden glance and guilty smile, I'd say I hit the bullseye. Those arms, the way he coached me, wow-sers.

'It was, wasn't it?'

I nod, confirming that I, too, have been reliving every

moment, glances, touches and kisses. I inhale sharply and exhale slowly.

'What's on your mind?' he asks, suddenly realizing something is up. The man reads me like a book.

'About Aaron...' I begin tentatively, not wanting to sound accusatory right off the bat.

His body tenses slightly. 'I apologize for him. Honestly, I don't know what drives him to act like he does sometimes,' he admits, his eyes avoiding mine. 'But don't worry, he won't be interrupting us again anytime soon. GPS deactivated.'

I had actually forgotten about that part. He thinks this conversation is about Aaron interrupting us. Crap.

I take a deep breath, carefully considering my words.

'Madi saw him at a club getting cozy with another woman... after discussing taking their relationship to the next level. Like he was *trying* to hurt her.'

'Yeah, that sounds like him.' An uncomfortable smile accompanies his response.

'Is that something you condone? Intentionally hurting a woman? Ghosting her? Cheating within eyesight?' I press, feeling conflicted about even asking the questions because the man stopped my wedding because of a cheater.

He sighs, stopping what he's doing and running a hand through his hair before walking the few steps to me at the bar. He meets my gaze, resting his hands on the island countertop.

'Of course not,' he says. 'I don't condone cheating in any form,' he says. 'Every girlfriend I've ever had has cheated on me. But Aaron's always been impulsive and reckless. I can't control him.'

'I know you can't control him, I'm not suggesting that. But surely this is a situation where you have to correct your brother?

I mean, does Madi mean anything to him or is she just another conquest?' I ask, frustration in my tone.

'I—' He shifts uncomfortably. 'I'd like to believe that deep down, there's a part of him that cares for her,' he replies cautiously. 'But, truthfully, I'm not sure.'

'Would you tell me if you knew he was doing something stupid behind her back?'

Asher's eyes flicker with a mixture of emotions – frustration, concern and a hint of resignation. 'Honestly, I try not to get involved in his drama.'

'You got involved when Brandon cheated on me,' I remind him.

'That was different,' he says with a pained expression. 'We have a history together. My loyalty lies with you.'

'You have a history with Aaron, you're family.'

'Exactly. So, who do I choose? You, a woman sweeping me off my feet by the minute? Or my little brother who's never not had my back? I feel like this should stay between them.'

'Except it's not just their problem,' I argue. 'He's your brother, and she's like the sister I never had. He hunted you down and interrupted our date – that seemed to upset you. And after it was cut short by drama we didn't create, I spent the whole night trying to lift Madi up. Now it affects me too.'

I can see his internal struggle. He wants to protect Aaron but also to spare me from the chaos that comes with him. I understand, but I can't be in the dark about things that affect me, him *and* my friend.

'It's not that simple,' he says. 'I care about both of you, but this is their issue to resolve – not ours.'

'I get that, Ash. But if you see him heading down a destructive path that would hurt *my* friend, someone important to me, wouldn't you want to intervene?' I push. 'If she were doing this to Aaron, I'd be on her case.'

His jaw tightens, a fleeting shadow of guilt crossing his features. 'Of course, I wouldn't stand by and watch him self-destruct or intentionally hurt anyone. But Aaron is stubborn. He doesn't listen to reason. None of this is abnormal for him and we warned her about him. I told you this would happen.'

I told you? Did he just 'I told you so' me? *Everything is fine, Luce, you're having a grown-up conversation and even grown-ups don't always say the exact right thing.*

'You did warn us. And I thank you for that because it helps to know. But I refuse to sit back and watch Madison get hurt, knowing you could tell Aaron he's in the wrong and at least make him aware of what he's doing, so he can break it off without destroying her,' I declare fiercely, a steely resolve settling within me. 'She's already been through that once and I don't know how well she'll fare a second time.'

He crosses his arms over his chest, his sleeves taut around his tattooed biceps. Not gonna lie; I'd much rather have those arms around me than get all defensive as they are.

'So, we're fighting because they are?'

'No,' I say firmly, meeting his gaze with determination. 'We're not *fighting*. We're discussing a situation affecting our friends *and* us. We're also stepping into something more than friends and I want to ensure we're on the same page regarding things like this because I've been burned, Ash. Bad. So have you. I don't want to wake up one day two years into this and find out you've been keeping secrets from me like Brandon did. I don't know if I'd ever recover.'

His eyes soften as he takes in my words, understanding dawning on his face. He reaches out and grasps my hand, a silent apology in his touch. 'I would never keep secrets from you,' he says.

I raise an eyebrow skeptically. 'I didn't think he would either – then he became a professional liar.'

In that instant, I see the gears turning in his mind, and I know he comprehends the weight of my words and the terror lurking beneath them. But before we can delve further into this conversation, a jolt of alarm shoots through my wrist via my Apple Watch: a Zoom call in five minutes.

'Perhaps we can revisit this later because right now I have a crucial meeting with a top-tier client,' I say.

As I turn to leave the kitchen, I feel his eyes burning holes into my back, but he remains silent, as if paralyzed by the whole situation.

God, ma'am, sir, whatever, please, help. It's too late to stop from falling for Ash. I'm there. I want to love the hell out of that man. Please make it easier.

## 36

## ASHER

Fucking, Aaron. Despite Lucy's reassurances that we were just in discussion, yesterday felt like our first real fight. All because of Aaron and his fuckboy ways. I hated it, feeling like I'd somehow let her down. I would never hurt Lucy, and now I've got to make sure Aaron doesn't via Madi? It's so fucking complicated. I already warned him about this, yet his mind is on himself as usual, and now he's fucking up my life too. She's not wrong about that.

She and Madi spent last night together, probably burning Aaron's voodoo doll in a trash can somewhere; who knows? He didn't call me last night either, so I'm totally in the dark here because I tried contacting Lucy, but she hasn't answered my calls, which is understandable considering she's been busy. When she finally did respond to my text messages, her responses were short.

My emotions are in turmoil – I've fallen hard for this girl, and now I'm a complete mess. I don't want to lose her already. A part of me hopes she needs time to process her thoughts and recognize my innocence. She had her heart broken recently. I get that, and I'm willing to prove whatever she needs and go as slow as necessary to reassure her that I'm on her side. She deserves that.

Yet, I just spent an entire night with my mind swirling, while doubt and uncertainty took hold of me, and now I'm questioning whether I have unknowingly contributed to this predicament without realizing it. I tell Aaron to shut up when he's crude. But it doesn't stop. Maybe I need to be a better brother and dig a little deeper. And I've got the perfect opportunity to do just that because he and I are at the restaurant officially moving in, putting the final touches on everything. Our soft opening is in two weeks. I wanted to test the waters before I put the word 'grand' on anything – that's scheduled six months out.

I meticulously place my prized collection of knives on the magnetic strip next to my station, each blade gleaming and reflecting the warm glow of the kitchen lights as I wait for him to arrive.

'Moving day!' Aaron calls as he walks in the front door.

'Moving day,' I repeat, forcing a smile at his enthusiasm, trying to push aside the tension that lingers between us – tension he probably doesn't even feel because, for him, blocking a number solves all his problems.

We both get to work setting up the kitchen. I steal glances at him occasionally, wondering if he even realizes the impact of his actions on my budding relationship. Occasionally, I catch his eyes flicker toward me, a glimmer of guilt dancing in them before he quickly averts his gaze. So, we're not talking. Got it.

'What'd you do last night?' he finally asks, his words slicing through the silence like a razor-sharp knife.

'Stared at my ceiling,' I mutter.

He raises an eyebrow in confusion. 'Sounds like a blast.'

'What about you?'

'I went to a club and almost became the lord of the dance,' he boasts with a smirk.

'You're definitely the lord of something,' I mutter under my breath, mentally adding 'idiots' to the end of the sentence.

'What was that?' he asks, giving me a stern look.

'I said—'

I choke on my words, feeling like a piece of gristly meat is stuck in my throat as I try to address the situation. God, I hate this. Fighting with people who I love. But I need to call him out for his womanizing ways.

Pause, Ash. Find the right approach. I notice all the knives on the butcher block before him and watch as he runs a cloth over them one by one until they shine. It gives me an idea.

'Would you rather be dismembered or mutilated?' I blurt out impulsively.

Playing 'Would You Rather' was our go-to game for killing time as kids. As adults we often play just for fun. I've heard all kinds of shit and thought of things I otherwise probably wouldn't have.

He rears his head back, looking at me with concern.

'Do I live if I'm mutilated?'

'You're horrifically maimed. Your face, once recognizable and "pretty" is now a grotesque jigsaw puzzle of scars and disfigurement,' I say. 'No one would ever recognize you.'

'Just dismember me then,' he says. 'My face is half of my personality, so if it's gone, butcher me like an animal and be done with it.'

'I suppose your precious manhood is the other half?'

He bristles at my words, wounded pride apparent in his eyes.

'Damn, bro, what's up with you?'

I shake my head as if nothing is up. But everything is. This man is fucking up my world and his.

'Would you rather murder or be murdered?'

He scrunches his face. 'You're morbid as hell today,' he spits out. 'I'd rather murder if I could get away with it.'

'You wouldn't. I'd turn you in without a doubt.'

He gasps. 'We are brothers. Your answer is supposed to be, "how deep should we bury them?"'

I shake my head.

'Would you rather be intelligent but hideous or stunningly beautiful but utterly dumb?'

He scoffs at my question. 'I'm already both,' he boasts arrogantly. 'Next question.'

'Are you, though?' I challenge him, knowing full well that his ego could use a good deflating.

'You're being a douche,' he snaps back at me.

I nod, smirking triumphantly. 'Would you rather have someone call you out on your stupidity or remain willfully ignorant?'

Finally, he stops what he's doing and turns to face me directly. His eyes narrow as he scrutinizes me.

'Do you have something to say, Wright?' he demands, sensing there's more behind my questions than idle curiosity.

'I do, actually.'

'Then fucking say it.'

I meet his gaze head-on and take a deep breath, ready to finally address the elephant in the room.

'Your toxic, fuckboy ways are creating possibly irreparable damage to my brand-new relationship,' I seethe.

'How's that?' he retorts.

I roll my eyes in exasperation. 'Let's see, you fucked her maid of honor the moment you met her. Now you're attempting to ghost the same woman after weeks of sleeping at her place five outta seven days, and the other two nights, she's at yours! You're basically living with her, and now, in true Aaron style, you're going to fake your own death and hope someone else might be dumb enough to fall for your playboy ways *again*?'

'I only faked my death once, for a good reason; that girl was nuts,' he says as if it's normal, hopping up onto the counter of his workspace.

'Stop manipulating, Madi. I'm tired of making excuses for you.'

'You don't make excuses for me,' he says.

'Yeah, I do; you just don't hear them because your mind is constantly in "get laid" mode. Women are not just objects for your pleasure to be tossed aside when you're done. Your constant display of horniness in front of any female is not only embarrassing but also downright disrespectful and I can't wait for the day when one of these girls gives you a "Brandon" moment.'

'Jeez, asshole, tell me how you really feel, would ya?'

'Great. I was hoping you'd say that 'cause I've still got some shit to say.'

His eyebrows shoot up his head with surprise.

'You have no regard for anyone else's feelings but your own selfish desires, making you a narcissistic, heartless man.'

He gasps. 'I am *not* selfish.'

Not selfish, but he doesn't argue the narcissism or heartless-ness? My jaw drops.

'You hunted me down while I was on a date to get my advice on something absolutely stupid because I didn't answer my phone. That's not selfish?'

He shrugs.

'Silence is golden, I like that. Listen closely. Your insatiable hunger for validation through manipulating women is disgusting and degrading. And, to top it off, you have a loyal girl who puts up with all of your bullshit, and yet you have the audacity to ignore her like she means nothing because you're scared of how you feel about her. Now, Lucy is questioning whether I condone this behavior – which I don't – and I'm pretty sure she's worrying that I'm like you.'

Aaron's face twists into a mask of fury as he listens to my tirade, finally understanding the depth of my anger. He looks like he's been slapped hard. 'You think I'm a terrible person, don't you?'

'No. But, I do think you might need a girl like Madi. She's smart, independent and likes your dumb ass. After all, brothers grow up and get their own lives. And one day—'

'You won't be around to keep me alive?'

I sigh. 'I'll always be around, but yeah. Eventually, we all gotta grow up. We've gone from sous chefs to this.' I motion around the restaurant. 'If you don't want to be with Madi, tell her. Use your big-boy words. If you actually like the woman like you've insinuated you do, worship her. She might be the only woman to see past your pretty exterior.'

'Fuck.' he groans. 'Why must you believe in love? And why did I get the looks and you get the emotional and mental stability?'

I roll my eyes. 'I even love you, toolbag.'

A hard edge replaces Aaron's usual easygoing demeanor. He seems on the verge of saying something for a moment, but then he clamps his jaw shut and turns back to his work. I watch as he cleans a knife with a furious intensity, each stroke more forceful than the last. And great, now I feel bad.

'I'm not saying you're a bad person, Aaron... just misguided,' I speak softly, trying to reason with him. 'It's fixable. We're men now, *real* adults. We can't ignore our problems or run from them because they'll always follow. We have to own up and fix ourselves because nobody's saving us. You need to confront whatever made you like this.'

He remains silent, eyes fixed on some distant point beyond me. I turn my attention to wiping down the countertops, trying to defuse the tension that has suddenly erupted between us. But as I work, a thought occurs to me. It's not just about whether or not Aaron will change his ways – though I desperately hope he will. It's about doing what's right and standing up for what I believe in, even if it means confronting family. Which is personal growth that I didn't expect considering I've never even been able to tell a cheating girlfriend off, yet here I am, having an intensely hard conversation with my little brother.

Aaron finally speaks, his voice heavy with emotion. 'Nothing made me like this, it's just who I am. Jesus, you definitely don't know what the fuck you're talking about.'

I stop wiping the counter and look at him. 'Then explain it.'

He sets down the knife he was cleaning and meets my gaze. 'You were already grown when Mom finally left Dad. Which means I got the worst of him out of the three of us.' he explains bitterly. 'You know he told me he needed to get laid more – when I was *twelve*. I didn't want to think about that shit. Then when I brought home my first girlfriend he handed me a condom and said *"startin' young, that's my boy, better buy these in bulk, son."* I was a thirteen-year-old asshole fuckboy yet the girls kept on coming. At the time, I had no idea what it meant, but something sprouted in here,' he motions to his heart, 'that convinced me that there is no love, only sex. So far, we're both proof of that.'

Well, not both of us.

'For my sixteenth birthday he literally bought me a box of

condoms. And not a small box, like a fucking case. You know every holiday he still gets drunk and insists that women don't belong in a man's life long term – they'll only fuck you over? Then he talks about his latest conquests – and the guy somehow pulls some seriously hot women. But you wouldn't know any of that because you never show up for holidays at Dad's.'

'It's because he's a liar. An ex-pro ball player. Or a tech CEO. He's an asshole. Assholes say whatever benefits them,' I counter. 'I'd bet money not a single story he tells is true.'

'It's felt true,' he replies with a shrug. 'You've seen my life; even if I like a girl, she flees within days.'

'That's because you make it clear you only want one thing,' I point out. 'And while some girls are cool with that, most want something more serious than just a physical relationship even if that's how it started. And I'm pretty sure Madi is there. She sees through your exterior.'

'That's my best side.' He sighs, running a hand through his hair. 'What the fuck do I have to give her? I'm a fucking sous chef. My best quality is my face. I've got no rules in life – zero morals, and you're my drive. What more could I possibly offer her?'

'Dude,' I say gently, patting him on the back. 'You're the co-owner of a restaurant. You're a hell of a chef. You're pretty. You've got to be good in bed considering the women you pull. And she already likes you. All you've got to do now is seal the deal. If you've discovered she's not the girl for you, I respect that, but at least tell her, and don't just avoid the conversation because it's uncomfortable.'

He's not looking at me, but I can tell he's listening because those knives have never looked better.

'Fine. Maybe you're right. I'm a fuckboy douche-wagon who's spent years disrespecting women and using them for my own pleasure. But I don't know how to change. It's like second nature to me now. I don't even realize I'm doing it half the time.'

'What Dad does is wrong. He is a terrible example, but it doesn't mean you need to live like him. Being a man-whore isn't genetic – look at the rooftop. It's completely romantic, and you did that. Plus, you always look after me. So, I know you've got a heart in there.' I jab at his chest. 'Maybe you should focus on healing it and what makes you happy, as opposed to always listening to that.' I glance down at the front of his pants.

'You think it's that simple? To change who I am?' There's a world of pain in his eyes as he looks at me.

I shake my head. 'No, it's not simple. But it's possible.'

'Then tell me how to start this changing, Mr Miyagi.'

'Yes, Daniel San.' I bow, mimicking the movie. 'First step of: "rehab Aaron's heart" should probably be you being honest with yourself whether you're into Madi in any other way besides the bedroom.'

He stares at me, silent, his brow furrowed in confusion.

'Are you?' I ask, wondering if his brain is smoking as the gears inside malfunction.

'She's pretty.' He holds up a finger. 'Smart – girl knows everything.' Finger two. 'Funny – like truly, I laugh at her jokes.' Three fingers. After a few silent moments, he drops his hand altogether. 'Yeah, I think I like her beyond the bedroom,' he responds with a slight smile.

'Well, there ya go. Why don't you devise a plan to try to make it work? Don't let your penis or Dad's words dictate your decisions, or you'll end up just like him, schooling some illegitimate kid about the wrong way to live his life. Strive to be someone's Miyagi.'

'Someone's Miyagi,' he repeats, his face softening as he takes in my words, nodding slowly in agreement. 'I think you're onto something.'

* * *

It's been two agonizing days since our 'discussion' about Aaron, and Lucy is still avoiding me. Every time I reach out, her responses are brief and distant. My insides twist with anxiety as I slice through the vegetables, my eyes darting to her empty chair at the kitchen island. She's never late for dinner, let alone absent without explanation.

Mitzi notices my unease and tries to reassure me with a smile, but I can't shake off the sinking feeling in my stomach.

'I'm sure she'll be here soon, sweetheart. She's in love with your cooking, remember?'

I hope that's not all she's in love with because, at this point, the woman literally owns me.

Just then, the doorbell rings, and my heart leaps with excitement.

'I'll get it,' I say, hastily wiping my hands on a nearby towel before heading to the front door like I live here.

As I swing open the door, my heart plummets. It's not Lucy, but a delivery man holding a bouquet of roses. Which I should have suspected because I bought them. Plus, Lucy lives here, so she wouldn't be ringing the doorbell to get in. I'm losing my mind over this woman.

'I have a delivery for... Lucy Gray?' he says, checking his clipboard.

'I'll take them,' I say, accepting the roses from the man before closing the door.

Mitzi's eyes widen as I walk back into the kitchen. Thirty white roses, not in a vase, partially wrapped in black and white paper – meant to say 'I'm sorry.' I Googled which flowers represented an apology, and these were the interweb's overwhelming conclusion.

'You do know how to pick flowers, don't you, darling? She's going to love them.'

'I hope she does.'

As I set the bouquet of roses on the kitchen island, I notice Mitzi studying me with a knowing look. Her eyes seem to pierce through my facade, seeing the turmoil I've been trying so hard to hide. I can't keep up this charade much longer; the tension in this house is suffocating, and Lucy's absence is deafening.

Mitzi gets up from her chair and riffles around in a drawer across the kitchen from me before setting a pad of paper and pen next to the flowers. 'She won't be back until late tonight. Write her a note and put these in her room.'

'A note?' I ask, wondering if the simple 'I'm sorry' I'd put on the bouquet card isn't enough.

Mitzi nods. 'Women adore love letters. I've gotten dozens throughout my life, and even though I only occasionally loved any of the men who wrote them, I've kept every single one to this day.'

I wonder how big a box that is.

'Really?' I ask, surprised to hear this. 'Do you still read them?'

'When I need a pick-me-up, yes. Trust me, dear. I've lived a lot of life; I know things. Write the note. She already loves you; she just needs confirmation she's not making another mistake. Stand out. Be the prince she's always dreamed of.'

The words of Madi in Vegas, flash through my mind suddenly. '*He's her prince.*' At the time, she was talking about Brandon, and we all know how that turned out. Is that what she's looking for? Because I can be that. I'm a blow the socks off that daydream prince.

* * *

So, after dinner, I grab the pen and paper, the weight of Mitzi's words heavy on my shoulders. Women adore love notes. I've never actually written one, so here goes nothing.

After what feels like an eternity, I finish, folding it neatly and slipping it into the bouquet – her name written across the front.

With a determined stride, I make my way to Lucy's room, pausing at the door as I've not yet been in her bedroom, and it feels slightly weird to do so without her here. But the door is already ajar, so I push it open slowly.

Her room is a soft oasis decorated in pastel colors and touches of floral patterns. The lace curtains billow gently in the breeze, the windows on either side of her bed casting a warm glow over the room. The walls are a pale lavender, casting a dreamy hue over the space. Her bed is neatly made with a plush comforter, and a stack of books sits on her bedside table. Trinkets and treasures line the shelves and dressers, including a photo of us that neither of us took, but we're at the bubble dance party, looking quite comfortable in one another's arms. If I had to guess, I'd bet Mitzi took this. And she framed it. In her room. Maybe she doesn't hate me if she's not burned this yet.

I carefully arrange the flowers and note in the middle of her bed, then leave her bedroom door as it was before. God, I hope every word I wrote will make her heart race a little faster, just like they did mine.

## 37

## LUCY

Sitting at the bar, Madi and I anxiously wait for her 'date' to arrive so we can put her plan into action. Plan – Make Aaron Jealous – to see if he actually has a heart or if sexual gratification is his only personality.

'Have you two talked yet?' Madi asks.

I shake my head. 'I'm sort of spooked, honestly. I don't want to make another mistake.'

As I recount my conversation with Asher, the storm of insecurities that Brandon left in his wake stirs to life. Is it normal for guys to pretend like Aaron's behavior is OK? Shouldn't men hold each other accountable instead of looking the other way? These questions swirl through my mind like a hurricane getting ready to level up, causing me to second-guess everything I thought I knew about Asher and our relationship. If someone had said something to Brandon, would it have mattered?

'Ash is probably different,' she reassures me.

'Probably doesn't help me not worry.'

'I know,' she moans, taking a sip of her drink. 'Aaron is a grown man and can make his own choices – Asher is not responsible for that. However, if someone is deliberately disrespecting or degrading a woman, it is the responsibility of all men to speak out against it – especially if they're brothers.' The words tumble out of her mouth in a rush, frustration and determination filling her voice.

'That's what I think,' I say. 'Honesty is one of the qualities I admire in Asher. I mean, he wouldn't let me marry someone unfaithful. Why is he suddenly drawing a line with his brother?'

'Did you tell him that?'

'I did. And then I was interrupted by work, and since then, I can't bring myself to talk to the guy because I'm terrified he's been hiding the kind of man I'm trying to avoid. If that's true, at this point, my heart will break forever, not just temporarily...'

'Forever,' Madi sets her drink down, the look of shock on her face. 'No more man ban?'

I shake my head. 'Or maybe a permanent man ban if this works out for the best. I think I'm in love with him.'

She gasps, holding a hand over her mouth. 'Love?'

I nod.

'Holy shit, I've intruded with my ridiculousness, haven't I?' she asks suddenly.

'No,' I reassure her. 'Friends come before guys.'

'I can't believe you love him! Does he know?'

'Almost. Or I thought he did, and then this happened, and now I'm not sure.'

Just then, the door chimes as it opens, and in walks mister tall, dark, handsome and dull. Madi nudges me subtly, indicating that he's her target for the night.

'You called Tanner to help?' I whisper to her.

'Why not?' she replies with a shrug. 'He may be dry in conversation, but at least he's nice to look at. And that's kind of what I'm going for tonight.'

As he approaches the bar, Madi greets him like an old friend.

'Hey, Tanner! So glad you could make it. You remember, Lucy?'

He nods and flashes me a charming smile. 'Of course I do. How'd your hamster fare?'

I only crack a small smile.

'Now...' Madi turns to me as Tanner settles onto the stool beside her and orders a drink. 'You sit over there in the corner and keep watch. If things start getting heated when Aaron arrives, I'll pull the plug. I just want to see if he gets jealous, not cause a full-blown fight.'

'When will he be here?'

She glances at her phone. 'I texted him ten minutes ago and told him I'm not waiting on him to pull his head out of his ass and I'm going out with a real man – a gentleman, then "accidentally" sent him my location pin, so he should be here within the hour if he gives a crap.'

'You are evil but genius,' I laugh, grabbing my drink from the bar and heading to my dark corner to wait.

We're at a place named Lit. The atmosphere is cozy yet lively, with dim lighting provided by random neon signs and stylish Edison bulbs hanging over the bar. Their blue and orange hues illuminate the wooden countertops and stained concrete floors. Vintage posters and concert fliers decorate the walls, adding to the retro and edgy feel of the place. My crimson drink, expertly mixed and chilled, has a refreshing tang of cranberry and vodka with every sip. The buzz of people talking and music playing in the background makes it impossible to hear anything else from my table. All I can do is watch this possible train wreck.

My stomach growls, reminding me that I haven't been able to enjoy one of Asher's delicious dinners in a while. It's only been a couple of days since I last saw him, but I miss him more than I ever thought possible – which is conflicting with the things swirling through my head. While burning Brandon's 'soul' helped me heal, witnessing Ash defend his sleazy friend who hurt mine brought back the feeling I hate most: distrust.

I can't imagine what I would do if Aaron and Madi remained a couple, only for him to betray her while Asher knew and never mentioned it to me. I need reassurance that he won't keep secrets from me before I jump to conclusions based on my insecurities.

Why, universe? Why does betrayal plant a deeply ingrained fear that continues to haunt us even after we remove ourselves from the situation? I don't understand it and am unsure how to handle it. That's why I chose to take a slight step back from our relationship, not as drastically as Aaron did with Madi – we're still texting – but enough to give myself some distance and gain some perspective.

Initially, I intended to talk with him over dinner tonight. However, when Madi mentioned her plan to test whether Aaron has any emotions inside that overly pretty meat suit of his, I opted to act as a bodyguard instead. I didn't realize she was inviting an outsider, instead of picking a random dude when we got here. She doesn't really need me, but even if it's only by way of emotional support, I'm here for her because I know she'd drop everything for me. I'll catch Ash tonight while he preps for tomorrow and address my issue.

Fifteen minutes later, Aaron barges through the establishment's front door, causing the bell to chime loudly.

He stops, scanning the room. I quickly sip my drink and shift my head to avoid being noticed. However, Aaron's gaze never reaches me because he immediately spots Madi. He freezes momentarily, ruffling his hair and looking like someone just ran over his puppy. If I didn't know better, I believe his face could be classified as an emotion that is not sexual. More disappointment mixed with some 'fucked around and found out – shit.'

Madi has noticed him but is playing it off like she hasn't, cuddling up to Tanner in a way that makes me cringe. She starts chatting animatedly with him, tossing her hair back and laughing at something he's said. We all know Tanner is anything but funny. She should get an award for this performance.

Aaron's jaw clenches, his hands balling into fists at his sides. It's clear he's struggling to keep his composure as he watches Madi with another man. How did the guy ever think that him cozying up to some woman in front of Madi wouldn't make her feel the same way?

A wave of sympathy for him pours through me, despite everything, and I glance around the bar to see if there's anyone else who could distract him – a pity date, you could say – to make Madi jealous in return. That seems like him. But before I spot someone uncoupled and under the age of forty, Aaron strides purposefully toward Madi and Tanner, determination etched on his face.

Uh-oh.

Madi looks up in surprise as Aaron reaches them, his eyes blazing with an intensity that sends a shiver down my spine. Tanner stands, sensing the tension in the air, but Aaron speaks before he can say anything. I can't hear exactly what he says, but with his words, Madi's eyes widen in confusion.

Given how long he's been talking, it's pretty clear that Aaron's pouring his heart out to her – ignoring Tanner completely while he blocks his view of her by standing between their barstools. Madi's expression shifts from confusion to understanding, then softens with a mix of compassion and forgiveness.

Awkwardly now hovering on the sidelines, Tanner eventually takes a step back, realizing this is a conversation best left between Madi and Aaron, and before I know it, he's headed my direction.

'Your friend's nuts,' he says, sitting across from me.

'Aren't we all somehow?' I ask, wondering how our couple of interactions have turned into a weird acquaintance.

He nods. 'It's why I do what I do. Love makes you crazy.'

'Who said the word love?'

'She did.'

'What?!'

'Her exact words were, "I'm in love with a moron." But yeah, pretty sure that counts.'

'Oh my God,' I say in half a whisper. 'I knew she liked him, but love? That's huge!'

'The hugest,' he says. 'Speaking of love, what's going on with you? Why are you alone? Where's three?' He glances around the bar as if he must be here somewhere, but Ash doesn't even know where I am, and I feel bad about that.

'Why do you assume I'm in love?'

Tanner laughs, tapping his temple with his forefinger.

'I see things, remember. I don't understand why people think it's bull? Like you said, we're all nuts somehow.' He winks innocently.

I sigh heavily. 'Then I suppose I'll give you the satisfaction of knowing you're not wrong,' I admit. 'Love *is* involved with three. Whose name is actually Asher. So, perhaps your imaginary magical powers aren't so nuts after all.'

Tanner leans back, a smile growing on his face. 'I knew it.'

My phone dings with an incoming text finished with a heart.

ASHER

Miss u 🩶

I can't help but place a hand over my fluttering heart as a smile stretches across my face. He misses me? My God. *What* is he doing to me? How cute is this man?

'Speak of the devil,' Tanner says, lifting his hand to earn the bartender's attention, silently ordering another of whatever he left at the bar after Aaron moved in. 'What's he say?'

'That he misses me,' I say. 'We had a "disagreement" recently. I've been a little distant because of the whole "almost married" thing.'

'Go to him,' Tanner suggests, motioning me toward the door. 'I'll stay and watch Madi, just in case, but they look like they've resolved things too, so...'

I glance over and see Madi and Aaron have locked lips.

'You don't mind?'

'Nah, I could use a couple more drinks, honestly. No big deal.'

'Tanner, thank you. You're a godsend.'

And that's my cue, so I shoot Madi a text telling her, 'Congratulations!' and I'm leaving. I practically run to my car so I can get home and say the words my heart needs me to say.

\* \* \*

'Hello?' Setting my purse down on the table, I call out into the quietness. But there's no response from anyone. Damn it. I wondered why Ash's SUV wasn't out front. He left.

Suddenly, Mitzi appears from the dimly lit kitchen, her housecoat wrapped tightly around her and a bottle of water in hand.

'Good evening, dear,' she greets me warmly.

'Where's Ash?' I ask, knowing for sure he's not here if this is her outfit.

'He left after dinner.'

I exhale a guttural sigh. 'He didn't stay to prep?'

Mitzi's smile softens even more. 'I'm pretty sure he does that just to spend more time with you, darling.'

'Well, I needed to talk to him,' I tell her.

'I know,' she says as if she does indeed know, but I didn't tell, so it had to be Ash. 'He left something for you in your room.'

My stomach flips with excitement. I hope it's himself. I rush past Mitzi toward my room like a teenager in love and push open the door, but the room is dark. I flip on a light near my bed, and as the soft glow fills the room, my eyes land on a bouquet and a handwritten note resting on my bed.

I grab the note, written on a simple piece of white lined paper torn from a spiral notebook. Anticipation buzzes through me as I delicately unfold it and reveal a page half-filled with his handwritten words.

*Luce,*

*Originally, the card to these said, 'I'm sorry.' But when you didn't show up for dinner tonight, I stared at that empty chair, feeling like my heart was missing and knew I needed more than two words – so here are many.*

*I love catching you admiring me with those beautiful golden-brown eyes.*

*I love that I have no idea what I thought about all the time before you.*

*I love that your smile lights up my world.*

*I love your laugh; your voice has become my favorite sound.*

*I love how you react to my food (or any food).*

*I love that you hold me accountable and make me a better man.*

*I love that I thought I knew what love was – until you.*

*I love that I've become a morning person because I can't wait to see you.*

*I guess I'm trying to say that you stole my entire heart, and today, I've decided to let you keep it. I love you like the moon loves the night, the sun loves the morning, and if you let me, I will love you until the end of time.*

*Please call me. I'm not too proud to beg.*

*PS – I love that I've never written a love note – until you.*

*Ash*

I sink onto the edge of the bed, my heart swelling with emotion as I read and reread Ash's words. Tears prick at the corners of my eyes as I clutch the note to my chest, feeling overwhelmed and incredibly loved in a way I've never experienced – he means every single word of this, and for a guy who claims to have never written a love note, he nailed it.

I reach for my phone, my fingers trembling slightly as I dial his number. The phone rings barely once before he picks up – like he's been waiting for me.

'Luce,' he exhales with relief.

'Thank you,' I say, my voice barely above a whisper so he doesn't realize he has me in tears over here – happy tears. 'I got your note.'

'I meant every single word.'

'And I adored all of them.'

'Also, you should know that Aaron and I had words. You were right; as a man, I should be stepping up when one of my friends, or my brother, acts like a jerk, especially if it triggers old wounds in the woman I love.'

The woman he loves – me. I think my heart may explode into fireworks if he keeps talking.

'You did?' I reply, feeling my heart flutter at his sincerity.

'I did.'

'Was it bad?'

'No. It was needed.'

'Are you busy right now?' My nerves start to kick in as I ask.

He chuckles nervously into the phone.

'I'd drop the whole world for you, Lucy. All weekend, I've worried about you – us. I know you're scared of all this, but you never need to be afraid of me. I'll always choose to make you happy. I'll do whatever it takes.'

My God, that is sweet.

'I need to see you. Can you come over? Tonight??'

'I'm leaving right now.'

\* \* \*

Without wasting another second, I hang up the phone and rush to get ready. I quickly change into a comfortable yet sexy outfit, my heart racing with anticipation.

As I hear the doorbell ring, I practically skip to the front door, swinging it open. There stands my prince – the real one this time – looking as handsome as ever in a white T-shirt, jeans, and a white hat with blue stitching that reads 'Loverboy.' I've never been so attracted to someone.

'Lucy,' he breathes out, his voice filled with so much love and adoration that my knees are weak.

With a flurry of urgency, and before I can even react, he's inside and pulling me into his arms. His touch is electric, sending sparks through my body as he presses his lips to mine in a passionate kiss.

He walks me backward, our lips still locked in a fiery embrace, and I melt into him. He trails kisses down my neck, igniting a trail of fire along my skin.

'My God, I missed you,' he murmurs against my hair, his words sending shivers down my spine.

I can barely form a coherent thought as his lips continue to work their magic on me.

'I missed you too,' I reply, my mind fizzing at his touch.

The door clicks shut behind us, sealing us off from the rest of the world. We stand there momentarily, our eyes locked in an intense gaze that might light the room on fire if we're not careful.

'I'm so sorry. I got scared,' I admit.

He takes a step back, his fingertips gliding down the backs of my arms to my hands where he grasps mine tightly.

He shakes his head. 'You were right. And when I realized that, I was terrified I might lose you. So, I want you to know, everything in that note is true. No woman has ever made me feel like you do, Luce. You should also know, because of that, I will never in a million years hurt you or let anyone else either. You never have to be afraid of me.'

'That's good, because I've realized I'm more in love with you than anything else,' I admit.

His smile grows soft and adoring.

'Yeah?'

I nod. 'Hell, yeah.'

He drops one of my hands grabbing his chest dramatically.

'Thank. God,' he replies, before cupping my face tenderly with his other and planting another searing kiss on my lips that could send any woman to the floor.

He's never kissed me like this. Until now, they've been sweet and longing, and this is passionately urgent. I can feel the heat radiating from his body as he pulls me closer. And I am on board with it. Every doubt and fear love has ever scarred me with fades away as I am enveloped in his arms. This man would never – in a million trillion years – hurt me in any way. I know it with every fiber of my being.

I eagerly kiss him back, reveling in the low moan that escapes from his throat. We cling to each other, lost in the intensity of our reunion, and I think this will be a long and satisfying one. And I am A-OK with that for the first time in a long time.

# 38

## ASHER

In the kitchen, I stand freshly showered, preparing breakfast for three – before 8 a.m. this time. But only because I woke up here. Memories of last night play in my head, and I can't help but feel like I'm floating.

As the sizzle of bacon fills the air, I can't shake the smile that's been etched on my face since last night – and, honestly, I don't want to. I'm savoring every single second. Lucy is amazingly beautiful in every way – even ways I'd never imagined until recently. Never has something felt so right in my life. And easy, like we'd done it a million times.

The sound of chirping birds outside create a symphony of contentment in the kitchen. I hum a tune under my breath, the words of a pop song lingering at the edge of my consciousness.

'Well, good morning, you,' Lucy says as she enters the kitchen, fresh-faced with pink cheeks that probably aren't from the exertion it took to walk out here looking as effortlessly beautiful as she does in a pair of worn jeans and a fitted T-shirt.

'Good morning, beautiful.'

'Good morning, *both* of you,' we hear as Mitzi rounds the corner into the kitchen from her room.

'Hi, Mitzi,' Lucy says as she works her magic on the espresso machine, filling the air with the rich aroma of coffee.

'I'll take two shots this morning, please,' I request, already feeling the need for caffeine coursing through my body.

'Tired, are you?' Mitzi asks suspiciously. 'You're here early today. What brought you by?' Her stare feels accusing and lingers between Lucy and me like we've been caught.

Lucy's eyes meet mine, the smirk of what we spent all night doing and saying probably flashing through our minds like a news headline. 'Asher and Lucy said the L word to one another and then had all the sex.'

I shoot her a wink as if all's OK, and her standing naked in front of me in the shower only moments ago is not playing in my mind's eye.

I clear my throat, attempting to devise a plausible excuse, but Lucy beats me.

'Actually, we were up late last night talking about the menu project,' she says smoothly, her hand brushing mine under the guise of passing me a cup of coffee. 'I wanted to make sure I got it exactly right.'

Mitzi raises an eyebrow, shooting a glance at me. 'Did she?'

'Absolutely,' I reply, hoping my poker face is in place. 'She had some great ideas that we probably need to spend more time discussing further to really put a touch of perfection on it.'

Mitzi narrows her eyes, a sly grin appearing on her face.

'Uh-huh. You two and your "menu project." Do you think I was born yesterday, darling?'

Lucy laughs. 'Do not ask for details, Mitzi.'

'Of course, I won't,' she says as if Lucy is nuts even to say those words. 'At least not while he's here.'

I chuckle nervously, feeling the heat rise to my cheeks under Mitzi's scrutinizing gaze. I'm thirty years old and embarrassed, like I'm wandering into a drugstore for a box of condoms as a teenager, and my grandmother just caught me.

I take a sip of my coffee, trying to steer the conversation away from whatever suspicions Mitzi seems to be harboring.

When the doorbell rings, cutting through the tension in the room like a knife, I breathe a sigh of relief.

Mitzi raises an eyebrow, clearly intrigued by the unexpected visitor at this early hour.

'More flowers?' she muses, glancing between us.

I shake my head as Lucy hurries to open the door.

'I need to talk to you two,' the male voice cuts through the air, its urgency evident as it paces through the living room.

'He's in the kitchen,' Lucy says, her steps following.

'You two are my friends, right?' Aaron asks, approaching me and peering into the pan before me. He looks around the place, nodding with approval. 'This place is dope.' He grabs a slice of sizzling bacon and tosses it like a hot potato between his hands before devouring it whole.

'Dope?' Mitzi asks with confusion, looking at Lucy. 'Who is this?'

'That's Aaron,' Lucy reminds her. 'Ash's little brother. You met him at the bubble dance.'

'Right,' she says with a nod, sipping her coffee.

'How'd you find me this time? I turned that GPS off. So, you should know, if you one day disappear, nobody's coming for ya.'

Aaron rolls his eyes. 'You weren't home and it's a weekday, that means you're here. Didn't need the GPS. Though I didn't expect you to be here so early. Did things go well?' he asks, glancing my way and waggling his eyebrows.

'I suppose you told Madi what I said?'

He nods, with a wide smile. 'We've got no secrets.'

'And apparently neither do we,' I chime in.

'Nope. Now, help me,' Aaron pleads with desperation in his words and eyes.

Lucy gives me a questioning look, silently asking if we should trust Aaron and help him with whatever he needs. I nod slightly, indicating that we should hear him out.

I examine him closely, raising an eyebrow at his outfit – a light pink T-shirt with a bright purple heart front and center and very skinny jeans.

'Them are some tight pants,' I comment, trying to avoid the bulge I can only hope is not one of his socks. 'Let me guess, are you channeling your inner Swayze and hearing a pottery wheel calling your name?'

He smirks, nodding like he's proud of me for remembering his hero's name. 'No, but I'm adding that to the month-aversary date list.'

'Month-aversary?' I ask, curious about where he's going with this.

He nods. 'Madi's idea and never again am I disagreeing with her so now it's a thing. But, to prove I'm serious, I need something romantic, that I came up with on my own, to prove I'm the guy she's sure I am.'

'That's what you need help with?'

'Yes. Tonight, at the restaurant, I cook, you wait, you bartend,' he says, pointing at each of us as he assigns roles.

'You think I know how to bartend?' Lucy retorts incredulously. 'I can barely use the espresso machine. Pouring a drink into a glass is about the extent of my skills.'

Aaron rolls his eyes. 'You think this shit is rocket science? This guy bartended as a second job for years,' he says, nodding at me once again like I'm an idiot.

'How about she waits, and I bartend then?' I suggest.

'Fine, just show up at six. Madi arrives at eight.'

'It's gonna take us two hours to cook?' I ask. 'What are you making?'

'That part is undecided yet, which is why I need time. And dress the part; I want this to be classy. Black tie.'

I choke a laugh. 'Black tie means tuxedo.'

Aaron nods. 'Better get to the rental store before they close then.'

Lucy shoots me an amused grin. 'Ooh, this is going to be just like prom,' she teases, her eyes sparkling with mischief.

I guess the restaurant is hosting its first guest.

# 39

## LUCY

A chaotic mound of dresses lay scattered on the floor, a testament to my failed attempts at finding the perfect outfit. I let out an exasperated sigh and begin rummaging through my closet, yanking out any dress that catches my eye. I feel like a princess trying to choose her royal attire for a grand ball – with my new prince.

'Can I come in, darling?' Mitzi asks, gently knocking on my door and peeking inside.

I open the door and her eyes immediately land on the pile of clothing by my feet.

'Wardrobe troubles?' she asks sympathetically.

'Nothing is perfect,' I sigh.

'I know that feeling all too well; it seems to run in the family. Back in my day, there were no walk-in closets, so I had to turn a spare bedroom into one. Whenever I threw a party, nothing in my wardrobe felt just right, so I would always go out and buy something new. Looking back now, I wish I had kept those items for you.'

'Considering you are the queen of parties, any suggestions?'

'I think I can help,' she says, walking back into the hallway and returning with a dress bag. 'Why don't you try this on?' she says, handing me the bag.

I can't help but hold back my excitement as she hands me the dress. She has impeccable taste, and I'm sure it will be stunning.

'Please don't tell me a ten-thousand-dollar diamond-studded cocktail dress is inside.'

She grins guiltily. 'I didn't go overboard; this one was only three digits. It's simple, elegant and has no connection to any past relationships. Perfect for brand-new love.'

'Were you ever in love, Mitzi?'

'Do you think I was a dinosaur?'

'No,' I say as I unzip the bag. 'I've just never heard the story if you were.' I take a deep breath as the dress falls out of the zipper. 'This is stunning.'

It's a simple yet elegant black mesh midi dress with a fitted silhouette. The flesh-colored lining adds an element of intrigue, stopping mid-thigh and giving the illusion of being naked underneath (something Ash will surely appreciate). The dress features a sweetheart neckline with ruching down to the mid-calf on one side and a wide slit stopping just below my hip on the other.

'Try it on,' Mitzi insists, sitting on my bed as I enter the closet to put it on. 'And yes, I was in love in 1975.'

I peek out of the closet, suddenly interested. 'Dad's dad?'

'Lord no,' she says. 'A man named Jesse. Oh, he was wonderful. Tall, dark, handsome, polite, employed – all the things women want. I was head over heels for that man. I truly thought nothing could change my mind.'

'What happened?'

'He felt the same way, about somebody else.' Her tone is soft, almost sad, and my heart drops.

'Oh, Mitzi. I'm so sorry. What did you do?'

'I let him go, darling. Because that's what you do when you truly want the best for someone and you're not it.'

How could someone not choose her? She's incredible. I want to hunt this Jesse down and shove him over, but only because he's likely in his eighties or nineties and doing anything more than knocking him down would probably be wrong.

'Do you regret it?' I ask, zipping the side of the dress, then smoothing it down in front of the mirror at the back of my closet.

'I dream of him, still, to this day. Sometimes I'll read the letters he wrote me. But he died happy a few years back, and happy is all I ever wanted for him.'

Tragic.

'What about you? Are you happy?' I ask, now concerned she has regrets.

'Dear girl, I've had eighty-something wonderful years. A son I love. A granddaughter I adore. I'm as rich as can be, and I don't mean by way of money – that part was a bonus. Now, I get to watch *you* fall in love, and that makes me happier than you'll ever know. I'm alright with living vicariously through you.'

Now I'm thinking back to the times Ash included her in this journey, and I understand why she was so joyful to go dancing and get flowers even though the man treating her was more interested in me. She's missed it, and I wish she wasn't alone, but there's not much I can do about that if she's truly happy.

When I walk out of the closet, she gasps.

'Beautiful, darling girl, like it was tailor-made for you. Asher won't be able to take his eyes off of you.'

And I'm perfectly OK with that. I like his eyes on me.

'You're right,' I say happily. 'And I have the perfect shoes to go with it.' I step back into my closet and come out with my favorite – barely worn – black rhinestone strappy heels.

'Wonderful choice,' Mitzi nods approvingly.

I twirl around in front of the mirror, feeling like a million bucks. Mitzi was right; this is the one. The way it hugs my curves and accentuates all the right places makes me feel radiant. And the slit reveals just enough to be alluring but not too much. This is it – the perfect dress.

'Back in my day, a dress like that would have turned every head in the room,' she reminisces, a wistfulness in her voice.

What will it be like when I can use that phrase – 'back in my day?' Will Ash still be in my life, reminiscing about this exact dress with me?

'It'll turn at least one,' I reply.

Mitzi chuckles and stands up, smoothing out an invisible wrinkle near my hip.

'You have your mother's charm and your grandmother's poise. You'll be the belle of the ball.'

'Do you want to come tonight?' I ask spontaneously. 'I'm sure Ash won't mind.'

'Oh, honey,' she laughs. 'I just started a *Supernatural* marathon, and those Winchester boys would miss me if I didn't spend the evening with them. Or perhaps I'd miss them? I'm unsure. What I do know is this should be *your* night. Let that sweet man knock you off your feet.'

'If he does any more, I'll fall off a cliff.'

She chuckles. 'He'll catch you.'

He will. I know he will.

I can hardly contain my excitement at seeing his reaction to me in this dress. And I don't have to wait long, as the doorbell rings just as I finish applying my favorite lipstick, *Hermès Rose Épicé.*

'I'll get it so you can make a grand entrance,' Mitzi suggests, leaving my room as quickly as an eighty-something woman can.

One last glance in the mirror, clutch in hand, and I head toward the living room. As I step into where he's waiting, his jaw drops at the sight of me. For a moment, he's speechless, taking in every detail.

'Wow,' he finally says, placing a hand on the back of his neck and giving me that same smoldering look from last night. 'Holy wow. You look... incredible. Beyond incredible,' he says. 'You're breathtaking – dazzling – radiant – enchanting – glowing. I'm gonna have a hard time focusing on anything but you.'

He hands me a small bouquet of bright red roses. I don't know what it is, but I hope he keeps being this sweet forty years in, too.

'Thank you,' I say, looking him over. 'And you aren't wearing polyester and ruffles!'

He pulls at the lapels of his very debonair all-black suit – tailored to perfection, hugging his muscular form in all the right places. I have never seen this man look hotter, except when he's wearing nothing. I feel like I'm going on a date with 007.

'I went all out and purchased this since I now have someone to do fancy things with,' he says, smoothing the jacket. 'But let's be real, you're going to steal every show.'

'You sweet, sweet, man,' I say, my heart doing cartwheels in my chest at his reaction. 'But no way,' I say, placing my hand on his chest and giving him a quick kiss on the lips. 'You're so hand-some, it's melting my brain.'

He smiles wide, pressing his lips to my forehead.

'I like that,' he says. 'Ready to help Aaron prove he's not a complete ass?'

I shake my head. 'I need to do one more thing...' I say, nodding in Mitzi's direction. I walk her way and hand her the bouquet.

'No, darling, I couldn't,' she says, her eyes on me.

'I insist. Jesse was an idiot not to choose you. I'd bet money he died dreaming of you too. And tomorrow, you can live vicariously through me because I'll give you every detail.'

'Thank you, Lucy.' She smiles wide, lifting the bouquet to her nose. 'Now, let me snap a picture,' she says, avoiding the fact that her eyes are glistening with tears.

God, I love her so much. She's the perfect woman to look up to for the rest of my life.

\* \* \*

'My God, what took you so long?' Aaron asks, frantically cooking up a storm and not in the black tie attire he requested.

Until recently, I've never witnessed Aaron nervous. He's usually so casual and free, but now, he's sweating, entirely focused and visibly fearful.

'Everything has to be perfect,' he declares, his eyes scanning us up and down before giving a nod of approval.

'Whoa, you guys really did talk. I think he *like* likes her,' I say, glancing at Ash, who nods.

To my knowledge, not a single man on the planet has gone to this type of effort for Madi, so I know without a doubt this is going to be a night she'll never forget. Maybe I prefer Ash over Aaron, but for her, he is perfect.

He grabs something from the counter and throws it in my direction.

Ash catches it in one hand before it smacks me in the face, considering I didn't even get a heads-up.

'It's an apron. Wear it,' he orders.

'Over this?' I gesture proudly to my dress.

'Ask her nicer,' Ash tosses the apron back at him, whacking him unexpectedly upside the head.

He stops stirring whatever he's got in that bowl and looks at us with a forced smile.

'Please could you wear this, so you'll look like a waitress and not just the guest-of-honor's friend?'

He tosses it back our way and Ash grabs it out of mid-air again. 'That's better,' he says, leaning in close as he hands it to me. 'I've always wanted to strip an apron off a woman.'

My heart races at his words as I eagerly tie on the apron like it's the most valuable thing in the world. 'Then obviously that's happening later.'

He nods, shooting me a wink as if he approves.

'What can I help with?' Ash offers, finally offering his brother help, removing his jacket and hanging it on the back of the office chair.

A garment bag hangs on the door, most likely containing Aaron's outfit for the evening.

'The two of you can set the table for two on the roof. Light the candles. Set the mood. Maybe some soft music – the eighties are my decade. And here put the gift I bought her on her plate.'

Again, he attempts to launch an item my way, but Ash grabs it first.

'Are we really in a toss-shit-around sort of hurry?' he asks.

'I'm nervous, I'm sorry. I've never *tried* to be romantic,' Aaron says with guilt plastered on his face.

He bought her a gift?

'If it's any help, I know Madi pretty well, she's going to love this, I promise.' I take the box from Asher. 'What did you buy her?' I ask, thrilled for Madi that he's going all out.

'A gift, flowers, wine and these bourbon balls she goes on and on about...' He points a finger in the direction of each item.

He'd have had her going steady with just the wine and bourbon balls.

'Well, this is a jewelry box,' I say, glancing at Ash, wondering what kind of talk these two had to motivate all this.

I lift the lid, and nestled on a velvet cushion is a delicate necklace with a glistening sapphire – her birthstone. It catches the light and shimmers as I admire it.

Aaron's eyes soften as he gazes at the piece, over my shoulder, a hint of a smile playing on his lips.

'Aaron, this is beautiful,' I exclaim. 'She will adore it.'

'You think so?' he asks, sounding uncertain. 'Is it too soon for jewelry?'

I shake my head. 'Darling, it's never too soon for jewelry,' I say as if I'm Mitzi. It's just something she would say. 'And you'll be the first to ever go this route. That'll be big for her.'

'I am fucking good!' he exclaims, pumping his fist in the air. 'Damn, I've got a real talent for this romance shit.'

Ash squeezes his fingers together. 'So close,' he chuckles. 'You realize you'll have to one day top all this.'

'What? Why?' he asks, panic on his face.

'Because you're setting the bar high, my friend.'

He looks at me, with sympathy. 'He didn't buy you jewelry yet, did he?'

I lift a shoulder. 'He wrote me a love note. It's good as gold, trust me.'

'Pffft. Loser,' he teases his brother.

As we make our way up to the rooftop to set up, I can't help but feel a rush of excitement for Aaron and Madi. Our first real date was up here, and I'm never going to forget a second of it.

The city lights twinkle below us as Ash and I work together

to set the table. A gentle evening breeze tousles my hair as I attempt to light the candles, finally getting them lit, creating a romantic ambiance under the starlit sky.

Ash's fingers brush against mine as we arrange the wine glasses, sending a jolt of electricity through me. I glance at him and catch his eye, a soft smile on his lips.

'Is it wrong that I'm more excited to leave here with you than help them?' he asks.

'If it is, we're both headed to the lake of fire because I'm feeling it too.'

'Even the lake of fire would be a good time with you,' he says.

'It's the company, not the location,' I say, repeating something Mitzi once said.

'Exactly.'

Once everything is set up to perfection, Ash steps back with a satisfied grin.

'I think we nailed it,' he says, glancing over at me.

I nod in agreement, feeling warm in my chest, knowing that we've helped create something special for our friends. 'Reminds me of our date up here,' I say, feeling like it was years ago because so much has happened since.

Just then, the door to the roof creaks open, and Aaron steps out, looking transformed in his sleek black suit. His eyes light up as he takes in the scene before him.

'Well, well, well,' Ash says with an approving nod. 'Look at you. I don't think I've ever seen you this way before.'

'Right back at ya, bud.' Aaron nods, a mischievous smile spreading across his face. 'Looking pretty dapper, aren't I?' he chuckles.

'Hell, yeah,' Ash says.

And I guess that's how men compliment one another.

'When will she be here?' I ask.

'Any minute,' he says nervously. 'After we're settled, I expect you both to disappear,' he instructs, pointing toward the door. 'Exit the whole building.'

'That won't be a problem,' Ash says, grinning my way.

'I'm sure we'll be able to find *something* to do,' I tease, my gaze on the most handsome man I've ever seen.

'Enough of the lovesick bedroom eyes,' Aaron says, straightening up the gift on Madi's plate. 'Lucy, you wait for her downstairs and bring her up when she gets here. I've plated the food; all you'll need to do is bring it up. Ash, make two drinks, something fancy and pretty for her and a double on ice for me, whatever you choose.'

He's planned this out like he might have heavy feelings for her, and I love every second of it. Madi is going to be thrilled he's gone to this much effort to prove he's not just into her naked.

'Consider it done,' Ash says as if he's Aaron's butler.

The two of us return downstairs, and I hover by the front door, awaiting my best friend. I watch Ash mix a couple of cocktails, shaking them skillfully to prove he has mastered the bartender field, because he knows I'm watching, and it's totally hot, then he expertly pours them into pretty glasses before making two more, presumably one for him and another for Aaron.

'My lady,' he says, handing me one of the cocktails. 'I tentatively named this one "The Lucy" because it's sweet, pretty and relaxing. Tell me what you think.'

'Really?' I ask, loving his definition of me. I think relaxing is a good thing. 'I didn't see this in your email for the menus.'

'I wanted to wait to see if you like it first.'

I take a sip and nearly go weak in the knees. Something

raspberry with a lemon round setting on the top of the pinkish purple liquid. 'That is to die for, what is it?'

'It's a raspberry lemon drop, and the vodka is infused with lavender.'

I take another sip, tasting every flavor. 'Also known as heaven.'

'Which is exactly where we'll be disappearing to later. I'll be back for you in a few,' he says, sipping the drink he made for him before carrying the other two up to the rooftop.

When I see Madi, looking gorgeous in a bright blue fitted dress, practically skipping up the sidewalk, I open the restaurant door before she can even knock.

'Welcome to Fire and Spice,' I say as if I work there.

'What are you—?'

I laugh at her shock of seeing me. 'Just helping out a friend,' I say, hooking my elbow through hers and leading her toward the stairs to the roof.

'Wow,' she says, glancing around the place. 'This is gorgeous. Can you believe they own this?'

'Totally cool, isn't it?'

'Yes. How do I look?' she asks nervously. 'Too much boob?'

'You know who you're here to see, right?' I ask with a laugh. 'I'm sure it's exactly the right amount of boob.'

'I'm a little on edge,' she says. 'And I don't know why, because I wanted this. Love is terrifying.'

I nod, completely agreeing. 'We're never truly ready to meet someone who turns our world upside down and makes us vulnerable, are we?' I ask, using her words against her from the day she secretly set me up with Tanner.

She smirks. 'I know. I know.'

'Can I just tell you one thing before you see him?'

She breathes out a nervous breath. 'As long as it's not bad and if it is, necessary.'

'Nothing bad. Truthfully, I think Aaron might be a diamond in the rough. And watching him set this up, I can see that he really, *really* likes you.'

With my words, she beams. 'Luce, I love him.'

'I know. Tanner told me and you know he's never wrong.'

We both laugh. That was certainly something I didn't expect.

'Don't be nervous, OK? He's done a lot to make this perfect.'

'No promises,' she says as we reach the door to the roof. 'What're the chances that we – best friends – fall in love with brothers? Oh my God, we could have a double wedding!'

'Slow down,' I laugh. 'Let's savor the journey. For now—' I twist the knob, opening the door, '— enjoy this...'

Her eyes widen in surprise at the sight before her – probably exactly the same way mine did when Ash first brought me up here. The flickering candlelight, the elegantly set table, and Aaron standing in his best suit with a nervous, yet hopeful, expression.

'Ma'am.' Ash hands her the beautifully crafted cocktail, and she smiles gratefully, her gaze moving around the scene before landing on Aaron.

He freezes in place, his eyes widening as he takes in the sight of her. Madi's face lights up in a radiant smile as she sees Aaron standing there, a look of awe on his face. This is so stinking cute. I glance at Ash, and he's mesmerized by them, too. Is this how we look to others? If so, I don't hate it.

'This is amazing,' she whispers, her voice filled with emotion.

'You look beautiful,' Aaron breathes out.

Madi blushes, a soft giggle escaping her lips. 'And you look so handsome,' she replies, stepping closer to him and straightening his tie.

That's our cue. We leave the roof, and I do as I was told, bringing up the plates of food and delivering them without them ever noticing, as their eyes are only on one another.

* * *

As I get back downstairs, the chandeliers are sparkling, the bar is glowing, and our graffiti wall looks amazing bordered above and below with black lighting that makes it stand out amongst everything – we made that.

'What do you think?' Ash says, walking around the corner from the kitchen into the dining room. 'This is the first time I've had it lit like it will be when we're open.'

'It's gorgeous. If this is what the inside of your head looks like, I'm in the right place.'

He pulls his phone from his pocket and taps at the screen, the room filling with the sound of our youth. A song we danced to at the prom all those years ago.

'Going all out with the memories, are ya?'

We glide across the floor without a plan or skill, just moving with one another however feels right.

'I'd say Aaron inspired me, but that was all you.'

Good, God. This man. 'Are you going to be sweet like this always, or…?'

'Or nothing. This is for always, Luce. I'm not even trying; this is just me around you. I'm in love with everything about you, remember?' he asks as if he needs a reminder.

'I remember everything,' I say, repeating back the phrase he used as he tried to convince me that prom way back when was not a pity date. He just wanted to see me smile.

He kisses me softly, sweetly, sliding a hand up my neck and only pulling away for a second before pecking another on my lips. 'I've been wanting to do that all night.'

'You and me both,' I say, licking the taste of Jack Daniel's from my lips. 'I sort of wish we'd have re-met years ago.'

'That would've changed where we are right now. And I love where we are. I love who we were. I love most of where we've been. But the universe had plans for us and the fact that we've been through what we have set us up for this moment,' he says.

Be still my heart. This man.

'This may sound completely ridiculous,' he continues. 'But I was sort of wondering if maybe you wanted to be my official girlfriend?'

He looks worried, as if there may be a chance I'd say no. Is he insane?! I'm having to stop myself from cartwheeling through the room right now.

I look up at him, my heart swelling ten sizes as I meet his gaze. He truly loves me; I've never been surer of anything.

'Ash,' I say, my voice barely above a whisper. 'I would *love* to be your official girlfriend.'

He pulls me into a tight embrace, holding me close as if never wanting to let go. And I hope he never does.

'You know, I was going to tell you this last night, but we got — busy,' he laughs. 'Anyway, you were right.'

'About what?'

'That *was* a thirtieth birthday I'll never forget. It may have been chaotic and confusing, but it brought me the greatest gift I've ever had – you. From here on out, all my birthday wishes will be about you.'

No. *Now*, be still my heart.

'If we're being cheesy – and FYI, I sort of like cheesy love –

you should know that every star I wish on will be about you,' I say in return.

They haven't failed me yet, so why stop now?

As we sway together in the empty dining room, I feel like everything has fallen into place. Aaron and Madi's love blossoming on the rooftop (in a place I can't see) only adds to the magic of this evening. And so, feeling like the luckiest woman in the world, I rest my head against his chest, listening to the steady beat of his heart under the soft glow of the restaurant lights. This is my happy place. And I never saw it coming. Not in a million years would I have guessed that Asher Wright would be the one to make me believe in love again. He's unlocked a part of me that I never thought was possible – a love that is pure, strong and secure. I don't know the right words to describe how I feel right now – content, loved, in love, safe and blissful – all at once. But whatever they are, that's exactly how I always want to feel in Asher's arms.

# EPILOGUE
## ASHER

*Six Months Later*

'If anyone can show just cause why these two should not be wed, speak now or forever hold your peace...'

I hold Lucy's hand tightly and silently.

'I can't believe they're doing this,' she whispers.

That's right. Aaron sweet-talked us into going on our yearly Vegas trip as a 'double date,' and we're currently stone-cold sober while Aaron and Madi get married. I had no idea they were doing this, but here we are. We have an itinerary. They've made plans. All it took for Aaron to man up was a strong woman.

As the officiant waits for a response, Lucy's hand trembles in mine – anxiety. She's had a hard time back in Vegas, and when they told us what they were doing today, she pretty much froze in fear.

And just as the weight of the silence becomes almost unbearable, a voice rings out from the back of the chapel.

'I object...'

Our heads snap to the back, hearts standing still, especially poor Lucy's – I know because she's now gripping my hand like a vice.

'...To *not* officiating this wedding,' the voice continues, now making his way up the aisle and removing the current officiant, taking his place. 'Traffic was a bitch. Now, let's fall in love.'

Thank all the Gods that it's not some ex-partner but only Elvis insisting he officiates the wedding.

'I think my heart stopped for a second,' Luce whispers, her free hand raises to her chest.

I'd warn her that it might stop later tonight, but I don't want to ruin the surprise.

I steal a glance at Aaron and Madi, standing side by side with beaming smiles on their faces. It was their dream for Elvis to marry them in Sin City, where they began. Finally, Aaron looks at peace, like a man who has found his place in the world.

As he slips the ring onto Madi's finger, a sense of happiness fills the room, and I can feel the genuine love between them radiating outwards. It's infectious.

A soft smile plays on Lucy's lips as she leans her head on my shoulder, her fingers intertwined with mine. The ceremony carries on around us, but in that moment, it feels like we are the only two people in the room. I want her to be beside me for every moment of my life.

Yes, I have a plan and a ring box tucked away in Aaron's jacket pocket for safekeeping until the timing is right. There's not a chance Lucy's going home this weekend without replacing a bad memory with a great one. But I want our moment to be ours and not shared with the whole world like the last time she was in Vegas.

The ceremony concludes with Aaron and Madi sealing their

vows with a kiss. We and the chapel employees burst into cheers and applause as the newlyweds make their way down the aisle, Elvis leading the way with a guitar in hand.

'How lovely do they look?' Mitzi says, throwing wedding chapel-shaped confetti at the couple as they walk past.

Yep, we brought Mitzi. She's such a huge part of our lives that there's not a lot we don't do with her. In Vegas she spends most of her time in the hotel we're staying in, meandering around buffets and casino floors, but she couldn't miss this.

Without a word, we both rise from our seats and follow the crowd outside. The neon lights of the Vegas strip illuminate the night as we step onto the bustling sidewalk.

'Did you ever imagine we'd end up here together? Or that my best friend and your brother would marry one another?' Lucy asks as we walk hand in hand, the sounds of the city swirling around us.

'I never imagined it, but I'm grateful for every twist and turn that brought us here,' I reply, squeezing her hand gently.

A car pulls up next to us, and I stop, heading its way.

'What are you doing?' Lucy asks, pointing at Aaron and Madi, who are at least a block ahead of us and clearly on a mission.

'We've got one more stop, and we're Ubering there, for Mitzi's sake.'

She looks between me and Mitzi, confusion plastered on her face. 'OK...' she says, getting into the Uber's back seat and sliding over for me.

We're headed to the Neon Boneyard, usually open to the public this time of year, but Mitzi and Paul have reserved it tonight for a party of six. Really, it's the backdrop of the beginning of the rest of Lucy and my life. I hope.

The closer we get, the more nervous I become. I've never

been this anxious, actually. Except when visiting Paul at his office and feeling like he was prosecuting *me* as I asked to do this. I knew it was important to Lucy, and this time, he didn't even threaten me like he did Brandon. Mostly because I'm not a demon in disguise, but also because there is no question, I love his daughter with everything in me.

We arrive at the site, where vintage neon signs cast a colorful glow over the night. As we walk in, we're greeted by Aaron and Madi dancing under the flickering lights of a giant martini glass sign as Elvis serenades them with a classic love song.

Lucy's eyes light up at the scene before us, and she squeezes my hand excitedly. 'This is amazing,' she whispers, leaning in close as we watch our friends celebrate their love.

It doesn't take long for Mitzi to be twirling on Elvis' hand with a glass of champagne in hers, her infectious laughter filling the air.

'Want to look around?' I ask, motioning to the paths through the glowing discarded signs.

Aaron and Madi came first because they were setting the stage. In front of the famous Stardust sign is a flower petal heart dotted with flickering candles waiting for us. There is also a photographer to capture every second because I know she's not expecting this right now and she's going to want to remember everything.

Truthfully, none of this was originally in my plan, but when I walked into the jeweler with Aaron to help pick out Madi's ring a few weeks ago, one stood out above the rest, and it wasn't meant for Madi. Like everything else about us, it seemed like it was meant to be.

'How beautiful is this?' Lucy asks as we walk through the signs. After a few minutes, she moves away from me with perfect timing, her phone in her hand, camera on, and the neon lights shining in her eyes.

I take the opportunity to round the corner without her and take a breath, waiting for her to find me.

'Wait, Ash?' she calls my name. 'Where are y— *Dad*!? What are *you* doing he—' Her words stop, and I know things are getting real because Paul just stepped into his part of the plan.

Her voice fades, and around another corner comes Madi, Aaron and Mitzi, all ready with confetti poppers to celebrate what hopefully is a giant 'yes' to the question I'm about to ask.

'You nervous?' Aaron asks under his breath, pulling the ring from his inside jacket pocket and setting it in my hand.

I grip the box tightly. 'Incredibly so.'

'Why? She's saying yes,' Madi says, smoothing down the veil now thrown back over her hair. 'No question about that.'

'I know. Just the option of no is squeezing my heart like someone's trying to tie a knot in it.'

*Breathe, Ash. You know she loves you, and all she's ever wanted in life is to have this moment with the right man, and you are him. She'll say yes.*

God. She has to say yes, or my entire world will screech to a halt.

'Holy—' Her words stop again when she rounds the corner, her hand in her father's as they walk my way.

She doesn't see me until I take a step forward from the edge of the sign, my heart pounding in my chest. She looks at me, then Paul, then back to me, her eyes filled with a whirlwind of emotions. I can see the moment she realizes what is happening.

A tear escapes down her cheek as she nods slightly, already answering the question I've yet to ask, unable to form the words that I know are swimming in her mind, while I drop down to one knee. I'll get on both knees if I must – that's how much I love this woman.

'Lucy,' I begin, my voice barely above a whisper yet echoing in the silent night around us. 'From the moment I met you for the third time, my life has been brighter, more vibrant... more complete. Every memory that ties us together is worth it right now. And I want a million more moments with you, so what do you think of maybe spending the rest of your life with me?'

For a second, time stands still as Lucy stares at me, her hand flying up to cover her mouth in shock. The world fades away until all that exists is the two of us in this neon-lit haven of discarded memories and new beginnings.

'Marry me?' I ask, my heart finally slowing from the race it was on as I see the word 'yes' all over her face.

With tears streaming down her face and a radiant smile breaking through, she nods vigorously. 'Yes! You crazy, amazing man,' she says, dropping to her knees in front of me and throwing her arms around my neck, nearly knocking me over.

Pops from the confetti poppers startle her, causing her to pull away, sitting back on her knees. Her gaze lands on the ring still gripped tightly in my hand.

'Oh my God, it's gorgeous,' she says, her eyes locking with mine.

'A gorgeous ring for a gorgeous girl,' I say, pulling the it from the box.

I've never seen her happier as she allows me to slide the ring on her finger.

She holds her hand in front of her, not even noticing our friends around us. 'This is beautiful. You're beautiful!' she exclaims.

I laugh, getting to my feet and helping her up.

'I love you so much,' I whisper to just her. 'Thank you for saying yes.'

'No wasn't even an option,' she says, her voice filled with emotion once again, wrapping her arms tightly around my neck.

Elvis strikes up a celebratory tune on his guitar.

'I can't believe this is happening!' Madi exclaims, tears of joy streaming down her face.

I wrap my arms tightly around Lucy, holding her close as the music, cheers and applause of our friends and family fill the Neon Boneyard. Mitzi is practically jumping with joy, Elvis is singing even louder, and I can feel Paul's proud gaze on us.

The ring sparkles on Lucy's finger in the neon lights as she celebrates with her family and friends.

'Congratulations, son,' Paul says, clapping me on the back. 'I've no doubt you're the one she's been looking for all these years.'

'I am,' I say, sure of it myself.

My God, she said yes. She wants to spend eternity with me. Wow. Suddenly, the world seems to spin a little slower, as if savoring this precious moment in time.

'I love you,' Lucy says as she steps back into my arms. 'We're getting married!' she says. 'Not in Vegas, I hope...?' she asks nervously.

'Anywhere you want. Tomorrow or a year from now. I don't care, as long as you're there.'

She beams. 'It's gonna be perfect.'

'Just like you,' I say, pecking another kiss on her lips.

The rest of the night is a blur of laughter, music and celebration as we dance under the neon lights, our hearts full to bursting with love for each other and for the friends who have become family. As Elvis sings another ballad and Mitzi twirls around with Aaron, I know that this moment will be etched in my memory forever as the best day of my life. Until the next one, when she walks down the aisle and becomes my wife.

\* \* \*

## MORE FROM AIMEE BROWN

Another gorgeously funny romantic comedy from Aimee Brown, *Still the One*, is available to order now here: https://mybook.to/StillTheOneBackAd

# ACKNOWLEDGEMENTS

Hi, readers! First and foremost, you are the most important part of this adventure. So, thank you for reading *Third Time Lucky* (unless this is a pirate copy, then no thanks to you). I hope, at minimum, I made you smile, possibly laugh, and hopefully fall in love with Ash and Lucy (and Aaron and Madi!). These couples saved me from worrying... about everything lately. Like a lot of folks right now, I prefer fiction over reality so if anyone has a spell to jump into this story and stay, lemme know.

*Third Time Lucky* is my ninth published book. Don't go look and count, or anything, because my earliest three have had rights reverted back to me so I'm working on a plan to re-release them soon. But anyway... my ninth book. NINE. Just one story away from double digits. That's a small amount in comparison to others but a huge amount for me. I remember attempting to write my first book over a decade ago now. Which was easily 1,567 different versions, took ten-plus years, and still never made it past chapter six. Never, in a million years did I think I'd be staring down the barrel at book number ten. But here I am.

I'm not gonna lie, publishing isn't for the weak, impatient or thin-skinned (people can be SO mean when sitting at a keyboard hidden behind a screen). But I've made it nine books deep and for me that's something to be proud of. Now I'm not rich, by any means. My royalties aren't flying me to Cancun every weekend. And not every reader knows my name, but you know what? That's OK. Because the readers that do have been absolutely amazingly supportive and I could never thank you enough for taking a chance on me and my stories.

The world is going through a massive shift right now, one I've never witnessed in all my forty-seven years. Truth be told, it's made me appreciate books and fictional worlds more and more, just to escape the chaos. So, please, even though the world seems on fire right now, I'd like to encourage my fellow writers to keep writing and my fellow readers to keep reading. We will make it through this and until we do, I hope the words of your favorite stories keep you smiling.

Thank you to my publishing team at Boldwood Books; editors, proofreaders, designers, marketing, formatting, and all the folks in the background (audiobook narrators and producers, etc.), thank you. Without you this book would be a file in my computer never to see the light of day again.

To Andie Newton and Sandy Barker (amazing authors BTW – you should buy their books) who read my first drafts and know exactly how badly I can write given the chance (lol), THANK YOU. Your words are always so helpful and kind and your encouragement has thus far kept me in the business. No one could ask for better friends and co-workers. You two make my books better.

Fun fact: I hide easter eggs from my other books in all my books. Have fun spotting them!

P.S. Every single book I write takes place mostly in Portland, Oregon, my soul city. I'm Oregon born and raised, all of my extended family is still there, and I lived in PDX for many years. Despite the fact that its reputation has taken a hit over the last decade, I write about both the Portland I knew and parts of what it's become. I've been to Powell's Books, 19,000 times, minimum. I raised my littles into tweens in this city. Shared fun local experiences with my family and friends. Worked with some amazing people. Had tragedies and celebrations. And pranced around the city day or night with my bestie – Staci – going to concerts, having drinks, and enjoying our twenties/early thirties in the best way we knew how. I'll never look back and not be thankful for the experiences Portland (Oregon in general) gave me and one day, maybe we'll be back? Who knows. It's a crazy world and anything is possible. All my love to Portland, and my PDX readers who are the BEST. 🩶